DEMON DISGRACE

Also by
M.J. Haag

Fairy Tale Retellings
(ALL IN THE SAME WORLD)

BEASTLY TALES

Depravity

Deceit

Devastation

TALES OF CINDER

Disowned (prequel)

Defiant

Disdain

Damnation

RESURRECTION CHRONICLES
(hottie demons!)

Demon Ember   *Demon Escape*   *Demon Dawn*

Demon Flames   *Demon Deception*   *Dmeon Disgrace*

Demon Ash   *Demon Night*   *Demon Fall*

DEMON
DISGRACE
THE RESURRECTION CHRONICLES

M.J. HAAG

Shattered Glass
—— PUBLISHING ——

ISBN 978-1-943051-58-8 (eBook Edition)
ISBN 978-1-943051-62-5 (Paperback Edition)

Editing by Ulva Eldridge
Cover design by Shattered Glass Publishing LLC
© Depositphotos.com

Version 2020.10.14

To everyone struggling,
You can overcome.
You're not as alone as you feel.

More than two months ago, earthquakes unleashed hellhounds on an unsuspecting mankind. The bite of a hound changes humans, turning people into flesh-craving infected.

The hellhounds weren't the only things to emerge from the earthen caverns. Demon men with grey skin and reptilian eyes have been trapped underground for thousands of years. They alone can kill the hellhounds and help bring a stop to the plague. They only ask for one thing in return: a chance to meet women who might be willing to love them as they are.

CHAPTER ONE

I STOOD UNDER THE HOT SPRAY OF THE SHOWER AND LET MYSELF imagine a lie. In my lie, the world wasn't irrevocably changed. The steaming water raining down on me wasn't due to the solar panels on the roof but the work of a perfectly functioning utility grid. And, at any moment now, my sister would pound on the door to demand that I stop hogging the bathroom and the hot water.

I could almost hear her yelling, "Hannah," as she drew out the last syllable of my name.

Pain pierced my middle. The world I'd once known was gone, and I struggled to endure the reality that persisted. There was no reliable utility grid. There was no sister. The dregs of humanity that remained huddled in fear of the black dogs with glowing red eyes and the infected that wanted to eat us alive. Fear was just part of life now, and yesterday had proved that death always waited just two heartbeats away.

Lovely reality.

I turned off the water and went through the motions of getting ready for the day as if I had somewhere to go. Jeans paired with a cute top. It was an outfit I would have loved wearing before the earthquakes. Now, along with most everything else, I hated it. None of what I put on was mine. Like all the people in Tolerance, I wore what had been collected from the homes the fey searched for supplies. Remnants and reminders from those already claimed by this new reality of fear and death.

And sacrifice.

So much sacrifice. How much more would we need to give before the infected and the hounds were dead?

With a bitter tilt forming at the corner of my mouth, I recalled the tiny ember of hope that had flared to life the moment the fey had appeared. That hope had begun to fade when I realized a simple truth. There were too many hounds and infected out there. And those creatures that craved human flesh would continue to return, day after day, relentless in their determination to kill us all. Yesterday's breach had proved that. It had also extinguished any remaining hint of hope.

I already knew the end of humanity's story, and it wasn't pretty. It would be filled with fear, blood, and death. What then was the point of the continual struggle to exist?

With trembling fingers, I combed through my drying blonde curls then left the bathroom. Downstairs, Emily moved around in the kitchen.

"You look like you didn't sleep well," she said, noticing me. "Me neither. I couldn't stop seeing yesterday." She lifted the bowl of mush she was stirring. "I'm making dog food meatloaf for Merdon as a thank you. Want to help?"

With a shuddering look at the pinkish mash, I shook my head and fetched my morning glass. The cupboard above the stove didn't have much of a selection anymore. I was down to vodka. Not my drink of choice, but it would do. The last three fingers from the bottle looked pathetic in my cup. More so after I took a large swallow.

"I still can't believe how Merdon came out of nowhere like that," Emily continued. "I mean, I know the fey move fast, but he was almost a blur. Without him there..." She shook her head and flipped the mush into a pan.

I tipped back the rest of the vodka, trying to drown out the memories. It didn't work. Images from the day before, breach day, flooded my mind.

Hordes of infected had gotten in and stormed the streets of our supposed safe haven. A woman with a huge chunk of her cheek missing had run straight toward Emily and me. Had it not been for Merdon, Emily and I wouldn't be in the kitchen now. We'd be a headless mass of decaying corpses tossed out in the trees somewhere.

The thought didn't upset me. After all, that was where we'd end up at some point. What did upset me was another day of the struggle to exist. If not for Merdon, I'd already be at peace.

Another sharp pang of regret and loss pierced me, and I set the empty glass on the counter to double-check the cupboards.

"This is going to take a while to bake," Emily said, sliding the dogloaf into the oven. "Want to go check on James and Mary with me? They'd probably appreciate the company after yesterday."

"They're going to want to recap what happened. I'll pass." Frustrated with the lack of alcohol, I closed the cupboard door and faced Emily.

"I think we should have another get-together. To celebrate the lives of those we lost," I added so I wouldn't sound insensitive.

She tipped her head, studying me.

"I've been with you for months now, Hannah. I know you better than anyone else. I see the way your hand is shaking.

You're not okay. Is it because of yesterday, or did you have another bad night?"

I fisted my hands and sat on the kitchen stool.

"Both," I admitted. "Last night was the worst yet." My gaze darted to the cupboards. I needed to keep better track of our alcohol stock. How had we run so low?

"And what happened yesterday didn't help," Emily said in soft understanding.

Of all the people who'd been in that RV with me, she'd been the only one who hadn't found another roommate when we'd arrived here. James and Mary, the older couple who'd been in the RV with us, had a reason to need their own place. Oldness. While our group had been together, the couple hadn't complained about my nightmares or my screaming, which made them okay. Just not today.

I moved to the door and slipped into my coat and boots as I spoke.

"You should go check on James and Mary. I'll walk around and see who might be interested in coming over."

"Okay, but stress that we're asking for more than just alcohol. And spread the word that anyone without food should arrive after dark. I'll see if any of the other girls want to join us."

I waved in acknowledgment and quickly left.

Outside, evidence of the day before painted the trampled snow red in places. The few swallows of vodka sitting in my stomach hadn't even come close to dulling my senses enough to unsee the reminder of the devastation. The screams echoed in my head.

Don't think about it. I plastered a happy smile on my face and started making my way around the neighborhood. *Just make it through today, and you'll be fine.*

Keeping my eyes off the bloodied ground, I waved to the fey I knew, which were most of them, and paused to talk to the ones who'd provided what I needed in the past.

"Hey, Fyllo. Any chance you still have some of that scotch left? We're having another get-together tonight."

"I gave you the last one. But there is another bottle like it that I could bring. It's new."

Since the fey couldn't read, the bottle could be anything from fancy cooking oil to sparkling grape juice.

"Nope. Nothing new unless it's tested ahead of time," I said, pretending to look upset by the news. "If you have a roast or something, that could work, too. Emily wants someone to bring something edible. But only one person. We don't want to waste food by making too much."

He blinked at me, a common quirk the fey all seemed to share when they were deciding how to respond.

"I have no meat. I do have cheese toes."

"We'll pass on the junk food. Maybe you'll find something that meets the requirements before tonight," I hinted. "You know what I like."

He nodded thoughtfully then took off at a jog toward the wall.

What I liked and what Emily liked were two different things. We'd agreed to set food and booze as the price of an invitation to our little gatherings. She thought the fey brought mostly booze because they knew I liked it, which I did, not because it was the sole item I encouraged.

Watching Fyllo go, I exhaled slowly and kept my smile in place. Hopefully, he'd find a bottle of something good and not a stupid roast.

I continued along the sidewalk until I saw Tor and waved for him to join me. He was always good for something liquid.

"Just the fey I wanted to see," I said with a smile that hurt my face.

He smiled in return, showing his pointed teeth.

"Hello, Hannah. Why did you want to see me?"

"Emily and I are having a get-together tonight, and I sure could use some of that brandy you found."

He nodded.

"I've been saving it for this," he said. "We can play your games, and I will win a kiss."

"You got it, big guy." I winked and waved goodbye.

The moment I turned my back to him, my well-known, thousand-watt smile dimmed. There was no way I was going to kiss anyone tonight. "Stage five clinger" didn't even come close to describing the level of clingy, needy infatuation mouth to mouth contact could elicit from a fey. I'd long ago drawn the line at hair touching and friendly hugs. Even that tended to create cleedy fey.

Mentally cringing away from the memory of the one time I'd offered more to one of the fey, I looked around for my next target. Movement to the side caught my attention, and I met Merdon's steady gaze as he emerged from between two houses.

Unlike the rest of the fey, I didn't know this one well and had no interest in changing that. I didn't care that he'd been shunned by the rest of his kind or that he and his friend, Thallirin, had killed more hellhounds between them than the rest of the fey put together. My apathy toward this fey lay in my inability to read him.

Merdon never smiled. Ever. No matter what wattage I threw his way.

He stopped moving and just...watched me. Something he'd been doing a lot since he'd witnessed the one time I'd suggested more than a friendly hug. Hearing me offer to have Shax's baby and Shax's rejection had probably given Merdon ideas that I was up for grabs. Not now. Not ever again.

I sighed at the tiny bubble of regret that welled up at the thought of what I'd lost. Shax would have brought me anything for just a touch. Granted, he was also why I had the no kissing rule. Just one stupid kiss, and he'd been annoyingly obsessed with me. In hindsight, I wished I would have appreciated his willingness to do anything for me while I'd had his attention. When his interest had turned to someone else, I'd lost my most reliable source of alcohol. I didn't begrudge him Angel, though. If people could be happy in this shit-show of a world, more power to them.

That level of blind ignorance wasn't for me. And neither was acquiring another love-struck fool.

Looking away from Merdon, I continued walking. He'd wander away again. He always did. He probably stared because he'd never seen a blonde with my level of curls before. Yet, his behavior yesterday niggled at my mind for half a second before I dismissed it. Any fey would have rushed to save us. They were all girl-hungry like that. I told myself that Merdon's conveniently close proximity and his timely intervention weren't an indication of another saran-man in the making.

He was just another protective fey trying to get close. Like Shax.

I forced away my regret at losing Shax and fixed my signature happy-Hannah expression on my face while I looked for my next target.

Several other fey stopped to talk to me as I made a slow loop around Tolerance. I let them know the price of admission to that night's party, stressing we only needed one roast for the evening. It seemed that word had already spread because there were far too many offers to bring food. The last thing I wanted was all meat and no booze.

After having spoken to a dozen fey, I knew news of the party would continue to spread, and by nightfall, we'd have a decent showing. Tired of pretending to be happy, I headed home before the sun even reached its zenith.

Emily was still gone when I let myself in. No surprise there, given who she'd gone to visit. I kicked off my shoes and looked around the house for something to do. There was far too much time until the party, and idleness was my worst enemy.

A fey passed by one of the side windows on his way through our yard.

The image of the first infected I'd ever seen clouded my mind, pulling me under, drowning me in a memory. Like the fey just now, the infected had shuffled past the window. I could vividly recall his whiskered profile and the way the light had glinted oddly in his eye, making it look milky white.

I tried not to remember the moment the familiar face turned, and I'd seen the flap of scalp dangling over the bloody patch that should have been his ear. He'd looked in the window, but after a beat, he'd turned and continued his shamble through our yard.

That was the last time I'd seen my father. He'd gone outside to see whose dog was running loose. In hindsight, I now knew it hadn't been a dog but a hellhound.

Releasing a shuddering breath, I moved away from the windows and went to search the cupboards again, hoping I'd overlooked a bottle. I wasn't that lucky. I never was.

Hands shaking, I fluffed my hair and started for the door. Some fey out there had to have something. A knock sounded before I reached the front entrance. I hurried to answer and smiled at Fyllo as he held up two bottles. As I'd guessed, one was garlic and rosemary-infused oil. The other bottle, though, had me extending a hand.

He surrendered the sherry and watched me open it and take a long drink.

"Will that work for tonight?" he asked.

"It sure will. You're officially in, but Emily said no one should come before dark. I'll just hold onto it until then, okay?"

He nodded and smiled. I gave a quick smile in return, closed the door on him, then did my best to drown the memories in sherry.

The door opened, pulling me from my semi-stupor.

"Hey, Hannah," Emily called. "I brought goodies from Mary."

I sat up from my comfortably prone position on the couch and dutifully looked at Emily, who was holding up a plate of baked goods.

Merdon closed the door behind her and met my gaze.

"A stray followed you in," I said, not paying any attention to the food she carried.

"Be nice," she said with a laugh. "I told you I was making dinner for Merdon." She glanced back at the fey. "Shoes off at the door, please. You can hang your jacket on the hooks there."

While she instructed him, I resumed my relaxed recline and let my world continue to drift. The sherry was gone, and the buzz from it was starting to fade. But I wasn't worried. It was almost dark, and people would start showing up soon enough.

"Hannah, come join us," Emily called.

"No, thank you. I'm not hungry for dogloaf."

"Good, because that's just for Merdon. Get your butt over here and eat something, or I'm turning everyone away tonight."

Sitting up again, I narrowed my eyes at her then got up to help her set the table. Sometimes Emily's mothering stifled me to the point I wanted to tell her to lay off. In the end, I could never bring myself to say the words. She put up with a lot from me. Putting up with a little from her was the least I could do.

"Mary said you should come over tomorrow," Emily said, placing the dogloaf on the table. "She said she has something special set aside for you."

I hoped "special" was code for aged Cognac. She and James had gifted me with a nice bottle once before. That stuff had kicked my ass hard.

"I'll try to stop by tomorrow," I said, not committing.

Emily pulled something else from the oven. Wrapped in foil, the food was a mystery until she removed the covering and revealed a stir fry looking jumble of veggies and chicken.

"You're welcome to try this, too, Merdon," she said, "But I know most of you don't enjoy your veggies."

She took the seat nearest the kitchen and gestured to the chair to her right. Merdon sat and glanced at me. Suppressing my sigh, I sat across from Emily, to his right. Hopefully, the position would make it harder for him to stare at me throughout the meal.

"This smells amazing," Emily said, scooping a large portion of stir fry onto her plate. She was obviously hungry.

"Here," she said, handing the plate to Merdon. "Pass that to Hannah. Hannah, I'll take your plate."

My stomach twisted as I stared at the mound of food. If I ate it all, I'd have no room for dessert of the liquid variety.

Disgruntled, but knowing better than to argue, I surrendered my empty plate to Merdon in exchange for the full one.

Emily did her typical hostess shtick where she made conversation.

"What's it like outside the wall today? I haven't heard a single moan," she said to Merdon.

I zoned out and focused on the food.

Methodically, I chewed, swallowed, and scooped up some more, working my way around the plate and shrinking the pile. I didn't taste the meal. Food had lost its flavor long ago. When I'd eaten at least half, I pushed my plate away.

"I can't eat more. If I do, I'll throw up."

"Hannah—"

"I'm serious, Emily. That was a lot. Big meals are a relic from before the quakes. My stomach can't handle all of that at once. I'll save what's left for later."

She glanced at my plate then at Merdon's. The dogloaf pan was empty, and his plate was clean.

My stomach gave a threatening heave.

"I'm not a starving fey, so don't even try to compare us," I said in annoyance.

The first knock of the night echoed on the front door, and I sprang up to answer it.

Behind me, Emily explained to Merdon that we were having a get-together to remember the people who'd died. Then, she invited him to stay.

I rolled my eyes. Of course she'd invite him; he hadn't been following *her* around all morning.

Fyllo smiled at me from outside and held up another bottle of sherry.

"I had more," he said.

"That's great! Come on in. Just set the bottle on the counter."

As interested as I was in another drink, I knew there'd be better options.

Behind him, more fey emerged from the dark. A good number of them carried bottles. I chose not to notice how many held some kind of dish. Leaving the door open, I selected one of the mellower vinyls from our collection and went to the turntable. In no time, smooth music filled the air.

While Emily welcomed guests, I began pouring drinks in the kitchen. Generally, the fey didn't care for the burn of alcohol, which meant more liquor for those who did like to drink it.

Greedily eyeing the few extra inches of alcohol that I'd given myself, I lifted my cup to my lips and took a large swallow. It didn't burn on the way down, but it did warm my stomach. The mellowness I needed would soon follow, and I settled a hip against the counter to patiently wait for it.

As I drank some more, I looked around the room. Fey outnumbered the few human females brave enough to attend. No surprise there. Of the human survivors, fewer than half were females. And fewer than half of those lived in our fey-friendly community of Tolerance. Emily had done her job well, though, and there were new female faces in the crowd. Most of them hung out around the food table, sampling what the fey had procured, as the fey tried to make conversation with them.

I wondered how many of these new girls wished they hadn't agreed to stay here after yesterday's blood bath. Given they were alive and being fed, probably none of them. We lived in a "take what you can get" kind of world after all.

I snorted into my cup and continued to look around.

Green and gold eyes locked onto mine from across the room. Merdon was watching me again. I flashed him my bright smile since it always paid to be welcoming to the fey, no matter how annoying they were, then turned my back on him and tipped my glass.

"Hannah," Emily said, coming to me with a new girl in tow. "This is Cheri. She's new here."

Someone caught Emily's eye, or at least that's what she pretended happened, and she excused herself. Pawning off guests was a skill Emily had probably perfected before the quakes. She was a social queen like that. After all, if she let one person monopolize her time, how would she ever get to talk to everyone?

"Hi, Cheri," I said brightly as I handed her a drink. "Sorry, I don't remember seeing your face with the Whiteman people. Are you liking living in Tolerance so far?"

She gave me a strained smile.

"It's an adjustment."

I gave a humorless laugh. "It's the apocalypse. Of course it's an adjustment."

"You're right. Sorry. I shouldn't complain."

"Nah. Complain away. I'm all ears."

She shot me a confused look, obviously trying to figure out if I was being sarcastic or sincere. I kept my Hannah-loves-everyone smile firmly in place and waited.

"I appreciate the food and the safety. I really do. But the attention's a little overwhelming. My roommate stands outside the bathroom door when I'm in there." She flushed and glanced across the room at one of the fey.

"Yeah, he's probably picturing you naked. Or hoping you'll walk out naked. Don't overthink it. The fey are harmless. I promise. Drink up and relax."

She nodded, took the first sip of her drink, and coughed.

"What is this?"

I glanced at the bottles on the counter.

"It's either brandy or whiskey."

"Straight?"

True humor lifted my lips.

"The end of the world isn't watered down; why should the drinks be?"

She gave a tentative smile and lifted her cup to her lips again. I glanced across the room at Farco and winked. He flashed his teeth at me, knowing he'd be carrying his newly acquired roommate home. Oh, I had no concerns about Cheri's safety. He'd carry her home, remove her shoes, and tuck her into bed like a good fey. They never took more than what was offered. It wasn't their way. Just holding her in his arms would be enough for him.

The fey hadn't yet lost their hope. Not like I had.

An ache started in my chest, and I drank deeply again, hating that feelings from the past kept trying to surface. It was time to drown them completely.

"Who's ready for some games?" I called over the soft music.

While the fey hurriedly started rearranging the furniture, I locked my arm through Cheri's and led her to the table.

"The games are fun," I said. "And a great way to get to know the fey. They love betting small things like holding your hand or touching your hair, in exchange for pretty much whatever you want." I leaned in closer to her. "Just don't bet kisses unless you're willing to have another fey standing outside the bathroom door."

She gave me a worried look then nodded.

The next hour passed in a blur of laughter and betting. Cheri couldn't hold her liquor and ended up in Farco's arms as I'd predicted. At the door, Emily gave him a stern talk to only remove Cheri's shoes, stating that anything else without consent would ruin his chances with the girl. He looked down at the girl, complete adoration in his eyes, and I snorted softly. He wouldn't have the balls to do anything that would jeopardize his chances with her. Come morning, not only would he likely apologize for touching her feet while she was passed out, but he'd also be running all over Tolerance to find her pain reliever for the bitch of a headache she'd have. If she was smart, she'd realize she had the key to whatever she wants.

I turned and almost ran into a fey.

"Sorry," I said, lifting my head to offer a smile.

Merdon looked down at me, his expression inscrutable.

"Are you having a good time?" I asked, trying to be pleasant while also attempting to recall if he'd joined the games.

He didn't answer. Instead, he breathed in deeply, his nostrils flaring slightly before his gaze flicked to the cup I held. My smile slipped a little at the feeling I was being judged.

"If you need anything, let Emily know," I said, stepping around him.

In the kitchen, the dregs of the brandy went into my glass, and I turned the remaining bottles so all the labels were facing forward. The fey had done their jobs well and supplied enough alcohol to last a while. They were also providing a nice distraction.

Rejoining the games, I bet a walk around Tolerance (with hand-holding) against a container of "just add water" waffle mix, a package of breakfast sausages, and a canister of dried eggs. Emily rooted for me as I let the quarter roll off my nose into the cup, knocked back the contents, then slammed the empty cup on the table. I grinned as the fey's cup hit the surface a second later than mine. They might have mad skills at running and killing shit, but they couldn't stand the burn of liquor.

"We're eating a real breakfast tomorrow," Emily crowed.

I laughed and moved out of the way so the next person could bet. My limbs and face felt pleasantly numb as the room tilted and wobbled around me.

A hand wrapped around my upper arm.

"You look unsteady."

Tipping my head back with my smile still lingering on my lips, I met Merdon's gaze.

"I've never been steadier. Would you like something to drink?"

He didn't answer.

Rolling my eyes, I tugged my arm from his hold.

"Suit yourself."

I shuffled to the kitchen and looked at my pretty line up of bottles.

"Tempting little hussies," I whispered to them then giggled.

Taking the open one, I sloshed some of the contents into my cup. A hand reached around me and plucked the bottle from my grasp before I was finished.

"Hey."

"You've had enough."

Bleary-eyed, I squinted at Merdon.

"Is my speech impaired?"

"No."

I touched my finger to my nose.

"Did I miss my nose when trying to touch it?"

He didn't answer.

"Exactly," I said. "I'm fine. Please focus your attention elsewhere for the evening unless you want to bet something at the table."

His gaze flicked from my face to the bottle he held. Instead of taking up my challenge, he set the booze on the counter and walked away.

"That's what I thought," I mumbled.

Fluffing my hair and noting my steady hand, I grinned and rejoined the games.

CHAPTER TWO

THE NEED TO PEE FORCED ME FROM BED AROUND DAWN. Disoriented and still tipsy, I shuffled toward my adjoining bathroom and landed my bare ass half off the toilet seat. My bladder refused to wait for an adjustment in position, but thankfully, I heard the splashdown a second later and knew I wouldn't be scrubbing the floor.

I closed my eyes and drifted in a pleasant haze while recalling the night before. Snippets of betting and drinking floated in my mind along with the memory of winning some good food. Food always made Emily happy. What made me happy were the bottles that still sat on the counter when I'd stumbled to bed well after midnight.

I vaguely recalled a new bottle of something that had tempted me. I might have taken a little sample of it before I went back to bed. I couldn't remember.

After quickly washing, I left my bedroom. My steps weren't quite steady, but the carpeted stairs didn't make a sound under my feet as I clung to the railing. It was a good thing because Emily was a light sleeper, and I didn't want to be caught going down to look at our haul. Well, my haul.

The light above the sink guided me to the tidy kitchen. All evidence of a party was gone, including the bottles.

Confused, I spun in a slow circle. My eyes had to be seeing things wrong, or maybe I was drunker than I'd thought. The alcohol couldn't be gone. There had been at least seven bottles sitting right there when I'd gone to bed. I squinted at the counter for a moment then smiled.

Emily had probably put them away. She was always cleaning up like that.

Trying to be as quiet as possible, I opened the cupboard above the stove and peered into the inky emptiness. Undeterred, I continued searching until every single door in the kitchen gaped open. There wasn't a single bottle of liquor in any of them.

Gripping the counter to stay upright, I struggled to cope with what this meant. There would be no escape from the pain and memories once I sobered. If I sobered—

I heard a muted rustle behind me and froze. How many times had I been in this situation since the quakes? Hearing something and knowing what was coming for me? After all, that whisper of noise was usually the only indication a person had before becoming infected.

I should have been afraid. But I wasn't. The only thing I felt was tired...of everything.

Pivoting to face the living room, I peered into the gloom and watched a form slowly sit up on the couch. It didn't do anything more than that, though, which was unusual. Infected typically ran at their next meal.

I flicked on the light and felt like I'd been gut-punched when Merdon blinked back at me.

"What are you doing?" I whispered harshly.

"I was sleeping. What are you doing in the kitchen, Hannah?"

"Shh. Why are you sleeping on our couch? Go sleep on your own."

"I have no couch. Or home. That is why Emily told me to sleep here."

I almost swore. Emily's soft heart was going to screw us over. Just like a person should never feed a gremlin after midnight, a smart human never invited a fey to sleep over. The grey men tended not to want to leave. No way I wanted to be stuck with a stray fey.

Instead of cursing, I pasted on a smile and moved to the front door.

"I'm glad you were able to stay warm while you slept. I'll ask around to see if someone has an open couch for you tonight."

I opened the door and waited, expectantly. He didn't stand up to leave like a normal person would have. Annoyingly, he just stared at me. I held my ground, letting my toes go cold. It didn't take long for the furnace to kick on.

"This is where you leave, Merdon," I said finally.

Fey didn't always understand human subtleties.

He rose from the couch, unfolding to an impressive height, and prowled toward me. Dawn's pink light painted his grey skin, making him appear almost human if not for the pointed ears and freakishly yellowed eyes.

He stopped before me, towering over my diminutive height.

"I'm not impressed," I said. "But I am cold. Could you just leave already?"

He tilted his head, studying me.

"You are very used to getting what you want."

I snorted.

"If that were true, I would have a drink in my hand right now."

I didn't let myself think of what I really wanted.

"You drink too much."

Anger spiked up, and I grabbed his bicep to turn him toward the exit. Unfortunately, a human couldn't move a fey unless the fey wanted to move, and this one was being stubborn.

"Stopping that infected from killing me doesn't mean you own me or have a right to tell me what I should or shouldn't be doing. You've overstayed your welcome. It's time to leave." I gestured to the snow-covered outdoors. "If you find any of that fun stuff you think I drink too much of, you're welcome to come back. Until then, don't."

He blinked at me, and for a brief moment, I thought he'd say something judgmental again. Fortunately, Merdon had some sense and left.

I shook my head and closed the door. The fey were so predictable, trying to boss a girl around in hopes of establishing some kind of claim. Luckily, I wasn't dumb enough to fall for that bullshit.

My righteousness only lasted a few seconds before I realized I had bigger issues. Where was I going to find more alcohol? I'd been careful with the parties that Emily and I threw. If I instigated too many, we would draw Mya's attention. Or worse, I would tick off Emily.

Exhaling resignedly, I gauged my level of buzz. There was still enough tingle in the tank to knock me out for a few more hours. I'd take it. Shuffling back the way I'd come, I crawled into bed and let the alcohol pull me under.

It felt like I'd barely closed my eyes when Emily shook my shoulder.

"What time is it?" I asked, struggling to swallow because of a severe case of dry mouth.

"Past breakfast. Don't worry, I saved you some. Come on. Get up. You said you'd visit Mary and James today."

I forced myself to sit up.

"I'm awake."

She crossed her arms and stared at me, knowing me well enough to not leave the room.

Groaning, I slid out of bed and followed her downstairs where she had a plate waiting for me on the island. A small pile of yellow sat next to a waffle and a breakfast sausage.

"There's syrup, too." She pushed a jar toward me. "Real maple."

Forcing a smile, I dutifully used the syrup and took a bite of everything.

"I hope you don't mind, but I let Merdon use the couch last night. Don't worry, he's already gone." Her placating tone didn't match the sheepish look that crossed her features. "I think he might be back today because all the cupboard doors were open when I came downstairs."

"Why do you think that means he'll be back?" I asked, admitting nothing.

"He was obviously taking stock of our supplies to see what he could provide. I know how you feel about inviting too much attention from any one of the fey, so I'll make sure to let him know his consideration isn't necessary if he shows up."

"You know the fey don't take hints well. You should have never let him sleep on the couch."

"Hannah, it was the right thing to do after he risked his life to save us."

"If you want to show him gratitude, whatever. But don't pull me into it. To be clear, dinners and sleepovers in the house we share definitely pulls me into it. I always check with you before inviting anyone over, and the parties we throw work well enough to get us supplies without any kind of fey commitment."

"I know. You're right. I'm sorry."

"Don't worry about it. If he comes back, we'll handle it together. How'd we do with supplies last night?"

I didn't give a damn about the food. I wanted to know what happened to my bottles.

"The losers started dropping off their losses as soon as I turned the porch light on. It's enough for a few days. It sucks there's not any alcohol left for the next party. We could have asked for canned goods as an entry fee then."

The news curdled the food in my stomach, and I toyed with the remains of my eggs.

"You know the drinking games are the only way to win with them," I said. "I can't believe we went through all that liquor. I thought there were at least six bottles still on the counter when I went to bed."

"Those were empty," she said, sounding as upset as I felt.

"A few days of supplies means we'll need to plan another gathering soon. Unless you have another idea," I said. The key to making the parties happen was to sound as if I didn't care about them.

"Every idea I come up with breaks our rules."

The rules were simple, but effective, for keeping us fed and unencumbered by unwanted fey attention. The first rule was no one-on-one time with a fey. That gave them ideas. The second rule was no accepting handouts from a fey. The same logic applied to the second rule as the first. By playing the games, we were "earning" the items, not accepting handouts. Also, the party scene kept us from any one-on-one time.

"Let me know when you want to plan it," I said. "I'll spread the word."

"Yeah, I want to keep thinking on it more. You have to do a lot of drinking to win sometimes. That can't be good for your liver."

I snorted.

"Just one more hazard of surviving the apocalypse."

She gave me a sad look that quickly vanished.

"Why don't you take your time with breakfast and meet me at James and Mary's when you're done?"

"Sure."

As soon as she left, I scraped the remnants of my breakfast into the garbage and returned to my room. The bed called to me despite the numerous hours I'd already spent in it. While some would succumb to the lure of a few more Z's, I knew better. The bed wasn't my friend.

Turning my back on the rumpled mass of bedding, I padded into the bathroom. I took my time, since I was in no hurry to get to James and Mary's. It wasn't like they were going anywhere. There was nowhere to go. What the hellhounds and infected hadn't destroyed, the idiots with the bombs had.

The fey and people like Mya were delusional to believe there was any kind of future for us. We humans were just fish in a barrel within Tolerance's walls.

With sobriety came the oppressive certainty that there was no point to any of this. Eating. Washing. Why do any of it just to die in a few days or weeks?

Shutting off the water, I left the enclosure and stared at myself in the foggy mirror.

What are you doing, Hannah? Are you living or just slowly dying?

The answer reflected back at me in the dark circles under my eyes and visibility of my rib bones. What little vitality I'd clung to had died long ago.

A single tear trailed down my cheek, and I wiped it away with a shaky hand before pushing back from the counter. My current train of thought needed to stop, and there was only one way to do that.

I bent to grab my jeans from the floor, intent on finding someone who might have an adult beverage to share. The sun coming through the window glinted at something peeking from under my bed. Leaning down, I saw the gold cap of a bottle of liquor.

"There you are," I murmured, pulling it out. "I remember you from last night." This had been the bottle I'd wanted to sample.

I twisted the top, listening to the seal break, and grinned.

No time like the present for a little taste.

"HANNAH."

If the persistent shaking hadn't penetrated the pleasant haze, the sharp annoyance in Emily's tone had. Blinking the fuzzy dusk of my room into focus, I squinted up at my housemate.

"Hey, Emily."

Her expression shifted from annoyed to angry.

"You didn't show," she accused. "You promised you would. Instead, I come home to find you passed out again. Did you drink this whole thing by yourself?"

I gave the empty bottle she held in her hand a quick side glance.

"It's not that big."

Her anger bled away, leaving a level of sorrow that made me want to close my eyes. I hated sorrow. It was just as bad as pity. I didn't need any of that bullshit.

Instead of scolding me more, Emily sat on the edge of my bed.

"Hannah, I'm worried. I think the drinking is making you worse. I'm not judging. I know life's not easy, and we're all desperate for a little escape. But I'm—"

"Worried. I get it. I don't need your worry or constant mothering. I'm fine. Or, I would be if you got off my case. It's just one dumb bottle. I'll find you some more."

"Hannah, I'm not mad that you drank this because I wanted it. I'm not mad at all. I'm scared for you, and I don't know what to do to help."

"You don't need to do anything, Emily. I'm not some pet project that needs fixing so you can distract yourself from how fucking shitty the world is."

A hurt look crossed her face before she stood.

"Fine. Wallow in your misery then."

"Thank you."

I closed my eyes and welcomed the darkness.

PANIC SUFFOCATED ME, *burning my lungs and straining my pulse.*

Behind us, the soft moans of a dozen infected were almost drowned out by our gasping breaths and the rustle of leaves under our feet. Even if we couldn't hear them, there was no doubting they were there. The stench of their rot carried on the wind that blew my hair into my face.

In front of us, the trees stretched endlessly, providing no protection.

My lungs burned with effort, and my side ached. I couldn't think. I didn't know what to do.

"Hannah," Katie panted. "I can't."

I tightened my hand on hers, pulling her along. Her weight dragged on my arm. She wasn't keeping up like she should.

"Keep going," I said.

The moans were getting closer. There was no stopping. Stopping would be death.

I glanced over my shoulder, catching so much detail in that brief look. Katie's wide, desperate eyes locked on me. The exhaustion pulling at her features. The horde of infected barely fifty feet behind us and gaining.

I sat up, gasping and shaking. The memory coated my mind, an unwanted stain on my thoughts. Scrambling out of bed, I got on my belly in the dark and searched frantically for another hidden bottle. There was no second miracle to be found, though. I curled in a ball and tried to hold myself together while I desperately waited for the images to fade. They didn't though. I saw it all play out again, and with a choked moan, I pulled at my hair.

It wouldn't leave me. It wouldn't stop. Ever.

I couldn't do it anymore.

Sobbing softly, I heaved myself to my knees then stumbled to the window. The sash lifted soundlessly, and I slipped through the opening. The brisk, night air shocked me enough to interrupt my tormented thoughts.

I looked over the quiet homes, blanketed in white, and focused on the lights illuminating the dark above the wall. The lights, powered by batteries that were charged using the solar panels retrofitted on the homes, kept the hellhounds out. But the lights wouldn't last forever. Then what? I didn't want to be here to find out.

Ignoring the bite of the snow on my bare feet, I climbed

higher on the roof. Numbness wrapped around me. From the cold or my resolution, I couldn't be sure. I walked along the peak, waiting for some sense of calm to settle in my soul. It never came.

I reached the edge and looked down at the dark yard below. Hopefully, I was high enough. Even if I wasn't, I deserved whatever pain I had to endure until death took me.

I thought of my sister, closed my eyes, and stepped off.

My stomach pitched as I dropped. I waited for the pain, ready to welcome it in order to embrace what would follow. Nothingness.

My back hit a hard ridge with bruising force half a moment before the back of my legs collided with the same. Strangely, the wind continued to rush past me as if I were still falling. I opened my eyes.

Yellow-gold eyes glinted down at me in the dark a second before my descent came to a joint-jarring stop. I bit my tongue, the copper tang of blood flooding my mouth as I stared at Merdon in horror.

He'd saved me. Again. No, not saved. Condemned me to continue my hellish existence.

Anger bled into my shredded soul.

"You fucking asshole."

The broken words had little effect on him. He blinked at me, which just pissed me off more. I pushed at his chest and tried to twist out of his arms. His grip was unyielding.

"Put me down."

He didn't move. Just continued to study me.

"Are you deaf?"

"No."

"No, what? No, you're not deaf, or no, you won't put me down?"

He tore his gaze from mine and started walking.

"You're not wearing shoes."

Shoes? He was worried about shoes after catching me because I'd jumped off a roof? I wrapped my arms around my middle, trying to hold myself together.

He jostled my weight more firmly against his chest and held me with one arm as he opened our back door. Once we were inside, he damn near dropped me in his haste to get me back onto my own feet.

I caught my balance and scowled at him.

"What the hell is your problem?"

He stepped closer to me, a move meant to intimidate. I wasn't intimidated. To prove it, I closed the space between us and bared my teeth.

"You do not own me, Merdon. Get out of my house, now."

He was silent for so long that I thought he wouldn't answer.

"I know what you're doing, Hannah, and I'll be watching you."

His gaze flicked over my face, not in the longing way that Shax used to look at me but in a cold, calculating way that had me wondering what the hell Merdon's comment meant. Before I could ask, he pivoted and left.

Glaring into the night, I stalked forward and slammed the door behind him.

"What's going on?" Emily asked.

I froze at the sound of her voice, cursing myself for my lack of sense.

"Sorry," I said, turning to face her. "That was Merdon again. He's got a case of the stalker."

"What happened?" she asked in concern as she came down the steps.

I made a split-second decision to tell a skeleton version of the truth.

"I had a bad dream and stepped out on the roof to clear my head. I slipped on the snow and fell. Merdon caught me then went all caveman on me. After almost dropping me on the floor, he told me he's watching me. As if I didn't already know that. He showed up out of nowhere on breach day and, since then, has been shadowing me whenever I leave the house."

She cringed.

"I'm really glad he was there to catch you, but I'm equally sorry I let him sleep on the couch. That probably didn't help."

I waved away her apology.

"Do you want to watch a movie?" she asked, knowing there'd be no more sleep for me because of the dream.

"No. I'm fine. You go back to bed. I'll find something quiet to do."

She yawned, gave my arm a squeeze then shuffled upstairs. The soft click of her door closing told me she'd believed everything.

The shredded remnants of my façade slipped away from me, and I slowly slid to the floor. Thoughts clawed at my brain, making me twitchy and desperate. Without alcohol, there was no muting it.

I cried.

CHAPTER THREE

HAIR STUCK TO THE SWEAT DRYING ON MY FACE AS I IMPASSIVELY took in my progress. It'd taken me hours to clean to the level that a germaphobe or someone with OCD would applaud. Every surface in the kitchen gleamed in the morning light. Yet, I felt no sense of pride at what I'd accomplished. I'd done it to keep Emily happy and to focus my thoughts on safely mundane topics such as what to scrub next.

Despite my efforts, a few thoughts had still crept in. Anger at Merdon, who I'd caught glimpses of whenever I'd looked out the window. Bitterness that I was still in this shit world, and without alcohol to boot.

Wiping at my hair with my forearm, I looked around for what to do next.

"Morning," Emily said in a chipper tone as she jogged down the stairs. "Wow, this is amazing, Hannah. It looks and smells great in here. Were you up all night?"

"Yeah. Figured I might as well use my time wisely."

"How about I make us some breakfast while you wash up?"

"Sure."

I didn't care about breakfast. I didn't care about being clean. In fact, I cared about very little except the heaviness that made each step more difficult than the last. It felt like my body no longer belonged to me.

Entering my bathroom, I glanced at the shower. I was sweaty and probably smelled, but I struggled to find a reason why I should be concerned. Because a normal person would care, and I needed to think like a normal person. If I behaved like a functioning person, Emily would be happy, and a happy Emily would agree to more parties.

In a state of emotional detachment, I forced myself to strip and went through the motions of washing. Was this how the infected felt? Disconnected from the world around them? Driven by a single, consuming need? While they wanted blood or brains or whatever, I desperately wanted a drink.

My hands shook as I wiped my face. Tears leaked from my eyes. Anger and bitterness surged forward again, the only feelings that managed to penetrate the numbness.

I realized I was staring at my razor and quickly averted my gaze, once again cursing Merdon's intervention.

The doorbell rang, interrupting my train of thought. Most of the human residents of Tolerance weren't up and wandering around this early. That meant a fey was at the door. More specifically, a fey with a delivery.

Hurrying from the bathroom, I grabbed whatever clothes were close and dressed. There was no murmur of voices as I went downstairs, which told me whoever had stopped by was already gone.

Emily's lone presence in the kitchen, along with the box on the counter before her, confirmed that assumption.

"Who was at the door?" I asked.

"Merdon. I know I shouldn't have taken anything from him, but he said it was payment for letting him sleep on the couch. Plus, look at what's on top." She lifted a bag of fresh carrots. "They aren't wilted or moldy or anything."

What little hope that had sprouted at the sound of the doorbell withered and died at the mention of Merdon's name and the sight of those roots. Woodenly, I moved closer and peered into the box. There wasn't a single bottle among the supplies.

My stomach churned sickeningly, and I fisted my hand so Emily wouldn't notice the tremble.

"Looks like some decent food. Hopefully, he doesn't try to leave anything tomorrow."

"Yeah."

Her agreement didn't sound that sincere.

"What?" I asked.

"Do you think we should do something to thank him for saving you last night?"

Weeks of hiding what I was really feeling was the only thing that kept my anger and frustration from showing.

"He carried me all the way to the house. You know how they are about touching. That much holding time was reward enough. Don't encourage him, Emily. That's the last thing we want."

"I know. You're right."

She started putting the supplies away.

"Instead of making breakfast here, I thought we could go eat with James and Mary. You know how Mary is about company. She'd love it."

"Sure," I said, dying just a little more inside.

When Emily finished, we both bundled up and trudged outside. She paused and looked back at the house.

"Too bad it snowed," she said.

I looked around, realizing I'd missed that little detail while I'd been cleaning.

"Why is that too bad? You miss seeing the bloodstains?"

"Of course not." She pointed to our roof. "I just wanted to see your epic wipeout mark."

"It wasn't that impressive," I mumbled, striding away.

She hurried to catch up to me.

"Sorry. I didn't mean to make light of it. It must have been scary, falling like that."

I noted a fey across the street and fixed a smile on my face as I waved at him.

"I don't want to talk about it. Okay?" There were too many ears to lie now and get away with it.

"Sure." Emily smiled at the fey and waved as well.

The rest of the walk to James and Mary's was made in silence. When we reached their house, Emily knocked twice then let herself in.

"Hello," she called. "It's Hannah and Emily."

"Come in, come in," James called. "You're just in time. Ma's cooking up a feast."

I shucked my jacket and boots and followed Emily to the living room where James was comfortably seated in the chair he favored.

"Hannah, we've missed you," he said.

I dutifully gave him a quick hug.

"I'm sorry about that. I got caught up in my own head again."

He nodded in understanding.

"It's an easy thing to do nowadays. Sit down. Ma said the food won't be ready for a bit."

"I think I'll go help her," Emily said, moving toward the kitchen.

The old couple had grabbed one of the more dated homes in the subdivision. The house hadn't been converted to an open concept living plan like so many of the others, which suited the pair just fine. After fifty-some years together, they valued their separate space as much as they enjoyed spending time together.

"You don't look like you're holding up," James said bluntly as I sat on the couch. "Dreaming again?"

"I never stopped."

He shook his head in that way old men did when they didn't like the news they were hearing.

"That's a damn shame. A girl your age should have happier thoughts in her head. Damn hellhounds and infected. Who would have thought we'd end up in a world like this?"

"Not me."

"Me, neither. Mary thought we'd get bored in our retirement." He snorted. "I'd welcome bored just about now."

We both knew that was a lie. While he didn't like the threat of death that the hellhounds or infected brought, neither he nor Mary minded the visitors. It was probably more than they'd had before the earthquakes.

"It's better not to play the 'what-if' game," I said, dully. "That kind of thinking can mess with your head."

James studied me for a long moment.

"Are you all right?"

"I've been up long enough to clean the entire kitchen, top to bottom. I'm just tired."

He grunted in a way that was far too reminiscent of the fey.

The door to the kitchen swung open, and Mary bustled out with a stack of plates, which she immediately left on the dining room table so she could come give me a hug.

"I was so worried about you," she said, smoothing her hands over my curls.

"I'm fine."

She clucked her tongue, her doubt clearly showing in the look she gave me.

"I'm fine," I repeated. "And I'm sorry for not showing up yesterday. I just got caught up in my own head." That was the standard excuse I gave when I slipped up.

Before the quakes, people always used to forget things in the rush of their own busy lives. My mom used to say it was because we were getting caught up in our own heads. With so much to do and think about, inevitably things were missed or forgotten.

Thinking of Mom hurt, so I focused on moving.

"I'll set the table," I said, pulling out of Mary's hold.

"Nonsense," she said.

"I insist. It's my way of apologizing for not visiting sooner."

Mary harrumphed and took a seat in the chair next to James. Emily emerged from the kitchen to help me set the table.

"I think there's an extra plate," I said, holding up the fifth in the pile.

"Nope. We have more company."

As if timed, the bathroom door down the hall opened, and Merdon stepped out with a towel around his waist.

"Now that it is a sight," Mary said, twisting in her chair to see the fey. "Merdon, darlin', your clothes are still in the washer. You're just going to need to sit down and have breakfast with us as you are."

I shot Emily a look. "Did you tell him we were coming here?"

She shook her head. "No. I swear."

I swiveled my angry gaze to Merdon.

"Are you following me?"

Mary made an impatient noise.

"He was here first, so he sure as fire didn't follow you. Behave, Hannah. Merdon is one of the many fey who doesn't have a home to call his own. They all know they're welcome here for a shower or a clean change of clothes whenever they want. It's the least we can do for the food they provide us."

James snorted.

"It's not the food. You like the views, Ma."

"Hush, Pa. It is too the food." A smile curved her lips, and she winked at us. "The views don't hurt none, though."

During all this byplay, Merdon watched me closely. His attention would have been understandable if there was even a hint of typical fey yearning in his steady, yellow gaze; but there wasn't. His indecipherable expression gave me no hint of what he was thinking when he looked at me. Yet, I felt judged and hated him for it. He had no idea what hells were tormenting me or what I'd survived.

"Do you mind not staring? It makes me uncomfortable," I said, keeping my tone light so Mary wouldn't scold me again.

His complete disregard of my request rekindled the temper he'd sparked to life with his unwanted interference earlier. A flush heated my neck then slowly crept higher.

"Hannah, come help fetch what Mary made for breakfast," Emily said, noting the stare-down Merdon and I were having.

"You are so sweet, Emily," Mary said. "My feet sure are tired."

James snorted again.

"And there's no view in the kitchen. Need your glasses, Ma?" James asked.

"Hush. Merdon, be a dear and help me to the table?"

I didn't flee to the kitchen fast enough to miss the way Mary petted Merdon's bulging bicep as he helped her to her feet.

"There's no way I can sit at that table and eat," I whispered to Emily.

She chuckled. "Mary's harmless. I think the way she treats the fey is funny. And Merdon probably enjoys the attention as much as the rest of the fey do."

"I didn't mean Mary's questionable fascination. Although that is a little stomach-turning. I meant I can't stay here with him. This might be a coincidence, or maybe he overheard us talking and planned it."

Emily didn't dismiss my concern. We both knew how sharp fey hearing was. In fact, Merdon was probably listening to us now. My gaze slid to the door.

"We'll eat fast. Take this."

She handed me a baking dish. The lid rattled, and I tried harder to hold it steady.

"Everything all right?" She asked, noticing.

"Fine. I wish everyone would stop asking. It's making me not fine."

"Sorry."

"Let's just hurry up and get this over with."

Emily shot me a hurt, surprised look. Before she even spoke, I was berating myself for letting too much of my anger slip.

"Mary and James are both looking forward to this. Be nice."

I turned on my smile, not all one thousand watts but one with just enough happy to back my words.

"I'm always nice."

I led the way out of the kitchen and saw Merdon was already seated on the far side of the table. With James on one end and Mary sitting beside her husband, opposite Merdon, that meant my options were to take the end seat next to Merdon or the one open next to Mary, across from him. Emily made the decision for me by taking the end seat.

It's just one meal, I told myself. *No big deal.*

I set the dish on the table, ignoring the way his unwavering gaze made my insides twitchy, and took my seat.

Mary removed the lids off the dishes, and my stomach roiled at the aroma wafting in steamy curls from the egg bake. There were no sour notes of food gone bad or poorly prepared to explain my reaction. Likely, it was just due to my general mood. Something a drink would soothe.

Knowing what was expected of me, I handed her my plate and watched her scoop out a moderate portion. She did the same for Emily and herself. James received a bit more, but Merdon's plate got the majority.

The meal had progressed only a few bites when Mary dropped her fork. It bounced off the edge of the table and fell to the floor.

"Damn this cold and my arthritis," she mumbled, already bending down to retrieve it.

I scooted my chair to the side to give her more room as her top half disappeared under the table.

A sudden bang against the surface set all the dishes rattling.

"Sweet mother of Jesus," Mary said loudly.

A moment later, she extracted herself, wide-eyed, with the fork clutched in her hand.

"Mary?" James asked.

"Yep. That one," Mary said vacantly, staring at Merdon, who, like the rest of us, was watching Mary and wondering what was going on.

"Spit it out, woman. What's wrong with you?" James said.

She turned her gaze to her husband.

"It's the size of my grandma's rolling pin. The one she hit grandpa with over the head because he'd stayed out drinking too late."

She swallowed hard and looked at Merdon.

"Bless you, boy. You're going to make some woman very happy someday."

Then, she began fanning herself vigorously with her free hand.

"You need to settle down, Ma," James said. "The last time you got this worked up, you almost broke *my* rolling pin."

My fork clattered to my plate. I felt traumatized on more levels than I could count. I couldn't even look at Merdon to see if he understood what had just happened because he'd sat at Mary's table while wearing nothing but a towel.

James's gaze swept over his guests.

"Mmm," he mumbled. "It looks like we could all settle down. Maybe just a breakfast nip."

He got up from the table and shuffled to a sideboard that looked like it was from the 1970s. Sliding the panel front to the side, he revealed a cache of bottles that made me want to weep with joy. With my mouth drying by the second, I watched him select an aged brandy.

"For the orange juice," he said, catching my stare.

I could have kissed the old man. Instead, I got up to help him pour.

Mary drank hers straight, having already drained her juice, and held out her glass for a bit more. As much as I wanted to do the same, I drank my diluted brandy, fully aware of Merdon's persistent scrutiny.

It was a relief when Mary and James finished their meals and Emily started to clear everyone's plates.

"Not much of an appetite, dear?" Mary asked, noting I still had more than half of my meal left.

"I drank too much juice. Where'd you find it?"

"The fey bring us all sorts of supplies," James said. "Especially the liquid kind. They know the alcohol helps with the aches and pains Mary and I have. Medicinal, you know."

There was no need to justify the merits of alcohol to me. Thanks to James, I'd discovered its benefits not long after the world fell to shit.

A buzz went off somewhere in the house.

"Merdon, that's the washer. Do you remember how to switch over to the dryer, or should I help you?" Mary asked.

James snorted.

"The man remembers. You stay in your chair, Ma, or you'll give yourself a fit."

Merdon left the room, and Mary leaned toward me.

"The towel fell off of Tor when he was here. He's not quite as big as Merdon but thick." She shook her head and made num-num noises that someone her age shouldn't make. At least, not around someone my age.

She straightened away and took my plate. "I'll just wrap this up for you. I'm sure you'll want it later."

She disappeared into the kitchen, leaving me alone with James. Without asking, I grabbed the bottle and went to put it away.

"You have a hefty collection here," I said, returning it to its place. "I'm surprised that the cabinet's supporting all the weight."

"You and me both. If you see something you like, feel free to take it." He gave me a considering look. "You're over 21, right?"

I laughed. It was the same thing he'd asked me when he'd poured me my first shot in the RV after a bad dream.

"Not by a few years. But if you won't tell, I won't."

He pretended to lock his lips and throw away the key.

"The police won't be knocking on your door because of me," he said.

I turned before my expression could give away any of the pain those words caused. The bottles provided a good distraction from the reminder of the world we had lost.

"Do you have a kind you don't like?"

"Any of those big ones. That's too much for Mary and me to finish, and we know you girls like to have your get-togethers. Help yourself."

I selected a 1.75-liter vodka bottle that already had some missing from it.

"We'll help you finish this one off," I said, standing.

"Real kind of you." He winked at me before getting serious. "You girls need to take care of yourselves. Mary and I lost a lot, and I'm not sure we could handle any more."

"None of us can."

He nodded in agreement.

"Any chance you changed your mind about house-sharing with one of the fey? I think Emily wouldn't object if you were—"

"No."

"I'm not suggesting anything permanent like the other girls. What if you did something like Mary and me? A different fey every night so none of them get ideas."

I shook my head.

"You know why that won't work. A single night? A week? The length of time wouldn't matter; what matters is that Emily and I are over eighteen. We're fair game. You and Mary aren't. If we let a fey in, we're waving the flag that we're up for auction. I'm not going to be a broodmare for the next generation of feybies just to have a big, strong protector. No thanks.

"I appreciate the donation," I said, lifting the bottle, "but I think I'll get going. Please let Emily know I headed home."

James sighed and nodded.

Leaving him at the table, I grabbed my jacket and hurried out the door. My rush wasn't due to his nagging. After all, the topic of a fey roommate surfaced every time I visited the old couple. I really hadn't expected to escape it this time. No, my haste was due to my need to beat Emily home. The topic was just a perfect excuse for my departure, though.

With my prize safely tucked under my arm, I let myself into our house and went straight for the recycling. The bottles from our party were still there. Glad that Emily hadn't carried it to wherever she went with the recycling, I fished through for another vodka bottle, carefully rearranged the rest, then filled the bottle with water.

By the time she returned home, the fake bottle of liquor was stored above the stove, and I had two shots warming my belly while I lounged on the couch.

"We need more movies," I said. "I've watched all of these enough to repeat the lines, word for word."

"Why didn't you wait for me?"

"Because you were in the kitchen, cleaning up, and I was in the dining room, listening to James's 'you need a man' speech. It wasn't something I wanted Merdon to join in on." I lifted my head from the couch and met her gaze over the back. "Oh, and James sent home a mostly full bottle of vodka with me. I stashed it above the stove, figuring we could save it for the next party. I know we do food and booze as the buy-in for the parties, but what if we allowed a movie or two?"

Her concern melted away to a smile.

"I like that idea."

And just like that, I knew I'd reassured her.

Unlike me, Emily didn't drink outside of the parties. She'd never know the bottle wasn't real. I'd replace it long before then.

CHAPTER FOUR

A SPLASH OF UNWANTED ORANGE FLICKERED THROUGH MY EYELIDS and pulled me from my sleep. I rolled over to a more comfortable position, facing away from the window, and hit my forehead on something hard. Cracking my eyes open, I cringed at the sunlight glinting off the vodka bottle on my pillow.

I didn't remember removing it from its hiding place under my mattress after going to bed. Then again, I'd been pleasantly buzzed when I'd come up to my room, so who knew what I'd done once I crawled under the covers.

In fact, thanks to my bed-buddy, I was still blissfully insulated from the harshness of life. Unwilling to give up even a little of the ground I'd gained, I took a morning swig then stowed the bottle before closing myself in the bathroom.

When I saw myself in the mirror, I realized my bloodshot eyes were sending out a warning beacon. Emily would take one look and know I'd been drinking. Since her harping was the last thing I wanted to listen to, I wet a washcloth and held the cold compress to them. It took several applications before the redness faded. I even went the extra step to brush my teeth and comb my hair.

Feeling pretty confident that my appearance passed as normal, I left my room and noticed Emily's door was still closed. Good. It would give me more time to figure out what to do with myself. Yesterday, I'd gotten away with just lying on the couch because she'd assumed I was tired from being up most of the previous night. Going to bed early also hadn't been questioned.

I knew better than to think I'd get away with the same today. At least, not without Emily thinking something was wrong with me. I mean, obviously, there was, but her motherly smothering wouldn't fix it. Nothing would.

That thought had me craving another drink, which started an internal debate over whether I should. I knew I needed to conserve the alcohol I had left until I figured out how to quietly get more. In addition to the issue of gaining a better supply, there was also the problem of Emily. She worried and watched me far too closely. Although she hadn't commented on my quiet trips to my bedroom yesterday, she'd likely question it today.

Even if I had an endless supply of alcohol, I wouldn't get away with drinking myself into a constant state of numbness with her around. That meant I either needed to go somewhere else and drink—not happening with so many fey around—or find some way to distract myself from the burning thirst drying my throat.

I decided to keep cleaning. It'd been something my family had done every Saturday morning. We'd all take a room and clean the hell out of it. As my sister got older, she and I competed to see who could get done first. It'd been fun.

The small smile on my lips died with the memory, and regret and guilt clouded my mind.

Emily didn't comment on my dusting when she finally came

downstairs or when I changed to washing light switches and doorknobs. Moving from room to room gave me an excuse to duck into my own for a quick drink without raising suspicion.

"You have a lot of energy today," Emily commented when I returned to the kitchen with the cleaning rag. "Did you sleep better last night?"

"Yep. No dreams that I remember."

"Good. Do you want to get out and do something? I was thinking about catching a fey ride over to Tenacity to check it out."

From all accounts, Tenacity was just like Tolerance, a massive cluster of homes that the fey made "safe" for habitation by building a wall around them. Since I didn't care for my current prison, I didn't see the point of going to tour another one.

"I'll pass. We haven't made a cake in a while. I think I'll go to the supply shed and see if there's a box mix."

"I heard it's pretty low, but there are groups going out for supply runs every morning. If you can't find anything today, there might be something tomorrow. Are you sure you don't want to go with me?"

"I'm sure. Don't worry. You go do you. I'll be fine."

I pulled the vacuum out of the supply closet and pretended I couldn't feel her staring at me.

As soon as she left, I stopped cleaning and poured myself a cup of vodka. I didn't bother mixing it with anything because if Emily returned before my drink was gone, it'd look like water. At least, that was the reason I told myself.

Wandering the house, I sipped and studied all the empty nail holes in the walls. There were boxes in the basement filled with the previous family's belongings. Based on all the holes, there had to be a lot of pictures. Unable to help myself, I crept downstairs. The basement ran the width of the house, its length divided by the stairs. One side had once been used as an exercise room, based on the equipment drowning amidst the clutter.

At the bottom of the steps, I flicked on the overhead lights that did little to dispel the long shadows cast by the stacks of boxes and totes. I went to the nearest box and lifted the flap. A picture, carefully cushioned by newspaper, lay on top. A family of four posed against a green backdrop of trees, the parents standing behind the children. I studied the happy boy and girl, barely into their teens, and took a bigger drink.

As much as I wanted to believe the family had made it to somewhere safe, I knew better. There wasn't anywhere safe, and families didn't survive. At least, not intact.

The light from the nearest basement window dimmed for a brief moment. Fear and resignation kept me from looking up. Instead, I took another long drink and continued to gaze at the happy family that reminded me so much of mine.

The light grew brighter. Hand trembling, I put the picture back in the box and glared at the leather-clad legs as they vanished from sight.

I hated the way the fey moved around aimlessly just like the infected. Just like my family. My sister.

My bitter thoughts weighed on me so much that just breathing became hard. I hated this world. It offered only anger and fear to those who still survived. With the constant presence of those two emotions, I felt like I was always two seconds from drowning.

I took a bigger drink and thought again how this wasn't living. It was a suspended state of death. There was no blissful peace, just never-ending time to contemplate how I would meet my end.

Back upstairs, instead of going for the cake mix, I went for a refill.

"YOU'RE NEVER GOING to believe what I heard," Emily called the moment she opened the door.

I didn't bother sitting up. It was too much work.

"What?" I asked. Had that come out a little too slow and relaxed?

"The plane that's been going out to look for Molev spotted some survivors. Can you believe that? It's not just us and the Whiteman folks anymore."

A fear settled in my chest, and I forced myself to sit up and look at her.

"What do you mean?"

"There's a bunch of them. The pilot wasn't able to count accurately, but at least a dozen people came out to wave when the plane flew overhead."

She was excited about a dozen waving humans? I lay back down on the couch and closed my eyes against the spinning and the subtle heartache. A dozen more survivors wouldn't do shit. They weren't some miracle find but fate throwing the dregs together to make the slaughter more convenient for the infected.

Emily babbled on, relating all the juicy details from her amazing visit to ward number two. I made non-committal noises whenever she paused. Prodded by what she perceived as interest, she continued her gossip, barely noticing me.

When she finally headed to the kitchen to put something together for dinner, I mumbled an excuse about a long day of cleaning and turned in early. I wasn't even sure what time it was when I fell into the bed and pulled out my bottle. I didn't care about conserving as I took a long pull; I only cared about my unacceptable state of consciousness.

It was dark when I jerked awake.

Heart pounding, but not sure why, I sat up in bed and looked around the room. There was nothing there. Yet, the panicked feeling continued to grow.

Taking my bottle, I went into the bathroom and sat in the dry shower, hugging my knees. I thought of my family, of my sister, and the fear continued to swell. I did the only thing I could to stop it and took a drink. Then, another. My throat burned when the next one went down the wrong way. I coughed and went back for more.

At some point, the alcohol did its job, and with the cold tile of the bathroom cradling me, I returned to the peace of oblivion.

A knock at the bathroom door startled me awake.

"Hannah?" Emily called.

"Yeah," I croaked.

"Are you okay?"

For a bleary moment, I wasn't sure. I didn't know where I was or who was at the door. Unfolding from my huddled position, I winced at the stiffness in my back and the numbness of my ass. Pieces clicked into place. Mostly that it was Emily outside the bathroom door, trying to mother me again.

"Yep. I'm fine. Did you need something or do you just enjoy sending me to turtle town?"

"Oh, sorry! I'll talk to you downstairs."

I rubbed my hand over my face then carefully climbed to my feet. My knees popped.

What in the hell had happened to me last night?

Going to the sink, I rinsed out my mouth and tried to

remember. A big blank nothing between going to bed and Emily knocking on the door was all I could manage. It should have felt like a win. Nothingness was far better than dreams of Katie. But my life was too far removed from that of a winner.

Turning away from my sallow reflection, my gaze caught on the vodka sitting in the center of the shower. Why had I carried it in here? I frowned, trying again to remember what had happened last night. Maybe it was better that I didn't.

Mid-morning light streamed through my bedroom windows when I emerged from the bathroom. It didn't bode well that I'd slept in that long. It also explained why Emily had come looking for me. No doubt she would scrutinize every damn thing about me once I went downstairs. Annoyed, I returned the bottle to its place under my bed and did my best not to notice how there was less than half of it left.

Skipping a shower since I'd already spent enough time in it, I changed into something I found on my floor then twisted my hair into a sloppy bun. The look had been cute, once upon a time, and I hoped Emily would think that's what I was going for.

Leaving my room, my stomach lurched at the smell of whatever Emily was making. Why did she always have to cook?

"Hope you're hungry," she said, hearing me on the stairs. "I'm making scrambled eggs and toast. We had another box of food this morning with bread in it."

She looked up as I entered the kitchen.

"You look..." Her gaze swept over my face as she obviously searched for the right word to describe my appearance.

Obviously, my half-hearted attempt at cute had failed by a mile.

"Like I slept like shit? I did. Thanks for noticing."

"Sorry."

Feeling agitated and disagreeable, I sat on the stool.

"You say that too much. Don't be sorry. Just be thankful it's not you."

"I wish it were me," she said quietly. "I hate seeing you like this."

"Then don't look."

Instead of guilt, her expression of hurt irritated me more.

"You know what? I'll spare us both and just go back to bed unless you need something."

"Wait," she said, stopping my move to stand. "I have a better idea than spending the day in bed."

The rest of her suggestion was lost on me as I noted someone through the window to our backyard. He'd been standing so still beside the tree that he almost blended with it.

"Fucking bullshit," I said as I recognized Merdon.

"We don't have to go," Emily said, regaining my attention.

"Not you. Him."

I nodded toward the window. Emily followed my gaze.

"I can't deal with him right now," I said. "Get rid of him. Make sure he knows not to come back."

Turning away from him and Emily, I went upstairs. However, instead of heading to my room, I moved down the hall, looking for a good spot to spectate.

The space by the tree was empty, but I wasn't a fool. He was out there somewhere. Even as I had that thought, something creaked overhead. I looked up to glare at the ceiling as Emily called Merdon's name outside.

Emily appeared as I glanced at the yard through a sheer curtain.

"Merdon?" she called again.

A dark shape fell past the window and landed right beside

her, making my heart race. Merdon smoothly straightened from his crouch, facing Emily, who'd whirled as soon as he'd touched ground.

She started talking, and I resented that I couldn't hear her tell him off or, at least, see his fallen expression. Settling for watching body language, I waited for his shoulders to slump, needing to see his dejected defeat. But the bastard just crossed his arms when she stopped talking. The way she continued to stare at him let me know she was listening. What was he saying? Shit. Was he telling her I jumped?

I hurried downstairs and yanked open the back door at the same time she reached it. There was no sign of Merdon behind her.

"Is he gone?" I asked. "Or back on the roof? What did he say to you?"

She stepped inside and took off her jacket, not meeting my gaze.

"He said you're drinking too much. And I told him he shouldn't base his opinions on what he saw at the party."

Relief coursed through me.

"Good."

I started to turn, and she caught my arm.

"He said he wasn't, Hannah. I know you're drinking too much, too. I can smell it on you."

I faced her and rolled my eyes. "I slept like shit and grabbed clothes off the floor because I'm lazy and tired and in a mood. I'm wearing the same stuff I wore on party night. Instead of going back to bed, I'll do laundry."

She reluctantly released me, and I could see in her eyes she wasn't buying my bullshit anymore.

"That's not what you were wearing."

"Now you're the clothes police? Whatever, Emily. I'll clean up and stop stinking up your air. If I continue to be offensive, just say the word and I'll find somewhere else to go."

"You know that's not what I'm suggesting."

"Right. I better get started on my laundry."

Even knowing that she could smell it on me, I needed another drink. When I reached my room, I pulled all the shades so my creeper wouldn't spy on me and took several gulps. Then I stripped naked, wrapped myself in a blanket toga, and spent the morning as a drunk washerwoman.

Around lunch, Emily tried to get me to eat some mashed-up crap that looked too much like vomit. It was an easy pass for me. Dinner, a simple baked potato with butter and cheese, didn't appeal to me any more than lunch. She only asked once before leaving me to my rerun of *Drop Dead Fred*.

At some time during the night, I woke up on the couch with my bladder screaming at me. I fell when I tried to get up, then banged my knee on the damn end table when I tried to navigate to the guest bathroom. None of it hurt. Probably because my world was still spinning. I sat with a sigh and stared at the window as I peed.

A face appeared.

"Jesus fucking shit!"

I fell off the toilet mid-piss and got it everywhere.

Even drunk off my ass, I knew enough to be angry as I stood, shorts and underwear around my ankles, and yanked the shade down. Kicking off my wet bottoms, I stumbled from the room.

PEOPLE RAN. *Their screams filled the air, almost muting the groans of the infected that sprinted in the streets. Fear congealed the blood in my veins. I'd be an idiot not to feel it. But I didn't run like the rest. Not when Emily called my name or when she tugged on my arm. Rooted, I watched the woman with the torn off cheek turn toward us. A sense of acceptance joined my fear as I faced my impending death.*

The dream shifted.

Arms around Emily, I watched the massacre below. The cheekless woman was dead on our lawn. Others still ran after humans or broke into houses. I could hear fighting in our living room. Emily shook. I probably did too. I couldn't really tell. Most of my attention was on the people running outside.

A woman stumbled and went down to her knees. I could see the panic in her wide eyes, so like Katie. Fear crawled its way up my spine, wrapping around my lungs. Squeezing.

I tried to shut my eyes but couldn't.

The infected lunged for the woman.

But it wasn't the woman anymore. It was Emily that the infected bit again and again. Emily's screams that filled my ears.

I jerked away from the person I still held. She tilted her tear-streaked face up to look at me.

"You left her," Katie whispered with sad eyes.

THERE WAS no transition from sleeping to waking. Not really. The sobbing and screams that had escaped during the nightmare continued as I slowly became aware of my bedroom, daylight, and the open door.

Emily sat on the edge of my bed, softly saying nonsensical things like, "It's okay," and "you're safe." We knew both were lies.

"I'm fine," I said through my snot-filled sobs. "You can go."

She exhaled heavily.

"I think you're so used to saying that that you don't stop and ask yourself if you really are, Hannah." She took my hand before I could get angry. "I cleaned up the urine all over the downstairs bathroom and washed your clothes."

Last night came flooding back, and I did get mad. Pulling my hand from hers, I scowled.

"I was mid-pee when that asshole, Merdon, looked through the fucking window. Given recent happenings, the sudden appearance of a face scared me so bad I fell off the toilet. I doubt you would have reacted any differently."

She studied me for a moment.

"I would have been aware enough to close the curtain before using the bathroom," she said softly then stood. "I'll make us something to eat."

"I'm not hungry," I said, feeling thirsty more than anything.

"You need to eat, Hannah."

"You need to stop acting like my mom. She's dead."

Instead of giving me a hurt look, she nodded and left.

Whatever. I didn't need her weirdness right now.

The dream still clung to me, making my skin itch and tingle. I reached under my bed, grateful I'd actually hidden the vodka before falling asleep. Helping myself to a large drink of it, I ignored how little remained in the bottle and did my best to erase the dream.

It didn't fade easily. The bad ones never did.

Pacing to the window, I looked out at the street where the woman had died a few days ago. Instead of seeing the slightly trampled but still pristine white snow, I saw Emily laying in a pool of her own blood.

Shuddering, I gulped more vodka.

How long before that really did happen? Today? Tomorrow? It didn't matter. I didn't want to be around to see it. I couldn't.

Just as I let the curtain fall back into place, Merdon stepped into view.

I could feel his gaze shift from my face to the bottle in my hand. I gave him the finger, hoping the gesture wasn't completely lost on him.

CHAPTER FIVE

I WAS OUT. NOT A DROP REMAINED IN THE BOTTLE AFTER yesterday's binge drinking because of that messed up dream.

Making a face at myself in the mirror, I dabbed another layer of concealer under my eyes and gave my wet curls another scrunch. Hopefully, the effort would be worthwhile. After all of Emily's condemning looks yesterday, I needed to at least pretend to have my act together if I wanted to fool Mary and James.

Exhaustion pulled at me as I made my way downstairs. Too little sleep could do that to a person if they let it. I wasn't about to let it. There was a lot to do today even if dawn's light was barely creeping over the wall.

In the kitchen, I whipped up a batch of biscuits as quietly as possible. While they were baking, I started on the powdered eggs and sausage. It wasn't much, but Emily would know effort went into it.

While I waited for her to wake up, I opened the curtains of every window in the house for the show.

Look at Hannah not drinking.

Fucking Merdon.

With everything in place, I sat down on the couch and waited. My mind raced along all the possible ways today might end. There was only one outcome I wanted, me in bed with a bottle snuggled close. Not that I planned on broadcasting that. No, I'd give everyone what they wanted. A picture-perfect Hannah, happy with her place in this shitty world.

The soft smile I'd practiced in the mirror slipped into place with ease when I heard Emily on the stairs.

"Morning," I said, standing. "I made egg biscuits."

Her steps slowed as I hurried to the oven and withdrew the two plates I'd kept warm.

"I made them from memory, so I hope they taste okay. It's been a while."

I swallowed hard, remembering the exact last time I'd made them. It'd been with my mom, two days before the quakes. We'd girl-talked our way through the process. She'd asked questions about my plans to celebrate my birthday with my friends that night, and I'd filled her in on the latest school drama and my plans for college.

Keeping my smile in place, I set the plate before Emily. She didn't look happy.

"Hannah, I know this song and dance. You don't need to pretend things are fine."

My false humor slipped a little.

"You're right. Things aren't fine. But I tried acting like they weren't fine, and it didn't make things any better, did it?"

She sighed.

"No. It didn't."

"Exactly. So, which version of me do you want?"

Rather than answering, she took a bite of her sandwich.

"This is really good," she mumbled around a mouthful.

My smile widened, hurting my cheeks.

"Thank you."

I sat beside her and forced myself to eat. It tasted like dust and ash mixed with a little water.

"So what do we want to do today?" I asked. "I'm tired of being in the house."

Emily chewed thoughtfully for a moment, and I could feel her wary gaze on me.

"We could do the rounds," she said. "End at James and Mary's for dinner?"

That answer was the one I both anticipated and dreaded.

"Sounds good to me."

The last thing I wanted to do was spend the day talking to people. But I really, really needed face to face time with James and Mary. Well, just James. And, I couldn't get the latter without the former, so I'd just need to suck it up for a day. No problem.

An hour later, hands tucked between my knees to hide the trembling, I questioned how badly I wanted a drink as I listened to this new girl whine about her roommate.

"It's not that he's doing anything bad, really," she said. "It's all the creepy watching."

She glanced through the patio doors to where the fey stood on the deck, doing the creepy watching thing she just mentioned.

"Curtains," I said with a smile I didn't feel. "Everything that's see-through needs them."

She shook her head slightly.

"I think he watches me sleep. Listen, I like the food and all, but since the infected got in here and not in Tenacity, I think I'm changing teams again. I don't feel safe here, anymore."

I snorted softly, and Emily gave me a quick, censuring look before taking the girl's hand.

"The fey aren't mind readers. You have to set clear boundaries with them. If it's bothering you that he's watching you while you sleep, tell him. Warn him that you're considering leaving because his obsessive hovering is stifling. I haven't met a fey yet who wouldn't adjust what he's doing to be more accommodating. Especially if his actions might risk a female leaving."

"What she's saying is that he wants you here and will do anything you want to get you to stay. The one thing fey don't do is force," I said. "They don't have the balls for that."

Emily cut me another warning look.

"What? You know that's true."

I looked at the fey on the patio. Since the girl had said she wanted to leave, he'd gotten that slumped-shouldered, defeated look of rejection. Seriously, how could Emily think he had balls?

Shaking my head a little and wishing the visit over, I refocused on Emily as she coached the girl on how to have the conversation with her roommate.

Five minutes later, we let ourselves out, and I breathed a sigh of relief.

"I really hope they aren't all going to be that whiny," I said.

"Talking about your feelings isn't whiny, Hannah. It's healthy."

"Then why do I feel sick after listening to it?"

She rolled her eyes at me, and I tucked my hands into my jacket as we trudged to the next house on her list.

"What's the point to these visits?" I asked as we neared Cheri's house. "We're telling everyone the same things we told them when they first moved here."

"Change is hard. Sometimes a friendly face and a little advice, even if it's a repeat, can go a long way. Besides, it's in our best interest that these girls stay."

I frowned in confusion.

"Why's that? They're taking up the supplies."

"They're also taking up the attention. Unless you've changed your mind and want—"

"Nope," I said quickly. "No fey; no way. That's my campaign slogan. Seriously, look at how miserable the last girl was. Who, in her right mind, would want that?"

Emily shrugged slightly and knocked on the door.

"Hey, Farco," she said to the fey who answered. "Is Cheri here?"

He grunted and let us inside where we found Cheri sitting in the living room. Curled comfortably in a chair with a stack of books on the floor next to her, she looked up from her reading as we entered.

"Library time?" I asked.

She grinned.

"Farco went out and found a bunch of books for me when I wasn't feeling well after the party." She glanced at him, her smile warming. "I mentioned how much I like reading."

"When you read those, I will find more," he promised.

I could see it in her eyes. She was falling for him. It wasn't a complete shock. After all, she wasn't the first human female to fall for a fey. But over books? Come on. She could have asked for anything, like a remodel of the basement to include a bowling alley. Instead, she was giving in to a life of breeding for books.

"Farco, would you mind going somewhere else so we can have a private girl talk?" I asked.

He grunted and looked at Cheri.

"I will find some chips for you."

Cheri's adoration grew three times too big for my cynical

heart. The door had barely closed when I opened my mouth to tell her the truth.

"I'm so happy for you," Emily said, beating me.

"Thank you. Coming here was the best decision ever. If not for your party and my killer hangover, I don't think I would have given Farco a chance. He was so incredibly sweet, though, when I was puking out my guts. He cleaned up everything like it was no big deal then just played with my hair because it made my head feel better."

I snorted.

"He was playing with your hair because he wanted to touch you."

Cheri shrugged.

"I don't mind if he got a little something out of it. Last night, I got the best foot rub of my life." A blush flared to life in her cheeks. "He's so attentive."

"Let me guess," I said. "You groaned a little, and he started in on your calves. When you groaned again, he went a little higher."

She looked shocked then hurt.

"So it's a game?" she asked.

"Don't mind Hannah," Emily said, quickly cutting me off. "It's not a game. But keep in mind that the fey didn't even know what a woman was until after the quakes. We're so new to them, and they're so clueless about what makes us tick. When one of them finds something a girl likes, they do information share. It's not a game; it's an honest effort to learn what makes us happy because they really do want to make us happy."

Cheri's glance slid to me, looking for confirmation.

"It's true. Happy girls want to stay. But girls who stay tend to get knocked up. You ready for his feyby?"

She cringed a little, and Emily reached out to pat her leg.

"Don't worry about babies. Just take things slow and see if you enjoy his company, first. Fey really are attentive."

Cheri gave a slow nod, a little more troubled looking than before, as Emily hustled us out the door.

"We spent thirty minutes listening to the last one whine, and now you're rushing? Not enough whining from Cheri for you?" I asked.

Emily shot me a dark look.

"Just because you're miserable doesn't mean you need to make everyone else miserable."

"Whoa, that is not what I was doing. I was telling her the truth."

Emily exhaled heavily.

"The truth delivered in a negative way to stir drama."

I snorted.

"Pot calling the kettle there."

"What's that supposed to mean?" she asked.

"We're focused on all the houses that have new girls so you can prod them into giving the fey a chance. If that isn't stirring drama, I don't know what is."

"It's me caring about them enough during a time of transition to check in on their mental wellbeing. This shit isn't easy on anyone, Hannah. Maybe you should try looking beyond yourself and your own misery for a while."

Shit. I was losing her.

Taking a deep breath, I walked by her side for the count of twenty then spoke.

"You're right. I'm sorry. It's not about me. I'm just worried that, if all the girls and fey start matching up, we'll be next."

"I know, Hannah. But did you ever stop to consider what that would mean for us? No more parties. Constant food. Would that be so bad?"

"If that's what you want from this life, no, that wouldn't be bad. It's not what I want though, so don't ask me to go there."

"Fair enough."

No matter how much my hands shook or my stomach twisted or my head hurt, I behaved for the remainder of the day. And I was full of relief when we left the last house and headed for James and Mary's place.

"I'm really hoping for something good," I said a little breathlessly. Nothing felt good, and all of the walking around was making it worse.

"Me too," Emily said. "Those cookies were too salty."

I made a non-committal noise. Not only was I not talking about food, but I'd also had the smarts not to eat the deformed balls Emily had.

James called for us to enter after Emily's first knock. We let ourselves in and took off our jackets and boots.

"Well, this is a surprise," James said when he saw me. "Twice in a week."

"It's a new week," I deadpanned.

He laughed. "Could be. But, I didn't think I'd see you again so soon. Glad you're here, though. Now Ma can stop scolding me about keeping my mouth shut."

A true smile lifted my lips. He and Mary thought I'd left because of his fey talk. Perfect. Guilt was good.

"What have you two been up to today?" he asked. "Ma said she saw you earlier."

"Saw us?" Emily asked.

"She went to the supply shed. There was a good supply run

and more on the shelves, and I think she misses shopping. She saw you two while she was out."

"We'll need to go check it out," Emily said enthusiastically.

Just the thought of food made my stomach turn.

"We were out talking to the new girls," I said, steering the conversation to a safer topic until my stomach settled.

Mary swept into the room from the kitchen. Her face lit up when she saw us.

"I'm so glad I made a double batch of macaroni and cheese," she said, coming to hug us. "You're staying for dinner, right?"

Emily looked at me. I smiled and nodded my head. Mary beamed with delight, and I could only hope the dinner would stay down long enough to get what I'd come for.

While Emily went to help Mary with the place settings, I followed James to the table. Easy conversation flowed during the meal, making it possible to eat less and talk more. Especially when Emily shared that we'd learned that most of the girls weren't liking their fey roommates.

"That's a shame," Mary said. "Those fey are all so sweet and deserve a little bit of happiness in their lives."

"What about happiness in our lives?" I asked. "Why do we have to give up everything for their little bit of happy?"

"Oh, I'm not saying you should," Mary reassured me. "It's just that some of those girls really seem like they could use a man in their lives. Someone to lean on in times of trouble. You two have each other. James and I aren't judging."

I almost spit out the small bite I'd reluctantly taken.

"Mary, we're not lesbians," Emily said.

"Of course you aren't, dear." Mary's curious gaze settled on me, and I swallowed.

"You know what? If it gets me out of future talks about how I need a man in my life, yep, I'm gay."

James made a choked sound that I was sure was a laugh.

"While I was on my way to the supply shed," Mary said, "I saw one of those girls yelling at poor Sain to leave her the bleep alone."

"Bleep?"

Emily and Mary ignored me as Emily made a sympathetic sound.

"Sain is such a teddy bear," Emily said. "So shy. I'll have to stop by his place tomorrow."

"That's a wonderful idea. I'm sure if she just got a chance to know him like we do, she'd love him. Oh, I have the perfect idea."

"Now, I doubt that," James mumbled, keeping his head down as Mary shot him a dirty look.

"Remember that show *The Dating Game*? We should come up with some questions for the girls to ask the fey to get to know them."

"I think that show was before our time," I said, having no clue about the reference.

Mary waved a hand at me and focused on Emily, who was nodding.

"Premade questions would be good. Especially if we can turn it into some kind of game. The fey love games, and it might make the girls more willing to go along."

Their animated conversation drew them away from the table. James shook his head and leaned back in his chair, his plate empty. I looked at the other two plates and saw they were bare, too. Taking a quick bite, I stacked my plate on top of Mary's and collected the rest.

"You hightailing it out of here?" James asked, watching me.

"As fast as I can."

James chuckled.

"They mean well."

I didn't reply. Spilling my thoughts earlier had almost cost me my opportunity. I wasn't going to potentially screw it up again.

Taking the dishes to the kitchen, I rushed through washing them and left everything in the drainer to air dry. James was in his chair again. The one facing the liquor cabinet.

"I washed the dishes, figuring they'd be at it a while," I said, hearing Emily and Mary's voices coming from the basement.

"Thank you."

"No problem. Just stick up for me when Emily gets mad that I left without her again."

He chuckled and winked at me.

I smiled and moved to the door, my palms sweating with need. My hands shook as I zipped my jacket.

"Oh," I said, turning as if a thought had just occurred to me. "And thank you for that bottle of vodka. Let me know if you ever need me to make room for more. The last party wiped out our supply so we have plenty of room."

He waved at the cabinet.

"Grab a few now. We see at least one new bottle a day. Anything that looks strong enough to clean out a cut, we've been sending to Cassie's for real medicinal purposes."

"Hopefully, she gets to use it."

His expression turned thoughtful.

"Not sure I understand your meaning."

"Most hurts now aren't the kind that a disinfectant can fix. They're the kind that turn you."

He nodded slowly.

"Yeah, then let's hope she gets a chance to use it."

I moved from the door and made a show of helping myself to a bottle of brandy. Then, turning my back to him, I moved a few bottles and slid the door closed. When I straightened, I took the single bottle from the top of the sideboard.

"Thanks for this," I said, lifting the bottle slightly.

He nodded and reclined back in his chair, ready for his after-dinner nap.

Every nerve tingled as I let myself out of his house and walked down the street, openly carrying the brandy. I could already taste it. My mouth watered. I imagined myself taking off the top and lifting it to my lips. Need didn't completely cloud my thoughts into making a hasty decision, though. I waited until I was home where all the curtains still gaped wide.

Kicking off my shoes, I crossed to the kitchen. Instead of opening the bottle, I opened the cabinet and put the precious win inside, right beside an empty vodka bottle that had a sticky note on it.

I know this was water.

I got angry, but I didn't show it. That Emily knew didn't matter. I wasn't going to make the same mistake twice. Closing the door, I went up to my room and closed my curtains.

Once I was alone, I pulled the second bottle from my jacket. It wasn't big, but it would do. Unscrewing the top, I took a long swig and exhaled heavily.

I felt no guilt that I'd taken it. James had given me an open invitation to do so. And I felt no guilt that I was hiding it. In fact, I was feeling something I hadn't felt in a good, long while. Pride.

Emily and Merdon's judgmental views of my drinking wouldn't oppress me.

As I'd proven time and again, I was the queen of drinking games.

CHAPTER SIX

THE BOTTLE WITH THE STICKY NOTE WAS ON THE COUNTER ALONG with its new, unopened, partner, when I came downstairs the next morning. I knew an ambush when I saw one.

"Do we really need to do this?" I called out.

Emily popped up from behind the island.

"Yes. We do."

I looked her over with the same intensity she was looking me over.

"Why, exactly, were you hiding?" I asked after the moment stretched long enough.

"To see your reaction to the bottles."

My gaze shifted to the bottles then the note on the empty one.

"They're bottles. Do you want me to start leaving love notes on them, too?"

"You know that isn't a love note, Hannah." She pulled the vibrant yellow paper off and thrust it at me. "It's a problem."

"Yeah it is, and so is hiding behind a counter. Better watch how you're acting or people will start thinking there's something wrong with you. It's a judgy place around here."

Her shoulders slumped for a moment then she slapped the note down onto the counter.

"I'm not judging. I'm afraid. Afraid of losing you and being alone again."

Her words made the storm inside of me thunder louder.

"Don't you get it yet?" I asked. "It's never been about if we'll die but about when we'll die. You will lose me." My thoughts collided as I realized something so very obvious. "We were always meant to die. From the day we were born. The only thing that's changed is how. Instead of old age, it'll be infection or a hound."

The idea that my mortality had always been there, that my life had always been meant to end, sent my mind into a spiral. I gripped the counter against the onslaught of questions. How could anyone live knowing they were already dying? How were we all not running around in fear even before the quakes? What the fuck was the point of living at all?

"Hannah? You don't look good. Are you okay? Are you going to be sick?"

I shook my head and stumbled away from her, unable to deal with her questions any more than I was able to deal with my own.

"I need some air." I grabbed my jacket, my hands shaking so bad that I knew there was no hiding it from her. "The new bottle is still sealed, by the way, but feel free to break it open and take a sip if you don't trust me. I'll be back later."

I left the house and took a few stumbling steps down the front walk as I struggled to breathe. It felt like something was growing inside of me, taking up the room that I needed and stealing my air. A choked sound escaped me, then another.

Across the street, a fey stopped walking to look at me; and just like that, I inhaled and my walk smoothed out. I waved, not even knowing how I'd managed the bright smile I wore, and crossed the street.

"Good morning, Tor," I said when I neared. Then, I broke eye contact and kept walking.

Awareness tingled along my spine, and I looked back, thinking Tor might have followed me in a bid for conversation. However, it wasn't Tor I saw watching me.

Merdon stood near the tree in my front yard.

I faced forward again and continued on my way, not knowing where I was headed until I arrived at Mary and James's place.

Despite the early hour, James still called out in welcome after my second knock.

"Didn't think we'd see you again so soon," James said from his chair.

"Yeah, me either. Emily and I had a fight, and I needed somewhere quiet to think."

James considered me for a moment then asked, "Do you want to talk about it?"

I almost said that I didn't but realized I was with the one person who might be able to help me. Sitting in the chair beside him, I exhaled slowly and tucked my hands between my knees.

"I'm going to die," I said, looking at him. "These walls might delay it; but someday, somehow, I'm going to die."

He nodded slowly.

"I didn't figure that out until I was in my thirties. I can still remember how that made me feel. The fear." He stood and went to the decanter on the sideboard and poured us both a small amount. Without another word, he handed me a glass. I gulped down the contents and held out the cup for more. He obliged.

With the alcohol warming my stomach, some of the shaking eased.

"What is the point of all this, James?" I asked before I could stop myself. "The struggle to keep going when you know there's just another round of pain hiding behind the next corner?"

"It's not about the pain but about the happiness in between," James said kindly. "Don't worry. The fear will fade, and you'll see."

I doubted that very much.

I was about to stand and excuse myself when Mary peeked out from the kitchen.

"I thought I heard someone," she said, emerging to give me a hug. "I could use a helper."

It wasn't her earnest expression that had me staying but James's murmured, "I'll get you a refill," that decided me. I was where I needed to be.

My certainty dimmed as I spent the next two hours hand-laminating ridiculous question cards Mary had spent most of the night making. That James had capped the decanter after my third drink added to my doubt.

Placing the last card on the stack, I quickly stood. The drinks had warmed my belly and taken the edge off the worst of my thoughts, but I knew what would happen if I didn't find something more soon. I did not want to be sober.

"I better get going," I said. "I don't want Emily to worry about me."

"She loves you so much," Mary said with a pat to my shoulder before she scooped up the cards and disappeared into the kitchen.

"How disappointed will she be when she figures out that Emily and I aren't gay?" I asked James.

He chuckled.

"She'll be thrilled. It'll mean she can add your names to the dating fishbowl." He pointed to a glass jar that had folded pieces of paper in them.

"Not ever happening," I said, grabbing my jacket.

"She's right, though, about Emily. That girl cares about everyone, but she worries about you more than the rest. You should take another bottle of liquor home. I think she's worried you won't have enough."

I'd started toward the cabinet at his suggestion but paused at the last statement.

"Why would you think that?" I asked.

"She was asking how many shots are in a bottle and how long a bottle would last. She knows how you like your gatherings and knows that one bottle won't do much."

"Ah. Well, I don't think I'll be in the mood for a gathering for a while. I have a lot to wrap my head around."

He nodded in understanding.

"Come back whenever you'd like. We'll find you a quiet place to sit and think here." He frowned and glanced at the kitchen door where Mary had disappeared. "Well, maybe not here. I have a feeling we'll be hosting Mary's version of The Dating Game soon."

"I doubt that," I said. "Despite Emily's meddling, most of the girls aren't too keen on living with the fey."

Mary's head popped out of the kitchen. "They just need incentive to give them a chance. Be a dear, and start asking the fey to bring any extra canned goods here. Emily is going to use that as payment for a date."

I stared at the old woman for a disbelieving moment then agreed.

"Sure. I'll talk to the fey for you."

I called my farewell and rushed out the door. Did I agree with what Mary and Emily were doing? Hell no. But, whether I helped or not, they'd go ahead with their plan and likely get a few desperate females to agree to their dumb game. So why not improve my drinkless position? Since Emily was obviously watching the bottle in the cabinet and would likely ask James if I'd taken more from him when she learned I'd visited, I really didn't have much of a choice, anyway.

Outside, I waved to the first fey I saw, who happened to be Tor again. He smiled broadly and jogged my way.

"Hello, Hannah."

"What are the odds that you're the first fey I see when I walk out the door. That's twice today. Are you stalking me?" I asked jokingly.

He blinked at me, and his smile fell. Crap. They were sensitive about the word "stalker."

"I'm kidding," I said, tapping his arm playfully. "I actually have some really exciting news. Mary and Emily are pulling something together to give you guys a chance to get to know the humans. Do you want me to add your name to the list? It only costs one bottle."

The smile lit his face again.

"I will pay that. When should I give you the bottle?"

"Tomorrow. Spread the word, okay? Any fey who wants some one-on-one time with a female should bring a bottle to my place tomorrow to get scheduled."

He nodded and took off at a jog. The thing taking up space and robbing me of air twisted inside of me again, and I wished I could call him back and ask for something today. But I couldn't. First, I needed to deal with Emily.

The first words she said to me when I walked in the door just confirmed it.

"Have fun drinking with James?" she asked.

I stared at her for a moment then took off my jacket. It wasn't like her to be so confrontational.

"No, I didn't. I laminated over one hundred stupid question cards. But Mary seemed happy about it if that matters."

Emily's expression wavered then fell.

"Of course it matters. I think it's great that you went there to help."

"I didn't go there to help. I went there because you obviously wanted a fight, and I didn't. Yes, James offered me a drink. Yes, I accepted. No, I didn't take another stupid bottle from him. Can we be done with this now?"

She studied me for a minute then nodded.

"I just want you to be okay," she said. "The drinking—"

"Isn't a problem. But, how you're going to bribe girls into hanging out with the fey so they can play fifty questions is. The fey are going to get their hopes up at the idea of a dinner with a girl. Meanwhile, all the girls are going to rush through the questions so they get paid and can get out of there. It's not fair because the expectations aren't clear."

"You have a different idea, don't you?"

"I do. And it involves alcohol." I lifted my hand as if she was going to object. "Now just hear me out."

She made an annoyed sound. "I don't have a problem with drinking, Hannah, I'm just worried that you were going too far."

She had no idea.

"Back to the point. We shouldn't call this a dating game. We should call it a date because that's what the fey really want, and we should be upfront with the girls agreeing to this. And make it less like a payoff because that's like whoring."

Emily's mouth popped open a little.

"Instead of promising canned goods, promise a full meal. As much as they want to eat for as long as they want to stay. That alone will promote lingering and conversation. The cards can be on the table just to help the conversation if it lulls. And, let's be honest. With the fey, it will lull.

"What do you think?" I asked.

She chewed her lip for a minute then agreed it might be a better idea.

"Good. I already started spreading the word among the fey. They're going to show up here tomorrow to schedule a day. How many a day do you think we can do?"

She frowned, and I piped up again.

"I was thinking that Mary would want to host and cook for the couples. She's the one in love with the idea of pairing them up. Plus, James has the liquor cabinet that'll be needed to calm a lot of nerves."

"The girls aren't that nervous. They're just uncomfortable."

"The ones already living with the fey aren't the ones who'd be tempted by an all-you-can-eat meal. I'm talking about all the single ladies at Tenacity."

Therein lay the beauty of my plan. In order to get enough females on board with this, Emily would need to spend a lot of time at Tenacity, talking to girls, and I would need to stay here to schedule the fey. She'd hear about the bottle payments eventually, but I'd worry about that later. Hopefully, I'd be drunk enough to no longer care. Or hear. Or feel.

"Hannah?"

I realized Emily had been talking to me.

"Sorry. Lost in my thoughts again."

"It's okay. This is a lot to think about. I asked if you mentioned any of this to Mary."

"Nope. I did my time there today. I'll leave that to you."

"You know that she won't be able to do all the cooking and cleaning alone, right?"

"Yep. I'm sure there are other matchmakers who'd be willing to pitch in so they can watch the love-show."

Emily was already walking to the door.

"I'm going to go talk to Mary."

I waved her away and waited for the door to close before running upstairs for my small, empty bottle. James wasn't the only one with a supply of spare booze, and thanks to him, I knew where to go.

A few minutes later, Kerr opened their door, his expression not it's usually stoic mask.

"Looking a little harassed there, Kerr," I said. "Everything okay?"

"Everything is fine. Are you looking for Cassie?"

"Please."

He stepped aside to let me in and revealed a wall covered with colorful marker swirls. There was also a bucket and a scrub brush next to a little girl with tear-streaked cheeks.

"Nice artwork," I commented.

"Cassie is not happy," Kerr said quietly.

"I bet not."

The little girl snuffled as we walked past to the kitchen. Cassie was at the stove, angry-cooking by the looks of things. I almost smiled.

"Maybe I should come back later."

Cassie glanced at me and shook her head.

"No. I could use a break." Her gaze met Kerr's. "Cleaning is an appropriate punishment. Even if you didn't know the rules, she did."

Without another word, Cassie strode from the kitchen. It didn't take a genius to figure out what had happened.

"Hope they weren't permanent," I said.

"They were!" Cassie yelled from down the hall. Upstairs, a baby started to cry.

I hurried after Cassie and found her pacing a small room with a narrow bed. I studied her for a moment.

"You've been around the fey enough to understand they don't know all the rules," I said.

She let out a slow breath.

"I have. But, it's not the rules. This isn't our house. We're wrecking someone else's things."

The wailing increased.

"Just a second," she said before rushing from the room.

I quietly opened cupboards until I found what I needed. By the time she returned, I was standing where she'd left me, and she looked a little calmer.

"I'm sorry, Hannah. I shouldn't have unloaded on you. How can I help you?"

"Just checking back in to see if you have anything for sleep yet."

She considered me for a moment.

"Nothing I'm confident enough to give you. Have you tried exercise like I suggested?"

"No, but thanks anyway."

She caught my arm as I moved to leave.

"My offer is still open," she said. "Sometimes talking about—"

"No," I said more forcefully. "Talking won't fix this."

She released me, and I left quickly, hating that I'd ever admitted to her that I wasn't sleeping because of nightmares of the past. Hearing stupid shit like post-traumatic stress had made me want to slap her. Instead, I'd smiled and nodded and told her I'd come back if it got any worse.

Outside the air cooled my anger, and I managed a normal pace as I set out for home. Inside my coat, the liquid in the now full bottle sloshed against my breast. My mouth felt so dry. I couldn't wait to hide up in my room and take a drink. I desperately needed some escape.

A shadow crossed my path. It was the only warning I had before I collided with someone.

"I'm so sorr—"

The words died as I lifted my head and looked at Merdon.

"You did that on purpose," I said, jerking back a few steps.

I could see in his gaze that I was right and that he didn't care if I knew it.

"Stop following me around."

He tilted his head, studying me.

"Or what?" he asked.

My mouth fell open, and he prowled forward, closing the space between us.

"You don't have the balls to do anything about it," he said, close to my ear.

My eyes went wide, and I remembered I'd said those words just the day before. Obviously, Merdon had been doing more than just following me around. He'd been listening to my conversations, too.

Before I could respond, he walked away.

I stood there, seething for a moment, then hurried home. Safely inside with the curtains pulled shut, I slammed half the bottle down, not giving a damn if Emily found out or not. I just couldn't deal with the level of crazy in this world anymore.

Thankfully, Emily stayed at Mary and James's place most of

the day and didn't question my position on the couch when she came home well after dinner. Honestly, for the first few minutes, I wasn't even sure she was aware I was really there. She talked non-stop about how she and Mary had the logistics figured out. The fey were already bringing supplies to Mary's place, and Emily had already found a fey to take her over to Tenacity. On and on it went, with no conversational response necessary from me.

When the enthusiastic retelling of her day halted abruptly, I sat up and gave her a questioning look. There was no excitement in her expression, only worry.

"A little birdy told me you went to Cassie's today. Everything okay?" she asked.

"Seriously, when are you going to stop asking that?" I asked, feigning my best bored tone. "No, shit's not okay. You hear me scream at night. Since you don't like me drinking, I went to see if she had something to help me sleep."

"Did she?"

"No. Nothing she's comfortable administering, anyway. And if you're behind the reason why Merdon was following me around today, I'm not sure we can be friends anymore."

"I didn't ask him to follow you around. I think he's just worried about you. Besides, you know he's harmless."

"Do I? When I told him to stop, he told me I didn't have the balls to do anything about it. He's following me around *and* listening to our conversations."

Emily cringed, and I flopped back onto the couch.

"I told you it was a mistake to let him sleep here."

She didn't answer. It wasn't like her to not answer. It also wasn't like her to be hedgy, but that was exactly the expression on her face when I sat up to look at her again.

"What?" I asked.

"Nothing. I'm going to go draw up a schedule for you to use tomorrow then go to bed." She hurried from the room before I could press her for a real answer.

Had I cared enough, I would have chased after her. But I was pleasantly buzzed, and the only fuck I had left to give was that I'd sufficiently reassured Emily enough for her to leave tomorrow so I could bathe in the booze the fey were about to bring me.

CHAPTER SEVEN

SINCE SLEEP WAS A HARD-WON COMMODITY, MORNINGS USUALLY didn't do much for me. Especially when I'd gone to bed drunk. Today was different, though. Today was my b-day. Booze Day. I hurriedly tugged on a new-to-me dress from my closet and shuffled downstairs.

As I'd hoped, Emily was already gone. A note waited for me on the counter of the tidied kitchen.

I set up the living room for you and left the schedule. First come, first served, to keep it fair! See you around dinner. Breakfast is in the oven.

Glancing at the living room, I saw that she'd pushed everything aside and had a table in the middle of the space, like when we hosted the gatherings. A chair waited at each side of the table, the setup reminiscent of an interview. On the table, a huge board had "Dating Schedule" written on the top and blank spots where I was supposed to add fey names.

Ignoring that responsibility for the moment, I checked the oven. More eggs waited for me. I made a face and put the plate on the table, planning on offering it to the first fey who walked in.

Ready for a drink, I opened the front door. Tor had truly spread the word. Dozens of fey waited outside, each one of them holding a bottle of some sort. My mouth watered as fey after fey entered with their lovely payments.

I smiled at Tor and offered him my eggs as I got a glass and opened the brandy he'd handed me. The subtly sweet liquid warmed my throat with the first large swallow. Exhaling contentedly, I faced the fey.

"So, Tor, tell me what you're looking for in a woman. Big boobs? Childbearing hips?"

"Yes," he said.

"Really? You're going to be that picky?"

His expression turned troubled, and I chuckled.

"I'm just teasing you, Tor. If you want that, I'll make sure to let Emily know to match you up with someone like that."

"I won't be picky," he said. "Emily can match me with any female."

Of course she could. None of these fey were picky. They'd take anything with a hole. I didn't say that, though. Instead, I wrote his name in the slot, promised Emily would do her best, which I knew she would, then called the next fey and his tribute forward.

The chart filled up in no time, and I turned away the rest of the gathered fey with a promise that we'd do it again sometime. It sucked saying "no" to so much good booze, but I didn't want to rile them up by collecting and not delivering. Alone in the house, I turned to look at my b-day haul. I could already taste all of it. In fact, I itched to open another bottle just to do so. But I didn't.

The bottles of tequila I put in the cupboard above the stove. The rest, I hid in my room.

My logic about dividing my supply was simple. The fey

talked, so Emily would know that they'd brought booze here. However, Emily wouldn't know that each one had brought a bottle. That meant I could lead her to believe what was above the stove was it. She could keep an eye on that supply and think that my drinking had slowed while I continued to self-medicate in my room.

It'd be fine.

Someone knocked on the door. I took another quick drink from my brandy before going to answer it and turn away whichever fey hadn't yet heard that the dating schedule was full for now.

The smile on my face melted away as I focused on the one fey I didn't want to see. Merdon filled the space, looking down at me with his judgmental gaze.

"Why do you need thirteen bottles of alcohol?"

"First, that's none of your business. Second, when did you learn to count?"

He glowered at me mutely.

"Fine. Whatever. Don't answer. I'll return the favor."

I moved to shut the door, but he stopped me by placing a hand on the panel. That's all it took. One hand, and I couldn't budge it. He watched me steadily like a cat toying with a mouse. Did he seriously think I could do nothing?

His comment from yesterday roared in my ears, and I lost it. Jerking the door open wide, I got in his space.

"You don't think I have the balls to face-off with you? Try me," I all but growled at him.

We remained locked in a staring contest until he retreated a step.

"Emily will know," he said.

I slammed the door shut in his face, showing him just how

much I cared about his stupid threat. And to make sure he understood, because the fey were a little slow sometimes, I opened the curtain wide, grabbed the nearest bottle, and chugged until I ran out of breath.

If he was going to tattle, I was going to make the trouble worth my while.

He crossed his arms as he watched me and leaned against the tree, showing me he wasn't leaving.

"Fine," I said, taking another long drink from the bottle.

Then, I settled in to enjoy my day.

"HOLY SHIT!"

The exclamation didn't fully pull me from oblivion, but the clank of glass-on-glass did. My eye popped open just as Emily's barely audible words reached my ears.

"Are you sure you got it all?"

Disoriented, I tried to piece together where I was and what was happening. I lifted my head and looked down at myself. I was tucked into my bed and still wearing my dress. There wasn't any light coming from the window, so it was either really early or late. Frowning, I tried to recall which, but all I could come up with was day-drinking my ass off, possibly letting Thallirin use our shower, and definitely flipping off Merdon repeatedly through the front window because he wouldn't leave.

Were Thallirin and Brenna still here? And, more importantly, why wasn't Emily shaking me awake and demanding to know how much I drank?

I hesitated, debating whether or not to get out of bed. The way the room was spinning ever so slightly and the complete mellowness I felt let me know I was still buzzing strong. It would be easy for me to curl up and pass out again. But only for the short term. Keeping the peace now would make my life easier in the long run.

Slithering from the bed, I held the wall for a moment to gain my balance then carefully made my way to the stairs.

"...angry about this. You better go before she wakes up. Are you sure you got all of it?" Emily asked.

"Yes."

I frowned at the low answer. That didn't sound like Thallirin. Again, I heard the faint sound of clinking.

"Thanks again for your help, Merdon."

My mouth fell open, and I almost fell down the stairs in my hurry to get to the kitchen. The door closed before I reached the bottom. Emily was by herself.

"What is going on?" I asked, gaze flicking between her and the door. "Was that Merdon?"

"It was," Emily said.

I was expecting her to look pissed because of the booze. The worried expression on her face was even better. Worried was easier to channel in the right direction.

"So he already tattled about my day drinking?" I asked.

She nodded.

"I only did it to piss him off because he came in here being all judgmental."

"No you didn't," she said softly. "You drank because you need to drink. It stops now."

"Yeah, I know. That's why I left all the bottles in the cabinet." I nodded to the one above the stove.

She shook her head slightly and looked down at her hands.

"No, you didn't, Hannah. You hid some in your room, too."

She looked up at me, her gaze steely. "Merdon found the bottles and took those along with the ones above the cabinet. There's nothing left in the house. He also told me he'll spread the word so you won't be able to pull the stunt you did today. The fey deserve better from us, Hannah. You used them."

"Betrayal seems to be going around," I said. Anger didn't begin to describe what I felt at the one person I'd thought was my friend.

She gave me a sad look.

"Fuck you and your pity," I growled.

Turning my back on her as she'd just turned hers on me, I went back upstairs. I had to know. Surely, she'd been exaggerating. She hadn't really let Merdon search my room while I was in it, had she?

The bottle under my bed was gone, but that was fine. It'd been a decoy bottle anyway.

However, the bottles I'd hidden in the bath towels, in the closet, in the shoes, and in the damn toilet tank were gone, too. That thing inside me twisted and grew, taking up so much space I couldn't breathe. My gaze flicked around the room as I gasped for air. There was nothing left to save me from what I knew was coming without my bottles. The memories already tugged at me, demanding their due.

My eyes started to water, and my hands shook.

"It'll be okay, Hannah," Emily said from behind me.

I whirled on her, my fear hardening into a furious outrage.

"Get out!"

She backpedaled into the hall before I had a chance to push her out. Robbed of the satisfaction, I slammed the door in her face instead. My anger evaporated as the painful truth of my situation crashed down on me once more. I slid to the floor as the first sob escaped me.

They'd taken the only peace I'd had.

I had nothing.

No one.

I curled around myself, the pain bleeding out through my tears and whimpers. How could Emily betray me like she had? She knew how bad things were. She heard me at night. She cared. At least, I thought she had. Just like I'd thought she'd been my friend.

Betrayed. The word wouldn't stop echoing through my mind, not even after the tears dried up and my throat went hoarse. Did I deserve any less? No.

I just lay there, staring vacantly ahead as the sky outside my window gradually lightened.

A knock at my door broke through my numbness.

"Hannah, I made some breakfast if you're hungry."

My temper reignited, and I only barely managed to swallow my response to her. Further confrontation would not improve my circumstances. I needed to be smarter, less emotional. Emotions were for at night when I had no control.

When I didn't answer, she walked away, her steps soft on the hall carpet. Determination wormed its way inside me. I was not going to let Emily and Merdon get away with manipulating my life. If Merdon wanted balls, I'd show him balls. And once I brought him to his knees, I'd take back my bottles.

Pulling myself up off the floor, I stumbled to the bathroom, intent on making myself presentable. The dress fell in a pool around me, and I happened to catch a glance of myself in the mirror before I quickly turned away. The skeletal glimpse wasn't the pre-quake version of myself that still lingered in my mind. But, we were all thin now. It wasn't a big deal.

Under the spray of the shower, I wet my hair. My fragile determination slipped fractionally as darker thoughts slipped in. Why go through all the effort? The alcohol was a bandage. There was only one real cure. Ending it all. The roof didn't work. There were other methods.

Even as I mentally cringed away from the thought, my gaze slid to where I kept my razor. It was gone. Frowning, I turned off the water to check the drawer. Everything sharp was gone.

I stood there, dripping water all over as mental pieces fell into place. Merdon's presence this morning. Emily's overreaction. Now, the missing razor.

Merdon told Emily about the roof.

Panic consumed me, and I gripped the countertop for support as my mind raced. The desperation of my situation had never been higher. I really needed those bottles. I couldn't cope with Emily knowing, not without them.

Grabbing a towel, I dried quickly and dressed. I didn't bother with my hair or makeup. I needed to find Merdon, fast, before he blabbed to someone else. Given the fey's love to gossip, it was likely already too late. My stomach churned at the thought. What would I do if everyone knew? No one would help me, then.

Rushing out the door, I nearly plowed Emily over in my hurry.

"Where are you going?" she said, rushing after me.

"Trying to fix your fuck-up," I said, lifting my jacket from the hook as I flew out the door.

My first impulse was to start yelling Merdon's name. He'd already proven the superiority of his hearing with his fey ears, so I knew he'd hear me wherever he was within the walls. As would every other fey, and I didn't really want to call attention to the need behind my rush to find him if he'd actually kept his mouth shut.

Taking off at a jog, I started down the road. The snow crunched under my feet, and my breath misted in front of me.

The fey I passed nodded at me normally enough, not that I could count on that as an indicator of anything. Very little fazed them to the point that they would act differently. Playing along, I waved and smiled like normal and continued jogging as if my side wasn't splitting in two or my breathing labored.

At the end of the road, I paused, panting as I looked around for the ass who'd been following me around for days. Where in the hell was he? I struggled not to let my anger show and forced my fisted hands to relax. Rather than running around and collapsing in the snow, I waved down a single fey.

"Hey, have you seen Merdon?"

"What do you need, Hannah?" the bastard asked from behind me.

I whirled around with a glare.

He nodded to the fey, who jogged away, before looking down at me.

"I want you to return what you stole."

"No."

"It wasn't yours to take. I know you understand what stealing means and that it's wrong. Now, give it all back."

"I did."

I wanted to pull all the hair from his head.

"You did what?"

"I gave it back to the fey you tricked into giving it to you." He stepped closer, menacingly. "I know you understand what trickery is and that it's wrong. Now, go home, Hannah."

I shook with my need to swing out and throat punch him. All I would do was hurt myself, though. Damn their strength and durability.

"You have no idea how much I wish I had the strength to hurt you right now."

"I do know. I also know that hurting me will not make you feel better."

"Oh? I think we should give it a try. Mind staying here while I go find a hammer?"

I smiled sweetly at him.

"Die and go to hell, Merdon."

Pivoting on my heel, I stalked off in the other direction. At least, the confrontation had satisfied one need. I now knew where to find my booze. All I needed to do was sweet talk a few fey into giving it back to me.

I waved to the first one I recognized.

"Hey! I heard that Merdon returned the bottle you gave me. He and I are having a little misunderstanding. Would you be willing to return it to me?"

The fey shook his head.

"Merdon said too much alcohol poisons a human's body, and all those bottles would make you sicker."

"I'm not sick."

He shrugged. "I already poured it out."

I definitely felt sick, hearing his admission.

"Why would you do that? It's not like anyone is making more."

"Good. I don't want to poison any humans."

I held out my arms.

"Do I look poisoned to you?"

He studied me far too long for my comfort.

"You are a different version of the Hannah who Ghua carried from the RV. That Hannah swore and had fire in her eyes. There's no fire there now. Only sadness, even when you smile."

I understood then that I hadn't been fooling anyone. Well, at least not any of the fey. I let my smile fall.

"Of course I'm not the same person. My world has been destroyed, and everything familiar is gone. I'm sure you're not the same person you were either."

"I am not sad; I am happy."

"Sure. You gained knowledge of and access to women. What's not to love about that? But what did humans get? Death and destruction. Don't expect everyone to be as joyful as you. Humans were dealt a far shittier hand."

He blinked at me, and I knew I was wasting my time, trying to justify myself to him.

"If you find any more alcohol, please keep me in mind."

With a wave, I walked off to find the others. However, I received about the same response from all of them. They either poured the alcohol out after hearing Merdon say it was poison, gave it to Cassie to clean wounds, or just flat out refused to return it to me.

Frustrated beyond measure and feeling more than a little nauseous, I went in search of my last hope. Tor.

I found him lingering by James and Mary's house. He straightened away from the tree when he saw me.

"I will not return the bottle," he said without preamble.

I rolled my eyes and leaned a shoulder against the tree.

"Let me guess. It is poison and will kill me. If it's so poisonous, why give it to James and Mary? Why let Cassie use it to clean wounds? It's only poisonous in large amounts. And even though I had all those bottles, I wasn't dumb enough to try drinking them all at once or by myself. You know the games we play at the parties."

I could see a flicker of doubt in his eyes.

"I can't, Hannah. I—"

"Are you excited for your date?"

His regret melted away, and he nodded, his gaze sliding to Mary and James's house.

"I chose to go last so I would have more time to learn."

"Learn?"

"Yes. I will watch my brothers attempt to win their females and learn from their mistakes."

"Smart. If you want, I can help you."

"You can?"

"Sure. We can have date dinners at my house, and you can practice on me."

Stomach twisting and desperation clawing at my insides, I stepped closer to him and ran my fingers over his forearm.

"Anything you want to practice," I whispered, my voice surprisingly steady.

His pupils dilated, and from my peripheral, I saw the front of his pants twitch.

"But I need something in return," I continued.

His expression fell slightly.

"Hannah, I cannot return the bottle to you."

"Not the same one, but you can get others. And you can control how much I drink so you know I'm not poisoning myself."

His hand closed over mine, his fingers trailing over my skin before he gently removed my touch.

"I cannot help you," he said softly. "Merdon is your best hope. I am sorry, Hannah."

My lower lip trembled.

"Merdon is my best hope?" I let out an angry, harsh laugh. "Merdon isn't trying to help me; he's trying to kill me. And I wouldn't be the first one he's killed, would I?"

Turning my back on Tor's shocked expression, I found Merdon watching me from several houses down. I hated him so badly.

"What was your friend's name again?" I asked over my shoulder. "The one that Merdon and Thallirin killed?"

"Oelm."

I faced Merdon.

"Yeah. Oelm."

If my words hurt Merdon, he didn't show it. And that made me even madder. Averting my gaze as if he wasn't there, I headed home, seething and fighting not to throw up.

Sweat coated my skin when I let myself inside and found Emily pacing the living room. Her worried expression turned more so as she watched me take off my jacket. I could imagine how I looked. Like shit because that's how I felt. I didn't understand why I was sweating when it had been cold outside. The shaking I was used to popping up on occasion. A drink usually steadied me. But that was out, thanks to Emily.

The nausea was the worst, though. I couldn't even tell her off for staring at me as I made my way upstairs. Closing myself into my bathroom, I barely made it to my knees in front of the toilet before I emptied what little there was in my stomach.

Again and again, I heaved. The muscles ached from the bruising force. By the time I stopped, I had no energy left in me and collapsed to the floor.

"Hannah?" Emily's voice came through the door. "Do you need anything?"

A tear slipped from my eyes. She knew damn well what I needed.

"Fuck you. Go away."

The words were barely more than a rasp from my raw throat. Why couldn't I just die already?

Oh, right. I hadn't suffered enough yet.

CHAPTER EIGHT

PANIC SUFFOCATED ME, MAKING MY HEART RACE AND SQUEEZING THE *air from my lungs.*

The moans of the infected rang in my ears, and their rancid smell of decay filled my nose. I ran, knowing we were almost out of time. I ran even as I knew it was pointless.

In front of us, the trees stretched endlessly, providing no protection.

"Hannah," Katie panted from behind me. "I can't."

Her fingers were barely grasping mine as I pulled her along. She wasn't keeping up like she should.

"Keep going," I said.

I glanced over my shoulder even though I desperately didn't want to. I already knew what I'd see. Katie's wide, desperate eyes locked on me, silently pleading for me to help her. The white ring around her lips and the exhaustion pulling at her features.

Behind her, the infected were closer. Less than ten yards now. We were both going to die.

She stumbled.

Her hand started to slip through mine. I tightened my hold, but the weight of her pulled at my arm as she completely lost her footing.

Her wide eyes were still locked on mine.

I knew what was next and screamed.

Screams tore through me, and I flailed violently, trying to pull myself free from the memory.

"Hannah, it's okay."

Hands clamped down on my wrists, holding me in place as I opened my eyes and blindly tried to focus on my surroundings. The image of Katie's eyes didn't immediately fade, though. I trembled with a force that made my bones hurt.

"It's okay, Hannah. It's okay."

The voice penetrated the pain.

Blinking, I looked up at Emily.

"Get the fuck away from me," I said thickly.

"Why? You'd rather stay flopping around in your own vomit?" She stood and held out a hand to me.

I slapped it away and stayed right where I was, giving her my answer.

She shook her head and started for the door.

"I hope you didn't throw away your earplugs," I said before she got too far, "because things are going to get intense. Unless I'm a considerate roommate and just try to stay awake all the time, again. I mean, that worked out well last time. A little sleep deprivation is way healthier than a few drinks, right?"

She paused in the doorway, her back to me. Instead of having the guts to admit she'd screwed me over and apologize, she left the bathroom.

I lifted myself from the floor and peeled off the clothes that I had indeed vomited on at some point. Not bothering with a shower, I walked back into my room and grabbed something clean, dressed, and sat on the chair in the corner of my room. It was dusk. Time for sleep.

I refused to do that to myself.

Instead, I stared at the stars through the curtain and tried to think of nothing. The memory was too close to the surface to allow that, though. Thoughts of my mother crept in. After seeing Dad shuffle through the yard, she'd wanted to go out to him. Katie and I had pleaded with her to stay and watch first. Together, the three of us witnessed what an infected would do if they found us. It'd only taken one sound from our neighbor for Dad to turn on him.

Hands shaking, I covered my ears and hummed, trying to drown out the cries for help that still echoed in my ears. How hadn't I known then what I knew now? I couldn't help anyone. Not even myself.

Unable to take the idleness, I stood and paced the confines of my room. The movement didn't exorcise the restless energy boiling inside of me or the agitation. The space was too small to do that. So, I left my room and went downstairs, drifting from room to room, looking for something to soothe me. But there was nothing. It wasn't until every door and drawer in the kitchen gaped open that I realized more than my precious bottles were missing. So were the knives and the forks.

The fucking forks.

I slammed every single door hard, and Emily came racing downstairs, barely awake.

"What's wrong?" I asked with fake concern before she could utter the question. "Can't sleep?"

"Hannah, you're not even trying."

I wished I had some kind of mental power that could squish her head.

"Trying what? To sleep? Been there, done that. Trying to mind my own business and be as amiable as possible in this hell we call real life? Also tried that. Apparently, I wasn't minding my own business well enough and, for some reason, you decided you could mind it better. How's that working for you?"

Her gaze shifted behind me for the briefest of moments that I almost didn't notice.

"I'm going back to bed. Goodnight, Hannah."

"Enjoy your sleep," I said, slamming another door angrily.

I turned to glare out the kitchen window. As I'd guessed, Merdon stood in the shadows of our backyard. I flipped him off and pulled the shade.

By dawn, the odd bouts of sweats were more infrequent, and I felt less queasy. My stomach hurt like a bitch, though; and I couldn't stop thinking about finding something to drink. Throwing on my jacket, I went to the one place I hadn't had the time to try yesterday before I got sick.

James called for me to enter after the first knock. He was still in his long underwear and white t-shirt and just reaching his chair when I let myself in.

My gaze flicked to the cabinet, and my mind raced with scenarios as I focused on him once more.

"Morning, Hannah," he said sleepily.

"I'm sorry I woke you," I said. "Would you have any spare coffee you'd be willing to share? We're out, and I've had a rough night."

James exhaled slowly, really studying me. Then, without a word, he hoisted himself out of the chair and went straight to the liquor cabinet.

"We both know you're not here for coffee, sweetheart."

My mouth watered shamelessly as he took a glass and poured a bare fingerful of brandy into it.

"Here. Drink this. It'll help take the edge off. I warned Emily that cutting it out completely might be rough on you."

He held out the glass. I didn't immediately take it. I was too angry that Emily had been here and worse, talked to James and Mary about me.

"Did she talk to you before or after she had Merdon sneak into my room and steal my things?"

"Honey, they removed the alcohol so you wouldn't be tempted. They're trying to help."

"Before or after?" I repeated angrily.

"Before. She wanted to make sure we knew what she was doing and supported her so we wouldn't undermine any progress you made."

They were all in on it.

I wished I could take the glass and throw it at him, but I couldn't. I needed that meager drink too badly. Angrily swiping it from his grasp, I gulped the liquid and slammed the cup back on the cabinet.

"He didn't just take my bottles. The way they are infringing on my rights wouldn't stand in the old world. How can you support what they're doing?"

"It's not the old world anymore," he said gently.

"No kidding. I barely noticed."

"And Mary and I care about you too much to continue excusing what we've been watching happen over these past few weeks."

"Then don't watch."

I left the house in a righteous rage, and almost face-planted right into Merdon's chest.

"Psychopath. Get a new hobby."

He caught me by the back of my neck and pulled me close. I'd been close to my share of fey, thanks to drinking games. But usually, when they were almost nose to nose with me, there was a healthy dose of desire in their eyes. The hard glint in Merdon's eyes did not hint at desire. No, there was a lot of anger there.

"What the hell do you think you're doing?" I tried ducking out of his hold and pulling his hand off me, but his grip was iron.

He inhaled deeply.

"You drank something," he all but growled in my face.

"No shit. Just a little FYI, I'm an adult and can do what I want."

"No drinking."

"No being a fucking dick." I stomped on his foot, and he didn't even flinch.

"Do not do that again."

The growled warning sent a shiver of real fear through me. Merdon wasn't playing by the normal fey rules. He wasn't listening, wasn't being nice, and above all, wasn't manipulable like the rest.

So, I did what I've come to do best.

I screamed in his face. A panicked, someone-is-ripping-my-arm-off-and-going-to-rape-me-with-it kind of scream.

His face registered complete shock before I started struggling in earnest.

"Let me go! Let me go! I don't want this!"

It took him two seconds to release me and step back.

I shot him a brief, triumphant look before I bolted with a look of fear on my face for all the fey bystanders who'd come running. Adding to the effect, I glanced back as if afraid Merdon would give chase. He didn't. The angry way he strode toward James and Mary's place didn't bode well for the old couple. Not my problem, though.

Focusing on the road ahead of me, I retraced my route. The fey watched my passing without interfering, their friendly waves absent. My world had irrevocably changed again. I could feel that certainty in my bones, and I didn't know how to deal with it.

I reached the house and hesitated, a weight of dread settling into me. I couldn't go back in there for another day of nothing but my own thoughts.

Standing in the wide open, I suddenly felt so stifled I couldn't breathe.

The curtain in the front window moved, and I saw Emily looking out at me. Worry pulled her features.

Turning my back on her, I walked off again. There had to be something for me within these walls. Something that would take away the pain that lived and breathed inside of me, a beast with claws that tore me apart from the inside when I let my guard down.

I ambled toward the storage shed, which was really a house that was used to store supplies, already knowing that I wouldn't find any alcohol in there. Desperation had me opening the door, regardless. I walked through the aisles of racks in the living room, not really seeing the shelves overflowing with food. Farther in, a spare bedroom was being used for toiletries. My eyes lingered on a tube of toothpaste then lifted to the mouthwash above it.

That dread twisted inside of me more firmly. Was I so desperate?

My hands shook, and tears wet my cheeks as I helplessly reached for my salvation and possibly my death. I wasn't sure which I was hoping for when I uncapped the bottle and took my first drink. It burned in a different way, and I coughed before taking another gulp.

My stomach revolted slightly, and I burped mint.

I looked down at the bottle in my hands. How had I gotten here? When had I sunk low enough to drink mouthwash? I thought of the moment on the roof and had my answer. When I'd stepped off, that had been me giving up.

I was good at giving up, I thought bitterly.

Lifting the bottle to my lips, I took another drink as I cried. A scratch of noise was my only warning before the door opened in the main room. I capped the bottle, quickly replaced it on the shelf, and scooped up the box at my feet. Tampons. Perfect.

Moving away from those supplies, I picked up pads and some toilet bowl cleaner. How long had it been since I'd had my last period? I frowned, trying to remember, but since the RV rescue, my days all just seemed to blur together. It couldn't have been that long ago, could it?

"What are you doing, Hannah?" Merdon asked from behind me.

I turned and found him a healthy distance away. Maybe I couldn't manipulate him, but it seemed he might be trainable. It gave me hope.

"I'm trying to figure out when I had my last period. I think I'm overdue."

He tilted his head at me. His expression didn't give a lot away, but I didn't need it to know he didn't believe me.

"Let me guess. You're trying to figure out if I'm lying? I'm not. That's what I was thinking, and I really am not sure. Now, are you trapping me in here or are you going to let me keep shopping?"

He stepped to the side, and I held my breath as I walked past, hoping he wouldn't smell mouthwash on me.

I pretended to consider what was on the shelves as my mind raced. Thanks to Emily and Merdon, I'd have a hard time finding supplies in Tolerance. James's liquor cabinet was out since he was always home. Even if they both left, there were too many fey roaming around. And the big grey idiots were too willing to listen to Merdon instead of helping me out anymore.

Briefly, I considered Cassie's again.

"What are you looking for?" Merdon asked from behind me.

"Nothing and anything, all at the same time. Can't you go be someone else's pain in the ass for a while? There's no damn booze here to tempt me."

He didn't answer, and I didn't turn to look at him. Knowing the only way to get rid of him was to be done, I put a bunch of random shit in the box then started for the door.

The ass reached around me and plucked the box from my arms.

"What the hell? Now I'm not allowed food and toiletries?"

He looked through the box and plucked the toilet bowl cleaner from the contents. With a challenging stare, he handed the box back to me.

Humiliation flamed my cheeks.

"I drink because I don't want to suffer, idiot. I wouldn't drink that."

He said nothing, just continued to stare at me.

"You know what? Fuck you, and fuck the supplies." I tossed the box to the floor. "I don't need them."

I felt like I was constantly turning my back on him and storming off. Why in the hell couldn't he get the message and leave me alone already?

He wasn't the only thorn in my side.

Emily opened our front door before I reached it.

"Are you hungry? I made some mac and cheese for lunch."

I gave her a cold glare as I passed her.

"Save it for your new best friend, Merdon. He's right behind me."

And he had been--the entire way back to the house. But when I glanced back, he wasn't following me inside. He stood on the snow-covered lawn, his arms crossed as he met Emily's sad stare.

"Why don't you just screw already and fuck each other over instead of me?"

Emily's mouth dropped open as she shot me an angry look.

"There's no need to be mean," she said, closing the door.

"How old am I, Emily?"

"Eighteen," she said.

"An adult, then. Yet, you and that grey-skinned, cave-dwelling reject are treating me like a child incapable of making my own decisions."

"Because you are."

"Why? Just because you disagree with my choices doesn't mean you have the right to make them for me. That kind of shit is why people start fighting at Christmas dinner. Better yet, Hitler, that's how wars start. Do you want a war?"

"No. I want you safe, Hannah."

"No one is fucking safe, Emily. When are you going to get that through your fucking head?" I calmed myself slightly and shook my head at her. "I pity you for your delusions. I might want to drink the truth away, but at least I acknowledge it's there."

"That's why you drink? Because you think you're not safe?"

I threw my hands in the air.

"Go ask your dumb questions to the body pile the fey buried because of the breach. They'll be able to answer you better than I can."

She didn't say anything more as I climbed the stairs.

MY STOMACH GURGLED SICKENINGLY as the scent of whatever Emily was making for dinner penetrated my room. I rushed for the bathroom and threw up bile and mint. Stupid mouthwash.

The sweats were starting again by the time I finished heaving and rinsed my mouth out. Desperate for fresh air, I opened my window and leaned out. The lights were already on along the wall, and shadows moved along the streets. Looking over the houses and the soft glows illuminating their windows, I let myself believe, for just a moment, that this was a normal winter night.

The illusion burst before it could start when a fey stepped into the light and stared up at me. Then another. And another.

I retreated and closed the window.

Ignoring the watchful presence I had outside and Emily's hesitant knock at my door, I paced the confines of my room.

The tremors weren't horrible. The random sweats sucked. But, it was the moments I swore I heard Katie whispering my name that were the worst. The pleading tone was too real. During those times, I'd curl into a ball and cover my ears and hum. When it was over, I'd get back up and pace some more. No matter what, I didn't lay on the bed. I couldn't fall asleep. I wouldn't.

Dawn's early light was a relief. Exhausted but determined, I once again left my room in search of something that would help me.

I asked every fey I found if they had anything for me to drink or if they would be willing to find me something. Each and every damn one of them told me no. I pleaded with most of them, crying for a few and seducing any I'd thought might be receptive to it, but nothing worked. Not even when I started snarling threats to rip off their sacs and watch them choke on their own testicles.

Word seemed to spread after that, and the fey made themselves scarce. Good. I was tired of their hovering presences anyway.

Tor found me when the sun had almost reached its zenith.

"Hey, Hannah," he said amiably. "I don't have any alcohol for you, but I know where you can get some."

"I'm listening."

"Mary and Emily are looking for volunteers to test their dating game meals. The first one is now, but no girls are showing up. Emily promised there would be a drink."

"Yes. A thousand times, yes. Will you give me a lift?"

He nodded and picked me up, taking off running before I could bury my face. We were in front of Mary and James's place in seconds.

"Thank you, Tor. I owe you for this," I said as he put me down.

"You're helping me," he said. "I cannot have my turn until the rest have theirs. And they cannot have theirs until Mary and Emily know that this will work."

"Fair enough." I patted his arm then moved up the sidewalk, glad he wasn't going to try to call in a favor later.

My two knocks on the door were immediately answered by James, in person, instead of a shout from his usual place in his chair.

"This is a surprise," I said, looking at his neat button-down shirt and crisply ironed pants.

His gaze swept over me as he stepped aside and helped me out of my coat.

"A surprise in equal measure," he murmured. "Do you want to go home and change first?"

I looked down at myself. Yesterday's clothes looked a bit rumpled. Or were these the clothes from two days ago? I couldn't remember anymore. My gaze caught on the dribble marks going down my front. Vomit? Maybe.

"No, I'm good. I know Mary probably already has the meal ready and doesn't want it to get cold."

He nodded slowly, still watching me closely. He took a breath like he was going to say more, then hesitated.

Finally, he stepped aside and said, "Your dining companion is already here."

I smiled my thousand-watt smile and lifted my gaze to take in the room, fully prepared to drink myself silly at their dumb test run of the dating game.

I wasn't prepared for the sight of Merdon standing next to a candlelit table.

"Fate fucking hates me."

CHAPTER NINE

"Hannah, behave," James warned. "Merdon is our guest."

I exhaled through my nose and mentally braced myself. I could do this. My gaze shifted to the bottle on the table. Brandy. The good stuff. Yep, I could definitely sit through a mock dinner date with Merdon.

"All right. Tell me what to do."

"You've never been on a date before?" James asked.

"Of course I have."

"Then you know what to do."

I rolled my eyes and headed toward the table.

"Merdon, it's so nice to see you." Not even a little. "I'm glad Emily talked you into this." I'd rather spoon my eye out. "Are you ready to start?"

I delivered each word with flawless sincerity and a perfect smile, keeping my internal jabs all to myself. It was easy to play nice when my goal was seductively singing to me from the table's top.

"You smell," Merdon said flatly.

The smile almost slipped.

"Thank you for noticing," I said brightly. "It's a new scent I'm trying, called 'Life in Hell.' It's very easy to obtain now. Would you like some?"

"Hannah," James said warningly.

I cut him a look.

"Merdon started it."

"He doesn't know any better."

I snorted and looked at Merdon.

"He knows very well what he said was offensive. That's why he said it, James."

Merdon remained quiet, his almost angry gaze locked on me. His lack of denial proved my words correct.

James cleared his throat.

"I'll just tell Mary that you're here. Why don't you both sit? I think we can skip the whole helping with the chair routine this round."

"Thank you," I said dryly, taking my own seat.

Merdon did the same, only he did it with a goading look on his face. My fingers curled with the urge to claw his damn judgy eyes out, and suddenly the width of the table didn't seem far enough apart.

As soon as James disappeared into the kitchen, I propped my forearms on the table and glared at Merdon.

"Was it your idea, or Emily's, to be my dinner partner?" I asked.

"Why?" The smooth tones of his voice gave nothing away.

"So I know who to kill in their sleep," I said sweetly.

He leaned forward in his chair.

"I don't sleep." He tilted his head. "It looks like you don't either."

Two more inches closer, and his disapproving eyes were mine.

"Thanks to you and Emily."

He grunted and sat back just before the kitchen door swung open.

Emily emerged with a welcoming smile on her face and those stupid plastic cards in her hand.

"Thank you for joining us. Tonight, we'll be cooking duck with orange glaze, baby potatoes bathed in butter, and dilled carrots as our main course. It takes a while to prepare, so make yourselves comfortable. We'll start you off with an appetizer and soup of the chef's choice in a bit. While you wait, we would like you to ask each other questions. If you can't think of any, you can use these."

She held out the cards to me.

I stared at her, my mouth slightly open in disbelief for so many reasons. First, that she thought I'd actually use her stupid cards. I'd read the inane questions on them when I'd laminated them. Like "what's your favorite color?" I didn't give a damn about Merdon's favorite anything. I wanted my drink and to get out of there.

"Are you kidding me?" I said. "The food's not even done yet?"

When I didn't take the cards, she shifted to hold them out to Merdon. He took them from her with a nod.

"The food isn't even started," he said as she fled back to the kitchen.

I glared at him then decided I'd find a silver lining in that tempting little bottle before me. I reached for it.

"Fine. I can wait."

The bottle disappeared from the table. I blinked and saw it in his hand.

"You'll need to earn this," he said, watching me closely. The anger and judgment were absent in his gaze. He almost looked —turned on?

My stomach pitched. While I was fine making out with some random fey for a drink, there was no way I could do that with Merdon. No matter how bad it got, I knew he wasn't an option. He didn't play by fey rules, and that spelled big trouble. He'd proven that again and again.

"No, thanks." The words came out breathy and more than a little shaky.

He blinked at me and tilted his head.

"You don't know what you need to do to earn it. Why refuse what you want most?"

I snorted and crossed my arms protectively in front of me.

"I can guess what you want. It's the same thing all you fey want. Pussy, right?"

"Hannah!" Mary scolded from the other side of the door.

I flushed but kept my arms belligerently over my chest. Damn eavesdropper. I should have known she was standing with her ear pressed to the kitchen door so she could find out if her little experiment was working. She should have picked more agreeable test subjects.

"You can talk about rolling pins, but I can't say the truth?" I called back to her.

Mary poked her head out of the door. Her pouf of white hair was neatly pinned back, and her cheeks tinted a vibrant shade of pink. She'd gone all out for this.

"This is different," she said. "It's a date. Act like it."

"It's not a date. It's practice."

"Then practice or leave." Her hard tone brooked no argument.

Unfolding my arms, I swallowed down my resentment and

faced Merdon. A heavy weight settled in my stomach, but I told myself what he wanted didn't matter. If he wanted to make out or even have sex, I'd ensure I drank enough first so it'd all be fine. That's what I did best. Drink everything away so the pain didn't matter.

"How can I earn my drink?" I asked, my tone dead.

"You can answer my questions."

My gaze flicked to the cards on the table.

"I thought fey couldn't read."

"We can't. The cards are for the humans. Since you didn't want them, I'll ask the questions, and you can earn the alcohol you crave so deeply."

Again with the judgment. I saw it in his eyes and heard it in his tone. Asshole.

"Fine. Start asking. I'm thirsty."

"Where did you live before Tolerance?"

"You mean before the earthquakes that freed you and destroyed everything good in the world? I lived in Broken Arrow, Oklahoma." I slid my glass across the table to him. "Fill her up, buttercup."

He dribbled a few drips into the glass. I seethed but was careful to keep that reaction from my expression and my tone.

"That's not much of a drink," I commented.

"That wasn't much of an answer. Did you have family?"

"Yes." I looked pointedly at the glass.

He didn't move.

"I answered."

"With one word."

"First, when I answered with more words, you barely poured anything. Second, if you don't want one-word answers, don't ask yes or no questions."

"Did you have a family and what were their names? What did they look like?"

A vise-like pressure squeezed my chest at the thought of talking about them. I should have kept my mouth shut about the simple questions. Staring at the bottle in his hand, I disconnected myself from the moment as best as I could and answered.

"My dad's name was Dylan. He was fifty-three years old, had a goatee, sandy blonde hair, and loved cats. My mom's name was Heather. She was forty-five years old, short, had wavy dark brown hair, and was adopted when she was seven. They were the best parents ever, and now they're dead. Would you like to bring up something else painful? You should ask how they died."

I shifted my gaze to his. He didn't blink as he poured a tiny bit more into my glass without commenting on my suggestion.

"What do you miss?" he asked when he finished.

"Fucking privacy."

For a moment, I thought he wouldn't pour. But he did. Cheaply again.

"What do you dream about at night?" he asked.

"Puppies and rainbows. Stop being cheap with those dribbles."

Despite my warning, he only added maybe five more drops to my glass.

"Stop giving me fake answers," he countered.

"Fine. I dream of death. Of blood and infected and the hell I've lived since those fucking earthquakes. Want more detail?"

He gave me a healthier dose, but not by much.

"I want to know why you jumped."

The words were like a fist to my gut. I struggled to breathe for a moment as I stared at him.

"You don't really care about the reason. You only want to

know how to fix the broken baby-maker. Every vagina counts, right? Even the ones attached to fucked up people. Give me my drink. I've earned what's in that glass."

He didn't push it toward me, but I didn't let that little fact stop me from grabbing it myself and slamming back the contents. It wasn't much more than a swallow. The liquid burned in the best way, and I closed my eyes to focus on the sensation rather than my overwhelming need to cry.

"Emily thinks you will hurt less if you speak about what hurts you. I think you are angry and mean because you enjoy being angry and mean."

My eyes flew open.

"What did you say?"

"Your ears work, Hannah. You heard me."

My fingers clamped onto the edge of the table. The need to flip the piece of furniture on him and jump on it, cartoon style, while he was pinned underneath it nearly overwhelmed me.

"I'm not small enough to hope you die," I said in a strained voice. "No, I hope you live. Live and watch as, one by one, your precious humans fall to the infected. All your hope of a future will be wiped out before your eyes and rotting as they moan for a bite of you."

"Food!" Emily practically shouted as she shoved out of the kitchen with two bowls in her hands.

She set them down before us, her gaze darting between Merdon and me.

"Is there anything else I can get you?" she asked.

"A new dinner partner," I said, still staring at Merdon.

"No. Thank you, Emily," Merdon said, turning his gaze from mine to nod at her.

She gave him a weak smile and fled back into the kitchen.

"Eat the soup, Hannah. I will give you more of your drink."

He had to know I was two seconds from getting up and walking out. Which was the only reason he'd dangled that carrot, and the alcohol was the only reason I stayed.

Staring at the bottle, I woodenly took my first bite of soup. My stomach turned a little even though the food didn't taste like anything. When was the last time I'd eaten anything? The eggs?

I managed four bites.

"I'll take that drink now," I said, setting down the spoon.

He trickled four drops into the cup.

"If you want more, eat more," he said.

I slowly nodded my head then got up from the table.

"I can see how this will go. No, thanks. Keep your pathetic attempts at bribery. They aren't worth putting up with you."

"Hannah, wait," Emily called as I strode toward my jacket.

"Screw you, Emily," I said without looking at her. "You were supposed to be my friend."

"I am."

I left before she could lie some more.

The wind cooled some of my anger. Just enough to keep me from screaming my frustration as I roamed the streets of Tolerance and ignored the fey who watched me. If only Merdon had kept his big mouth shut, then I wouldn't be walking around far too sober and sick to my stomach. That soup had to have been off.

Rubbing my stomach, I glanced around and wondered again where I'd find a drink in this place. What was that new girl's name? Cheri? Maybe I could have her ask the fey for booze. They'd give it to her, and I could go to her place and drink. My initial hopefulness withered as I realized that wouldn't work. Her fey would know what was happening and likely say something to Merdon before I managed one sip.

Damn Merdon.

"Hey, Hannah," Garrett said with a friendly smile and nod as he walked past me.

"Hey, Garrett." My tone was flat, and he heard it.

Pausing his stride, he looked at me.

"Everything okay?"

"Not really. We have all these supplies coming in, but none of what I really want."

He chuckled.

"I know what you mean. Brenna, Zach, and I just went to Tenacity this morning to trade some of our surplus. They're hard up over there and could use some extras if you have them."

A new plan began to form.

"Thanks, Garrett."

"Anytime."

With a little wave, he continued on his way, and I changed directions.

By the time Emily returned home, I was up in my room pacing. The box of goods that I had gathered from the storage shed sat by my locked bedroom door. All I had to do was make it through one night. I could do that. Tomorrow, I'd have what I needed to finally get some sleep. After that, I'd just take one day, or rather night, at a time. No problem.

A crawling, tingling sensation moved under my skin, contradicting my previous conviction. My stomach hadn't yet settled after those few bites of soup, either. It was going to be a long night.

Emily knocked on my door.

"Are you hungry?"

I rolled my eyes and continued pacing. Unless she was serving rum cake, I wasn't interested, and she knew it.

My hot, gritty gaze slid to the window. A wisp of daylight remained.

"I'm sorry I didn't tell you about lunch," she continued through the door. "I didn't think Merdon would be so blunt with his questions."

I stopped pacing to glare at the door. Her admission had just confirmed that Merdon had told the truth about Emily's part in what he'd been asking. I almost went to the door to tell her what I thought of her involvement. Quick thinking had me reconsidering the move. Sometimes, the best reaction was inaction. If tomorrow panned out like I hoped, tonight's sulking silence would conceal tomorrow's drunken silence.

Her footsteps whispered down the hall after a few moments, and I rubbed my tired eyes as I resumed my pacing.

I just needed to stay awake twelve more hours. No problem.

PANIC MADE MY HEART RACE, and my lungs screamed for air as I ran through the trees, pulling my sister along. I could feel the infected behind us and knew we were out of time. Running was pointless.

"Hannah," Katie panted. "I can't."

"Keep going," I said.

I glanced over my shoulder, already knowing what I'd see. Katie's wide, desperate eyes, pleading for me to help her. And, just behind her, the infected less than ten yards away.

She stumbled.

Her hand started to slip through mine. I tightened my hold, but the weight of her pulled at my arm as she completely lost her footing.

She fell to her knees.

Her wide eyes locked on mine.

The infected kept coming.

I pulled once, but she couldn't stand. She was too tired. Too out of breath.

I hesitated...

...then I released her.

"Hannah!"

She screamed my name as I turned and ran. Her scream echoed louder a moment later.

I looked back over my shoulder. The infected were no longer chasing me. They were converging on my sister.

One hand emerged through the mass of bodies.

"Hannah!"

I WOKE myself screaming then scrambled to the bathroom to throw up. Leaning on the toilet, I struggled to breathe through my self-loathing and tears. I hated. I hated Emily and Merdon for taking my bottles. I hated the fey for coming to the surface. But mostly, I just hated myself.

I couldn't do it anymore. I couldn't keep reliving my hell every time I closed my eyes.

Staggering to my feet, still sobbing, I went to the window. Maybe fate would be more kind this time. Maybe, like last night, Merdon would be gone.

I set my hands to the window and heaved upward. It didn't budge. I tried the locks, but they weren't latched. The window wasn't moving. I tried the other one, and it didn't move either.

Swearing and crying, I stumbled to my door. I'd find a different window.

"Don't bother," Emily said, scaring another scream from me.

Shaking so much I couldn't stay upright, I collapsed on the floor and looked at the chair in the dark corner near my bed. She sat there, her troubled expression barely lit by the dim light coming through the windows.

"Merdon nailed them shut from the outside." She leaned forward. "Talk to me, Hannah. I know something bad happened to you. Tell me. Let me help you."

I shook my head slowly and rested my cheek on the carpet.

"If you were my friend, you'd let me forget," I whispered.

"I can't. You're trying to kill yourself, Hannah. Drinking too much. Jumping off the roof. You can't see what you're doing, but I can. And I'm not going to let you go that route. We'll figure this out together."

"Why are you sitting in the chair?"

The shaking was starting to fade, but not the guilt. Never the guilt.

"You've been fighting sleep for too long. I knew you were going to crash tonight and wanted to be here for you."

"You should have woken me up," I whispered.

"I was hoping you'd want to talk about it."

She'd let me suffer on purpose. The tears started fresh.

"Leave me alone, Emily."

"I can't."

Anger replaced fear. Raging, I got to my feet.

"Get the fuck out!" I screamed at her.

She got the message and beat a hasty retreat. I slammed the door behind her and made sure I locked it. This time, I dragged the chair in front of it and flipped the mattress off the bed so I wouldn't be tempted by it again. Not like I would have been.

I could still hear my sister screaming my name.

CHAPTER TEN

Dawn's light was barely kissing the horizon when I snuck from my bedroom with my box of goods. I'd been more than a little surprised when I'd finally thought to check that the box was still in my room and found everything there. Apparently, the items had been all deemed safe by Mother Emily.

Dizzy and sick, I barely managed to get my coat and boots on. But I didn't linger until it passed. I didn't have the luxury of time. A cold sweat broke out over my skin as I carried the weighted box outside.

After collecting my supplies yesterday, I'd learned the fey left for supply runs every morning and met any humans who wanted to go with them by the wall. I didn't intend to join a supply run but figured it was the best way to hitch a ride over to Tenacity.

Thankfully, no one questioned my early-morning presence at the wall. Probably because I wasn't the only one with a box of supplies for trade. That and the fey were too busy talking about a cow run, whatever that meant.

When Ryan, Mya's brother, finally signaled that the few fey gathered were ready, I looked around at the familiar faces, relieved to see one missing. Merdon's continued absence would ensure I'd have a better day.

The fey who offered to give me a ride kept glancing at my supplies then at my face. At one time in my life, I would have told him to spit it out already. Now, I just didn't give a damn about whatever he had on his mind. My biggest concern was not throwing up from all the jostling.

We reached Tenacity in minutes, thankfully, and I followed a few other humans to a supply shed that Tenacity used for trading. Unlike the one in Tolerance, there were no overflowing shelves. There wasn't even enough food to feed a family of four for three days.

While we set up our tables, Ryan announced that he and the group of fey who'd brought us over would be back in a few hours and asked if there were any volunteers from Tenacity willing to go with them.

Looking out at the hungry faces that were already gathering, I saw no one was interested in leaving the safety of the wall to hunt for supplies. They'd rather slowly starve and fight over the meager offerings we were willing to trade than risk their immediate lives.

I felt a new level of hopelessness. What I'd said to Merdon about watching their pet humans die wasn't as far in the future as I'd thought.

"What will you take for that box of noodles?" a man asked me.

"Any kind of alcohol you have," I said after a quick glance around. It wasn't necessary, though. All the fey had left with Ryan.

"I have an apple," he offered.

"Did I say I wanted an apple? No. Booze only, people," I said loudly. There were a few grumbles. Several people broke away from my line to go to another. One guy just completely walked away.

Most remained to press forward and offer up something else as equally useless as the apple.

"Use your ears," I said. "Alcohol. I want alcohol."

Someone told me to fuck off. I gave him the finger. After several minutes of no one approaching me, the man I'd seen leave earlier approached with a glass jar. It had two inches of clear liquid in it.

"This is just a sample," he said quietly. "I don't want no one knowing what I have."

He uncapped the jar and held it out to me.

"If it's what you're looking for, you'll have to come get what you want for the whole box."

He nodded to my yet untouched supplies.

I took the jar and sniffed. The smell of alcohol was so strong it tickled the back of my throat and made me cough.

"Rubbing alcohol?" I asked.

"No, that stuff would kill you." He glanced around and leaned in close. "It's moonshine."

Liquid gold as far as I was concerned.

I lifted the jar to my lips and took a drink. It burned in the best way. I coughed lightly again then finished my sample.

"That's good. How much do you have?"

He looked around.

"Take a break and walk with me. We'll talk where it's quieter."

I nodded thoughtfully.

"Fine. But the supplies stay here for now."

"Deal."

I looked at my neighbor.

"Watch after my stuff, will you? And don't trade it. I know what I have."

He gave me a pissed off look. I wasn't worried. He was from Tolerance, which meant he was a rule follower. My supplies would be safe enough with him.

I waited until my new friend and I left the crowds behind to speak.

"How many of those jars do you have?" I asked.

"Enough to make this little walk worth your while," he said. "This moonshine is stronger than most anything you'd find in a bottle. Four jars this size," he held up the empty pint sample jar, "would equal one of those big economy bottles."

"Sounds like you're trying to negotiate low," I said. "Moonshine doesn't have much value. Food does. You're going to need to do better than four pints. I could easily trade what I have for eight quarts."

"If you could find the people with it. People who had liquor already drank it and are too afraid to go find more. And if they did leave, it wouldn't be to find a drink; it would be to find food."

"You haven't answered my original question."

"I have twelve quarts. But I'm not trading eight. Just like you know what you have, I know what I have. Supply and demand, sugar. We both have what the other wants, so let's try to keep it fair. Build a partnership if you will."

He was right. I needed to think long term. It was better to trade for a small batch, in case it was taken from me again, than a large one.

"If I settle lower, I need to know that you'll save the rest for me on the next trade."

He smiled and motioned to a nearby house.

"Let's step inside and negotiate."

A weird feeling tickled my stomach. I didn't like the way he was looking at me, all smug. He reminded me too much of Merdon. But this asshole was willing to give me a drink; the other one only took my drinks away.

"After you," I said.

I followed him into the house. It was toasty warm and very quiet. My nerves kicked up again, despite the moonshine already warming my belly.

He went straight to the kitchen, stepping around some supply boxes stacked on the floor, and opened a cupboard.

I spared the supplies a quick glance. He already had a lot of food. Why was he interested in my supplies? Not my problem or concern, I decided. If he wanted to trade and was willing to give up some of his moonshine, that was fine with me.

He turned to me with two, quart-sized jars in his hands.

"My housemates are out right now. But only for a little while. We need to hurry this up."

"Does that mean the moonshine isn't yours?" I asked, tearing my gaze from the boxes.

"It's partly mine. The part I'm trading with you." He winked.

What did I care if it wasn't his? He was giving it to me and getting something in return. By the time his housemates caught on, hopefully, I'd be long gone. Or, at the very least, long drunk.

"I need to sample both," I said. "I won't be tricked with water."

"Then we have a deal with two quarts?"

"We have a deal as long as you find a way to save the rest and agree only to trade them to me."

He smiled and uncapped both jars.

"Drink up, sugar."

I lifted the first jar to my lips and took two swallows. It was just as strong as the sample and burned its way down to my stomach. I took a slow, calming breath, already feeling it mute some of the emotions that had been clinging to me since I woke. Taking the second jar from him, I repeated the process.

He took a seat at the table while he waited.

"I've never seen a girl who drinks her shine as neat as you," he commented. "You're not new to it, are you?"

I flashed him my thousand-watt smile just because I felt like it and sank into a kitchen chair.

"I've been known to drink from time to time," I said.

Rather than capping the jar, I took another sip. The mellow was already setting in, weighing down my arms and legs in that pleasant way I'd come to love.

"What's your drink of choice?" he asked.

"There was this one bottle of cognac that was really good. Wouldn't mind more of that."

He laughed.

"You have expensive taste. I'm surprised you like the moonshine."

I shrugged lightly.

"It does the job."

"And what job's that?"

"Numbs the memories." Just saying it brought them back, and I took a longer drink, desperate to drown the pain.

"Sounds like you need some new memories. What's your name?"

"Hannah." I exhaled slowly, really feeling the moonshine kick in. The room even gave a little spin.

"Drink up, Hannah. You'll do just fine."

He was right. I would now that I had something to help. I took another drink, no longer feeling the burn.

"Do you have anyone who'll miss you, Hannah?"

I blinked at him. He didn't seem like Merdon now. He seemed nicer. Kinder. He'd given me moonshine, and when he asked about my people, it was in a simple, not so hurtful way.

"No. Everyone who'd miss me is already gone."

I heard the way my words slurred and didn't even care. I had a few hours before I'd be missed, and I planned to make the most of them.

With a smile at my host, I drank some more.

BLISS CAME in different forms for different people. Not many would call a screaming headache and a mouthful of ass-taste bliss, but it was pretty close for me. So was the fact that I couldn't remember anything after drinking from the man's jar. Not even his name.

I lifted my head, expecting to see a strange room. When I didn't, the familiar view of my own curtains confused me. I could have sworn I'd been in Tenacity.

A sinking feeling settled into my soul.

Where was my moonshine?

"Are you hurt?"

Emily had to repeat the question to gain my attention.

"Yep. My head. How did I get here?"

More importantly, where were my jars?

"I mean, did they hurt you?"

I frowned through the throbbing in my skull and tried to focus on Emily. She had the chair near the bed for some reason.

"Did who hurt me?"

Her expression, which was already sad, notched up the pity a few degrees.

"The men who kidnapped you."

I laughed, not a full out laugh—that would have hurt too much—but enough for Emily to know I didn't believe her. This headache needed to go. Sitting up a little, I looked around my room hopefully. Maybe someone had brought the jars with me.

"It's true," Emily said. "It was the same group who had Brenna and Eden."

My head just wasn't keeping up with her conversation. I needed a drink.

"Hannah," Emily said sternly. "Look at me."

I stopped scanning the room and focused on her.

"What?"

"You were kidnapped by rapists. Are you hurt?"

"If you're asking me if my cooter is sore, the answer is no, Mom. No unexpected pregnancies to inconvenience your future. Where are my supplies? I made a fair trade at Tenacity and want my jars."

"I'm sorry I can't help you, Hannah," she said softly. "I tried." She reached out and gave my hand a quick squeeze. "There's someone here to see you."

She walked out of the room, leaving the door open behind her.

Before I could get up to search for something to drink, Merdon strode in.

"Get out of bed."

His harsh tone and the way he stood over me grated on my last hungover nerve.

"Get the fuck out of my room, Merdon."

He leaned in close, bracing his hands on the mattress on either side of me.

"You smell worse than a cow," he growled at me. "Go shower."

"Piss off."

The blankets covering me abruptly disappeared. A moment later, I was over his shoulder, and he was striding across the room. It happened so fast that I didn't even have a chance to think about kicking him or screaming. Then, I was on my feet again in the bathroom.

"Shower," he said, shoving me toward the tiled enclosure.

"Back the fuck off," I said, pushing away his hands.

He was like a damn octopus, though. Hands everywhere, nudging me into the shower whether I wanted to go there or not.

I swore up a storm, calling him every vile thing I could think of. He didn't flinch at all. Or stop. Once I stood in the shower, I swung at his head. He caught my fist and reached around me.

Cold water blasted me.

"Mother fucker!"

He slammed the shower door shut and leaned his back against it.

"Bathe, Hannah."

Knowing full well Merdon would only turn it back on if I turned it off, I beat my fists against the glass until the water started to warm. Then, with a snarl, I stripped off my wet clothes. With satisfaction, I pushed the sopping wad over the top and watched it tumble over his head and shoulders.

He flicked it to the ground, unperturbed at the water now soaking his hair and shirt, and glanced back at me.

"Wash, Hannah. It will be more pleasant while the water is warm."

I slowly lifted my middle finger.

"Do you know what this means?" I all but snarled. "Go screw yourself, caveman, and crawl back under the rock you came from."

His lip curled in a small sardonic smile.

"If you would rather wait for the water to run cold again, that is your choice. I am a patient man."

He resumed his comfortable position, facing away from me, and I spit out every vile name I could come up with. Then, I washed.

"Under your arms, too," he said without looking. "You reek of—"

"Yeah, I get it," I yelled, already scrubbing my pits angrily.

I didn't stop calling him names the entire time. Somehow, he knew when I finished washing and left the bathroom before I managed to shut off the water.

Livid, I stood there, shaking. Cooling water dripped from my hair and down my back as I grappled with what had just happened. My tremor-inducing anger wasn't just because Merdon had forced me into the shower and made me strip like some hooker. It was that he was here, involved again, and ruining my life. Why did he keep showing up?

It had to be Emily. Just before he'd barged into my room, she'd apologized and said I had a visitor. Why apologize? The answer was obvious. It was because she'd invited him in. She'd done this to me.

Emily's betrayal was the biggest source of my anger and hurt. I obviously couldn't count on her to have my back anymore.

It was time to make a change. Tenacity had what I needed. Living in Tolerance with a hateful roommate and a psychotic fey, who couldn't mind his own business, no longer made any sense.

I wrapped a towel around my torso and strode into my room, focused on one goal. Packing my shit up to get the hell out of the viper's pit I found myself in. Given the light coming from the window, I could probably find someone at the wall to hitch a ride to Tenacity. But I needed to hurry.

Since I didn't have a suitcase, I started tossing clothes onto the bed. The plan was simple. I'd take what I could carry in the bundled up sheet.

"What are you doing?"

Hearing Merdon's voice made me see red. Enraged, I swung around, ready to fight.

My thoughts came to an abrupt halt as I caught sight of Eden standing beside him. Good. I needed a witness to how this Neanderthal was throwing his weight around.

"I'm packing my things to move to Tenacity where I won't be forced to do things I don't want to do. Now get out of my room, asshole."

He crossed his arms, his stance making it clear he wasn't about to go anywhere.

"Um, do you mind if we sit down for a minute?" Eden asked, without looking at Merdon. "There's something you should know before you pack up."

Since she'd asked nicely, I indicated the chair to her and perched on the bed.

"Sorry about the towel. I didn't have much of a choice in the matter."

"Yeah, I gathered as much from all the swearing."

She'd been here for the whole thing? Worse, she'd done nothing to try to intervene.

"What do you want?" I asked bluntly, losing my niceness.

"It's not what I want but what I don't want. I don't want you to end up like me. Or worse, like Brenna."

"I'm not following."

She looked at me with a sad thoughtfulness for a moment.

"Our lives went to shit after the quakes," she said. "I lost my parents in the first few weeks then got picked up by a group that promised safety. They weren't offering safety, though. They wanted women to breed with. They said it was their duty to preserve the human race."

So far, her story sounded crappily familiar.

"The fey are assholes like that," I agreed.

Eden shook her head.

"Not the fey. They don't take. These were humans. The same ones who starved Brenna and her brother until Brenna agreed to have sex with one of them. She was raped, Hannah. Those men took without asking. If I hadn't escaped them when I did, my fate would have been the same. Those were the men who had you. Do you understand? They baited you with moonshine and got you so drunk you wouldn't have woken up until after they'd carried you somewhere else. Then, they would have withheld food until you were willing to do whatever they wanted."

A sick feeling settled into my stomach at the picture she was painting. Mostly because they wouldn't have needed to starve me. It wasn't food I wanted.

"You weren't the only one they kidnapped yesterday. They managed to take Brenna again and a young girl. Brenna's quick thinking saved all three of you from a fate worse than death."

Would it have been, though? I would have had drinks. At least until they ran out.

"What do you want from me?" I asked, needing this conversation to be over.

"I want you to understand that Tenacity isn't safe. It doesn't matter that they haven't seen an infected outside the walls in over a week. It doesn't matter that there are more humans over there.

There's not enough food in Tenacity, and people do terrible things when they're starved, desperate, and afraid."

"Got it."

She gave me a doubtful look then glanced at Merdon as she left the room.

"Are you going to get out so I can dress?" I asked.

"Is that the life you want, Hannah? A life on your back while a human man pumps his seed into you again and again, against your will?"

Bile rose in my throat.

"None of this is the life I want," I said bitterly. "Do you really think one option is any better than the other to me?"

He grunted softly and studied the clothes already on my bed.

"Get comfortable here, Hannah. You won't be leaving for a long time."

Before the words fully sank in, he walked out, closing the door behind him.

I sat there for a stunned moment then rushed to let myself out. The knob wouldn't turn. I beat on the door and yelled every obscenity I could think of at him, then at Emily.

I hated them all.

CHAPTER ELEVEN

SWEAT COATED MY SKIN. I WIPED MY MOUTH WITH THE BACK OF MY hand and stumbled out of the bathroom without bothering to flush the toilet.

As I passed the bedroom door, I tried opening it again. The knob still didn't move.

"Assholes," I said under my breath.

I wasn't sure how long I'd been locked in. My mind tended to drift, something that had started happening with increasing frequency since waking up from my moonshine binge. Trapped as I was with nothing to do but lay in bed and stare at the walls and nailed-shut windows, it was no wonder, really. Yet, despite the drifting, I felt certain at least a day had passed.

Out of boredom and sickness, I'd fallen asleep twice. It had been dark the last time I'd woken from a dream of my mom. She'd come to me, materializing out of the darkness, to comfort me because even in my sleep, I hadn't been able to escape the way my middle cramped and my body ached.

I could still feel the echo of Mom's dream-hand stroking my

hair and hear her whispering for me to be strong. She'd told me I would survive. I was meant to live.

After waking from that dream, I'd curled into a ball and sobbed, hating that she'd felt so real. More so, I hated that I'd been pulled away from the comfort I so desperately wanted, something I hadn't had since the day she died.

Reaching the bed, I collapsed on the mattress and gave up trying to remember. I didn't honestly care that it was light outside now. I hurt and was thirsty, but the only thing I wanted to drink wasn't available to me.

With the exception of the magical appearance of food-filled bowls on my bedside table, Emily and Merdon left me alone. That suited me just fine. Other than dumping the peace offerings into the toilet along with my steady contribution of bile, I stayed in bed.

So I lay there, shaking, waiting for the time to pass and my misery to end, one way or another.

My mind started to drift again.

An image of my mother appeared in the corner of my room. She was smiling and waving for me to join her. Behind her, I saw the kitchen of our family home. My hands twitched on the covers. I wanted to throw them back so badly and help her bake cookies.

The image wavered, and my mom and the kitchen changed. This time, she was motioning for me to stay. It was a scene I remembered well. Her clothes were dirty, and the dimly lit kitchen was a mess. She was telling Katie and me to stay put while she snuck over to see if the neighbor, the one my dad had killed, had any food.

I shook my head, feeling the tears gather.

"Don't go," I whispered.

"I won't."

The words didn't match her lips, which were mouthing, "I'll be right back. Stay quiet and stay together."

I trembled as she turned her back on me and faded into nothing. Tears made slow treks down my cheeks. Everyone always left. Even me.

For a while, there was just a wall to stare at.

Then, Katie appeared. She was kneeling beside a bed, moving jerkily.

"No," I said loudly.

I curled into a ball, covering my head with my arms, and rocked and trembled. I didn't want to see that memory.

"Not that one," I panted. "Anything but that one."

Again, the dream of running through the trees returned, and I relived every terror-filled moment. Knowing how it would end made re-experiencing the moments before even more painful. I wanted to yell at myself to keep going, to push Katie ahead of me, or maybe to try climbing a tree. This dream didn't allow me any such kindness, though. It was no more than I deserved. So, I relived abandoning my sister, over and over, the pain cutting deeper and deeper into my soul.

I sobbed.

My mom returned again with her gentle hand smoothing over my sweat-slicked curls.

"Be strong. You will live."

I knew I would live, and that was my shame. I didn't deserve life.

"I don't want to live," I whispered. "I want to die."

The hand stilled.

"That's no longer a choice you can make."

She was right. Emily and Merdon had taken that from me.

"Soon," I whispered.

"Never."

The voice was right and wrong at the same time. Like the mismatched lips. I wished I could see her instead of just feel her.

Sighing, I waited for the memory and some of the pain to fade. When it did, so did her hand.

Exhausted, sick, and mind-numb from all the thoughts I didn't want to think, I almost missed the sound of the door opening. I shifted my gaze, wondering if this moment was real, and watched Emily as she entered and coughed lightly before covering her nose.

She left the door open behind her and moved toward the bathroom.

I pushed off my covers and forced myself to my feet. Freedom beckoned.

The toilet flushed, and I hurried toward the door. Just before I reached it, tall, dark, and pain-in-my-ass filled the space.

He stared at me impassively and crossed his arms.

I stretched my lips in a silent snarl, turned around, and crawled right back into bed. He continued to watch me, so I rolled over and gave him my back.

Didn't he have anywhere else to be?

There was a scrape of noise on my bedside table then footsteps retreating.

"She's not drinking or eating," Emily said softly. "I think she's giving up."

"If she was giving up, she wouldn't still be trying to leave."

The door closed on the rest of Merdon's words. Was he right? Was I not really giving up? I wanted to. I'd jumped off the damn roof, hadn't I? What more did I need to do to leave the pain of what I'd done behind?

Merdon abruptly entered my room again, a glass in one hand. "You need to drink."

Without waiting for my response, he slid an arm under my shoulder and brought the cup to my lips as he braced me up.

I kept my lips closed as I glared at him.

"You can do it yourself," he said in a deadly whisper, "or I can force you. Your choice."

I glared at him, my mouth firmly closed.

His expression shifted slightly, almost as if he was glad I was resisting. Then, he dumped most of the water right in my face.

I sputtered and swore at him. The glass clanked against my teeth, and water flooded my mouth. Faced with a choice of swallow or drown, I swallowed. Damn him.

He didn't let up, continuing his attempt to drown me until the water was gone. He straightened abruptly, letting me fall back onto the bed as I choked and gasped. Our gazes locked as I caught my air, and I made a noise between a hiss and a growl, ready to flip off his retreating form. He didn't give me the opportunity. Rather than leave, he sat in the chair, not far from my bed.

His angry gaze held mine.

"That water will stay in you. If it doesn't, I will do that again and again until it does stay. Do you understand, Hannah? I won't play your game. You will drink."

I hadn't spoken since they'd locked me in here, but Merdon's antagonistic words tempted me to break my silence. However, even if I had the balls to tell him to screw himself, after his little display of force, I knew better than to provoke him further.

Since the quakes, I'd learned a lot about myself and other people. Most had wanted pleasantness and smiles even in the face of complete desolation. They'd wanted to be lulled and lied to. It made them feel better, a false sense of security and normalcy.

Giving people what they needed gave me a certain level of power. I just needed to wait and figure out what it was that Merdon needed. Then I would be the one with the power.

If he thought he had patience, I had more.

Turning my back to him, I closed my eyes. It was bad enough being locked in my room, alone and with nothing to do. I didn't need the additional misery of Merdon's presence or the water in my stomach.

My middle cramped painfully and a pre-puke burp escaped me. I started breathing fast through my mouth, doing everything I could to keep it down. I did not want a repeat performance of the forced drinking process.

After a time, the cramping in my middle eased, and I swallowed hard. Merdon remained quiet behind me. So quiet that I was tempted to turn around and see if he was still here. I knew better than to give in to the temptation. He wouldn't win. I wouldn't let him.

When the door opened again, the lighting in the room had changed.

"Two glasses of water this time," Emily said quietly. "I think we should have Cassie look at her."

I wanted to snort. What the hell would Cassie do? By her own admission, she had only been a nurse in training before the quakes. She couldn't even figure out what kind of sleeping pill to give me.

Merdon grunted. Why the hell couldn't he just say "yes" or "no" like a normal person?

"Hannah, are you going to sit up and drink, or do I need to help you?" he asked instead.

Stubbornly, I didn't move.

"Leave, Emily," he said softly.

The door closed, and I braced myself, waiting for his arm under my shoulders. It never came.

Fingers clamped down on my jaw, digging into my cheeks with enough force that I unwillingly opened for him. Water gushed into my mouth and up my nose.

"I warned you," he said as I choked and spluttered.

After a moment, he let me up and held out the half-empty glass.

"This will be the last time I offer you a chance to keep your independence. Choose wisely."

Impotent rage boiled in my veins. We both knew he was strong enough to force me to drink. He'd just proven that. He'd also just proved he wasn't afraid to use that force on me. The fey were supposed to be nice and cater to anything with boobs. Merdon wasn't following the rules I knew. He had his own set, and that meant I needed to tread carefully. Anything was possible with him.

I glared at him, cheeks aching, then grabbed the glass from his hand.

"All of it," he warned lowly. "Not a drop spilled."

I took my sweet ass time drinking it, like a normal person. We glared at each other the whole time. When I finally drained what was left of that glass, he handed me the second one. The need to throw the empty one at his head rode me hard.

"I see what's inside you," he said, his expression shifting ever so subtly again.

It felt like he was laughing at me, which only made me grip the empty glass tighter as I glared at him.

"Have you reconsidered? Do you want me to help you?"

His tone remained the same, but I knew he was taunting me, not just with his words but his change in subject. What did he see inside of me? He was goading me to speak. I knew it.

Extending my hand with the empty cup, I waited until he moved to reach for it before opening my hand, mic-drop style. He moved with speed, catching the glass easily before it could shatter on the carpet. I had him just where I wanted him. While he was crouched in front of me, I shifted my weight back, planted both feet on his shoulders, and heaved with all my might.

He fell onto his ass with a satisfying thump.

Instead of looking pissed about it, he slowly stood and tilted his head at me. It was a gesture I'd seen countless times on other fey when they were clueless about something. Merdon didn't look clueless. He looked dangerous, and his next two words proved it.

"You spilled."

I looked down at my shirt, where barely a dribble wet the material, then back up at him. Anticipation lit his gaze and sent a jolt of panic through me. With his warning ringing in my ears, I quickly lifted the glass to my lips and slammed the contents.

"Good." This time, he held out his hand. "Should we try this again?"

He was daring me to repeat my trick.

Hell, no. I wasn't stupid. But I also didn't want him to think he'd won this contest of wills by meekly handing the glass to him like a trained monkey. More importantly, I didn't want him thinking I was afraid of him.

I stood, coming almost toe to toe with him because he'd been so close to my bed. He didn't step back, but then, I hadn't expected him to. Holding his gaze, I tossed the glass onto the far side of my bed.

He glanced at the cup then at my face. The moment he moved, so did I. He went for the glass, and I bolted for the door. He caught me before I laid a single hand on it.

Spinning me around, he slammed my back against the wood. One hand, pressed just at the base of my throat, pinned me in place. I could feel his thumb against my collarbone.

He lifted the glass he held in the other hand as if I needed proof of how fast he could be. My move hadn't been about me escaping although I would have if he'd tripped on his face or something. It had been about proving I wasn't afraid of him.

And that was my biggest mistake.

He leaned in close and growled low, right in my face.

"Hannah, I see what's inside of you, and you're already using it."

Before I could ask what that meant, he had me over his shoulder. This time, I fought him as he strode to the bathroom. Breaking my silence, I called him every hateful name I could think of just before he plopped me down and cold water blasted my back.

He once again resumed his leaning position outside of the glass door.

"Bathe. You reek of vomit."

I stood in the cold water, shaking with rage and reminding myself to have patience.

"Why are you doing this?" I demanded.

"Because you'll leave."

I lifted my hands and mimed myself choking the life out of the idiot.

"I didn't mean why are you standing outside the shower. I meant, why are you here? Why are you involved?"

Thankfully I'd put my hands down before he glanced over his shoulder and met my gaze.

"Because Emily asked."

"I see," I said neutrally, my thoughts already racing with what that meant and how I could use it.

"No. You don't, but you will."

He turned around, missing my glare.

"Wash, Hannah."

I gave his back the finger, then stripped out of my clothes and once again tossed them out on his head. He flicked them to the floor, as unbothered as he was the first time I'd done that, and waited with seemingly endless patience as I washed. I decided to test just how far that patience stretched and took my time with each limb. I lingered long after the water cooled and my fingers pruned. He just continued to lean there.

Giving in, I washed my hair.

Like the last time, he left the bathroom just before I shut off the water. Privacy was good. I needed to think without him watching me.

Merdon was here because Emily asked. A small, victorious smile tugged on my lips. He'd given me the key to my freedom with those three little words. I knew how obsessed fey could get over a girl. He would do anything Emily asked.

I toweled my hair and thought of my next move.

Swaying Emily into stopping this lockdown shouldn't be hard. She said all along that she only wanted to help me because she thought I was drinking too much. Pulling myself together and acting normal for a while wouldn't be a problem. I'd done it hundreds of times before. But because of that, convincing her my actions were real might take some time.

That thought exhausted me.

Resting a trembling hand on the countertop, I looked at myself in the mirror. I didn't look good. Dark shadows smudged the thin skin under my eyes; my overall hue could only be described as waxen and sickly; and I was far too thin, something that Emily had been worrying about for a while. As I stared, another face superimposed over mine, likewise sickly and waxen.

I quickly turned my back on the memory and clutched my head while humming a flat note. My mind wanted to wander back to *that* day. It whispered that I hadn't yet suffered nearly enough to make up for what I'd done. It was the small, hateful voice eating at my thoughts and stirring my misery that reaffirmed my plan. I needed out of this room so I could find enough booze to shut down the memories and the voice again.

It took another minute of rocking and humming for my head to clear enough for me to consider my next steps. Emily wouldn't believe I was better until I stopped looking like I was two breaths away from turning into an infected. That meant food.

The thought of eating something didn't appeal to me in the slightest, but by eating real food, bathing, and acting nice, Emily would see the change she wanted to see. She always had in the past. I'd be out of this room by tomorrow morning, latest. No problem.

With my mind set on a plan, I wrapped my towel around my torso and left the bathroom. I only made it a step into my room before pausing and blinking in confusion.

The mattress no longer had any sheets covering it, and Merdon wasn't sitting in his usual place in the chair beside my bed. The chair now waited by the closet with a TV tray set up next to it. Merdon leaned against the door, blocking any means of escape.

I looked at the soup waiting for me, the shirt and yoga pants set out on the mattress, then Merdon.

"Would you mind facing the door so I can change privately?"

He tilted his head, considering me, then moved so he was facing the window. If I stayed by the bathroom door and changed there, he wouldn't see me. It was at least something. Grabbing the clothes, I quickly dressed while glancing at the soup. There wasn't anything in it. No noodles or meat. How was I supposed to show Emily that I was better by drinking that?

"I'd like to talk to Emily," I said.

He grunted and returned to his original position, making no move to get her.

"The broth smells great and everything, but I was hoping for something a little more substantial. And maybe a cake. She knows I like cake."

"You don't need cake. Eat."

"I wouldn't be eating; I'd be drinking. I'd still like to talk to her."

He neither did nor said anything, just stood there.

Fine. I could get her attention without him.

"Emily!" I yelled at the top of my lungs.

"She won't answer you," Merdon said.

"Why not?"

"Because you're mean."

I wanted to kick him in the balls until they popped out of his mouth, make him swallow them, then do it all again.

"I'm not mean. I'm nice."

"Maybe you were once. Not anymore. Eat, Hannah, or I will help you."

We both knew what his version of helping meant. I sat and drank the broth. It wasn't easy. It almost came back up twice, and

I couldn't imagine what it would have been like if it had been real food.

When I finished, I looked at the bed.

"Is Emily washing everything?" I asked.

He shrugged.

"There should be another set of sheets in the hall closet. I can get them."

He just stared at me.

"What am I supposed to do?" I asked.

"Figure out how to live."

My fingers curled before I could stop myself. His gaze flicked to them, and that hint of amusement crept into his expression.

I didn't think it was possible to hate him more, but he always managed to up his game.

CHAPTER TWELVE

HOW LONG DID IT TAKE TO WASH SOME BEDDING? FOREVER. I considered just lying on the bare mattress, but I knew what Merdon and Emily were doing. They were testing my reaction when provoked.

Goading me was something that Merdon did very well. With his arms crossed over his massive chest, he leaned against the door and watched me. I didn't mind the watching. It was the damn judgmental look in his eyes. Like he knew exactly what I was thinking and doing. I hated it. More importantly, I hated him.

"I'm hungry," I lied. "Can I have some crackers or something?"

"No."

"I thought you wanted me to live, not starve to death."

He snorted. It wasn't an amused snort; it was a disparaging one. I barely kept my fingers from curling into the claw-his-eyes-out position they'd taken before.

"Nothing to eat. Nowhere to rest. And nothing to do. Since I'm not into Tibetan throat singing, providing me a book or some other activity would have been considerate." I wanted to add in a dig about him not being able to read but swallowed it down. I would not give him more fuel for his "mean Hannah" remarks.

He made no comment as I continued to pace the small confines of my room.

"Why can't I go downstairs and just watch a movie? It's not like I'd be able to leave with you dead-eying me all the time."

He grunted. I couldn't tell if he agreed that I would never get by him or rejected the movie watching. Probably both.

I glanced at the window again. It was already getting late. I hated this time of day, especially sober, because I knew what was next.

A soft knock on the door interrupted my thoughts.

"Emily?" I called.

There was no answer.

Merdon removed his weight from the panel and opened it to reveal an empty hallway.

"What the hell? Is she avoiding me?"

Merdon bent down to pick up the tray I hadn't noticed sitting on the ground.

"Yes."

That one word confirmed the failure of my plans. Without Emily, there would be no escape from my prison or my warden.

Seething, I glared at Merdon and moved without fully thinking. I couldn't. I was too focused on the pretty visual I had floating in my head of him falling face first into the bowl of broth. That lovely fantasy evaporated when he pivoted suddenly and caught my outstretched hands in a forceful grip.

"Can't blame a girl for trying," I said with a cheeky smile I didn't mean.

"Your attempts are pathetic and weak."

"If they're so pathetic, how did I manage to get you to the ground once already?"

He thrust me away with enough strength that I stumbled back a few steps and fell onto the bed.

When I looked up, the door was closed once more, and the bowl of soup rested in his open palm.

"Same choice," he said simply, holding the bowl out.

"I'm tired of your games," I said. "If you want me to eat, bring me real food."

"This is what you need."

"Screw you."

He was on me in an instant, his hand clamped on my jaw and the other forcing the bowl between my clenched teeth. I only struggled for a moment before I gave in and gulped the broth. My lips and jaw hurt, and I knew it could get worse if I fought harder. I didn't want worse; I wanted complacency and escape.

I thought giving in would make it better. It didn't.

As soon as I swallowed the last of the broth, I was over his shoulder again.

"Not the shower, you son of a—"

His hand landed on my ass with a thunderous crack. I squealed and squirmed.

He deposited me in the shower and turned on the water while I was still trying to rub out the sting.

"I just bathed, asshole."

"And spilled soup all over yourself. Wash."

"Fuck you."

Too angry and with my ass stinging too much to think clearly, I moved to the far corner of the shower and sat with my arms wrapped around my knees. I didn't care about the cold water beating down on me. I knew it would warm eventually. I only cared about not giving the grey douche canoe another inch. It helped that the tile cooled the sting on my butt cheek. I hadn't been spanked like that since I was six and got into Mom's shaving cream. I'd made a horrible mess on the carpet with it.

"Get up and wash, Hannah."

I looked up, water hitting my face. Through the drips, I saw him glaring at me. I returned the favor.

"You hurt me. Fey don't hit women."

"I didn't hit a woman. I spanked a child. Get up."

I knew what would happen. He'd proven himself to me already. Yet, I couldn't stop myself from slowly giving him the one-finger salute. I was done with him trying to control me.

His chest lifted in a large inhale, and I hoped that meant I was pissing him off as much as he was me. I rescinded that thought the moment he opened the door and stepped in. My butt couldn't take another spanking.

He had me off the floor and my shirt front full of soap before I could blink. He wasn't nice about the scrubbing, but he wasn't being a creeper about it, either. His touch was efficiently brief. And I fought it the whole time, hands and elbows flailing. I caught him hard enough to elicit an "oof" from him at least once before I was pinned against the cold wall, his hand buried in my hair, holding me in place.

I panted heavily. As soon as I caught my breath, I'd give him round two.

He leaned in, his mouth close to my ear.

"Pathetic and weak, Hannah. That's why you'll never leave this room."

Fire ignited in my soul. Forgetting about a break, I struggled in his hold. His chest pressed against my back, and I felt it vibrate with his mirth.

"Stay in your wet clothes or change. It's up to you. They're clean again."

Just as swiftly as he'd entered, he was gone.

It took every ounce of willpower to stay upright. Fighting Merdon had drained me beyond what I'd thought was possible. My legs felt like jelly and almost gave out when I peeled myself from the wall.

As I shed my wet clothes, I wondered if my act of defiance had proven anything more than he truly did control me. Bitterly, I faced the mirror. My skin was pink. Whether from the manhandling or the hot water, I couldn't be sure. What I'd hope to find was absent. Not a single bruising mark marred my skin. I couldn't understand how when all of me ached.

Taking a towel, I repeated the process of drying my hair for the second time that day. Nothing was working. I couldn't talk to Emily. I couldn't prove I was fine. I'd be stuck in this room forever. Why? What was the point of all of this? If Emily cared, she wouldn't have sicced her guard dog on me. There was no way she couldn't hear what he was doing to me. That she was okay with all of it spoke volumes. It also meant I needed to think of another way out.

I just didn't have the energy to come up with a single, useful thought. Even lifting my arms to scrunch my hair in the towel was too much. Letting the towel drop to the floor, I looked at my curls that were more frizz than spiraled. I remembered how much I'd hated frizz. It was an old emotion, one that didn't matter anymore, like so many others.

Completely naked and uncaring, I gave the mirror my back and shuffled to the door.

Before I reached it, I heard them and pressed my ear against the wood.

"...doesn't sound like it's going well."

"She's not making it easy."

The deep timbre of Merdon's voice was unmistakable and sounded very close. They were purposely trying to speak quietly. Why? So I wouldn't know Emily was in there and try to talk to her? She and I were past that possibility, and her next words proved it.

"We could try something else."

"No."

"Are you sure you're okay with this?"

There was a rustle of cloth, and I could picture her pressing up against him, ensuring he would be okay with whatever she wanted. I'd taught her that move. Traitor.

"What I want doesn't matter."

I gripped the knob and twisted. It didn't move, just like my bedroom door that first day.

"Emily!" I yelled, slamming my hand against the door. "When I get out of here, we're done. Do you hear me? You can't do this and expect things to ever be the same again."

I hit the door again and put my shoulder into it when I tried the knob again.

This time, I came spilling out, a tangle of limbs and naked skin as I fell to the floor. My knee took the brunt of the impact. The throbbing pain didn't slow me as I picked myself up and looked around the room for the pair.

Emily was already gone, the door closed, and the bed made. Lights from the wall were illuminating the dimly lit room. Merdon was returning the chair to its original place. He didn't look at me, for a change. I did. I looked down at myself and felt a sharp stab of humiliation.

Gracelessly getting to my feet, I hobbled over to the bed. My hands shook from exhaustion as I slid into the new yoga pants and shirt that waited. I didn't look up from what I was doing even when I heard Merdon move to look out the window.

My heart hurt more than ever before. Who was I anymore?

Without acknowledging him, I slid under the covers. My stomach made a sound like a waterbed as I finally settled against the mattress. I couldn't believe I'd kept the broth down through all of that. I frowned, realizing I actually felt a lot less sick.

Fucking Merdon.

I closed my eyes, ignoring the tears sliding down my cheeks.

TRAPPED IN MY OWN HELL, *I ran through the trees, towing my sister with me. The infected moaned behind us, their sounds almost drowning out our ragged breathing.*

The familiar panic and fear coursed through me, making my heart race.

I wanted to scream and rail against what I knew was coming. I tried to open my mouth and make some kind of sound. I tried so hard my throat hurt. My mouth never opened, and I continued running, and like all the times before, I helplessly relived the moment I left my sister behind.

I could almost feel the trails my tears should have made as I looked back at her and watched her disappear under the crush of infected. I tried harder to force myself to stay with her. To do something other than run away.

Yet, I turned, and I ran. I ignored her shrieks for help and the wet sounds that would forever haunt me. I ran until I collapsed. Then, I forced myself to my feet and stumbled into the home Katie and I had been using for days.

I huddled in the corner of the bedroom we'd shared, and I sobbed as my soul shattered. But I still didn't scream. I couldn't make that kind of noise. It wasn't safe.

The dream shifted.

My stomach cramped. I moved around the kitchen, looking for a scrap of anything we might have missed, but I knew it was all gone. It had been for days now. Since the day Katie and I had left our sanctuary to find a better place with more food.

Eyes watering, I closed the cupboard and looked outside. If I wanted to live, I'd need to leave. The thought terrified me, which is why I'd chosen to slowly starve myself for the last two and a half days. My stomach spasmed harder, letting me know that waiting any longer wasn't an option.

After drinking my fill of water, I took a knife from the kitchen and slipped out the door.

I couldn't stop shaking as I crossed the yard. We'd found a house in a small neighborhood in the middle of nowhere. There'd been decaying bodies, but no infected. Now I knew why; the infected had been attracted to the next town over.

Since Katie and I had already cleaned these houses out of food, I knew I needed to go farther. It took hours to cross the fields and find another house. My adrenaline sang through my veins the entire time I crouched in the bushes and watched the place.

The dream fragmented, showing me bits of what had happened. Me walking into that quiet house. The scratching noise coming from a back room. Me blocking that door. Me cleaning out the cupboards and packing food in a child-sized backpack.

The dream solidified again, settling on the moment where I was back in the messy kitchen of the house in the abandoned subdivision.

I opened a can of fruit and drank the juice. My stomach cramped and gurgled. I knew I needed to pace myself and set the can down. My hand shook as I wiped the juice from my mouth. I was tired. So tired. I glanced at the fading light in the window. I hated nights. Especially without Katie there. My throat closed, and I forced the thought away. But I couldn't escape my guilt and shame. It carved a hole in my middle every moment of every day.

I sniffled and wiped at my face again as I walked forward.

I could feel my fear build and tried to stop moving. My dream-self didn't listen.

Katie was standing in the middle of the room, her back to me. Her shirt was ripped and dirty and marked with blood. So much blood. I could see the bite marks covering her skin. I knew what she was even as hope bloomed in my chest.

"Katie?" I whispered.

She slowly turned, her milky eyes locking on me as her mouth opened and closed.

A sob escaped me.

She started forward.

"Forgive me," I rasped a moment before I plunged the knife I still gripped into her chest. She didn't die. Her hands locked around my biceps, and she lunged forward, mouth open.

I jerked the knife free and stabbed it right into her gaping maw.

She dropped to the floor, the blade pulling free as she fell. She didn't move.

I dropped the knife and stared at my blood-stained hands. Infected blood. My sister's blood.

I'd killed my sister. She'd come back for me, and I'd killed her instead of joining her like I should have the first time.

A tear splashed onto the center of my right palm, cleaning away the red.

I would never be clean again.

The pain of what I'd done ripped through me.

I wailed, and the dream shifted.

My mom hugged me, her hand running over my hair.

"The heartache will fade."

I remembered the moment. It was after my first boyfriend, ever, had dumped me in middle school. I'd been about the same age as Katie had been when she'd died.

"It will never fade," I said between sobs.

The dream drifted away, and I woke with wet sheets sticking to my face. My guilt would never fade, and neither would the pain of killing my sister.

Sobbing and shaking, it took a moment to realize the feeling of the hand on my head hadn't faded. It was real and continued to stroke over my hair. I turned toward it, desperate for the comfort it offered, and found Merdon leaning forward in his chair. He had crossed the distance with just his hand, to comfort me.

Our eyes met. His were missing the typical judgmental disapproval. He didn't speak. His gaze held mine steadily as his fingers moved again, lightly smoothing over my hair.

Everything hurt. My body. My thoughts. My heart and my soul. It all ached for what I'd suffered and what I'd done to my sister. I wanted it to stop. I needed it to stop. And, his gentle touch was slowly soothing away the worst of the edges.

I didn't question what I was doing when I pulled back the covers. I didn't stop to think what might happen when I crawled from bed and into his lap. All I knew was that I desperately needed to stop hurting.

He didn't touch me for a moment as I settled my weight against his hard chest. It rose and fell in a slow rhythm that further calmed me. I blinked, feeling the wetness of my lashes on my cheeks as my sobbing slowed and my breathing hitched.

His hand found my head again and continued its slow, stroking path over my hair.

I knew I should tell him to stop. This kind of touching always led to some type of emotional attachment for them. Except, with Merdon, it might not. He was Emily's problem. That meant I could let him keep petting my hair.

A shaky exhale escaped me.

His hand paused like the sound had surprised him. I leaned my cheek more firmly against his pectoral, and he resumed his comforting caress.

He didn't seem like the same person in the dark. He actually seemed...nice. I didn't let myself think about how I might leverage this change to my advantage. I was still too raw for that and wasn't willing to sacrifice what he was currently giving me.

His hand moved from my hair to my back. The pressure and rhythm remained the same, but the new path created an awareness that hadn't been there a moment ago. The opportunity to feel something other than pain compelled me to lift my head.

His hand stilled as our gazes met. My focus shifted to his mouth.

Could I? There were so many reasons not to. Emily. The potential that Merdon's infatuation might inadvertently shift to me. Being stuck in this room even longer. But the reason to kiss him was more compelling.

What wouldn't I do not to think or hurt for a few minutes? What haven't I already tried?

I licked my lips and slowly closed the distance.

At the last second, he turned his head.

His rejection stung for a brief moment. Then he spoke.

"You can't use me to numb your pain, Hannah. It won't work."

"How will we know if I don't try?"

He looked me in the eye, his expression hardening into that same judgmental one that grated on my last nerve.

"I said no."

"You know what? Screw you, Merdon. You're an idiot for passing up an opportunity with a woman. You thought your past lives empty? This one will be filled with days watching all your brothers pair up while you remain alone. You know why? Because you're an asshole, and women are smart enough to avoid that kind of man."

During my rant, I'd pushed off of his lap. Now, I headed to the bed.

He caught me by the arm and spun me around.

"And no one will ever want you because you're mean," he growled at me.

My temper snapped. I balled up my fist and swung at him.

He dodged, ducking low. I squawked when his shoulder bumped my middle and he stood. I knew this move. Kicking in an effort to get free, I beat on his back.

"I don't need a shower, you fucking son of a—"

His hand landed on the same damn, abused butt cheek as last time. I squealed and bucked to get off his shoulder.

"Stop moving or you'll hit your head."

"Fuck you, Merdon!"

He shifted my weight, and I felt us going down. I paused, moving to push the hair out of my face and look around.

We were out of my room and descending the steps.

"Where are we going?"

He didn't answer. I twisted around, looking for Emily, but the house was dark. There was no way she could have slept through me yelling. I arched my back to look up the stairs, before he turned the corner, and saw her door was still shut.

I opened my mouth to yell to her, but what could I say? She'd already shown she wasn't going to help me.

Merdon turned again, heading for the basement stairs. A spike of foreboding speared me. Why was he taking me there?

Because it will be quieter, my thoughts whispered.

"What are you doing?" I asked.

He kept walking.

"Take me back to my room."

He reached for the door, and I started squirming in earnest.

Merdon didn't follow the rules. He shoved me into the shower, force-fed me, and smacked my butt. He was rough and didn't care that it hurt me. Whatever he planned to do to me in the basement wouldn't be good.

He jogged down the basement stairs and flicked on the lights. Then, he tossed me to the ground like a bag of dirty laundry.

Stunned, I looked up at him, my heart hammering.

"Try to hit me again," he said, standing over me.

It felt like my eyes were going to pop out of my head.

"No, thank you," I said quickly. I might want to hurt him, but I didn't want him to pop my head off like I was an infected.

"Stand up, Hannah. Now."

I scrambled to my feet, only then noticing they weren't on the cold cement floor. Under them were black foam interlocking squares. Firm yet cushioned. My gaze flicked around the room, noting other changes. The boxes were all moved against the walls, perfectly stacked to block all the windows—no witnesses —and the gym equipment was unburied.

"What is this?" I asked.

"No muscles and slow here," he tapped his head.

I almost flipped him off, but I wasn't sure what was going on. Was he mad? Did he bring me down here to torture me in some new way?

He reached out, quick as lightning, and tapped my arm in a way that made it swing loosely at my side.

He chuckled.

"No muscle," he repeated.

I didn't react. I watched him as he circled me. He was stalking me like I was some type of prey. I only wished I knew why. His focus was freaking me out.

Lightning fast, he rushed me, and I found myself on my back again.

"Where is your fight now, Hannah? Will you give up? Will you let me do whatever I want?"

I swallowed hard. What was the right answer? What was he thinking?

In a blink, I found myself face down on the mat. One of his big hands held my thigh. My eyes went wide in understanding a moment before his other hand came down on the same damn butt cheek. I couldn't even squeal, it hurt so much.

"Does your backside sting?" he whispered in my ear.

CHAPTER THIRTEEN

RAGE FUELED MY SO-CALLED WEAK MUSCLES. I TWISTED OUT OF Merdon's hold and scrambled to my feet.

With a feral smile, he bared his teeth.

"Make me pay, Hannah," he goaded.

I flew at him. My fists bombarded his chest for a fleeting moment before I was on my back again. The stunned second it took for that to register was all he needed to flip me over. I swore, knowing what he meant to do, and tried to scramble away. But, I wasn't fast enough to avoid his iron hand.

The crack echoed in the basement.

Snarling, I struggled to my feet. This time, I didn't fly at him. We circled each other. When he lunged for me, I tried to swivel out of the way. Again, I wasn't fast enough. I was mean, though, just like he said. When he had me on my back, I bit him.

He retreated with a grunt, and I shot to my feet.

Now that I understood his game, I fought hard to stay off my back. When he did manage to get me there, I did everything I could to avoid being flipped to my stomach. Sometimes, I wasn't fast enough or strong enough or smart enough, and my ass felt the pain of that failure. Each smack refueled my rage and gave me more will to not end up on the floor.

We went on like this until my limbs shook with effort and sweat coated my skin.

I landed on my back, yet again, not even sure what I'd done wrong to get there, and quickly rolled to escape his grasp. It was a move I'd used before to avoid a spank and regain my footing. This time, everything felt slower, and when I tried to stand, my legs gave out. I tried once more and collapsed to my knees, panting.

"Enough," Merdon said.

I looked up. He wasn't crouched, ready to attack, but standing with his legs braced and arms crossed as he studied me. The bastard wasn't even winded.

"Go upstairs and shower."

My gaze went to the stairs, and my legs wanted to weep. I couldn't even stand; how in the hell was I going to manage two flights of steps?

"Or do you want me to carry you?"

I focused on Merdon. Everything ached, and I was exhausted beyond reason. I'd like nothing more than to be carried upstairs, but I knew his offers were always double-edged. There was no way I was in any condition to take him up on another challenge. I was certain that my ass was hot enough from all of his spankings to heat a living room in the Arctic.

"I'll walk," I managed.

It took two tries to get to my feet. He watched impassively, without making any offer to help as I shuffled forward. I wasn't sure my legs would handle the stairs. My thighs threatened mutiny after the third step, and I had to grip the railing like a lifeline as I continued to ascend.

He followed me quietly, his silence making me as nervous as

his proximity to my backside. There wasn't much I could do about the latter, and he and I weren't so good at the conversation thing.

The sight of my bed almost made me weep. I wanted nothing more than to crawl under the covers, but I knew what would happen if I tried to ignore Merdon's order to shower. My clothes stuck to my skin from all the sweating I'd done, and I could smell myself. It wasn't pretty.

I grabbed another clean outfit from the closet and shuffled toward the bathroom. It wasn't until I was in there that I realized I was alone. I shut the door, stripped, and piled my hair on top of my head. Hopefully, he wouldn't throw a fit about not washing that, too. It was a little sweaty, but I didn't think I'd be able to hold my arms above my head long enough to do any good.

Turning away from the mirror, I checked my backside. My mouth dropped open at the perfect outline of a gigantic, glowing red handprint. Merdon had marked me on purpose, smacking me in the exact same spot every time. I mentally called him several names as I climbed into the shower, too smart to say them aloud and antagonize him.

The soap job was rushed, so I put on deodorant as a precaution then dressed.

Merdon was sitting in the chair beside the bed again when I reemerged. I could feel his eyes on me as I hobbled across the room but refused to acknowledge him. He was a sadist, and all I wanted was sleep.

He didn't try to stop me as I slipped under the covers with a sigh. I closed my eyes, hoping this wasn't some trick and I wouldn't find myself on my stomach in two seconds.

"You've slept enough. Get out of bed."

Too fogged by sleep to think clearly, I ignored the warning and burrowed deeper.

A second later, the mattress tilted under me, and I tumbled from the bed to the floor. I landed on my side, tangled in the blankets that had fallen with me.

Lifting my head, I glared up at Merdon as he put the mattress back onto the frame.

"Are you getting up and coming downstairs on your own, or do you need help?"

I snarled at him. He showed me his teeth.

"You have five minutes."

He left the room.

Bastard.

In the middle of my angry thoughts, I realized what he'd finally given me. This was my chance to escape. I struggled free of the blankets and looked around the room. My windows were still nailed shut. I could break them, but I'd never be fast enough; I'd only end up sleeping in a freezing room tonight. I noted the early morning light before my gaze shifted to the hall.

Emily's room wasn't over the porch, but I could easily drop from the window to the ground without breaking anything. Maybe? I chewed my lip in indecision before I hurried to my dresser and pulled on two pairs of socks.

I was running out of time.

Before I finished, doubts began to eat at my urge to escape. Five minutes wasn't much of a head start, and I'd leave footprints in the snow. He'd be on me before I reached the wall. And if he wasn't? Then what? Did I really think some other fey would deliver me to Tenacity? I had to try, though, didn't I? What he and

Emily were doing was wrong. They couldn't just keep me locked up like this.

I crossed the hall, still trying to imagine what I'd do once I was on the ground. All the possibilities vanished the moment I tried the knob. Emily's door was locked. I stared at it in confusion. She never locked it.

"Emily is not in her room," Merdon said.

I slowly turned my head and found him watching me from the bottom of the stairs.

My stomach sank. Not only was hope of escape just a dream, I knew what waited for me if I walked down those stairs. I did not want to go to the basement with Merdon. Yet, what other choice did I have?

"I hate you," I whispered.

"I know."

Resolutely, I started down the stairs. My legs weren't okay. Last night's exertions had to have damaged them in some way. That was the only explanation for the bone deep ache echoing in my thighs.

Merdon silently watched me limp my way down to him. There was no pity in his gaze, and I knew he wouldn't go any easier on me today because of my aches. I cursed my impulsive stupidity for doubling up on socks and not underwear and pants, and I couldn't help but wonder if his handprint was still gracing my backside. If it wasn't now, it would be before long.

I reached the second to last step and stopped, unable to go farther because Merdon hadn't moved. Even with the additional height of the steps, I had to tip my head to meet his gaze.

"I hope the timer isn't still running," I said.

He blinked at me.

"For the five minutes," I clarified. "It's not fair if you block the way so I can't meet the requirements."

"Do you find anything fair?" he asked.

"Since the quakes? Never."

He grunted and stepped aside to let me pass. I hesitated, not trusting that it wasn't some kind of trick, then cautiously moved forward with narrow-eyed suspicion. I hoped he didn't think my hesitation was due to fear. It wasn't. It was due to a healthy respect for his big hand and fast reflexes.

When I veered to the basement stairs, he stopped me.

"No. Breakfast first."

I wasn't expecting that. I also wasn't expecting to see Emily in the kitchen despite his warning that she wasn't in her room.

Frowning suspiciously, I glanced back at Merdon as I made my way to the kitchen island. If Emily was cooking, had he locked her door because he'd known I would try to use her windows? I didn't want to think about the implication of him anticipating my actions when I was so clueless about his.

Emily didn't say her usual chipper 'good morning' as she set a plate of eggs and pancakes before me. Her silence suited me just fine. We had nothing to say to one another, except maybe goodbye.

Merdon took the seat beside me. He received a warm smile from her, which I pretended not to notice, and a plate full of reconstituted eggs. The heaping mess of yellow, crumbly goo made me cringe. I'd never be able to eat that much and keep it down. Even the amount on my plate, a third the size of his, would be a struggle. Especially if he intended to flip me around on the mats like he had the night before.

Maybe that was his plan. Make me slow and heavy with food and unable to save my backside. No, thank you.

I only planned to eat lightly because of that. But the first bite tasted way better than I remembered, and I was starving from yesterday's liquid diet. Before I knew it, every single bit of food was gone from my plate.

"Do you want more?" Merdon asked.

"No. Am I allowed to go to the bathroom, or will that get me tossed to the floor and spanked?" I asked, looking directly at him.

"Hannah, you're not a prisoner," Emily said, speaking for the first time.

"Tell my ass that," I said without breaking eye contact with my tormentor. "You might want to inform your muscle that he needs to take it down a few notches today or I won't be able to join you for another quaint family meal this evening."

She gave me a hurt look.

"Stop being mean to Emily. She's done nothing to deserve it."

I could hear the warning in Merdon's tone but didn't care. I leaned toward him, challengingly.

"Or what?"

His expression hardened.

"Use the bathroom upstairs then meet me in the basement. You have two minutes."

"And if I say no?"

A hint of anticipation lit his gaze.

"There's always the other side."

It took a moment for me to realize he meant my other butt cheek. My face flamed with anger, and I stood stiffly.

"I'll be right back."

My legs protested any form of hustle as I made my way upstairs, and they shook when I sat to use the toilet. They'd be fine in a few more days. Hopefully. I wasn't as certain about my backside, though, so I stuffed a fluffy hand towel in my pants.

Satisfied with my handiwork, I went back downstairs. Merdon

was waiting for me at the bottom of the steps again. Did he think I'd try to make a break for it if he wasn't there guarding me? He was probably right. I hated feeling this trapped even as I acknowledged there wasn't anywhere I'd be able to go where Merdon wouldn't find me. If I even got that far. Stupid fey.

Ignoring both Emily and Merdon, I marched to the basement. I could feel him behind me the entire way. When I reached the mat, I turned and watched him, unwilling to walk onto the black mat with him at my back.

He didn't stop until he reached the middle and faced me.

"Are you ready?" he asked.

"For another beating? No. I'd rather not repeat that."

"You know what to do to avoid it. Don't let me get you on your back."

He crouched slightly, letting me know that the ass whooping was about to begin.

"I didn't realize fey had fetishes," I said, assuming the same stance but far warier. "Spanking, I could see, but the need to dominate a species that had no chance of possibly besting you is just sick."

"I am not doing this to dominate you."

"It *is* just about the spankings?" I straightened. "Then put me over your knee and get it done. My legs are too sore from last night to put up a fight anyway."

"I am not doing this to spank you."

"My ass begs to differ. It feels like your handprint is still there. And you were far too excited in the kitchen about the prospect of spanking the other side. Admit it. You liked spanking me. Does Emily know?"

I was on my back in a second. I tried to bite him, but he arched out of the way and had me on my stomach in the next second. His hand came down on my other cheek just as he'd promised. The sting wasn't as sharp as last night, and I grinned at my forethought...until I realized his hand was still on my butt. And, that it moved in a slow circle.

"What the hell are you doing, pervert?" I tried bucking off his hold, but he had one hand in the center of my back, pinning me in place.

His hand traveled up to my waistband. I knew I was in trouble the moment his fingers dipped into the elastic.

"Emily! He's going to ass rape me, damn you!"

Merdon ignored me and tugged the hand towel free. I let my head fall to the mat in defeat. There'd be no sitting later today.

"This is cheating," he said softly, tossing the towel on the mat near my face. "You will learn nothing without the sting of failure."

"I'm learning nothing now, other than you're a sadistic asshole. If you want me to learn something, teach me; don't beat me."

His hand left my back, and he lifted me to my feet like I weighed nothing.

"I get that life isn't fair, in general, but you getting me on my back is a sure thing."

"Is it?"

"You know it is."

"Yet you managed to avoid it a few times last night."

"Because I got lucky, played dirty, and was desperate not to get spanked."

"So, do it again."

"It wasn't easy!" I let my frustration bleed through. Mostly because if we were talking, he wasn't smacking my ass.

"It's not supposed to be. You're too slow, too weak, and aren't thinking. You need to get better at all three if you want to have any chance."

I fisted my hands as he crouched.

"Don't just tell me why I'm failing. Show me how to fix it."

"Crouch low, anchor your feet, and be ready. When I come at you, read how I'm coming at you. If I'm aiming high, go low. If I'm going low, go high."

"Go high? That's your advice? I'm not fey. I can't jump like you."

"So don't."

He charged at me, going slower than normal. His gaze was on my face. His hands reached for my arms. He was going high. I dropped and rolled. Instead of rolling away, I tumbled toward him, tripping up his feet.

Had he been less nimble, I would have liked to believe that he would have fallen on his face. I wasn't that lucky, though. He recovered his balance. Springing to my feet, I ignored the protest in my legs and braced myself for another attack.

"That was good," he said. "You saw what I intended and did the opposite. Rolling toward the danger isn't smart, though. Use your head."

"Says you. You're too fast. Rolling toward you was to try to trip you up. Rolling away from you wouldn't have done any good. You would have still caught me. This gave me a chance to get to my feet."

He grunted and got back in the crouch position.

"No spankings. Today, I'll bite."

"What!"

He moved. I barely had time to pivot to the left and run, squealing.

"Good," he said, returning to the center of the mat.

I unwedged myself from between a stack of boxes and looked at the insane grey man calmly regarding me.

"Good?" I demanded. "You just told me you were going to bite me. That is not okay. I want the spankings back. No biting."

"I won't break the skin."

I couldn't even respond to that. In no way was I reassured.

"Why are you doing this?"

"You said you wanted me to teach you."

I snarled at him, knowing he was purposely misunderstanding me. He took the snarl as go-time because he immediately dropped into a crouch and charged me. Thankfully, he was continuing to hold back. I dropped to my knees this time and aimed a fist for his dick.

He quickly spun out of the way with a growl, and I popped to my feet to watch him.

"Good." The word was grudgingly given. "That won't always work, though."

"I don't need it to always work. I only need it to work enough to not get bitten."

He grunted and crouched.

I wanted to scream in frustration. This wasn't teaching me anything useful. No matter what he said, he had to be getting some kind of sick pleasure from chasing me around and beating me. And now, biting me, apparently. I really, really didn't want that to happen.

He shifted his weight. That split-second warning was what I needed to bolt in the opposite direction as he came at me. My pride at seeing what he intended quickly evaporated as he adjusted course and was on me in a blur.

My back hit the mat. Panic and desperation flooded me. I couldn't be bitten.

I used everything. Fists, nails, knees, hips. I bucked, and I twisted, and I fought like a wild cat. None of it stopped him from grabbing both my hands, settling his weight on my torso to pin me, and biting down on my bicep.

It fucking hurt. I cried out and struggled harder.

He got off of me and stared down as I glared up at him.

"You failed because you panicked."

"I failed because you're bigger, stronger, and a mean son of a—"

The bastard flipped me over and spanked me. Hard.

I squealed and scrambled to a sitting position.

"You said no spankings!"

"Stop being mean."

I glared at him in silent mutiny, my backside stinging with the irony in his statement.

"If you don't want to be bitten, keep my mouth away from you. Hitting me and kicking me are useless. You know none of that will stop me, so why do it?"

I hated him for biting me. I hated him for forcing me to do this. But mostly, I hated him for repeating what I'd been trying to tell him all along. I had no chance of winning against him. Oblivious to my growing anger, he continued.

"Think, Hannah. Don't panic."

He motioned for me to get up.

I wanted revenge so badly that I snapped. I didn't just get up; I flew at him. His eyes went wide as he caught me. I opened my mouth, ready to bite his nipple clean off since it was the closest thing at the moment. But, he blocked me with a forearm under my chin.

My teeth clacked together as he nudged upward and back. I stumbled away, effectively stopped from succeeding. Instead of getting angry about it, I grinned ferally. He was teaching me something.

"Finally," I growled.

He blinked at me, and surprise registered on his face as I flew at him again. I went for the same nipple. There was a good chance he wouldn't repeat the previous blocking move. But, he seemed to always do the exact opposite of whatever I thought he'd do.

Finally, I got something right.

He thrust his hand out. I could see that he meant to plant it in my chest. I ducked, mouth open. His middle finger deep-throated the hell out of me. I swallowed my gag and clamped down.

All motion stopped.

A breath hissed out of him.

He didn't try to pull his finger free. He probably would have ripped my teeth out if he had. And, I didn't let go. I was biting down on his fucking finger for all it was worth.

"Bis is whab ib feews wike," I said. "Nah goob, inna?"

He wasn't looking at my face. He was staring at his lost middle finger.

"I suggest you stop now, Hannah," he said, his voice rough.

When he looked up, the cold, calculating look in his eyes terrified me. I immediately released him and gagged when his finger brushed my uvula on the way out.

He didn't speak. Didn't move. Just stared at his finger.

Swallowing thickly, I looked down at the twin marks my front teeth had made just above the base of the third knuckle. It was bad. As in, almost-broke-the-skin bad.

"Go drink some water," he said, without looking up at me.

I tried not to let my surprise show and bolted for the stairs.

Freedom.

CHAPTER FOURTEEN

"Where's Merdon?" Emily asked suspiciously when I appeared without him.

"Downstairs."

I went for my coat and quickly shoved my feet into my boots.

"Where are you going?" she asked.

"Anywhere but here."

I had the door open and was making a run for it before I finished the last word.

How much of a head start would I have? Thirty seconds? A minute? I needed a plan. I needed help. As I ran, I looked around, but the ever-present, wandering fey were mysteriously absent.

No help, then.

I sprinted for the wall.

An arm circled around my waist. The steel band close-lined me, flipped me, and spun me around. My stomach gave a queasy lurch and threatened to heave breakfast as it met a hard, familiar shoulder.

I went limp, arms swinging free, as Merdon turned around and started for the house.

"Smarter," he said. "But not smart enough."

Anger pushed aside defeat, and I considered his butt. It was extremely firm and tight. Could I bite it?

"Do you need help, Merdon?"

I jerked my head up and, bracing my hands on Merdon's lower back, glared at Tor.

"Does he need help? Seriously? I'm the one who ran for her life and is being dragged back to her one-room prison."

Merdon's hand settled on my butt. Right over the spot he'd smacked today.

I stiffened and wanted to swear.

"Do you have anything else to say, Hannah?" he asked.

I kept my mouth firmly shut.

"I don't need any help, yet. Thank you for watching her, Tor."

Tor smiled, waved at Merdon, and jogged away.

"Watching me?" I hissed at Merdon, twisting around to try to see his face.

His hand twitched on my backside, a reminder of his control over me. I stopped moving around and used my head. If Tor had been watching me, and all the other fey were hiding, then I'd been right about Merdon having the support of the other fey to keep me within the walls of Tolerance. I truly was a prisoner.

Merdon was right. I needed to be smarter.

He patted my butt, smoothed his hand over it, then surprised the hell out of me.

"Would you like to walk?" he asked.

"Yes."

He actually put me down. Nicely.

I pushed my hair out of my face and looked at him, trying to guess his motivation.

"Was I too heavy?" I asked.

"You weigh nothing."

"Why are you letting me walk?"

He took a step toward me, and I retreated with my hands raised.

"I'm walking! I'm walking." I hustled back to the house with Merdon trailing two steps behind me.

Emily was at the door, waiting for us.

"Everything okay?" she asked, looking at Merdon.

It stung.

"Everything is fine," Merdon said.

"Sure, for both of you," I muttered, kicking off my shoes and tossing my jacket to the floor. "Not the second-class occupant of this house."

I glared at Emily, who was refusing to meet my gaze.

"He bit me. That's what you're allowing him to do when he drags me down there. What in the hell has happened to you?"

Merdon grabbed my arm and towed me to the basement without a word.

I hated his protectiveness over her dumb feelings. Five minutes alone with her, and I would have her coming around to my way of thinking. I always did. Instead, she was standing there, looking at her toes while he dragged me back down to the basement of doom.

Tugging at his hold did nothing to free my arm. I stumbled after him, down the steps and onto the mat.

He didn't even give me a chance to get ready. He crouched low and came at me. I thrust my hand up, heel first, and hit the bottom of his jaw. It was like smacking stone. Still, he backed off briefly before coming at me from a different angle. I didn't try the same move. This time, I ducked and tumbled around his legs, springing up behind him.

I knew very well he was moving at "normal" speed and could have grabbed me if he'd wanted to.

On and on it went until I was panting for air and my limbs were shaking.

"I need to stop."

"Again."

"Damn your 'again.' What is the point of trying to kill me after stopping me from doing it myself?"

He stalked across the mat. I backpedaled my way into a stack of boxes, cornered. He crouched, and I thought he was going to come at me once more. Instead, he got right up in my face.

My pulse spiked. He'd pulled too much shit for me not to be wary.

"I am not trying to kill you, Hannah," he said with soft menace. "I am saving you."

It wasn't easy to find my voice and enough backbone to say what I needed to say.

"I'm tired. I'm hungry. And I hurt all over. This doesn't feel like a save."

He leaned down farther so we were eye to eye. His slit pupils narrowed to thin lines as he studied me.

"You are not tired. You will eat again when you are tired. And you have suffered much more than the minor aches you experience now."

I flinched away from the reminder of what I'd endured. Yet the thought made me realize that, since the dream last night, all this tumbling around had given me something else to focus on. It shocked me to recognize I hadn't thought of Katie once since then. Guilt hit me hard.

"No," Merdon said, giving me a rough shake.

When had he grabbed me?

"Lose focus, and you fail. Do you understand?"

Fail meant spanking. Or did it mean biting now? Either way, I didn't want to fail, so I nodded and focused completely on Merdon.

"Good."

He released me and strode to the center of the mat.

"Again."

Fuck my apocalyptic life.

I COULD DO IT. No, I *would* do it.

"Do you want help?"

"I don't like your version of help."

Merdon grunted behind me and waited patiently as I forced my foot onto the next stair. I'd never been physically pushed to the point of muscle failure, but I was there now. My limbs quaked with exhaustion, and I feared sitting to eat lunch. I'd never get up again. As lovely as melting into a puddle in the kitchen sounded, I knew better than to believe Merdon would allow it. He'd been clear that this was a lunch break only.

My stomach growled ominously, demanding it's due.

"Lift the other foot."

"I wish I had the energy to turn around and push you down the steps."

He tapped my butt with the back of his hand.

"Be nice."

"Says the guy who bit me at least a dozen times."

"You were too slow."

And he was sick in the head, but I was smart enough to keep that opinion to myself. After hours in the basement with him,

I'd caught on that he had a low tolerance for certain types of sass.

His hand nudged the back of my knee, and I forced myself upward another step. Just two more to go. No problem.

It took me a full minute, during which time Merdon said nothing. He was a weird mix of patience and drive that I doubted I'd ever understand.

When I reached the top, he clasped my arms and steered me to a stool at the kitchen island. I'd never been more grateful for the help. But it weirded me out at the same time. His version of "help" hadn't ever ended well for me before. I eyed him warily as he sat beside me.

"I hope this is okay," Emily said, sliding a bowl in front of me and stealing my attention.

I looked down at the stew and actually salivated.

Too hungry to answer, I picked up the spoon and started eating. Even that was too much work. I propped an elbow on the table so I could hold my head up while I fed myself. My eyes closed as I chewed.

How did he expect me to keep going? I had nothing left to give.

During the next spoonful, my sleeve slipped back to expose the bite on my wrist. The general redness was already fading, leaving behind the round dots of his sharp canines. Fey bites weren't fun. I bitterly hoped his middle finger got infected. It would serve him right.

"Are you finished?" Merdon asked.

I realized I'd stalled my eating with my tired thoughts and started back up again.

He scraped the bottom of his bowl then took it to the sink.

"Watch her," he said. "I'll be right back."

I looked up from my food as he walked down the hall to the bathroom.

Still hungry but too desperate to care, I pushed my bowl away and slid from the stool to a mostly upright position.

"You going to try to run again?" Emily asked quietly.

I snorted. I could barely lift my spoon. How in the hell did she think I'd get to the door? One unsteady step toward the living room nearly brought me to my knees.

"Please, don't do this, Hannah," Emily whispered.

Eyes on my prize, I continued forward, doing my best to hurry.

The couch beckoned. I didn't try to walk around it. I reached the arm and just fell forward. The cushions welcomed me like a long-absent lover. I sighed and closed my eyes. The black abyss of oblivion pulled me into its welcoming embrace.

Mom came to me again. She stroked my hair even though I couldn't see her.

"You're strong and intelligent. You will choose to live."

I wanted to ask her to tell Merdon how smart and strong I was, but my lips wouldn't move. Even in sleep, I was too tired. So, I quietly drifted in the feel of her touch while dishes clanked in the background, noise I associated with home and better times. I exhaled contentedly.

Bits of conversation drifted in and out of my awareness.

"...good she's eating."

"...manipulative. Don't trust..."

"...biting necessary?"

"Do you trust me?"

I tried to ignore it all, but the words kept worming their way in. Pressure on my arm tugged at my consciousness, demanding my attention. But sleep held me tightly until the loud crackle of velcro jolted me awake.

I blinked, disoriented, and tried to focus.

"Her vitals are good. But what you did was dangerous. People are supposed to be weaned."

I couldn't place the woman's voice.

"Not Hannah."

I definitely knew Merdon's. Fighting the remnants of exhaustion that still wanted to pull me back under, I struggled to sit up.

"How are you feeling, Hannah?" Cassie asked, moving close enough that I could see her.

"Tired."

"I bet. Emily said that you're exercising with Merdon. That's really good. Make sure you eat and drink more, though, to compensate."

I nodded like I understood her, but my brain was still stuck on how tired I was.

Cassie patted my leg and moved away from me. I wilted back into the cushions, my eyes already closing again.

"She's lucky to have you both in her corner. Be careful with the biting, Merdon. Fey teeth are much sharper than human teeth, and our skin is fragile compared to yours. And she needs rest as much as exercise. Her body needs time to heal."

Teeth? Biting?

My eyes popped open, all traces of exhaustion gone, as the door closed.

I swiveled around and found Merdon watching me from the front entry.

"People know you're biting me, and they're okay with it?"

He didn't answer.

I looked at Emily, who was in the kitchen, mixing something up. Surely, she couldn't be okay with that.

"I'm making biscuits to go with dinner," she said hesitantly, avoiding my question.

"Unbelievable."

I flopped back onto the couch and stared at the ceiling. What had the world come to that everyone was completely calm about some grey creature from myth biting me? None of what was happening should even be real.

My mind had barely begun to question the level of insanity in my life when Merdon's face appeared over me.

"Get up. You've rested enough."

"Cassie said I needed rest to heal. Are you saying you think I'm healthy now?"

He blinked at me, and I knew I had him.

"Because if I'm healthy, you have no reason to keep me a prisoner here." I got to my feet. "I think I'll go for a walk."

He didn't try to stop me from bundling up or leaving the house. But he did follow me. I could live with that.

It was easy to ignore my shadow when it felt so good to be outside. Now that I wasn't running, I paid more attention to everything around me and noticed the fey were still present. They were just working extra hard to stay out of my sight. Traitor chickens.

A low moo brought me up short. I listened and heard it again.

I looked back at Merdon in disbelief.

"Was that a cow?"

He came to stand beside me, his suspicious gaze sweeping over my face.

"Yes."

"How?" I demanded.

"One of the new arrivals in Tenacity knew where to find the cows. We went to get them the night before you were kidnapped."

I'd forgotten about that, somehow, and the reminder stirred some things I wasn't ready to feel. Pushing aside the regret and shame, I focused on what livestock might mean for the humans here.

"Cows?" I asked. "As in more than one?"

"Many."

"Where?"

Merdon led me toward a pair of vacant lots on the corner of one of the cul-de-sacs. At least ten cows meandered there, chomping grassy looking stuff from loose piles placed on top of the trampled snow.

"We have cows and cow food?"

"Some. Ryan is going out to the farms to look for more. The animals eat a lot."

A smile started and grew. It wasn't one of my fake smiles but a real one filled with fragile hope. Animals were alive. That had to mean something. At the very least, we would avoid eventual starvation when the existing food supply ran out.

I hugged my arms around myself and just watched the animals graze. They did eat a lot. Would Ryan be able to find what the cows needed? Granted, Mya's brother had been leading supply runs since we had settled here and seemed to know what he was doing. He always came back with what we needed. The quantity wasn't always there, though, not even with the help of his band of merry-fey.

But, if Ryan was a town kid like me, would he even know how much food to bring back for the cows? I knew nothing about cows other than that they could be eaten, and the moms could be milked.

"Are they milk cows?" I asked after a while.

"Not yet. They all have baby cows in them."

"More cows?" The words were barely a whisper. I was already seeing a herd rather than just the few we had. And if one of the cows was a male, we'd have even more.

A tear spilled down my cheek, and I quickly wiped it away.

"Do you like cows?"

I nodded, not wanting to look at him. He'd seen the tear, obviously, and I didn't want pity. Not from him.

"Do you think there might be other animals out there?" I asked.

"Angel told Shax she heard a bird."

It was still weird hearing Shax's name associated with another girl. How quickly he'd fallen out of infatuation with me. I wondered if the fey would be as obsessed with pregnant cows as they were with humans.

"Birds are good," I said, reining in my thoughts. "Pigs, goats, and chickens would be better."

"There is a chicken at Tenacity."

One chicken wasn't enough, but seeing the cows in front of me, I thought that we might have real hope of surviving. If only...

An ache exploded in my chest as I thought of Katie. My smile faded, and the urge to cry grew stronger. She should have been standing there with me. She should have had the chance to see what the world would look like if the fey managed to kill all the hellhounds.

"Enough rest," Merdon said, stepping in front of me with that judgy, angry expression back on his face.

Before I could respond, he bent down in a familiar move. My eyes went wide, and I reacted as his words about going high echoed in my ears.

My knee rammed into his chest at the same time my fingers closed over the end of one of his pointy ears. I'd accidentally discovered how sensitive fey ears were long ago.

Giving the pliable grey end a sharp twist, I pulled hard.

Merdon grunted and went down to one knee. Any triumph I felt withered as his hand clamped around my wrist and pulled my fingers free. When he looked up, there was real anger in his eyes.

"Be nice."

The low warning in those words made my bladder quiver in fear. Ignoring the sensation, I met his gaze with a glare.

"Ask to carry me, and I will be nice."

He slowly got to his feet, not loosening his hold on my wrist.

"I don't need your permission."

"Yes, you do. You don't own me. Stop acting like it."

He said nothing for a moment, considering me with an intensity that I found intimidating as hell. What worried me more was that he thought my consent was optional. Why was I stuck with the broken fey? Why couldn't one of the nice ones be interested in Emily?

With obvious reluctance, he released my wrist.

"Walk back to the house quickly if you don't want to be carried."

"Does everything need to be a threat with you?"

"Does everything need to be a fight with you?"

I gave him one last glare then turned on my heel and started back toward the house. A cow mooed its farewell, and I wondered if Emily knew about them. Of course she did. Emily tended to know everything that was going on inside both the walled towns. Had I not been locked in my room, she probably would have told me about the cows.

Bitterly, I thought of my ex-friend and wished I had someone I could count on like Cassie had said.

"Faster," Merdon said, nudging me from behind.

"I am going fast," I snapped, trying to lengthen my stride.

"No, you're thinking too much and slow."

"First, you complain I'm not smart. Now, you're complaining that I'm thinking? Make up your mind. What do you want me to do?"

Hands landed on my shoulder, and he spun me around.

Angry eyes held mine as he leaned in and whispered one little word that sent my pulse racing.

"Run."

My brain shorted out for a second too long because he started to growl. Pivoting, I took off at a sprint. I could hear him right behind me. The fear, the sound of being chased, and the knowledge that there was no one around to help, it brought everything back in full force. Panic ate at my chest. My legs and arms pumped in unison, desperation giving me fuel.

I didn't look back. I refused to see what I was leaving behind.

The door opened before I reached it. I didn't slow. Emily barely got out of my way as I barreled inside. I kept running. My snow-wet shoes skidded on the carpet as I made the sharp turn for the stairs.

I barely heard her call to Merdon as I thundered up the steps. My bedroom beckoned, a place of safety rather than the prison I'd imagined it to be. I cleared the opening and slammed the door shut behind me.

The sound resonated in the small space. Panting for air, I whirled and faced the door. Panic clung to me, coating my thoughts. It took several breaths for me to calm enough to realize an infected wasn't going to open the door. I wasn't sure knowing it would be Merdon was any better.

Had I really just slammed the door in his face?

I cringed and crept closer to place my ear against the wood panel.

There wasn't a sound from the other side. Carefully, I tried the doorknob. It didn't turn.

Shit. I was back to being locked in.

Annoyed, I kicked off my shoes and removed my jacket. Emily was going to be pissed that I ran through the house with my shoes on. A little bit of guilt poked me in the middle at the thought of her downstairs, blotting up water or scrubbing dirt stains. I pushed those thoughts aside and concentrated on my predicament.

Exercising in the basement with Merdon sucked, but it was better than being locked in my room all the time. I paced the confining space. How long would Emily want to keep me locked in here? I hadn't had anything alcoholic to drink in days and was eating now. Wasn't that enough to earn my freedom?

In a moment of brutal clarity, I knew it wouldn't be.

I'd pushed Emily too far. Obviously, I had if she was letting her boy toy spank and bite me. I sighed, knowing she'd seen my problem for what it was. She wouldn't let me loose to drink the pain away again. She'd want me to talk it out.

I turned toward the window, withering on the inside. I'd never speak my shame out loud. Ever.

The faint murmur of voices drew me to the door. I pressed my ear against it again.

"...resentment will only grow if you keep her locked in her room all the time. Would letting her have a little freedom be so bad? She was fine today, wasn't she?"

"She was fine because I was there."

"And you aren't going anywhere, right?"

There was a moment of silence and a rustle of cloth against cloth. I could imagine him hugging her.

"No, I'm not going anywhere."

"Good. Please consider letting her outside some more. Fresh air is good for us."

I frowned, trying to understand what I was hearing. Emily wasn't making the calls? Merdon was?

I was royally fucked.

CHAPTER FIFTEEN

REGRET DIDN'T COME CLOSE TO HOW I FELT ABOUT THE EAR TWIST I gave Merdon. I'd be lucky if he ever let me out of the room again.

Knowing that it was Merdon keeping me here also confused the hell out of me. Were his actions some sort of warped way of giving Emily what she wanted? I mean, she wanted me sober and mentally healthy. She'd made that pretty clear leading up to this lock in. While she and I both knew my sobriety and mental health weren't things she could just snap her fingers and fix, did he? I bet not.

Emily really did screw herself over hard by picking him as a beyfriend. He was way too forceful. She needed someone less prone to living life two seconds away from a rage. I wished I knew what she was thinking. More than that, I wished I knew what he was planning. How did he think he was going to fix me to her liking when he wasn't listening to her?

The adrenaline spike that had fueled my run of terror faded, leaving me tired. I sat on the bed. I knew if I lay down, I'd fall asleep. Somehow, I didn't think Merdon wanted that yet, no matter how much the idea of another dream-free day-nap tempted me.

I looked at the fading light outside and wondered what new version of hell the night would bring.

The door opened.

"Come."

Just one angry word. That was all I got before Merdon stepped aside expectantly.

I stood, my eyes going to his ear. The one I'd tugged was still a little darker than its twin.

"I'm sorry," I said quickly. "I shouldn't have tugged on your ear."

He was in front of me in a second, showing how fast he could move when he wanted.

"You brought me to my knee because of pain. What if I didn't feel pain? What would you have done then?"

"Probably yelled, kicked, and hit you as you carried me away."

"You would give up? Explain."

"You're stronger and faster. The only thing that even gives me a chance is that you can be hurt. If I couldn't hurt you, there'd be no way to stop you."

"You could kill me."

I jerked back.

"What are you saying?"

He took a slow, big breath before answering.

"You're getting smarter. That is all."

I blinked at him, feeling ridiculously like a fey in doing so. But he'd just confused the hell out of me. Was he saying that he'd known I would have to hurt him to stop him? Or that he was waiting for me to do that?

"Come," he repeated, stepping aside once more.

I led the way down to the kitchen, my thoughts still trying to work out our conversation upstairs.

"Do you want to eat first or go to the basement?" Emily asked from the kitchen.

"Basement first," Merdon said from behind me.

My stomach growled in protest.

"Okay. But not too long. Everything will be ready in an hour."

He nudged me to keep walking. I trudged toward my doom, recalling that before the ear pull, I'd also bitten his finger.

"Do I have to go to the basement? Can't we just eat like normal people?"

"No." He gave me another nudge.

I made a small sound of denial and started down the steps. I was still tired from the first round. What exactly did he think would happen in a repeat round? Was this just to take out some of his rage from all the shit I'd pulled? I hoped not.

When I reached the mat, I turned toward him. As low as I was on energy, I still felt a surge of adrenaline when he stepped toward me.

"Do we have to do this?" I asked again. "Can't we just hug it out or something?"

He paused mid-step and tilted his head at me.

"Hug what out?"

"Whatever emotion is driving you to torture me with spankings and biting. My legs are barely managing to walk. I don't think they're up for more squats and rolling. I just want dinner then sleep."

"No. You've rested enough to try again."

"Try what?" I asked in exasperation.

"To not be bitten."

He showed me his pointy teeth and got into a crouch. I quickly did the same, faltering at the way my legs protested.

"Focus," he said.

He came at me. It was noticeable how much he had slowed down after his little display upstairs. I pivoted to the side, barely avoiding his reaching grab, though.

"Good. Again." He returned to his starting position. "You're only safe when you're off the mat."

My eyes widened as I understood the change. He was going to keep coming after me unless I got away-away from him.

My brain barely got out an "aw, hell" before he came at me again. Knowing better than to repeat the move, I fell to my knees, rolled, then sprang to my feet. Or, I tried to. My legs gave out, refusing to participate in his bullshit anymore.

He was on me in a second.

Back pressed into the mat, I brought my forearm up to brace against his throat and grabbed his shoulder to steady the move. At the same time, I went for his ear with my free hand. Was I stupid? Probably. Yet, he hadn't exactly yelled at me for abusing his ear the first time. In fact, that conversation had ended with him saying I was getting smarter because I'd known pain was the only way to stop him.

His lips quirked, the only warning he gave that he'd read my intention. He caught my hand, and our gazes held as he pulled it to his mouth.

All I could think of was how I'd bitten him. Was this a revenge bite? Given his power and the sharp edges of his teeth, he could nip one of my fingers clean off if he wanted.

My eyes went wide, and panic surged through me. Feeling the weight of his hips on mine, I bucked hard. He grunted painfully but didn't move.

My pulse spiked into panic mode, and I struggled harder.

"Don't bite me," I yelled.

He continued to tug my hand closer as I fought against it.

At the last second, I changed my mind and thrust my hand toward him. Our combined strength meant that I hit harder than I would have on my own. One of my fingers jabbed right up his nose, and he grunted as he rolled away.

Eyes wide, I scrambled to my feet.

Merdon didn't come after me. He stayed where he was, head hung low. When he looked up, his nose was bleeding. He wiped the back of his hand over his upper lip and looked at the stain on his skin for a long, silent moment.

I'd drawn first blood. I had no doubt this would change the rules.

"Shit." The word escaped on an exhale.

He continued looking at me, a slight smear of red still under his nose. At least, it wasn't gushing. That had to count for something. Right?

"Are you afraid, Hannah?" he asked softly.

"I'd be stupid not to be," I said, tense and ready for him to spring on me.

"You would be," he agreed with an unusual calm as he got to his feet.

With slow steps, he stalked toward me.

"I don't want to do this anymore," I whispered, backing away.

"I know."

He said it almost soothingly, and that just made it worse. My stomach pitched with trepidation. I hated not knowing what was going to happen. How mad was he?

I skirted around him, sticking to the edges of the mat. He circled me.

"What are you most afraid of?" he asked.

"That you're angry and you're going to bite really hard."

"You're smart to fear being bitten."

That just made my stomach dive lower, and I fisted my hand, wondering which finger I'd be saying goodbye to. I hoped he'd leave me my middle ones. I needed those to tell the world what I thought of it once Cassie stopped the bleeding.

"You're breathing too fast," Merdon said.

"No shit. I don't want to lose my fingers."

He tilted his head at me but didn't stop his slow perusal of me.

"Come here, Hannah."

I shook my head.

"I won't bite your fingers."

"Oh, well, in that case..."

I'd circled enough that I was near the basement stairs. I bolted for them, hoping I'd get to the top like I did last time. I wasn't that lucky.

An arm circled my waist before I made it two steps.

My feet left the ground, and the panic riding me intensified. A weightlessness engulfed me, and I flailed mid-air, his hands still gripping me, before I landed on my back. My breath whooshed out. Before I could be grateful for the mats, his weight settled over me.

Lifting my gaze, I met his focused, yellow eyes. He didn't give me a moment to think. With little effort, he trapped my hands above my head and grabbed a handful of hair.

I couldn't move. I tried. Frantically, desperately, until sweat damped my skin, I tried. Through it all, he held me and watched. When I had nothing left, I lay still under him, defeated.

"You failed."

I wanted to hurl some sass back at him, but I couldn't. I knew what failure meant.

Air wheezed into my fear-constricted lungs as he lowered his face toward my neck. A whimper of fear squeaked out of my throat at the feel of his breath on my exposed collarbone. He hadn't yet set his mouth on me, but I could already feel the bite of his teeth breaking my skin. I could imagine the pain. The agony of being bitten again and again was something I thought about often.

I started to shake. Squeezing my eyes closed, I braced myself. A tear slipped out.

His nose grazed the side of my neck, a soft brush of skin to skin that was gone before it began. But, a weird tingle of awareness remained even as he tugged my head out of the way. When his teeth settled onto my skin, I wasn't as afraid as I was confused. I felt his lips and the heat of his breath more than the points of his teeth.

What the ever-living hell was going on?

I was about to ask him if he was going to bite me or what when his teeth closed down on my skin. A spark of pain ignited, but it was small in comparison to the jolt of pleasure that rushed from the collarbone to my core.

Air whooshed out of me along with another sound.

Merdon jerked his head back and looked at me.

I returned his stare equally as shocked. Had I really just moaned while he was biting me?

The silence grew, and I let it. What the hell was I going to say after that? My brain had short-circuited and wasn't rewiring itself into coherent thought. The only thing floating around in that numb void was wondering if I should ask him to do it again...just to see if it would happen a second time.

"Never turn your back on your attacker," Merdon said, finally. "That was your mistake."

He got up and pulled me to my feet. It was a first.

"Get to the kitchen and eat."

I couldn't do more than nod and hustle up the stairs on wobbly legs.

"I hope you're hungry," Emily said as I sat on an island stool.

"I don't like any of this," I said desperately.

She looked at the food she was putting on my plate.

"Not the food; the treatment. Locking me in my room. Not talking to me. Letting *him* do things to me."

I could feel that corrosive combination of fear, panic, and guilt writhing to life in my middle. Only this time, it had nothing to do with Katie. What I suffered now was because I'd treated Emily like crap and because I'd tried to hurt myself. It sucked seeing the truth for what it was. Worse than seeing the reality of my situation was not knowing what to do about it.

"Help me," I begged.

Her eyes started to water. Her gaze shifted from my face to something behind me just before Merdon's hands settled on my shoulders.

"Enough, Hannah. Emily is helping you. Eat."

Emily swallowed hard and pushed my plate toward me. I didn't reach for it. I couldn't. The feel of his fingers resting over the spot where he'd bitten me immobilized me. My pulse started to kick up.

The pressure on my shoulders increased infinitesimally as he leaned forward. His exhale moved the hair by my ear.

"Eat or I will help you eat."

With a trembling hand, I forked a heap of food into my mouth. He grunted and sat beside me. It wasn't until I'd hurriedly cleared half my plate that I realized he'd changed things up. He hadn't made me shower before eating. Why?

I paused with my half-eaten biscuit in my hand and glanced at him.

He was eating more slowly than usual. When he felt my attention, he immediately looked up. I could only stare at him a moment before I crammed the rest of the biscuit into my mouth. It took all my water to get it down.

Emily noticed how fast I was eating.

"Do you want more?" she asked. "There's still some left."

I almost said no. I'd packed away a plate of thick stew and two biscuits. I should be ready to pop. Instead, it barely felt like I ate anything.

"If we don't need to save it, I'll eat it," I said.

She smiled at me and emptied the remnants of the pot onto my plate. The portion was only a third of the size of my first helping, and I polished it off quickly.

Emily moved to grab my plate, but I shot from my seat and hurried to the sink myself. I didn't know what Merdon had planned for after-dinner fun that would allow me to skip a pre-dinner shower, but I didn't want anything to do with it. If my basement time taught me anything, it was to be ready and on my feet. It made for a faster getaway.

"Are you tired, Hannah?" Merdon asked.

"Exhausted."

He grunted. I rinsed faster.

As soon as I was done, I said, "I'm going to go shower," and bolted for the stairs.

My heart continued to race even after I was in my own room and had the door locked. The irony of using the lock wasn't lost on me. While I could accept my fickle nature when it came to wanting to be locked in my room, I was having a hard time accepting my reaction in the basement.

Troubled, I closed myself in the bathroom and paced.

It was the feel of his nose on my skin that had started the problem. I hadn't expected the soft touch, and it had taken me by surprise and created an unexpected moment of awareness. He was a male and had been manhandling me for two days. That was all. My brain just connected things in a weird way. What I'd felt hadn't meant anything and didn't mean I had a thing for the guy tormenting me.

Facing the mirror, I nodded to myself then took a calming breath. Everything was fine.

I turned away before I could see the doubt and worry in my reflection. How ardently had Shax professed his devotion to me, only to have that affection evaporate practically overnight because of Angel? Was I going to be Emily's Angel? I hoped not. I might not understand her reason for picking Merdon, but I wasn't about to get between the two of them.

Stepping under the spray of hot water, I did my best to wash away my doubt along with my dried sweat. I stayed until my fingers pruned and the temperature cooled.

Dressed in clean pajamas, I left the bathroom with my hair still wrapped in a towel. The room was dark despite the lights shining along the wall. My bed beckoned.

Tired from what felt like the longest day of my life, I crawled under the covers.

The last thought I had before I was pulled under was that after the hell I put up with during my waking hours, I better get respite during my sleep. I should have known better. Life never played that fair.

Dreams tortured me, leading me from the sprint through the

woods all the way to the moment where I plunged the knife into my sister's mouth. I woke, panting and shaking, fear clouding my mind so much that I didn't know where I was when I looked around.

When a shape moved in the chair beside the bed, I screamed.

"Hannah."

The sharp sound of my name in that deep, familiar voice broke through the worst of my panic. I fought my way out of the covers and stumbled to the only shelter I had. Huddled in Merdon's lap, I sobbed against his chest, clutching his shirt. One arm anchored me to him.

He didn't rock me or make soothing sounds, but he did run a hand over my hair again and again. I focused on that feeling, blocking out everything else. My breathing slowly calmed, only disturbed by an occasional hitch.

"The humans in Tenacity fear to leave the protection of their walls," Merdon said, his hand continuing its languid path. "They fear the wrong thing. They believe they are safe if they stay where the infected can't get to them, but it won't be the infected that kill them. The walls, and eventual starvation, will be their end. Like you, they are dying from the inside and refuse to see it."

I lifted my head, my face inches from his, as I met his gaze. There was no judgment in them. Maybe a hint of anger.

It was the other emotion I saw that had me pulling away from his hold. I didn't need or want his concern.

Without a word, I returned to my bed and nestled under the blankets. Fear of more dreams kept me awake until the sky started to lighten.

A BIG HAND shook my shoulder roughly.

"Wake up. You've slept enough."

I groaned and rolled away from the offensive appendage.

"I need to learn how to use a bow so I can shoot you," I mumbled.

Merdon made a noise that sounded suspiciously like a snort.

"You have five minutes to meet me downstairs."

"Why do you hate me?" I complained, burrowing deeper. "I need rest. Cassie told you."

"You also need food and have already missed breakfast. Five minutes," he repeated before walking out of the room.

I huffed, never opening my eyes. That was my first mistake. The second was falling back to sleep.

Arms scooped under me. My eyes flew open. I barely registered what was happening before Merdon had me over his shoulder. My full bladder protested at the pressure.

"What is wrong with you? Why can't you wake me up like a normal person? I need to pee."

"I did wake you up like a normal person. You chose to ignore me."

"No, I was tired and fell back asleep. Tired people do that."

Each downward step drove his shoulder further into my over-expanded organ.

"Seriously, Merdon, I will pee on you if you don't put me down now, and it won't be my fault because you're choosing to ignore me."

He grunted and set me on my feet in the kitchen.

"Bathroom then food."

I hurriedly nodded and waddle-walked to the bathroom. I barely made it to the bowl. Mentally calling him every name imaginable because he'd almost made me pee myself a second time, I glared at the closed door.

The damn man needed to understand personal boundaries. If he wanted to get up in some woman's business, he could focus on Emily.

Opening the door with force, I stomped my way to the kitchen where Merdon waited beside the island. He regarded me with a singular focus. Ignoring him, I marched over to Emily, who was watching something through the oven door.

"If you want a fey in your life so bad, then you spend time with him. I'm not here to keep your beyfriend entertained." She glanced at me in shock, but I didn't stop. "Thanks to you, I'm losing half my night to my fucking dreams; and when I finally get to sleep, he's waking me up. We both know sleep deprivation is just as bad as alcohol."

Her gaze shifted from me to Merdon and back again.

"Beyfriend?" she echoed, fixating on the wrong thing. "He's not my anything."

I opened my mouth to tell her to pay attention to what I was saying when her words settled into my mind. Not hers? If he wasn't here to fix me for Emily, then why in the hell was he torturing me?

Her gaze flicked to him. I looked at him, too.

His steady gaze met mine. For a brief moment, I saw the truth there before his expression shuttered.

"No," I said slowly. "I'm not yours."

He didn't speak; he didn't need to. His lack of denial said it all. He wasn't here for Emily.

The over-forceful and prone to sadism fey was here for me.

CHAPTER SIXTEEN

"COME," MERDON SAID, HOLDING OUT HIS HAND.

I backpedaled a step, shaking my head. It wasn't just his command that I was denying; it was all of him.

"No, I'm not yours. I don't want you here. You need to leave."

He crossed the room in a flash, standing tall in front of me.

"You need to eat. Will you sit with, or without, help?"

I swallowed hard, struggling to catch my breath as my heart raced in my chest. I knew that steely glint in his eyes. He wasn't going to give an inch, let alone just leave.

"You don't want me. I'm too mean, remember?"

His lips curled slightly.

"Too mean for my brothers, not for me."

He leaned toward me, bending until we were close to eye-level.

"You are mine, Hannah."

"I don't want you."

"I know."

"Then go away."

He straightened, crossing his arms.

"No. Last chance. Go eat. Now."

I snarled my frustration, and he snarled back. To avoid another caveman carry, I skirted around him and went to the island. Emily watched us with wide eyes.

"This is all your fault," I hissed at her. "He's way past stage five."

Her gaze darted to Merdon, who was slowly making his way to the seat beside me.

"Be nice, Hannah," he warned.

I dropped my gaze to my plate and angrily ate what was there. It wasn't like I had a lot of choice. If I tried to leave, he'd return me to my seat. Forcefully. If I refused to eat, he'd feed me. It wouldn't be pretty. As he'd confirmed on more than one occasion, consent wasn't required for what he deemed necessary.

When I finished, I set my fork aside and turned to him.

"What now, my malevolent master?"

"Change and meet me in the basement in—"

"Let me guess. In five minutes?" I curled my hands into fists. If he wanted me down there, fine. But there'd be no boundaries because of fear. Today, I'd rip his fucking ears off. It wasn't like he used them, anyway.

"Merdon, would it be possible for me to borrow Hannah for an hour or so today? James and Mary are worried about her, and a visit would ease their minds."

My thoughts raced with the possibilities. There was more than a potential reprieve from fighting with Merdon to be found by going to James and Mary's. I might get the help I needed.

Keeping any hint of the hope from my expression, I met Merdon's gaze as he considered me for a long moment.

"Maybe we could go before she gets all sweaty and tired?" Emily added, a hopeful note lacing her words.

"You choose, Hannah," he said softly. "Do you want to speak with James and Mary or spend time in the basement?"

Like it was even a choice.

"Visit."

"Go dress. If you're not down here, ready, in two minutes, I'll know you changed your mind."

I fled the kitchen, pulling my top off before I even cleared my bedroom door. I didn't know if it was guilt that had Emily throwing me a lifeline, but I'd take it, whatever the cause. James and Mary were kind and cared about me. If they found out what Merdon was doing, they'd put a stop to it. They had to.

Not only did I dress in record time, but I also managed to spritz my hair into manageable ringlets before bounding down the stairs.

Merdon waited at the bottom, his hard gaze taking in every detail of the short-sleeved dress that exposed the faint bruising from yesterday's bites. Unfortunately, there was no handprint on my butt that I'd be able to show to reinforce my abuse.

His gaze lingered on the darker crescent shape on my bicep. That one had hurt more because I'd tried yanking my arm away when he'd already been clamped down.

"I know what you're doing," he said calmly. "You'll be disappointed in the end." He motioned to the front door.

I wasn't sure what he meant and didn't stop to ask. It was after lunch, and I wanted Merdon out of my house and my life by dinner time.

Emily didn't say anything as I joined her by the door and grabbed my jacket and shoes, which were once again on the rug. When I was ready, she led the way. Merdon followed. I wasn't deterred.

Breathing deeply, I immersed myself in my momentary

freedom and imagined how I'd spend the next day. Maybe watching movies and flipping Merdon off through the window as I drank myself silly in the living room. The idea of giving him the finger throughout the day was more appealing than the drinking.

James called out his welcome as soon as Emily knocked. His face lit up when he saw me, and he yelled for Mary. She came out of the kitchen just as Merdon closed the door behind us.

"Well, this is a welcome surprise. How are you feeling, Hannah?" she asked.

The timing of her question couldn't have been better. I finished taking off my coat and held out my arms.

"Not well. Merdon is biting me and forcing me to do things I don't want to do."

Mary tsked and hurried toward me. She wrapped me in a tight hug, and I let out a relieved exhale.

"I can't imagine the biting feels good, but you'll get stronger. He won't get away with so many then," she said, still holding me.

I looked at James, confused.

"Merdon is smart for teaching you how to avoid being bitten by an infected, and you're brave for undertaking such demanding training." He looked at Merdon. "The nips look a might bit hard, though."

"Pain is motivation to try harder," Merdon said.

"I imagine so," James agreed. "Just remember she's human."

I jerked in Mary's arms as I realized what was happening. Again. They were all okay with what was happening.

Mary released me and patted my cheek affectionately.

"He's not teaching me how to avoid being bitten," I said emphatically.

"Of course he is," she said with a chuckle. "Unless those are love bites?"

"They aren't love bites! They're bites from an asshole who gets sick pleasure from torturing me while convincing everyone around me that it's for my own good. What's wrong with you people? Why do you refuse to see what's really going on?"

Mary gave me a sad look.

"We aren't the ones refusing to see things the way they are, sweetie."

I fisted my hands at my sides at the same time Merdon's hands settled on my shoulders. I stilled, my impotent rage consolidating in my middle.

"That's enough, Hannah."

I whirled on him.

"Or what? You'll force-feed me? Throw me into the shower? Hold me down and bite me? What more can you really do to me, Merdon? What new level of hell will I be forced to endure?"

That hard glint returned to his eyes.

"Do you want to find out?"

My fingers curled into claws. I wanted to hurt him. I wanted it so much I could barely breathe.

"All right, you two," James said. "Save the training for your house. We like our furniture. Ma, why don't you get your menu plans? Tor was already by this morning, asking if we had any news about the schedule."

"I'm not sure we're ready for that yet," Emily said.

"I agree," Merdon said.

I turned my back to him, not caring what he thought, then realized I had no idea what they were even talking about.

"Ready for what?" I asked.

"Our dating game dinners," Mary said. "The fey are anxious to get started, but it didn't feel right moving ahead with those plans when you were struggling so. But if you're feeling better, you can help us. If not and you'd rather stay with Merdon, I'll just steal Emily away for a few hours."

None of it felt real. How had we gone from me accusing Merdon of abusing me to dinner plans for the fey?

"Unbelievable," I breathed. My focus shifted to James. "I thought I could count on you."

Both he and Mary started talking. I didn't listen. Numb to everything, I turned to walk out the door.

Merdon blocked my way.

"You chose to visit. So, visit."

I looked up at him, feeling dead inside.

"No."

I held his gaze, daring him to show James and Mary what he was really like. When he did nothing, I skirted him and let myself outside.

The wind immediately bit my exposed skin. Rather than going back for my jacket, I wrapped my arms around myself and trudged on.

Merdon's warning that I'd be disappointed rang in my ears with each step. He'd known. He'd spoken to them at some point. That or Emily had. Anger curled in my middle at how it'd probably been Emily. She'd paved the way for the madman plaguing me. She'd given him the key to keeping me prisoner. And, as far as I could tell, there was no way out for me. Not anymore.

Lost, I stopped walking and tipped my head up to the light blue sky. Clarity often came with retrospection, and I thought again of Tenacity. I'd been a fool to go there for a drink. I should have packed up all my shit and moved there permanently while I'd had the chance.

No, my mistake was long before that. I should have pushed Katie ahead of me and given myself to the infected in her place.

An angry, rough voice cut into my thoughts.

"Keep walking."

"No." I turned toward Merdon, knowing it was the only way. "I don't care anymore. You can have me until I die if that's what you want. Hopefully, it will be over sooner than either of us expect."

Anger washed over his features. He bared his teeth and stalked close to me.

"You will not give up."

"I already have."

"No, this is a lie like all the other lies you tell yourself and others."

He began to circle me.

"I see what's inside you. I know your anger. It calls to my own. I recognize your pain. I've lived with my own for many lifetimes. You will not give up because, like me, you don't know how. You will cling to this life even when it's one you don't want."

He stopped behind me, and the weight of my jacket settled over my shoulders.

"I don't need your submission. You will choose to be mine."

His words sparked my temper. I tried to smother it, to bring back the numbness that let me not care, but he was right. I couldn't seem to let go.

Turning, I lifted my gaze to his.

"Never."

A slow grin spread over his lips in response to my whispered word.

"Fight it, Hannah. Fight it with every breath. Give me your fire."

I'd give him something.

I balled my fist and punched him. My knuckles cracked against his rock-hard abs. He chuckled low.

"Again."

So I did.

I hit him over and over, right then left, using him like a punching bag even as I knew my mighty blows were no more damaging than a gnat to him. My jacket fell from my shoulders.

Sweat beaded my upper lip, despite the temperature, by the time I stopped. Spent, I tipped forward, resting my forehead on his sternum.

His hand settled on my crown. After a moment, it smoothed over my hair. I couldn't bring myself to pull away because I needed his familiar, comforting touch. Could I be any more twisted? I'd just pummeled his stomach because I didn't want him laying claim to me, and now I was docilely lingering in his hold.

"This doesn't mean anything," I said.

"I know."

"Good."

He stroked my hair until I pulled away and picked up my jacket. We walked back to the house in silence.

I wasn't sure what to expect when the door closed behind us, but it sure wasn't an angry order to go change and meet him in the basement within his stupid five-minute limit.

"How do you even know when five minutes have passed?" I asked, not moving.

"I don't."

"You're ridiculous. And so are your stupid, made-up rules."

"Four minutes."

I glared at him. His gaze raked over me from head to toe.

"The skirt is going to slow you down."

Whirling, I raced upstairs. The ass needed to be taken down a few pegs. But how? I wished there was a way to slow him down. Maybe then I'd have a chance to hit him in the balls.

"Three minutes," he called from below.

Oh, how I wished I could watch him choke on his own testicles.

I stripped from the dress and tugged on a pair of leggings and a long-sleeved shirt. Bite protection. Rushing, I twisted my hair into a knot at the top of my head then left my room.

Merdon was already in the basement when I jogged downstairs. I briefly considered the front door, but I no longer felt an urge to run. Maybe it was because I knew I wouldn't get anywhere. Or maybe I just wanted to face off with Merdon in the basement. Oh, I knew he planned to put me through hell, but the need to give back more than he gave overrode any good sense I had left.

I shook my head at my pathetic attempt to rationalize why I wasn't trying to leave and forced myself to admit the truth. When I was fighting Merdon, I wasn't thinking of the past or how to survive the future. I was in the moment, dealing with just one problem. Him. Even with the spankings and the biting, facing him was easier than facing any of my other issues.

He was waiting for me at the bottom of the stairs and didn't say anything as I walked past him to take my place on the center of the mat. That was good. I didn't want words. I wanted action. I wanted to feel like I had a chance to influence the outcome, for a change.

I crouched low, initiating the start for the first round.

He studied me for a moment then mimicked the move.

We watched each other, both waiting for the tell that would give away the other's thoughts. Since I wasn't thinking, I doubted he was getting much from me, so I settled in for a wait, however long it might be.

"Patience?" he asked. "We both know you don't have any. Where are your balls now?"

I smiled. "Your goading isn't going to work. Not this time."

"It will. I only need to find the right words."

He shifted his weight, sliding a step to the right. I turned slightly, following him.

"Go ahead. There's nothing you can—"

"Whose death do you carry? Who haunts your dreams?"

I flew at him, letting all the raw pain that his words evoked well up and fuel my moves. Spinning on my heel just before I reached him, I drove my elbow into his middle at the same time I stomped down on his instep. He grunted, and I felt him bend ever so slightly. It wasn't enough to throw my head back into his nose, so I turned again, facing him, and brought my knee up.

Only his quick reflexes prevented a full-on bashing of his precious feyby-making testicles. The partial graze was effective enough to sap the strength from his knees. He slowly folded in, resting in a prayerful pose...if cupping one's groin was common in prayer.

I whooped and fist-pumped the air.

"Yes! How does that feel? Failure means pain, Merdon. Suck on that."

He growled as he lifted his head.

I only had time to think "oh, shit," before he launched himself at me. His shoulder hit my knees, and I crashed to the mat like a felled tree.

Air whooshed out of me. He didn't give me a moment to catch my breath. Weighing me down with his torso, he grabbed my hands and slammed them into the mat above my head.

"That is why no one else will want you. You laugh at another's pain or ignore it completely. You are a selfish creature, blind to what could be because of what was."

His harsh words hurt, and I tugged on my hands, wishing I could lash out. He laughed at my attempt and held me tighter.

"Your need to hurt me tells me the truth. Were you always like this, Hannah? Mean and selfish?"

An unbidden tear leaked from the corner of my eye.

"Were you always this big of a hypocritical asshole?"

He frowned at me.

"Yeah, that's right," I said angrily. "Hypocrite. You call me mean even as you're holding me down. How many bruises do I have because of you? How many times have you forced me to do something I didn't want to do?"

He snarled and changed his hold on my hands. His fingers bit into my skin as he grabbed my jaw.

"The only thing I've forced you to do is live. You will live. I will not lose what is mine."

Before I could guess what he intended, his lips came down on mine. I fought to turn away, but his hold on my jaw kept me in place as the pressure of his fingers forced me to open for him. He swallowed my sound of protest and struck me senseless with the first swipe of his tongue.

It was a harsh, punishing kiss, but heat flared out from my middle, regardless. I forgot to keep trying to pull my hands free and lost myself to the hungry stroke of his tongue and the way his legs were trapping mine.

He surrounded me, consumed me, and stirred a hunger hardly explored. And, he laid bare a need I didn't even know existed.

With a growl, he tore his lips from mine and stood.

"Stay here."

Then, he was gone.

I lay on the mat, panting for air and shaking all over. Lifting a hand, I touched my lips and wondered what the hell had just happened.

I'd thought my reaction to his bite a fluke, but it wasn't. My body wanted Merdon even when my brain told me to run far and fast from that fey. I'd made a grave mistake in thinking that Merdon was an easy problem to solve. He was anything but easy.

Running my fingers over my puffy lips, I wondered what I was supposed to do about this new discovery. How could I fight what I felt when I didn't fully understand what I wanted?

It took several minutes for the trembling to stop and another minute before I could stand. I made it up the stairs and as far as the couch before I had to sit again. Staring blankly at the dark television, I tried to string two logical thoughts together.

Merdon believed I was his. But, I didn't want to belong to any fey. Why? Because the fey were needy, and I didn't want needy. I wanted freedom. Why? So I could drink myself to death.

That last thought ground everything to a halt.

No, I didn't want to drink myself to death; I just wanted to have a little peace while I slept. At least, that was how the drinking had started. Just a glass or two before bed. The amount in my cups had gradually increased whenever the dreams had started creeping back in until I was passing out every night. Then, I'd started drinking during the day to drown out the guilt that haunted me during my waking hours.

I rubbed a hand over my face, hating that one dumb kiss had exposed so many ugly truths. My life was just one big pile of fucked-up-ness, and the instigator of my latest mind-fuck was out roaming the streets of Tolerance. He was probably coming up with some new, evil plan to make me miserable and mess with my head further.

He had to go. My life didn't need more complications; it needed fewer.

But how was I supposed to get rid of a guy who didn't respect boundaries or listen to what I wanted?

I sat there, determined to think of an answer. However, nothing inspiring came to mind as the house grew darker and I lost feeling in my butt. Eyelids heavy, I slapped my cheeks and tried to stay awake. I didn't want to go to sleep in an empty house. That was worse than going to sleep sober.

A knock on the door rescued me from my dilemma.

Angel smiled at me from the front step, and I felt an uncalled-for sense of disappointment that it wasn't Merdon.

"Hoping for someone else?" Angel asked, reading my expression.

"Not really. What can I do for you?"

"Merdon sent me. He's arranging some time for you to practice with Brenna tomorrow."

It took a second for me to understand.

"You mean with a bow?"

"Yep. He said you wanted to learn to shoot. Would it be okay if I tagged along?"

"Um, sure."

Was it awkward that my ex-stalker's new girlfriend wanted to hang out with me? Maybe a little.

"We're supposed to come up with a meeting place and let Brenna know. The fey don't want us anywhere near the cows. No accidental hamburgers in our future." She laughed.

She was always happy. The real kind of happy, not my fake kind. I envied her.

"I'm not sure where to practice. I don't even know how much room we need," I admitted.

"A decent amount. I'll check with Brenna and see if she has any ideas. Are you going to be up for a while?"

"Yeah. Probably. Merdon left kind of angry, and I'd rather be awake when he gets back." Retribution might be a bitch, and I'd prefer to be alert for it.

"Angry? I think this is a conversation best done in the kitchen. Have any chips?"

I found myself letting her in and following her to the kitchen.

"I honestly don't know what we have," I said. "Emily does the cooking."

Angel draped her jacket over a kitchen chair and started checking cupboards. There was a crazy amount of food in them now, including an unopened bag of chips.

"I've been craving chips," she said with a quick grin over her shoulder. "So why was Merdon angry when he left?"

She took a seat at the table and opened the bag, holding it out to me. I took a chip and joined her.

"I hit him in the dick."

Her laughter echoed off the walls.

"What'd he do to deserve that?"

"He's been spanking me and biting me, supposedly all in the name of teaching me to avoid infection. I think he just likes being a mean asshole."

"Would a mean asshole set up time for you to learn to shoot a bow?" she asked before crunching on a chip.

"I don't know. I'm still trying to figure that out."

"He's doing it because you asked him to."

Stunned, I remembered saying it when he woke me this morning.

"I can't believe he took me seriously."

Angel's humor faded a bit.

"There's nothing he takes more seriously. And, for the record, he wasn't mad when he came to talk to me."

"Why did he come talk to you and not Brenna?"

"Because he wanted to know if I thought you'd really shoot him with a bow if you knew how."

Angel's previous question poked at my mind. He was worried I'd try to shoot him and still wanted me to learn? Merdon was confusing the hell out of me, and I didn't like it.

"I think I have the perfect place to practice," I said with a sudden smile.

"Where?"

"Tell Brenna we'll meet by the burned dildo pile."

CHAPTER SEVENTEEN

I WOKE WITH A GASP, MY HEART THUNDERING IN MY EARS AS I bolted upright in my bed and looked at my hand. The feel of the knife lingered in my palm, but nothing was there. No sticky blood and no knife. A shaky exhale turned into a sob. Why wouldn't the dreams stop? How many times did I need to relive those moments for it to be enough?

Something to my left rustled, and I swiveled, my panic rising once more.

Merdon was leaning forward in his chair, his elbows braced on his knees as he watched me.

For a confused moment, I stared back. I itched to climb out of bed and crawl into his lap. I knew he'd comfort me. But I couldn't forget the kiss he'd given me. If I went to him now, knowing what he was thinking, I'd be signing away the tattered remnants of my soul.

"Tell me what you dream," he said softly.

Guilt and shame raged inside of me, and I suddenly understood why I still dreamed. What I'd done was so horrible, it belonged in the dark. So it would stay there, always.

Turning my back on him, I snuggled under the covers and tried to tell myself everything was fine. It wasn't until my breathing calmed and my tears dried that I wondered how I'd gotten to my bed. After Angel had left, I'd turned on a movie. Obviously, I'd lost the fight and fallen asleep.

I closed my eyes, knowing the answer to my question sat in the chair beside my bed.

I STRETCHED MYSELF AWAKE, then froze as I realized how wrong that was. Cautiously opening my eyes, I looked around my room. Daylight streamed into my window, and the chair was empty. I sat up, not believing my eyes.

What new game was Merdon playing?

Worried, I got out of bed and quickly dressed before jogging downstairs.

"Morning," Emily said cheerily from her place in the kitchen.

I scanned the room.

"He's not here," Emily said. "He left when I woke up but said he'd see you later. Are you really meeting up with Brenna for archery lessons?"

"Yeah, I guess so."

I sat at the island and watched Emily move around. She had corned beef hash frying on the stove and was pulling a platter of pancakes out of the oven.

"Where'd we get all the food?" I asked, recalling the stuffed cupboards.

Emily smiled.

"The supply shed is overflowing. The group that leaves to find provisions located a distribution center, full to the rafters with all kinds of food. Ryan tried getting Matt to take half, but he refused, so the fey are distributing everything to make room in the supply shed. If you're craving something more than chips, just let me know. I can probably get it."

"I'm not craving anything, but I'll keep that in mind."

She dished me up two pancakes and a healthy serving of hash and set the plate before me.

"Thanks," I said before digging in.

The sound of a sniffle had me looking up at Emily's tearing eyes.

"You okay?" I asked.

She nodded and wiped at her nose with the back of her hand.

"Fine. I'm just really happy. Do you want anything else?"

I looked down at the plate and shook my head while trying not to feel more guilt. I wasn't stupid. I understood her tears.

"Was I really that bad?" I asked.

"There was a stretch where you didn't eat anything for two days. That was before you tried jumping from the roof."

I mentally cringed away from what she said, but she noticed.

"We don't have to talk about it. You're doing better, and that's all that matters."

But was I? The dreams were still there, and if Emily set a bottle of whiskey on the counter, I wasn't so sure I'd be able to resist it. That desire to numb all the pain and worry was seductively tempting.

"Thanks for making breakfast," I said, unable to dwell on what I'd done or how I'd behaved.

"Any time," she said. "Seriously. If you're hungry for anything, just say the word. You know I like cooking, and I wouldn't mind the practice before Mary and I start making fancy meals for other people."

"How soon is that going to start up?" I asked. "You were at Mary's a long time yesterday."

Emily's face lit up, and she animatedly went on about the test dinner they made for James and what all still needs to happen before the real dinner.

"The trip to Tenacity went fine, but I really need to get back there to confirm and reassure."

"With all these supplies, you should bake something to take with you. You know, like cookies or something that's a little extra to show that they'd be well-fed if they agree to it."

"That's a perfect idea. Let me know if you want to tag along," she said, already reaching for the cookbook she kept on the counter. She froze mid-reach and looked at me guiltily.

"Forget that I said that. I mean, I know you're busy and ..."

A flush crept into her cheeks.

"You're worried that I'd find something to drink if I went with you."

The flush deepened.

"As if Merdon would let me out of his sight," I said bitterly. "Don't worry about it. Go talk to people. I'll be here." I finished my last bite, impressed that I'd packed it in so quickly. "I gotta go meet up with Brenna and Angel. Thanks again for breakfast. It was good."

She smiled and watched me leave.

Outside, I paused for a moment and lifted my face to the sun. Without the wind, it actually felt warm. I soaked it up and tried not to resent Emily's freedom. After all, Merdon wasn't following me now. And while I might not be able to leave Tolerance, I could still do what I wanted.

A smile tugged at my lips as I thought of today's goal.

Content for the moment, I started out. When I happened to

see a fey, I smiled and waved. They waved back, and things felt normal, but a better version of normal. I was on my way to learn how to shoot arrows at some dicks. Hopefully, with Merdon watching. That was way better than baking cookies or hitching a ride to Tenacity.

Brenna and Angel were already waiting for me by the melted mound of dildos. This wasn't the first time I'd seen the deformed pile of colorful plastics. I still couldn't get over how many it must have taken to make the waist-high heap. It was a miracle Eden was still with Ghua.

"Hey, Hannah," Angel said brightly when she saw me. "You ready to shoot some dicks?"

"So ready," I answered.

I glanced around and noted the area was spectator free. Including the top of the nearby wall.

"It's a little quiet, isn't it?" I asked.

Brenna snorted. "You know how word spreads. Once the fey found out what we were going to do, they ghosted."

"Shax didn't even want to come with," Angel said with a grin. "And I can usually talk him into anything."

Yep, still awkward.

"Merdon and Thallirin were talking in hushed tones in the kitchen this morning," Brenna said. "Merdon warned the others that you were angry at all the fey and were learning to shoot an arrow at fake human penises."

"You must have died laughing," Angel said.

"No, I was more curious why Hannah would be mad at all the fey. Thallirin wasn't very forthcoming."

I didn't know Brenna well, only that she was about my age and tended to be pretty serious. The solemn expression on her face and her tone of voice confirmed that assessment.

"I'm mad because they're all okay with how Merdon is treating me."

"How is he treating you?" she asked.

"He's force-fed me, made me try to get away from him in the basement, spanked me, bit me, and wasn't letting me leave the house until yesterday."

Brenna's face went white then red.

"Hold on," Angel said quickly. "Hannah, the fey talk, and I've heard something similar. But, there's more behind his behavior than what you're telling, isn't there?"

"You're saying you believe he's justified?" I asked, getting angry.

"No. I'm saying that you were trying to kill yourself with alcohol and Merdon's kept you inside so you could sober up away from temptation. He also set up a sparring area in your basement so you could get some exercise and take your mind off of withdrawals. To keep you very distracted, he taught you how to avoid infected bites. I'm not sure about the spankings. You'd need to ask him the reason for those. And the force-feeding I'm a little confused about as well, unless you were trying to starve yourself."

I stared at her in stunned silence, looking back at my interactions with Merdon in a different light. A distraction? The withdrawals hadn't been fun. I'd thrown up so much. I'd just been lying there in misery. That was why he'd forced me to drink and threatened to force me to eat. And it wasn't until after I was eating and drinking and over getting sick that he took me downstairs. Had it all been to distract me?

"My mom had problems with alcohol after the accident," Brenna said slowly. "It's a dangerous slope. I saw you when you let Thallirin use your shower and again when the men kidnapped us. You have a problem, and I hope that Merdon really is trying to help you. But if he isn't, if he's forcing you to do things, find me."

My eyes burned as I realized what she was saying. She would have my back if I needed someone to hold the body bag. Only, I wasn't sure anymore if that's what I needed. Still, I swallowed hard and nodded before looking at Angel.

"He was just doing stuff," I said. "He never said why. The reasons you gave sound good and make sense, but it didn't feel like that. It felt like he was being an asshole and getting off on it."

"Does that sound like any fey you know?" Angel asked softly.

"Yes. Merdon," I said firmly. "He doesn't act like all the rest of them. He walks around like someone pissed in his cereal."

"Thallirin was like that, too," Brenna said. "Angry all the time. Never talking about what was going on in his head. It made it hard to understand him. Talk to Merdon about what he's been doing. Get him to explain it to you."

It was my turn to snort.

"Right. Like he'd be forthcoming about anything. His favorite lines are 'I know' and 'you've slept enough.' The last one was why I told him I wanted to learn to shoot a bow. I'm tired of his method of waking me up."

"What's his method?" Angel asked.

"First, it was tossing me in a cold shower and telling me I stink. Then, it was just tipping the mattress so I fell out of bed."

Angel made a pitying face.

"That's harsh. You know you can change all that, though, right?"

"How?"

"Just sit on his face and ride his tongue like you would a horse. Whatever bug is up his ass will be gone by the time you're screaming his name, and he'll be ready to start worshipping the ground you walk on."

"First, I'm not 'with' Merdon. Second, isn't that a little backward?" I asked. "Aren't they supposed to worship us when they're the ones getting off?"

She gave me a wry smile. "That's human men. Fey are a different breed."

I huffed out a breath.

"A different breed with different rules. I hate being this lost."

"Don't worry. It'll work itself out."

"Communication is key," Brenna added. "Don't assume you know what Merdon's thinking. Ask. It's crazy how often we get the facts wrong because we're guessing the wrong thing."

"I don't want to work anything out. I want him to go away."

"Good luck with that," Brenna said. "Fey are stubbornly persistent. Do you know I threatened to shoot Thallirin when he wouldn't leave me alone, and he held his arms out and told me he'd stand still?"

"Damn. He's lucky he still has his babymaker," Angel said.

I agreed.

Brenna looked us both over.

"He is. They need to learn that their methods aren't always the best ones." She lifted her bow slightly. "You ready to learn how to use this?"

I'd never been readier.

MY ARM WAS SCREAMING in protest as I drew back for what felt like the hundredth time. Brenna had the patience of a saint and the eye of a hawk as she worked with me. If my elbow wasn't just right, I had to draw all over again. If I had a nose hair out of place when I took aim and exhaled, I had to start all over again. Fine, she wasn't that detailed but close.

"Focus, aim, exhale, release."

She made it sound so easy. It wasn't. I hadn't managed to hit the broad side of the melted penis pinnacle yet, and the sun was almost overhead.

Regardless, I did as she instructed and tried again. The twang of the release was almost cathartic, and I could see why she enjoyed archery. Maybe after a million hours of practice and a few bullseyes, I could too.

I watched the bolt fly toward the plastic and embed itself in one unmelted dick tip.

I squealed and spun around, a smile on my face.

"Did you see that?"

"About time," Angel said with a laugh. She'd managed to hit the target two attempts ago, her arrow bouncing off what looked like a left testicle. She'd howled with laughter for a good two minutes.

"Talk about an epic first hit," Brenna said, congratulating me. "I think you two are ready for bows of your own."

"We already have them," Angel said.

"We do?" I asked.

"Yep. Merdon and Thallirin started on them a while ago." She patted her belly. "I traded a fetal kick for a bow. Very lucrative currency in case either of you are interested."

"That's a big no, for me," Brenna said.

"You guys don't know what you're missing. Watch." She grinned then bellowed, "Shax, I'm hungry for some chips. Dill pickle, please."

Angel told Brenna to start counting. She'd just made it to forty-two when I spotted Shax sprinting toward us.

He stopped before Angel and handed her a bag of dill pickle potato chips.

"I couldn't find them. They were under the bed."

"Were they?" Angel asked with a teasing smile as she popped a chip into her mouth.

"Did you hide them?" he asked.

"I'll make it up to you later, babe. Promise."

His hands went to her belly, smoothing over it in a way that made me blush. When I averted my gaze, I found Merdon watching me from not far away. Thallirin, who'd been standing with him, broke away to go to Brenna. She lifted her lips for a kiss that made me want to fan myself.

There was way too much fey love going on around here.

My gaze shifted to Merdon again. As if my look had been some kind of signal, he started stalking toward me. I panicked.

"I'm gay. Only vagina will make me happy in the sack. No dick for me. Sorry. Looks like you're going to need to find someone else."

He stopped in front of me and crossed his arms.

"Prove it. Kiss Brenna."

"Hey, whoa," Brenna said, lowering her bow. "Don't bring me into this. I just figured out that I don't hate dick. A girl kiss might confuse me."

Thallirin protectively wrapped his arms around her while giving me a death glare.

"Don't look at me like that. I'm not the one who suggested kissing your woman. Merdon did. Might I suggest a swift punch to his ball sack in retribution?" I asked sweetly.

Angel buried her face in Shax's chest and was shaking so hard with laughter I was sure her water would break.

"You don't like females, Hannah," Merdon said.

"How do you know?"

"I can hear your lies with the beat of your heart." He reached out and tapped my chest. "It tells the truth."

"Yeah, well, maybe I want to try liking females."

He grunted, and I knew he wasn't buying it.

"Are you ready to go home?"

"Alone? Yes. With you? No. What does my heart say about that?"

He gave me a slow smile that made my insides go hot and cold.

"This has been fun," Angel said, "But I think I'm heading home for a nap."

I glanced at her as she looked up at Shax affectionately.

"What do you say, handsome? Feel like giving me a lift?"

Shax scooped her up into his arms and kissed her thoroughly. I had to glance away.

"Same time tomorrow," she called with a wave as he carried her away.

"I think we're going to get going too," Brenna said. "You all right on your own?"

It took everything I had not to look at Merdon.

"Yeah, I'll be fine. Thanks for the lesson."

"You're welcome. See you tomorrow."

Unlike Angel, Brenna didn't ask for a ride. But she did hold out her hand and twine her fingers in Thallirin's as they walked away.

"Why can't you be nice like them?" I asked, finally facing Merdon.

"Because you don't want nice. You're not done punishing yourself." He brushed the backs of his fingers over my cheek. "I saw you smile. It was real. You were real. I won't stop until you're that person again."

"That person was a lie, drowning in her own pain."

"Tell me your pain."

"No."

He didn't try to stop me as I started toward the house, and I wasn't surprised when he followed.

The house smelled like cookies when I opened the door.

"Any chance there are samples?" I called out as I kicked off my shoes.

"You're just in time. Lots of samples and a big lunch. I hope you're hungry."

"Very." It was weird to feel it. I hadn't been as hungry as I was now in ages. It was probably all the fresh air.

She slid a plate of cookies onto the counter and turned to get something out of the oven.

"This is one of the dishes that I'm considering for our date menu, and I really need some feedback on it. Is it too fancy? Does it work for both human and fey palates? That kind of stuff."

She set a pan of bloated pieces of meat wrapped with strings.

"What is it?" I asked suspiciously even as my mouth watered. It smelled good. Like roasted meat and something else.

"Not telling you until you take a bite."

"It better not be dog food."

"Be nice, Hannah," Merdon warned.

I shot him a disgruntled look.

"I was being nice. How would you like it if she snuck veggies in your food?"

He grunted and looked at her.

"Stop being babies, the both of you. Just try it. If you don't like it, you don't have to eat it."

She plated up two servings and passed them to us. I waited for Merdon to take the first bite. He chewed slowly, swallowed, and met my gaze.

"Eat."

"Are you telling me that because you're worried I won't eat or because you like bossing me around?"

He set down his fork and turned in his chair.

"Eat or I will help you."

I rolled my eyes at him and cut off a chunk, not nearly as large as the one he'd eaten.

"Make sure to get some of the middle," Emily said, her gaze shifting between us.

The part she was referencing was a pale green. I wasn't sure I trusted it. How many freezers had Katie and I opened only to gag and quickly close them because of rot?

Knowing they were both watching me, I shoved the bite in my mouth and tried to fast-chew. I paused on the second chomp as flavor hit my taste buds.

"Is that bacon?" I asked around my mouthful. "Pesto?"

She grinned and nodded. "Do you like it?"

I moaned and started cutting off another bite. "So good," I said before stuffing it in my mouth.

She danced her joy around the kitchen then nudged the plate of cookies closer to me before producing a glass of milk. It was heaven. Pure heaven. When I picked up the last crumbs with my finger, my stomach was ready to pop.

"Could I ask one more favor? I know you hated the questions we came up with before, so I want your opinion on these." She handed me a piece of paper. "It's a 'complete the sentence' kind of thing where the girl would ask the guy to complete it."

I looked down at the sheet.

The best part of living in Tolerance is...

I like it when you...

Right now I'm feeling...

I wish I could...

"If you think this method is better than the questions, I can come up with more," she added.

I looked up at her, realizing how hurtful I'd been toward her when she'd only been trying to help other people.

"Emily, the questions were fine. I was being a bitch."

"No, you were right. Some of them were lame, and some were too obvious. I don't want to make anyone uncomfortable."

"You know the fey have the ability to make anything uncomfortable, right?"

Her guilt-filled gaze shifted to Merdon. I looked at him, too, but didn't feel any guilt.

"Let's help Emily test this idea," I said, turning toward him. "Please finish the following sentence: The best part of living in Tolerance is?"

"The best part of living in Tolerance is being with my brothers again."

I glanced at Emily. "Not the answer I think most of the fey will give. I think most will say access to women."

"Yeah, you might be right," she agreed thoughtfully.

I turned back to Merdon.

"Okay, finish this one. I like it when you?"

"I like it when you sleep peacefully."

My chest tightened uncomfortably, and I glanced down at the paper.

"And this one? Right now I'm feeling..."

"Right now I'm feeling things you're not ready to hear."

Heart thundering, I stared at the paper. If not for the kiss, I would have thought the feelings he was hinting at were nice ones. Given his tone, tough, I was pretty sure that wasn't the case.

"The last one is 'I wish I could...'" Emily said softly.

"I wish I could take your pain, but I can't. It's yours to keep or let go." He stood. "Meet me downstairs in five minutes."

He stalked away, and I looked at Emily even though I knew she would be able to see my confusion. He said I was his. By fey standards, that should have meant his romantic interest. Instead, I got the feeling he meant I was his pain in the ass. But he'd said he liked it when I slept peacefully. That was a nice thing to say. Wasn't it?

How could those four little sentences get in my head so much?

"These are better than the questions," I said, sliding the paper back to Emily.

CHAPTER EIGHTEEN

Merdon paced, a restless prowl that stopped when he heard me on the basement steps. Emily's little game had obviously pissed him off, but I doubted he'd direct that anger at her. The way he was glowering in my direction said I'd be the target.

"Have you ever tried meditation?" I asked. "It's supposed to be really relaxing and calming."

His eyes narrowed, giving me the impression that I'd just poked the bear.

"Never mind," I mumbled, shuffling onto the mat. I really didn't want to be there. My stomach was too full.

"You're small and weak. Stop depending on strength when avoiding me. You need to be fast."

"Right. But we already established that I'm slow."

"You need to be faster."

"Tell me honestly. Are you doing this to teach me how to avoid being bitten by an infected or because you're angry at me and want a little revenge?"

"Are you asking so you can find a way to manipulate the situation to your advantage?"

I frowned at him.

"That's a horrible thing to say."

"Is it? Because it's true or because you don't want it to be true?"

"Why are you being so mean?"

"I've asked myself that same question about you countless times."

"Gah! You're such an asshole."

He crouched, showing he was ready for whatever I had to dish out.

"Fine, you don't want to admit what this is? Whatever. Do what you need to do." Rather than crouching, I just held my arms out wide and waved him forward.

His eyes narrowed fractionally then I was being flipped as I fell backward. A squawk ripped from my throat the moment I understood what was coming. I barely settled face first on the mat before his hand came cracking down on my ass cheek.

"What the hell is wrong with you?" I screeched. "I thought we were biting!"

He picked me up as I was still trying to rub away the sting, then he got right in my face.

"You weren't trying."

Only his fast reflexes prevented me from biting his nose off.

"You are the most infuriating son of a—"

Flip.

Spank.

"Dammit, Merdon!"

With his arms crossed, he watched me scramble to my feet.

"What do you want from me?" I asked, so furious I was close to tears.

"I want you to try."

"Fine."

I got into a crouch.

"Are we biting or spanking now?"

"Does it matter?"

"No, they're both equally painful and upsetting. Can we just punish each other with hugs?"

He made a sound, suspiciously close to a chuckle, before he came flying at me.

For the next several hours, I did my best to avoid spanking and bites. When I ran out of breath, he gave me a few minutes on the mat before goading me back onto my feet. When my legs gave out, he just provoked me until I stood again. He was relentless and merciless even as I whined and begged for him to stop.

Panting and face down on the mat, I questioned his sanity.

"You're the one who should be locked in a room," I rasped. "Spank me. Bite me. I don't care."

His hand came down on the same flaming spot that had been abused at least a dozen times already. I didn't flinch.

"Get up," he said.

"I can't. I'm done."

I closed my eyes, ready for the next smack or bite. It wasn't that I didn't care. I cared very much. So much that I was already trying to figure out how to get bitten by a radioactive spider and develop kickass superpowers so I could pulverize Merdon. It was just that I seriously couldn't move. I was spent. Beyond spent.

"You're not done. Get up."

"You're cute when you're crazy," I murmured, my breathing already slowing and my body feeling heavy. I knew this sensation. It was just like passing out. I was going under and hard.

"Night," I whispered.

He turned me over and picked me up. I didn't bother opening my eyes. I let him carry me upstairs.

"Are you going to shower, or do you need help?" he asked angrily.

I knew what he was trying to do, and I knew how much things were about to suck for me. Yet, there was only one real answer.

"I need help," I murmured.

He grunted.

A small part of me hoped he'd be nice. That part was stupid and naïve.

He turned on the water and walked into the shower with me. The cold blast shocked a gasp out of me and jumpstarted my system. I jerked in his arms and opened my eyes to look up at him.

"Thanks. I think I got it from here."

He grunted again and set me on my feet. He waited, watching to make sure I was steady before leaving to stand on the other side of the glass.

"What?" I stuttered. "No help s-soaping me up?"

He didn't answer. I didn't expect him to. Stripping out of my wet clothes was a chore and attempting to throw them over the top, far too much effort. I let everything fall to the bottom of the shower and reached for the soap as the water warmed. My legs gave out, and I sat hard on my wet clothes.

Merdon glanced back at me.

"No peeking now," I said. "You had your chance."

He grunted and faced away again.

I didn't care about him looking as much as I cared about him witnessing any attempt I made to try to stand back up. Naked, I could handle. Looking weak, I could not.

Getting to my knees wasn't too hard, but from my knees to my feet took some concentration. I felt dizzy by the time I was standing.

"I don't feel so good," I said, fumbling for the shut-off.

"You're fine," Merdon said, opening the door and thrusting a towel at me. "Dry off."

I bared my teeth at him, in a pathetic attempt at a snarl. He grunted and turned his back to me. It wasn't the reaction I'd wanted.

"Why are you still in here? You always leave before the shower turns off."

"You don't feel well."

"No shit. I just told you that. It doesn't explain why—"

I slipped and would have gone down if not for Merdon.

He was surprisingly good at gripping wet skin. The thought made my mind fling itself into the gutter with wild abandon.

"I need help," I muttered.

"I am helping."

He proved it by dumping me on my mattress, stalking to the closet, and throwing a shirt and shorts at me. I snorted then struggled into the clothes for the next several minutes.

Panting and slightly sweaty, I collapsed on the bed.

"You need to eat."

I opened one eye and found him staring down at me.

"Yep. I'm hungry. But I'm more tired than hungry, so that's going to win for now. You can spank me for it later."

I rolled over and curled into a ball on top of the covers, too tired to fix the problem.

I woke up gasping for air, my throat raw and tight from screaming. The need to run and the certainty of imminent danger consumed me. Wild-eyed, I looked around the room. Nothing was familiar. I couldn't remember where I was or how I'd gotten there.

My gaze locked onto the closet. Heart hammering, I flew out from under the covers and scrambled for the dark, small space. Even in my panic, I knew to be quiet as I wedged myself into a back corner and curled into a ball.

Straining to hear over the rapid beat of my pulse, I listened. Everything was quiet.

It took a moment to understand there weren't infected after me. That I'd been dreaming again. This time it'd been Katie leading me by the hand, and I'd been the one left behind. I could still feel the bites on my arms and legs.

A shadow moved outside the closet, and I smothered a terrified whimper. Towering and huge, the thing bent low until I recognized the fey squatting before me.

Merdon.

"You're safe."

The soft words were like a crack of thunder in the quiet room, making my fear flare again.

He held out his hand. "Come."

I put my hand in his, letting him pull me free from my hiding spot. But, the remnants of the dream continued to cloud my thinking and skew my judgment, and with my arms still aching from the bites, the bedroom felt too large and open. The lingering sensation of danger had me stepping into his arms when he released me.

There was a moment of hesitation on his part before his hand settled on my head, and he stroked my hair. A shuddering sigh escaped me, and I wrapped my arms around his waist. Face planted in his shirt, I stayed there, soaking up the comfort while I tried to separate dream from reality.

It took a few minutes for me to realize what I was doing and who I was doing it with. He didn't stop me when I pulled away. I tried not to notice how my head felt bare without his touch.

"Sorry," I mumbled.

He grunted.

I continued to stand there awkwardly. There was no way I could crawl back into bed. I also didn't want him to drag me downstairs again.

"Any chance I could eat now?" I asked hopefully.

"Yes."

With quiet relief, I followed him from the bedroom. Emily's door was closed tightly, and I wondered if she locked it at night because Merdon was in the house. Probably not. He could just break it down if he really wanted to get in. Luckily for her, he wasn't interested. Too bad for me, he was.

He sat at the island and watched me look through the cupboards. I found bags of cookies stored away, for Emily's visit to Tenacity, but left those alone and kept looking for something a little more nutritionally sound.

The search proved unnecessary when I discovered a plastic wrapped plate of food in the refrigerator. Meat, mashed potatoes with gravy, and carrots. My stomach growled loudly as I slipped it into the microwave. I stopped it before it could beep and started cutting the meat into manageable bites.

"Are you hungry?" I asked softly.

"No. Eat."

Everything was orders with him.

I took my time eating, letting the memory of the dream fade

as much as possible in the hopes that I'd be able to go back to sleep.

The complete silence accentuated the sound of my chewing, which I didn't like at all. It was sometimes like that now, though. Especially with the infected gone.

"How many days has it been since the breach?" I asked with a frown. All the days with Merdon were blending together.

"I don't know. Why are you asking?"

"It's weird for the infected to be gone this long, isn't it? I mean, it's been at least two weeks. Almost three, maybe. We've never gone that long without seeing an infected. What does that mean?"

"They are learning to stay away from us because we can kill them."

"Hmm. Are they still setting traps for the groups that go out for salvage runs?"

"Yes."

"Then I don't think they're staying away from here because they're avoiding you guys." It scared me to think that they might be planning something else.

I finished my food, trying not to focus on the noise I was making, then rinsed my plate to wash in the morning.

I didn't need to fake a yawn when I turned back to Merdon.

"Am I allowed to go back to bed, or are you in the mood for some wrestle time?"

He tilted his head, studying me for a long, intense moment.

"If you're looking for my vote, it's bed," I said with another yawn. "I feel like I could sleep for a day straight."

He stood and motioned for the stairs leading to the second floor. I didn't need to be told twice. Glad for the reprieve, I jogged up the stairs and was burrowed under my covers moments later.

With a sigh, I closed my eyes and let exhaustion pull me back under.

THOUGHTS DRIFTED in and out during my semi-conscious state of almost awake. One in particular had my eyes popping open, and I was momentarily blinded by the sunlight streaming in through the window. The light didn't banish my thoughts of last night's messed up dream or the blame for it.

Angry, I sat up and looked at the bite marks on my arms.

It'd been Merdon's bites I'd felt as the infected pulled me down. He'd wormed his way into my dream, twisting it so I suffered in Katie's place. Thanks to him, my imagination had supplied me with what I'd needed to make the dream seem so very real.

I twisted around to glare at him, but his chair was empty. Maybe I was finally getting lucky. That was two mornings in a row without him now.

Glancing at the sunlight again, I hurried out of bed and got dressed. I didn't want to miss my time with Brenna. I needed to learn to use that bow so I could shoot Merdon in his sleep.

I paused and glanced at the chair again. Did he sleep?

Shaking my head, I pulled on a sweater then jogged my way down to the kitchen.

"Morning," Emily said with a happy smile. "I saw you ate last night. I was worried when Merdon said you picked sleep over food."

"I didn't really have a choice. Sleep picked for me."

"Does that mean it's getting better?" she asked hesitantly.

"We both know it isn't," I said, knowing darn well she'd heard me last night. My throat still felt scratchy from all the screaming.

"Sorry." She slid a plate stacked with eggs—real ones, hash browns, and bacon—toward me. My mouth watered looking at it all.

"How?" I asked, pointing to the food with my fork.

"Ryan's farm raids. He found some chickens still alive in one of those big chicken farms. The place was a mess. It looked like a hellhound had gotten in and ripped open most of the cages. But, there were a few chickens surviving in the carnage."

I looked at my eggs, briefly wondering what the chickens had been eating with no one there to feed them, then decided I didn't care and dug in. It was heavenly.

"Where's Merdon this morning?" I asked between bites.

"Not sure. As soon as I came downstairs to start breakfast, he left without a word."

"If we're lucky, maybe he won't come back."

She made a non-committal noise that I knew from past experience came before much commenting.

"What?" I asked, giving in to the inevitable.

"Would we be lucky? I mean, we have food. We have the security of knowing he's here at night. You're doing better even if the dreams are still giving you trouble. Having him around has helped us."

Giving her a disbelieving stare, I pushed up my sleeves to show the light bruises from yesterday's bites.

"Thanks to Merdon, I was the one dying last night. No, we are not luckier having him around. I get that you wanted me to stop drinking. Fine, I'm off the booze, and I'm eating. Can't that be enough? Why does he need to stay here, tormenting me, just to make you feel better?"

"I think he means well but is going about things in the wrong way."

I snorted then finished my last bite.

"Thank you for breakfast. It was amazing. Your thoughts on Merdon, not so much. I'll be back around lunch if my keeper allows it."

I left her in the kitchen, looking guilty.

Outside, the sun warmed my face and the breeze played with my curls, tugging a few of the shorter ones free of their confines. Fey nodded or waved to me as I passed, not hiding as much as the day before. However, I spotted them less frequently as I approached our spot to practice archery.

There were a few more people waiting for me than the day before.

"Hey, Hannah," Angel said when she saw me. "Word's spreading."

I looked at Eden, who was already getting a quiet explanation from Brenna about the bow, then at the girl standing beside them. Her dark, curly hair was pulled back, showing the rapt attention in her dark eyes as she listened to Brenna. The girl was young, around Katie's age. And seeing her there made me feel awful things: guilt, panic, anger, and a shit-ton of shame.

"That's Tasha," Angel said, catching my stare. "She was the other girl kidnapped with you and Brenna. Brenna's family took her in. They're treating her like one of their own, teaching her archery and everything. She's loving it, and I think Brenna's enjoying having a little sister."

The words were a knife to my soul. Angel continued on, unaware of how deeply she'd just cut me.

"I know I love having Garrett in my life. Who would have

thought I'd find a family in this mess? It's kind of neat, all the adopting going on." She patted her belly.

Visions of Katie falling to a horde of infected surged forward in my mind. I'd had a family, and I'd turned my back on it. I'd killed it. I'd killed my sister.

I stared at the girl, Tasha, not seeing the differences between her and Katie but all of the similarities in the way she smiled at Brenna and hung on every word.

An invisible hand wrapped around my chest and squeezed. I couldn't breathe. I could only feel the anguish of what I'd done. It ripped at me, shredding my reason.

"Shut up," I whispered, staggering a step away from Angel.

"You okay?" she asked.

"Shut up!" I screamed and covered my ears. Everything was crumbling apart. Fire lit my insides, burning with a certainty that we were all dead like Katie. We just hadn't figured it out yet. The fey had trapped us in these flimsy tin walls, like cattle in a pen. We were infected food, waiting to happen.

Katie's screams filled my ears. Again and again, she called my name. I could feel the bites on my arms...on her arms. Panting, I wheeled around, looking for her.

"Hannah, stop."

I turned toward the voice. It wasn't Katie. It was *him*. Merdon. He did this to me.

"I hate you. I hate you for making me do this. I don't want to feel. Why can't you understand that? Why can't you just leave me alone?"

"Never."

I crouched automatically, not even realizing what I was doing. He shadowed the move a moment before I flew at him. I used everything. Teeth and nails on his skin whenever I managed to get close enough; fists and elbows planted in anything relatively soft. I kicked and I clawed and I didn't stop. I fought wildly for the freedom I needed. Freedom from the memories, the pain, and the guilt.

Time blurred. My side began to ache. My limbs started to shake. Fatigue slowed me but didn't cool my anger. I'd been fine before Merdon's self-imposed house arrest. Everything had been numb.

"I want it back," I yelled at him.

"No."

He shifted around me, trying to avoid me and making me work even harder to reach him. I remained focused until my legs gave out. The feel of my knees hitting the ground jarred me from my spiral enough to notice the people around me.

Thallirin had an arm protectively wrapped around Brenna, who was scowling at Merdon. When she met my gaze, I saw understanding I didn't need or deserve. I looked away and found the girl's shocked expression spoke volumes as did the sudden pallor to her caramel skin. Angel watched me with pity. Shax's expression echoed her own.

It was too much.

I bowed my head in defeat, understanding that I'd never be free from the fey or what I'd done.

Merdon came to me, grabbed an arm, and tossed me over his shoulder. I accepted the position in limp silence.

"I'm sorry, Merdon," Thallirin said.

"We cannot change the choices we've made; we can only learn to live with them. I must go."

Live with the choice he made in picking me? The broken, human female of Tolerance who was too mean for anyone else to want. Maybe I wasn't his choice. Maybe he'd gotten stuck with me by default.

My soul died further as he strode away with me over his shoulder. My heaving breaths turned into racking sobs before he reached the house.

"What happened?" Emily asked.

"It's nothing."

He set me down and grabbed my chin, forcing my attention to his angry face.

"Are you done, or do you need the basement?"

I swallowed hard, ignoring the snot running from my nose.

"I'm done."

"Good. Go upstairs and shower."

I nodded and shuffled upstairs. The bathroom mirror reflected my tear-streaked face and brought on a fresh round of pain and crying. Sniffling, I stripped and turned on the water. I tried not to think. It was easier to just function. Autopilot wasn't enough to stop the tears, though.

The shower had just warmed on my skin when Merdon walked in and looked at me through the glass.

"Why are you still crying?"

"I don't know how to stop. Did they make you pick me? Is that why Thallirin said he's sorry? Are you stuck with me?"

He stared at me through the glass for a long moment, his expression impossible to read.

"No, no one forced me to pick you."

The tears slowed.

"Thallirin was apologizing for the things he did lifetimes ago," he continued.

"What did he do?"

"After Oelm died, guilt consumed Thallirin. He sought to end his life. I stayed with him, watching him, keeping him alive. He fought me, and eventually, he forgave me for robbing him of the peace he sought."

Thallirin had been like me.

"Dry off. Get dressed. Mary and James invited us to eat with them. You need rest."

He angrily walked out of the room, leaving me wondering why exactly Merdon had a thing for saving people.

CHAPTER NINETEEN

EMOTIONALLY SPENT AND PHYSICALLY DRAINED, I DRESSED SLOWLY. How could just a few hours feel like a full day? Losing time seemed to be the theme for my stationary existence since the breach. No, not the breach, since Merdon barged in and started controlling my life.

While I was grateful for the upcoming reprieve from Merdon's focused attention, I was smart enough to know there was some agenda to James and Mary's lunch invitation. The old couple didn't demand our presence unless they needed something. It felt like I was trading one giant, agile devil for two smaller, slower ones. Yet, whatever it was the old couple wanted was better than any other option I had.

Bundled in a cozy sweater and wearing soft jeans, I made my way downstairs. I noticed Emily was in the kitchen, wrapping something up. Merdon wasn't with her, though. Instead, he stood staring at the dark TV in the living room.

"Works better if you turn it on," I said.

He glanced at me, his gaze sweeping me from head to toe before shifting to Emily.

"Are you ready?"

"Yep, all set," she answered.

She handed him the covered dish she'd been wrapping and went for her coat. I quickly joined her, slipped into my jacket and boots, then held the door for the pair. They looked so domestic together. Merdon, carrying the dish; Emily, smiling and thanking him.

He didn't even scowl angrily when he looked at her. Why did that annoy me?

"Did James and Mary say why they wanted us to come over?" I asked.

"No," Emily said. "Tor stopped by with the message, though, so I'm guessing it's about the dinner dates. Since I already had lunch made, I asked him to let Mary know I'd bring the food."

"Another dish for us to test?"

"Yep. I think you'll like this one, too."

My stomach growled its agreement, and she grinned at me. Merdon's frown deepened, which I ignored.

"I saw the cookies still in the house. When are you going to Tenacity to finalize the hookups?"

She wrinkled her nose.

"Let's think of something else to call it. Maybe something about the food so it doesn't seem so..."

"Like a sex hookup?"

She gave me a look and nodded her head toward Merdon as if he wasn't fully aware of the fey endgame. The only reason any of them wanted the dinner was to eventually have sex.

"What? That's why very few of the single women stayed in Tolerance when we gave them the choice between here and Tenacity. They already know what the fey's goals are and want nothing to do with them."

"Exactly. The women from Tenacity are rejecting the fey without even knowing anything about them except that they're different. That's the whole point of the dinners: to give them an opportunity to get to know the fey outside of the whole 'we want a woman' perception. Yes, the fey are hoping for a positive end result, but they also want to be accepted for who they are. And, Mary and I are hoping this is a start of a movement to change the general perception of the fey as seen by the female population of Tenacity. We need a better relationship for our communities to survive long-term."

A distant moo seemed to agree with her passionate outpouring. I hadn't realized how much these dinners meant to her.

"Then call it a 'dine and dash' so the women think that's all they'll need to do. Talk up the food and the conversation starter cards you have, and downplay the company they'll have at the table as no big deal. Make it sound like it's a painless escape and way to get fed, and they'll do it."

Emily gave me a grateful smile.

"Do you really think so?"

"Yes. And you're giving them food in the form of cookies just for talking to you. It's like one of those no purchase necessary contests. You're not forcing them to have dinner to get fed. They'll just get more food if they agree."

"Oh, I didn't think of it like that. Yeah, it's a good thing I made the cookies. Maybe I should make something else."

"A canned good would help open more doors and give you a reason to have a fey escort. A fey presence, in a helpful way, wouldn't be a bad thing."

"I know just the fey," she said.

I looked back at Merdon, who was following us.

In that single, sweeping glance, a new realization was born, and it had nothing to do with Emily's talk of changing the female perception of the fey. Though, ironically, that's what just happened because I'd noted the way his t-shirt clung to every hard muscle he owned and the way his worn buckskin pants encased his thighs. And most of all, how damn sexy all of that was, combined with the fact that he was still carrying Emily's dish of whatever.

The idea of Emily taking Merdon, and the fear of him actually going, filled me with jealousy. It didn't matter that he said I was his or I'd told him repeatedly that I didn't want him. My feelings weren't listening to my head. And, as much as I wanted to go back to the blind way I'd seen him before, I couldn't. Merdon was damn near lickable, and that shocked the hell out of me.

First that weird tingle, then the kiss, and now this? Was I Stockholming him? My stomach dipped and refused to settle down the rest of the way to James and Mary's place.

The door opened when we were two steps away, which I found as odd as James's serious expression.

"Is everything all right?" Emily asked, obviously noting the same things I had.

He nodded slowly, his gaze flicking to me.

"Yep. Everything's fine. Come on in. Ma's got the table set."

Emily and I took off our jackets by the door while Merdon carried the dish to the table.

"You are such a sweet man," Mary said from where she was pouring juice into our cups. "Any woman would be lucky to have you. Not just lucky but grateful."

That last word, spoken so forcefully, had me looking at Emily in question.

She gave me a slight "I have no idea" shrug before joining the others with me.

"Hannah and I were just talking about how I might get a few more volunteers for the dinners," Emily said chipperly.

"Oh?" Mary asked. The tone and stiff way she motioned everyone to sit made her seem almost angry. She'd scolded me plenty, but I'd never seen her looking this upset.

Emily frowned at her and repeated her earlier question. "Is everything all right?"

Mary gave Emily a quick smile. "Of course, dear. Tell me your ideas."

"Well, I'd baked the cookies as a way to soften up the ladies I plan to talk to and as an example of the food they'd get if they volunteered to attend the dinners. But Hannah made a good point about not wanting any of them to feel like they're being forced into a dinner in order to get fed. She suggested offering a canned good for anyone willing just to hear me out. No strings attached."

"Well, that seems nice. It's a good gesture." But Mary's grandmotherly doting expression fell into a truck stop wayside as she looked at me.

"I didn't think you had it in you to consider someone else's feelings."

The words stung harsher than any of Merdon's spankings. My mouth fell open in shock.

"Mary, that's enough," James said calmly. "What'd you bring to eat, Emily?"

Emily glanced from Mary to me and back again.

"Um, something I was thinking we could serve for one of the dinners. Merdon and Hannah both enjoyed yesterday's dish. I was going to have them test today's, too, but then figured we could all do that since it made more than I expected."

"That's so sweet of you, honey," Mary said. She looked at Merdon. "Isn't she sweet?"

He grunted, his gaze flicking to everyone at the table. His expression might not have shown it, but I could tell he was just as confused as I was by Mary's behavior.

"She'd make someone a fine partner for sure," Mary continued. "Kind, caring, nice childbearing hips, and breasts big enough for some decent milk."

Emily paused in the act of uncovering the dish she'd brought, a flush creeping into her cheeks.

"Ma, you're making her blush. Cut it out."

"I just think it's important to help the fey see what they should value in a potential partner." She turned to Merdon. "Make sure you let the rest know what I said."

"I will."

"The size of a girl's chest doesn't equate to milk production," Emily said hurriedly. "Please don't encourage false rumors." She shot Mary an imploring look. "We're going to have a hard enough time finding any willing girls, let alone ones with large busts and all the curves. Especially when we've been starved for weeks and are now barely eating the daily calories we need."

"I know, I know," Mary said. "I just don't want any of the men to think that the right woman is one who would attack him in public for no good reason."

My stomach dove to my toes as I realized why Mary was acting the way she was. Unable to look up and meet the accusation coming at me from across the table, I locked my gaze onto my plate.

"You should be ashamed of yourself, Hannah. I know you

were raised better than that. Merdon has done so much for you, taken care of you when you refused to take care of yourself, and that's how you repay him?"

"What's going on?" Emily asked.

"Hannah attacked Merdon this morning. You didn't notice the scratch on his face?"

Emily remained quiet. She had noticed but probably thought it'd come from one of our basement matches.

"He's a good man and deserves to be treated as such. Now, apologize."

My mind went completely blank for a moment before an overwhelming number of emotions and thoughts battered me. Yes, I'd lost my shit this morning. I shouldn't have lashed out the way I had, but it hadn't been a conscious choice. I didn't know how to cope with all the shit in my head without alcohol, which Merdon took away from me. How was it my fault I went crazy? Especially since Mary had just acknowledged something was wrong enough that someone else had to take care of me.

I was angry I was the one getting yelled at here, but over that anger was hurt. So much hurt. Mary and James were supposed to have been my support. Twice, now, they'd let me down.

"No," I said, lifting my head. "You both thought it was a good idea for Merdon to spank me and bite me, but when I do it back, I'm the one to blame? I'm not apologizing for reacting the way he's been teaching me to react. But I am sorry. I'm sorry I came here, and I'm sorry I ever believed you could care about me enough to help fill the place of everyone I've lost."

I stood and placed my napkin on the table.

"I'll try your dish at home if you want me to," I said to Emily.

James hurried to stand.

"I'll walk with you."

Ignoring him, I went to the door and grabbed my jacket. For a guy who usually didn't get up and answer the door, he had a lot of hustle as he followed me.

"Take pity on an old man, Hannah, and let me use your arm," he said when the door closed behind us.

Taking a calming breath, I stopped and helped him even though I didn't want to. I'd known James long enough to understand he was walking with me to put in his two cents.

"It might not seem like it now, but we love you, Hannah. Mary's just upset because she sees things differently than you. Honestly, we both do." He let out a weary sigh. "Mary and I are deadweight. We contribute nothing to our little community. We can't help get supplies, only eat them. We can't protect anyone." He nudged my arm he was clutching, "Hell, I can barely walk.

"Mary and I know we're a liability, but these fey have never once made us feel that way. Finding a girl to settle down with might consume every waking thought they have, but they still help us even knowing there's nothing Mary and I will ever be able to do to pay them back.

"They're good people, and Mary won't let poor treatment of such good people go without a strong word of discouragement."

"And my poor treatment? You both encouraged him. I wore his handprint for hours. You saw his bite marks."

"We also saw how bad it was getting and how much you've turned around in the weeks he's been with you. Don't you see? We were willing to do anything not to lose you. What's a few thrashings in exchange for you?"

"You wouldn't be saying that if it had been your backside," I mumbled.

"I would. I doubt he would have been as interested in

spanking me, though. Mary tried it once. Said I was too tough and didn't squeal enough."

I stopped walking to stare at him. He chuckled and winked at me.

"If you didn't have even a moment of fun with Merdon, he's not doing something right. Give him another chance. Or, ask him for a turn like Mary did to me."

The implication that he'd been spanking Mary prior to her spanking him made me want to stuff snow in my ears.

"Please, please stop talking about spankings."

"You're the one who brought them up."

"You have no idea how much I regret that now."

We continued walking, and he patted my arm.

"Just think about what I said."

"I'm trying not to."

He chuckled again.

"About the choice we made to allow Merdon to try to help you. We'd been trying and failing. You know you were sick, honey. You still are. And if you let yourself reflect on it, you'll see that you were taking your pain out on others, and that's not okay. Now, I'm not just talking about Merdon. I'm talking about Emily, too. That girl has stuck with you through thick and thin, and how have you repaid her?"

He wasn't scolding me in that same tone Mary had used. He was compassionate and softly spoken, all while patting my hand reassuringly.

"And what about Shax? That boy would have done anything for a scrap of your affection. You knew it, and what did you do?"

I swallowed hard, hating the way James was gently forcing me to see myself. Lifting my gaze, I focused on my house ahead and wished I could just shake loose of his hold and run for it. But, I couldn't. I couldn't be that past version of myself that he was painting for me.

He paused at the end of my sidewalk and released me.

"Look beyond yourself, Hannah. Everyone is struggling in some way. Your pain isn't special or new. That doesn't mean it's not real or that you have no right to feel it. It means you're not alone."

Turning, he lifted an arm.

"Any volunteers to give an old man a lift home?"

Several fey stepped out of their hiding places to offer their help.

"Fyllo, come on over here. I appreciate the ride," James said as the fey jogged over and gently lifted the old man. "We're having lunch at my place if you want to come in. Just don't take a shower first. Mary's been having issues with dropping her fork when you fey are sitting around the table in towels."

I shook my head and went inside, not knowing what to think about James's talk, mostly because I was just so damn tired of feeling guilty for everything. Mary had thought the worst about my fight with Merdon because of my past actions.

Yes, I'd used Shax. I'd known it at the time I was doing it and had told myself I'd been doing him a favor by giving him attention. Hadn't I hurled similar words at Merdon at one point? I'd treated all the fey like that. But, James was right. They were good people. I had always known that on some level. But, I'd let myself justify my actions because I'd been so fucked up in my head.

Hell, I still was. My skin crawled with the need to move, to escape all these awful feelings. I was angry, confused, guilt-ridden to the point of breaking, and...alone. Unwanted. Mean.

Standing just inside the door, I looked around at the empty

house and knew I didn't want to be there. I tugged off my boots and carried them through the house only to put them on again at the backdoor. I let myself out and headed for the nearest wall ladder.

No doubt, I had some fey trailing me. I didn't turn to see who it might be. I didn't want to see a fey I recognized and think about all the ways I might have wronged him. I also didn't want to be told to go home.

So I climbed the ladder and took a seat on the wall, letting my legs hang over the outside edge. Nothing moved out among the trees even though the snow around them was well trampled. It wasn't comforting that the infected weren't out there. Quite the opposite, actually. I shuddered at what changes might be happening that we weren't witnessing.

The cold of the metal underneath me slowly leached away my warmth. I began to shiver lightly but made no move to get up. I wasn't ready to return home. Instead, I lost myself in the company of the wind and trees.

"You're facing the wrong way if you're here for a good view of the sunset," a familiar voice said long after my toes had gone numb.

I looked over at Brenna, who was jogging atop the wall toward me.

"Not here for the view, just the solitude. No offense."

"None taken."

She also didn't take the hint because she sat down beside me.

"What I saw this morning wasn't pretty," she said.

I turned to stare, unable to believe she'd just sit down and say something like that. She met my gaze and shrugged.

"It wasn't, and you know it."

"Of course, I know it. What I don't know is why you're here rubbing it in?"

"Rubbing it in? Never. I wanted to tell you I know that look you were wearing. The anger. The fear. The guilt. I saw that in the mirror for weeks. It might not be due to the same experiences, or it might be. I'm not asking you to have a moment with me and bond over shared pain. But I'm here because I wanted you to know that I understand what I saw this morning, and I know what falling apart looks like. I've done it. My mom's done it. And I can say from experience that piecing yourself back together afterward can be rough. I'm here if you need a friendly ear or quiet company."

"Thanks."

"You don't mean that, but maybe you will when you see my offer for what it is. Don't isolate yourself. I promise you that closing yourself off is never the right choice."

She turned herself toward me, a forceful glint in her eye.

"Talk to someone about what's going on in your head even if you'd rather spoon your own eye out. In fact, the worse it feels to put it into the words, the more you probably need to talk about it. It won't be easy but is anything easy in this world?"

"Nope. Not since the quakes."

"If it was easy for you before the quakes, I envy you that. It wasn't easy for all of us."

She stood, shouldering her bow.

"Be at the dick pile tomorrow morning. One bad day doesn't mean you can quit."

She didn't wait for my answer but walked away. I stared after her for a moment before turning my attention to the fading light.

She, like Emily, wanted me to talk to someone. But how, when I didn't know the words to explain the thing eating me alive from the inside? It was volatile and uncompromisingly vicious when it stirred, and as today proved, it didn't just hurt me. It hurt everyone around me. And Brenna wanted me to talk about what woke it. No, thanks.

I'd heard what happened to her. Rape. And her mom had some sort of accident that landed her in a wheelchair. Things happened to them. Choices were taken away from them. No one took away my choice with Katie. I'd made that demon through my own actions. Brenna might think she understood my pain, but she didn't. Not really. No one could.

Except, maybe, Merdon.

He'd killed his friend. Someone who was supposedly like a brother to him. Yet, never once had Merdon shown any sign of guilt or regret. He didn't wake up screaming or strike out at people like I did. In fact, as James pointed out, Merdon was helpful. To everyone but me.

I folded my hands in my lap and looked down at my cold-numb fingers, trying to imagine telling Merdon about what had happened. He claimed I was his, and in normal fey-speak, that would mean kindness, compassion, and doting. None of that was Merdon.

He acted like he hated me and often reminded me how awful I was to everyone around me. While he might understand what I'd done, he obviously hadn't experienced the same remorse. He was, in general, cold and uncaring.

And he was my best option?

CHAPTER TWENTY

A FEY JUMPED UP NEXT TO ME, STARTLING ME SO BADLY THAT I almost toppled off the wall. A big grey hand clamped down on my shoulder, anchoring me as Shax took a seat beside me.

"What are you doing?" I couldn't help the suspicion in my tone or my glance over my shoulder at Tolerance.

"I am sitting with you. What are you doing?"

"Well, I'm wondering why you aren't with Angel."

"Merdon asked me to sit with you. He thought you might need a friend."

"That's confusing on so many levels."

Shax tilted his head at me, and I knew he needed an explanation.

"Well, Merdon just listened to Mary yell at me when what happened was partially his fault, and he didn't once stick up for me. Now, he's sent a 'friend' to me? And why you? Why not Emily?"

"Because you were nice to me once."

"Was I nice to you?" I asked softly.

I looked out over the trees, my heart hurting for myself.

"Am I really that awful? Do all the fey hate me?"

"No."

I snorted.

"Just the ones I used, right?" I asked ruefully. "I'm sorry for what I did to you, Shax. I knew what you wanted, so I used your infatuation to get what I wanted. I never meant to hurt you. I never meant to be so mean."

"It's okay. You helped me win Angel." A wistful note crept into his voice when he said her name.

It hurt to know I would never have anyone talk about me like Shax talked about Angel.

"You guys should let Merdon choose someone else. It's not fair to stick him with me just because no one else wants me."

Shax's silence became noticeable after a beat, and I looked over to meet his perplexed gaze.

"Many fey want you, Hannah, and Merdon has always been free to choose who he wants. He wants you. My brothers are respecting that decision." Shax's expression turned troubled. "Do you prefer a different fey?"

I could see how much the idea upset him.

"Honestly, I don't even like myself very much. How can I like anyone else?"

His gaze searched mine. Instead of asking questions, he simply wrapped an arm around my shoulders and pulled me close. It wasn't a move to get some girl-contact time. It was just a friendly, almost brotherly hug. And it was my undoing. Tears fell quietly as I let myself accept his offer of friendship even though I knew I didn't deserve it.

"You should like yourself," Shax said softly. "You will never be happy until you do."

"This wall is turning into a therapy couch," I said. "First

Brenna telling me to talk to someone, and now you telling me to like myself. I wish it was all that easy."

"It is. I like you. So do Angel and Brenna and Thallirin."

"Thallirin might be a stretch," I said sniffling.

Shax grunted.

"Yes. He is much taller than you."

I snorted a laugh and didn't try to correct him. Instead, I leaned my head on his shoulder and watched the light fade from the sky. He didn't get antsy even though I knew he was probably thinking about Angel.

"Thanks for the talk, Shax."

"Anytime."

"You should probably get back to Angel."

"Not until you come down from the wall. Do you want me to carry you home?"

"No, thanks. I'm tired of being carried. Merdon keeps throwing me over his shoulder. One of these days, I'm going to barf on his back just to spite him for being mean. I know you think he picked me, but I don't think he's happy about his choice." I stood, and Shax rose, too. "I still think you should encourage him to pick someone else. All I do is make him angry."

Shax blinked at me in the way fey did when they were either thinking or stumped. I wasn't sure which applied right then.

"Have you heard Merdon and Thallirin's story?" he asked finally. "Not about Oelm's death but about what happened to Merdon and Thallirin after they left the protection of Ernisi?"

"No."

"Let me help you down, and I'll tell you the story."

I nodded, and he picked me up nicely and jumped to the ground. His heat seeped into my numb legs, and I felt a little colder at the loss when he set me down again.

"Outside the walls of our home, only the light caves kept Merdon and Thallirin safe. Thallirin didn't want safety. He wanted to join Oelm. Because of Oelm's death, both Merdon and Thallirin understood that the crystals we wore were what brought us back to life. In the days after their exile, Thallirin tried removing his crystal many times.

"The hounds hunted them relentlessly. Thallirin would throw himself into their midst, and Merdon would need to fight them to get the crystal back on Thallirin before they both died. They were reborn together many times. Merdon never let Thallirin have what he wanted."

"Why?"

"Because each time Thallirin came back, he was more anguished."

"I don't understand. Merdon was purposely making Thallirin suffer?"

"Merdon believed that Oelm would not want them to follow him to a final death. To value Oelm's death, they needed to live as Oelm would have lived. Oelm was a good man, a strong hunter, and a fierce opponent. He would have thought a final death cowardly and would have been ashamed to call them brothers.

"After Merdon told Thallirin that, Thallirin still threw himself to the hounds, but he kept his crystal on and wouldn't allow himself the relief of rebirth. He would fight the hounds and win. And Merdon would need to drag him, bleeding and unable to walk, to the crystal cave to heal for many days. Thallirin chose to carry his scars as a reminder of what was lost to them. Merdon chose to do whatever was necessary to keep Thallirin from final death to honor Oelm."

I wasn't sure what to think of Shax's story. Was I just another Thallirin to Merdon? But why? Merdon didn't know my story. He didn't know who I'd wronged. Why had he stepped in to save me from the infected during the breach? Why had he caught me when I'd jumped from the roof?

Shax and I stopped in my backyard before I had any answers to my questions.

"Thank you for sharing their story."

"You're welcome. Go inside where it's warm. Angel is looking forward to practice tomorrow."

I nodded and gave him a small wave as I headed inside.

Merdon and Emily were in the kitchen. She was at the stove, and he stood near the end of the island where he could cross his arms and glare his disapproval of me at close range. I ignored him and gave Emily a small smile as I took off my boots.

"It smells good in here. Like something sweet." My nose was still too cold to identify the almost forgotten smell.

"I have some hot chocolate for you."

"Hot chocolate?"

"Yep. Made from a real packet, so it should taste good."

My mouth watered, and she poured a cup for me as soon as I had my jacket off. I wrapped my fingers around the mug and shivered at the warmth.

"I have food, too, if you want. I saved some of what we had for lunch, and dinner's almost done, too. I wasn't sure how hungry you'd be."

My stomach growled greedily in response to the idea that I'd be able to eat the meal I'd missed.

With his next words, Merdon ruined the bubble of happiness.

"It doesn't matter what she wants," he said. "Sit and eat, Hannah."

I didn't miss the look Emily shot him or the increasing anger in his scowl when I didn't immediately jump to follow his order.

"Would it be all right if I eat the leftovers while waiting for dinner?" I asked, choosing to remain focused on Emily.

"Of course. Have a seat. I'll warm it up for you."

I sat, sipped my cocoa greedily while trying not to burn my tongue, and watched her take a covered plate from the fridge. Merdon stalked around the counter and joined me. I pretended not to notice.

"What did everyone think of lunch?" I asked.

She flashed me a quick smile.

"I'll tell you after you try it for yourself."

"Are you going to tell me what it is?"

"Nope. But I think you'll know when you see it."

She pulled the plate from the microwave and set it before me. I started salivating at the sight of Shepard's Pie. Without needing to be coaxed, I dug in.

"So good," I said around a hot mouthful.

"Merdon liked it too," Emily said.

The fey beside me grunted.

"No corn?" I asked, digging in for another bite. I knew people made it differently, but my mom had always made ours with corn.

"Fey aren't a fan of tomato-based dishes or corn. Since meat is coveted by both sides right now, I'm trying to stick with meat-centric dishes."

"This definitely works. I can't imagine anyone saying 'no' to this."

She grinned.

"Great. I hope you like dinner just as much."

The feel of Merdon's stare didn't diminish the pleasure of eating one of my favorite meals. In fact, the growing intensity of his scowl as I made yum-yum sounds only enhanced the experience.

How Shax honestly believed that Merdon wanted me was beyond baffling. Anyone with eyes could see that Merdon was in a constant state of disapproval every time he looked at me. Yet, there were moments when he was almost nice. I would never understand his mercurial moods even if I tried, so I didn't bother. I just enjoyed my meal.

The oven beeped as I finished my last bite, and Emily pulled out another dish. Pot roast with carrots and potatoes.

"These meals are going to be a hit. You're using all the comfort foods that they would have a hard time making for themselves with the supplies they have." I paused for a moment as what I'd just said sunk in. "Do you think it will do the opposite of what you're hoping to accomplish?"

"What do you mean?"

"Well, you want to give the fey an opportunity to talk to women, but you are also working on building a bridge between the two towns. What if these generous meals are taken as a display of abundance and that we're not sharing?" I rested my chin in my hand and considered our options. "I think we should do something more than dinners. Something where both genders can benefit. If you want to build bridges, go all-in."

Emily was watching me with a slightly stunned look on her face.

"It'll be okay," I reassured her. "If we talk to Matt about our concern, he'll help us find a solution, and he'll back us. He wants his people fed, too. And the more survivors from Tenacity who come over to Team Fey, the more people there will be to go on supply runs for Tenacity. That means more food for both settlements. So it's a win-win all around."

"You want to help with this?" she asked. "Help me talk to Matt?"

I thought about it for a minute. I hated the idea that I'd created another perception for myself, the mean one that Merdon kept shoving in my face. How many fake smiles had I thrown out thinking I was so smart just to have everyone see through them? I didn't want to be that fake person anymore. I wanted to be helpful. Useful. Needed. Mostly, I wanted to be liked again.

"I think I do. Is that okay?"

She smiled, looking a little close to tears, and nodded.

"No," Merdon said abruptly. "This morning proved you're not ready. Leave your plate and get downstairs."

I whirled on him.

"What is your problem? Why can't you just be nice for one damn minute?"

He bared his teeth and slowly leaned toward me. I wasn't intimidated. I was too mad for that.

"You don't need nice. If you did, you'd be with Shax. Are you going downstairs, or do you need help?"

"Merdon," Emily said, "she just—"

He held up his hand, demanding her silence, his gaze never leaving mine.

"Fine. Downstairs time. Nice scratch on your face, by the way," I said before turning my back on him.

The smack across my ass robbed me of breath, and I faltered a step.

"Merdon!"

Emily's gasp of outrage fueled my anger. Without looking back, I continued to the basement.

Merdon didn't immediately follow me. I could hear the murmur of their voices overhead as I paced the mat. I was tired of his attitude and spankings. I was also tired in general and knew he'd have me shaking with exhaustion with no energy to eat.

He came down the steps on quiet feet, watching me closely.

"Wasn't this morning's impromptu session enough for today?"

"No." He began to crouch.

I marched over to him and grabbed his face. It wasn't an aggressive hold but an insistent one. I didn't want to end up face down on the mat.

"I've been humiliated twice today, yelled at, and guilted more times than I can count. I've cried, I've been angry, and I've been more thoughtful than I have been in a long time. I'm physically and emotionally wrung out. Please, don't do this. I really don't want to miss out on Emily's pot roast because I'd rather sleep than eat when you're done with me."

The muscle in his jaw twitched under my palm as I waited for his response. His fingers circled my wrists and gently tugged my hands free of his skin.

"No more spanking," he said softly.

My lips started to lift in a grateful smile.

"Biting only. I will try to break the skin."

"What!"

The word barely escaped my mouth before he crouched once more. I scrambled away, my brain chanting "oh-shit, oh-shit, oh-shit" as I realized the severity of my situation. Biting had been scary before. Knowing that he now wanted to draw blood was beyond terrifying. The sound of my heart thundered in my ears as I fought to control my panic so I could focus.

Merdon circled me slowly. I didn't take my eyes off of him. When he lunged at me, I tumbled into a roll and popped up on the other side, already putting distance between us. He grunted and backed off, only to charge at me anew.

Again and again, he came at me, a relentless assault that wore me down. It didn't take long before I was panting and struggling to stay out of his grasp. Aches and cramps tweaked my muscles, slowing me further. I knew landing on the mat was inevitable, and my mind raced with possible ways to avoid a bite after he brought me down.

The planning saved me more times than I cared to admit. One of the times, I managed a palm thrust under his chin, which made his teeth slip from my skin and clack together before he could draw blood. I throat punched him another time, which made him snarl at me that I couldn't depend on pain to stop an infected.

The comment brought me to a complete halt.

"You're right. But I can depend on you and all the other fey to stop them. So all of this is pointless. I'm going upstairs for pot roast while I can still walk."

I turned my back on him. It was a calculated risk after the spanking he'd delivered on the way down to the basement. But he let me walk away without any retribution. Well, it was more of a gimp than a walk.

Only the lingering smell of beef bolstered my energy enough to make it up the stairs. Emily was reading a book on the couch; but when she heard me, she popped up and took the foil-wrapped plates from the oven.

"You okay?" she asked sympathetically.

"He let me escape before he managed to draw blood, and I'm awake enough to eat. I'm great."

No one spoke after that. She went back to her book, and I worked through my dinner. The meat was perfectly tender and flawlessly seasoned. I wanted to drink the gravy from my plate when I was done, but there wasn't enough left. So I licked it clean instead.

I knew Merdon was watching me and didn't care. When I finished, I used my sleeve to wipe any stray gravy from my face, thanked Emily for making a dinner that would give my mom's a run for its money, and went upstairs.

Merdon didn't need to tell me to shower. I could smell myself and knew one was needed. He left me alone as I stripped and didn't stand guard as I started washing. I appreciated the small freedom immensely. Only the return of my razor would have topped it. I was starting to look a little sasquatchish.

With my hair piled on top of my head, it didn't take me long to finish washing. I wrapped the towel around my torso and went out to the main room to dig something clean out of the closet. The room was already dark, and Merdon sat in his usual spot in the chair beside the bed. Like he'd done another time, he had clothes laid out for me.

What was with his helpfulness at times and not at others?

"Thank you," I said, grabbing the underwear.

He grunted and looked away as I slid the garment on under the towel. I tugged the shirt over my head, covering all of my important bits, before removing the towel and putting on the shorts.

"Do you regret it?" I asked as I crawled under the covers.

"Regret what?"

"Your part in what happened with Oelm."

Merdon was silent for so long that I thought he wouldn't answer. When he did, I wasn't prepared for the pain in his voice.

"Every day."

KATIE'S PLEADING gaze moments before I released her haunted my sleep. The terror I felt running away from her consumed each breath. The smell of her rot when she found her way home days later clogged my nose. The wrongness of her once beautiful hair and the jerky way she moved wrapped around me in an inescapable blanket.

The dreams battered me as they shifted from one to the next in such vivid detail. I didn't see them for what they were; memories of a past I desperately wanted to forget. Instead, I sank into each moment, and the terror built, bleeding out into the real world.

I woke with a scream as I pulled the knife from my sister's decaying flesh. The twisted sheets clung to my sweat-dampened skin while I fought my way free of them. The need to run, to hide, rode me hard.

"You're safe," a voice said softly. "There's nothing here to harm you."

Half falling out of bed, I scrambled toward the sound and crawled into Merdon's lap. His arms wrapped around me, and his hand smoothed over my curls. I trembled and struggled to breathe quietly. Despite his assurance, I was still afraid of being heard.

Gradually, the dream released me enough for me to understand I'd been reliving my hell again.

"I can't keep doing this," I whispered.

"You can."

"You don't know. You don't understand. I can't."

I pressed closer to him, desperately wishing I could hide from the pain.

"Then make me understand."

The words were a challenge. I thought of Oelm's death and

Merdon's painful admission of regret. Brenna's advice to share the pain circled in my head. Was that really what I needed?

"I killed my sister," I said before I could stop myself. "The infected were chasing us. She couldn't keep up. I tried to pull her along, but she fell." The pain in my chest grew, and tears started raining down my cheeks all over again. "I ran. I could have tried to pick her up or to find something to protect us, but I left her. I can still hear her screaming my name and the sounds of the infected as they ate her."

I wiped the snot from my nose and made myself continue.

"She found me a few days later in the same house we'd been using. I killed her with a knife." I lifted my clean hand. "It feels like the blood is still here. I can feel its stickiness and the way the tissue clung to the blade as I yanked it out of her mouth."

I lifted my head and looked him in the eyes.

"I killed my sister. How do I live with that?"

"You would both be dead if you hadn't run. Your sister wouldn't have wanted that."

"My sister wouldn't have wanted to be bitten, turned, and killed by me."

"Guilt fades with time. You will learn to live with your past just as I have."

That was it? Live with what I'd done? What the hell did he think I'd been trying to do?

I scrambled off his lap.

"Get out."

"No."

"I told you everything like you wanted. You've nailed my window shut and taken away everything sharp. There's no reason for you to be in here anymore. Get out."

He leaned forward in his chair, bracing his elbows on his knees.

"Get back in bed and go to sleep, or we go down to the basement."

"God, I hate you."

"I know."

I crawled back into bed and glared at the window. I was so stupid for listening to Brenna and Shax. Merdon didn't have it in him to be nice. He was nothing but an asshole.

CHAPTER TWENTY-ONE

THE SNICK OF THE DOOR, JUST AFTER DAWN, PULLED ME OUT OF AN unintended doze. Thinking it was Emily coming into my room to speak with Merdon, I waited. Several long moments of silence passed before I gave in and twisted around to see what was happening.

Merdon's chair was empty.

Why leave now? Since I'd crawled back into bed, he'd been staring at me like a pain-in-the-ass hall monitor. And, I knew he hadn't slept because I'd watched him just as closely as he'd watched me. Or, at least, I had until exhaustion pulled me under shortly before dawn.

It didn't bode well for me that he'd waited for me to pass out before sneaking away. I realized he was probably going to relay everything I told him to Emily, and I began to panic. She'd kick me out, and I'd be forced to live in a house with Merdon, alone and in hell for the rest of my life.

I slithered from the bed and crept toward the door. Or, rather, I tried to. Everything felt weird. Not only in the way the room seemed to spin and twirl but how my movements were uncoordinated and slow. I was running on too little sleep because of last night.

I shook my head, trying to wake myself some more, then slowly and noiselessly let myself into the hall. Emily's door was closed. I didn't hear anything from her room, but I did hear the low rumble of Merdon's voice coming from the kitchen.

Knowing he had sharp hearing, I descended the steps to midway, stopping close enough to just make out words.

"...rough night. How is she doing?" Emily asked.

"She's restless."

"I hope that doesn't mean taking her to the basement again. I can't stand hearing you spank her or her yelps when you bite her. It's breaking my heart."

"I know."

There was that damn "I know" again. If he was so all-knowing, why couldn't he figure out that I saw his dumb pseudo-training for what it was? A strong fetish for ass abuse.

"I'm sorry, Merdon," Emily said.

Why was she apologizing to him? It was my ass that hurt. And my hand still felt tender from a bite.

"Are you all right?" she asked.

The worry in her voice confused the hell out of me as did Merdon's long, loud exhale.

"Your heart is breaking, but mine broke the first time I struck her. Now, I die a thousand deaths each time I harden her hate toward me."

My mouth fell open. That couldn't be right. I stuck a finger in my ear, certain it wasn't working, and gripped the railing tighter when my balance wobbled.

"Then tell her how you really feel," Emily said.

"You didn't see her when she jumped from the roof. She was

empty, ready for final death. Her anger gives her purpose. It is better she exists with hate than not exist at all."

It took a moment for his words to sink in. All those scowls? All the time in the basement? He'd done it because he thought making me hate him would keep me alive? No. He was an asshole. That wasn't a façade.

He'd locked me in my room, almost drowned me, forced me into a cold shower, spanked me, and bit me. He'd even threatened to break the skin.

He'd also made sure I ate, slept, and bathed, and he had comforted me after my worst dreams.

The echo of a memory wormed its way into my thoughts. I'd been dreaming of my mom's hand stroking my hair, but I'd woken to him comforting me. Then, there'd been the dream of my mom, a memory of the very last time I ever saw her, but her lips hadn't matched. She'd been about to leave, and I'd begged her not to go. I remembered what she said in real life, that she'd be right back; but in the dream, she'd promised not to leave me. Ever.

Another one tickled my memory. I'd told my mom I'd wanted to die, and she'd told me that was no longer my choice.

All those dreams of my mom while I was coming down from the drinking, had they all been him? Had he been the one telling me to be strong and that I needed to live?

"Go on and lie down," Emily said. "Sleep while you can. I'll listen and wake you as soon as I hear her moving around."

Stunned, I crept back up the stairs and sat on my bed where I tried to reconcile the two very different sides of the same man.

I die a thousand deaths each time I harden her hate toward me.

Then tell her how you really feel.

Those two phrases circled in my head. I wasn't simple. I knew what they were both getting at. Merdon was fey-crushing on me but "acting" like my worst enemy. Shax's story about Thallirin and Merdon's exile was the only possible explanation for Merdon's behavior shifts. He'd kept me alive, using whatever means he thought necessary because he would rather lose his chance with me than see me die.

Exhaustion tugged at my mind, and I slow-blinked while curling back under the covers. What was real? Was it the few times Merdon had been nice or the majority when he acted like the world's biggest asshole? If we were supposed to judge people based on their actions, and not their words, then everything I'd just heard was a lie.

"GET UP. You've slept long enough."

The angry voice immediately penetrated my sleep. Merdon. What I'd overheard earlier rattled in my mind, and I bolted upright with wide, panicked eyes.

His scowl faded, and he dropped the crossed-armed, power-pose to squat down beside the bed.

"You're safe, Hannah."

I blinked at the feel of his hand smoothing over my curls. There it was again, his comforting touch. Was it real? My body didn't seem to care if it was real or a lie because I wanted to lean into it and close my eyes. How could he make me feel safe with a simple stroke of my hair when I also bore faint marks from wrestling around with him in the basement? I had to be insane.

His yellow-green gaze held mine. There was no anger, but neither was there affection like when Shax looked at Angel. If anything, Merdon looked guarded. Did that, then, signify he really didn't want to be mean to me?

"Hannah?" he asked when I remained quiet, his voice gruff yet gentle.

"I don't know what's real anymore," I said, feeling desperate and confused as hell.

He tilted his head at me slightly.

"This room is real. Tolerance, your home, is real. The food that Emily makes for you is real."

He'd misunderstood and was trying to comfort me, behavior that aligned with how a fey would normally act toward someone he liked. Was this the real version of Merdon?

My gaze shifted from one of his alien eyes to the other as I tried to understand the implications of what his devotion would mean. Merdon, one of the most intense, no-boundaries fey I'd ever met, wanted me.

Suspicion began to cloud his gaze the longer I stared at him, and his hand retreated from my hair.

"It's time to get up," he repeated.

He didn't say it unpleasantly like he had before, but the way he was watching me closely made me nervous. He wanted me to hate him, and my stunned mind wasn't in angry-Hannah mode at the moment. Did he know? What would he do if he found out? *Please, not more spankings.*

Instead of getting out of the bed near him, I scooted to the far side, never taking my gaze from his.

"What are you doing?" he asked.

"I'm not sure."

He tilted his head again and took a step as if to go around the end of the bed. I retreated farther, creating more distance. He paused and frowned at me.

"I should change in the bathroom, alone," I said in a rush.

He grunted and crossed his arms.

I scurried to the closet, grabbed clothes at random, and bolted for the bathroom.

With a closed door safely between us, I took a calming breath and tried to gather my wits. I was acting weird, and he was noticing. I needed to cut it out and get my act together. Nothing had changed. Emily had confirmed Merdon was here because of me, what? Three days ago? After the initial panic had worn off, and he continued to be a jackass, I'd brushed my fears aside. I'd just do that again because he wasn't trying to get in my pants and trap me for life. He was just trying to make me hate him.

And hating Merdon was something I could do with ease.

Nodding to myself, I grabbed my brush and started to work through the worst knots in my hair. The memory of his hand on the strands wiggled its way into my head. I could still feel his touch and shivered lightly.

My brushing slowed as I remembered the time he'd held me just right in the basement and set places tingling that hadn't ever tingled like that. And what about that breath-stealing, angry kiss he'd given me? Or how I'd been jealous over the easy way he acted with Emily?

What was I doing? Was I as stupid and slow as he accused me of being?

I ran a hand over my face then studied myself in the mirror, trying to objectively view the "Hannah" everyone else saw. There were dark circles under my eyes, but I'd lost some of that haunted look I'd tried so hard to not see. Eating well these past few days and exercising had put some color back into my skin. But, I still looked sick and starved and troubled. Deeply troubled.

Why was I having any kind of romantic-type responses to

Merdon when I was still so messed up in my head? And talking to someone, like Brenna suggested, had backfired completely. Merdon's response to my confession had been the opposite of helpful.

Yet, after overhearing what I had, I couldn't help but wonder if he'd answered the way he had in order to further provoke me into hating him.

"Gah, this is so messed up."

A knock on the door resonated loudly and startled me into dropping the brush.

"Are you all right, Hannah?" Emily asked from the other side. "Merdon said you're acting a little weird this morning."

"I'm fine. I just need a minute. Too much going on in my head, you know?"

"Yeah, that's not reassuring me. Can I come in?"

"Nah, I'm coming out. I'm hungry and don't want to think anymore."

I quickly pulled on the clean shirt then left the bathroom. If Merdon had a problem with the sleep shorts, he'd just need to deal with it. He wasn't in the bedroom to notice, though.

Emily waited by the hall door. A look of relief crossed her features after she looked me over.

"Sorry," I said. "I didn't mean to worry you."

"It's okay. I know you didn't sleep well last night; I heard you. Maybe after breakfast, you can take a nap on the couch."

"Not sure Merdon will be okay with that," I said, following her from the room. I hoped he would. Naptime was far preferable to mat-time.

"You never know," she said with a shrug.

And the sad truth was that I really didn't know what to expect from him.

He was waiting for us in the kitchen and watched me closely as I forced myself to nonchalantly occupy my usual seat at the island. His hair was damp, and he wore new clothes. While I was sure he hadn't been wearing the same clothes for the past few weeks, given his penchant for my cleanliness, this was the first time I'd noticed the change. Why was I noticing?

I peeked at him from the corner of my eye. Were his biceps getting bigger? Did his pectoral just twitch? It couldn't possibly be as hard as it looked. I should check later.

Shit. *No checking, Hannah.*

"I made a pre-breakfast treat," Emily said, uncovering a plate of brownies.

My stomach growled hungrily at the sight of the dark brown squares, and I quickly grabbed two. Brownies were just the distraction I needed.

"I'm in heaven," I mumbled after a big bite. Chocolate was the best way to forget man-problems.

"I figured you might be," she said with a laugh. "What about you, Merdon? Are you willing to give them a try?"

I glanced at him as he took one from the plate. God, his hands were big. I mean, I knew they were big, but I hadn't really looked at them. They were crazy big. Like cover-my-face big.

That's not the only big thing, my brain whispered. The memory of the dropped fork incident at Mary's had me flushing as Merdon took a tentative bite from his brownie.

I had to look away from his mouth. Could I be any more messed up?

"You don't like it?" Emily asked after watching him for a moment.

Resisting the urge to peek at him again, I kept my focus firmly on Emily as he spoke.

"It's good, but Mya warned Drav that the chocolate supply is limited."

I'd forgotten about her chocolate cravings. Her current pregnant condition didn't mean she could call dibs on the world's remaining chocolate reserve, though. It wasn't fair to the rest of us, including the fey who were still trying to figure out what they did and didn't like to eat.

"It might be limited, but you can still have a brownie if you want it," I said, doing my best not to look at him. "It's not healthy for humans to eat too much of it. Moderation is the key. Just don't try telling a pregnant woman that. It won't end well for you."

Emily giggled.

"Pregnant women or a woman enduring shark week. You'll be mauled by both," she added.

I grinned at her and ate the rest of my brownies.

"I should feel guilty that you're doing all this cooking and offer to give you a break," I said to Emily, "but you're a far better cook."

"Not true. Your biscuits are amazing."

"Thanks."

"Maybe you'll consider making them to go with one of the meals?" she asked hopefully.

"Maybe," I said, not wanting to sound too eager when the reality was that I'd do anything that could get me out of basement time.

The main breakfast, a filling oatmeal with enough pumpkin and seasoning that it tasted like pie, topped the brownies I'd already eaten. I scraped the last of it from the bowl and stood to carry my dishes to the sink.

The hair on my legs tickled my skin as I walked, and I cringed. General fucked-up-ness aside, how could Merdon possibly be interested in a furry-legged, she-man in the making? I double-cringed that my head went to what he thought of me. What about what I thought? When was the last time I cared about myself enough to self-groom? I used to shave my legs religiously, hating the feel of stubble.

"Any chance I could get a razor to shave before I need to start braiding stuff?" I asked Emily as I rinsed my bowl.

Silence met my question, and I glanced back in time to see the pair sharing a look and Merdon shaking his head.

"Great," I said moodily. "I guess I'll just stick with long pants from now on."

"It won't be forever," Emily said, her voice laced with concern and regret.

I waved both away.

"Whatever. I better get ready or I'll be late meeting Brenna."

"No archery today," Merdon said, stopping my retreat.

Turning, I forced myself to look at him.

"What? Why not?"

"You're not ready. We'll practice in the basement."

The idea of rolling around on the mat with Merdon sent a jolt of panic through me and reignited my flush.

"Isn't there something else we can do? Something outside? Something that doesn't require touching?"

He tilted his head at me again. Crap. Could he hear the way my pulse was hammering? My palms grew sweaty.

"You're teaching me how to avoid being bitten, right? Isn't running the best option? How about I just go for a run around Tolerance?"

He shook his head slowly and then started toward me.

I retreated a step.

He moved faster.

I squealed and tried to bolt up the stairs.

His arm wrapped around my waist, and a moment later, I was draped over his shoulder in defeat. The position gave me an up-close view of how his pants hugged his perfectly shaped backside.

I rubbed my face and lifted my head to look back at Emily pleadingly.

"I'll make something good for lunch," she promised.

"No, find something for me to do that will keep me out of the basement."

Merdon swatted my backside sharply. I winced at the sting and at the way his hand lingered for just a fraction of a second after making contact. Had all those spankings been a way to cover up his secret desire for an ass grab?

A full-body flush consumed me, and I tried to fan my face as he descended the steps.

As soon as he reached the bottom, he set me on the mat. I bounded away from him, shaking my head to dislodge my thoughts. I needed to redirect them. This wasn't the time to start thinking about all the touching that was about to go down. Nope, definitely not the time.

"I can do this." I bounced lightly on my feet. "I can focus. Just focus. We're fighting. Nothing to it."

Merdon blinked slowly as he watched me.

"Do you still not know what is real?"

Great. Now he thought I was even crazier.

"Nope. You're real. The spankings are very real. And the bites suck. I'd rather avoid those. Got any new tips for me?"

"You're acting strange."

I stopped moving so much and gave him a pathetic look that truly reflected how I felt on the inside.

"I know. I don't know what to do about it. I'm trying, and it's not working."

He studied me for a moment then got into his "get ready for me" crouch. My nerves ratcheted up a notch, and I glanced at his pecs then his hands. My thoughts drifted back to touching, and I struggled to dislodge the topic with a new one.

"I was serious about the tips," I said as I copied him and tried to focus. "And about the running. The only reason I've avoided any of your attacks so far is because you are purposely being slower, and you're not using all your strength. You've said time and again that I can't depend on pain. Obviously, that's because pain doesn't register with the infected. So half my dirty moves are out. Wouldn't the smart thing be to work on my cardio so I can outrun them and avoid any bite-defense moves altogether?"

I listed to the side and dizzily realized I'd missed a few breaths during my nervous word spew.

"Focus, Hannah," Merdon warned.

A small "eep" escaped my lips as he launched himself at me. I should have moved, turned and run, or maybe executed my drop and roll number. Instead, I stood there like a deer in headlights. He brought me down to the mat, his body pressing the front of mine and his teeth grazing that sweet spot right over my collarbone.

I lifted my hands like I was welcoming a lover's embrace. He jerked his head up at the first touch of my fingers to his hair. My skin tingled where his mouth had been, and I licked my lips as I stared up at him.

His gaze flicked to my tongue, then his weight disappeared from me.

"Again," he said angrily. "This time, try."

Breathing hard, I scrambled to my feet.

"I'm sorry. I'll try."

He blinked at me then slowly got into his ready crouch.

"Remember, brace your forearm against my throat to keep my mouth away from you."

"What about your hands?" I asked as I attempted the same prepared position.

"What about them?"

"If you're trying to bite me, and I use my arm to stop you, what will your hands be doing?" My mind pictured some pretty intense petting with a bit of mild groping. "I mean, if you were an infected," I added quickly.

"I will try to move your arm."

"Right. You'll touch my arm. Got it."

He came at me again. I managed to get my arm up like he'd shown me, and my hand gripped his shoulder. But the feel of the muscles under my fingers distracted me. My grip slipped to his pectoral—it really was as hard as it looked—as he hooked a leg behind mine and brought me down to the mat again.

I landed with an oof, the feel of his chest ghosted my palm. His teeth nipped the back of my arm, which was closest to his mouth. There was no fancy tingle with that, just the stinging reminder that he was taking this seriously even if I wasn't.

His weight disappeared, and he jerked me to my feet.

"Again," he barked.

I nodded and watched him closely. His weight shifted to the left foot a moment before he came at me. I tried to spin away, but he caught me by the hair and tugged me close. Instead of blocking him with a forearm at the throat like I was supposed to, I brought my hands up.

My fingers grazed the column of his throat, and I became hyper-aware of the contact. The texture of his smooth, hard skin drew me in. It took a moment to realize I'd stopped trying and he'd stopped attacking.

Shit. I was staring at and petting his neck.

"Sorry," I mumbled, turning away. My cheeks were burning as I shook out my hands, trying to dislodge the feel of him. It wasn't working. What was wrong with me?

Hands settled on my shoulders, and I froze as my heart hammered in my chest.

I could hear him inhale deeply by my ear. He was smelling me? *Please don't smell how turned on I am,* I thought.

"I can go take a shower if I stink. I don't mind," I said rapidly.

His hold on my shoulders tightened, keeping me from running, and he turned me to face him. That spot he'd bitten tingled in time with my pulse.

His gaze swept over my flushed face, and he leaned in menacingly.

"What game are you playing?"

CHAPTER TWENTY-TWO

I COULDN'T BREATHE. I COULDN'T THINK. HE WAS TOO CLOSE, AND I was picturing me riding his face like Angel had suggested.

"I don't know," I stuttered. "I didn't get enough sleep. Nothing is making sense. I'm trying, but my head's not cooperating."

"Try harder. This isn't a game."

"Right," I agreed with an emphatic nod.

He didn't let go as he continued to scrutinize me with his narrow-eyed stare. The persistent heat from his hands on my shoulders seared its way into my awareness. How was I supposed to do this with him for hours? I'd never make it.

I needed space.

The answer to my need came with the ringing of the doorbell.

"I'll get it," I called.

I tried to bolt for the stairs, but Merdon's tight grip held me in place. His expression turned cold and angry, and I wanted to groan.

"Things are about to get really hard for me, aren't they?"

As soon as the words escaped my lips, I regretted them.

"I mean, you're going to be more ruthless now," I said,

growing flustered and fidgeting under his hold. "Did Emily turn up the heat? The basement feels warmer, doesn't it?"

A flicker of confusion showed on his face before disappearing.

"Whatever you're trying to do, it won't work," he said lowly.

I was saved from more. This time by Emily's voice.

"Brenna's here," she called from upstairs. "She wants to talk to Hannah."

I couldn't contain my hope as I stared up at Merdon.

"Go," he said. The soft menace and promise in his eyes let me know that I'd be paying for this escape later. I didn't care. Free, I bolted for the stairs and arrived at the top of them, breathless and perhaps a little wild-eyed.

Brenna adjusted her hold on her bow, her gaze flicking behind me before settling on my face.

"Everything okay?"

"Yep. Yeah. Yes. Everything's fine."

Her gaze briefly shifted behind me a second time.

"You sure? Because when we talked last, I was under the impression you were going to meet with me this morning to practice some more."

"Merdon wouldn't let me."

Oh, I knew I was stirring all sorts of trouble up with that comment, but it was the truth. And, it was worth it. No way was I going to lie and further enable whatever plans he had for me.

"Wouldn't let you?" she parroted.

This time her gaze stayed focused on the spot behind me.

"Are you keeping her here against her will?"

I couldn't help myself. I looked over my shoulder at Merdon. His angry gaze held mine.

"Yes," he said. "Yesterday proved she's a danger to herself and others."

Brenna snorted.

"Yesterday proved that she's a human with very human emotions. We're all dealing with some crazy shit. Not all of us were stolen away to the safety of your precious caves and spared from the hell of our world falling apart."

She looked at me.

"Do you want to hurt yourself?" she asked.

Guilt hit me hard.

"I might have in the past, but I don't want to anymore."

She nodded, no judgment in her gaze.

"And do you want to hurt anyone else?"

"Merdon, sometimes, but it's only when he bites hard."

Brenna's gaze narrowed slightly on Merdon.

"Go get dressed, Hannah. I'll wait for you."

I fought not to grin as I fled upstairs. There was no way Merdon would stand up to Brenna because she was part of a package deal, and Thallirin wouldn't take kindly to Merdon trying to boss around his woman.

It only took a minute for me to put on pants, toss my hair up, and throw on a sweater. Brenna was still by the door, glaring at Merdon when I returned.

"All set," I said, noticing Emily's worried expression too late to dampen my chipper tone. "I'll be back in time for lunch. Promise."

She nodded, her gaze shifting to Merdon. Brenna noticed.

"You're welcome to come with us," she said.

"No, that's okay. I have stuff to do here. I'm planning to take a few things to Tenacity later, and it'll need a bit of coordinating."

"The cookies?" I asked.

She nodded.

"I'd love to help. If I'm allowed to go with you." I looked pointedly at Merdon. "Am I?"

He stared at me, his expression impassive.

"Of course you're allowed," Brenna said. "A trip to Tenacity sounds fun. I think I'll join in."

"Perfect." I grabbed my coat. "I'll see you guys later."

Brenna held the door for me and closed it behind us as we left.

"Your timing couldn't have been better," I said with a grin.

"So I gathered. Does Merdon often keep you from leaving?"

I lost some of my humor.

"He did the first few days when I was going through withdrawals. Once those were over, he let me out but always keeps a close eye on me."

She was quiet for a long moment.

"My mom drank a lot after the accident. She wanted to forget the pain and what she'd lost," she said. "It's a tempting solution, at first glance. But a person never really forgets, you know?"

I did know. Even when I was drunk, I still knew why I was drinking. My sins were always there in my head, condemning me. The alcohol just made me care a little less at the time.

"I tried what you said," I said, changing the subject. "Talking about stuff didn't help."

"Since I just mentioned that yesterday, I think it's a little premature to decide if it was helpful or not. Especially if you tried with someone in your house. Not sure those two are the right crowd."

I wasn't sure anyone was.

We walked toward the practice circle in silence until Brenna swore under her breath.

"What?" I asked.

"He's already there."

"Who?"

She gave me a troubled frown.

"Merdon. Who else?"

I shrugged lightly.

"Fey follow women around. It's just what they do."

She stopped walking and grabbed my arm.

"They don't try to trap them in their houses or bite them."

"Yeah, the normal ones don't. Merdon's not like the rest. But then, neither am I." I gave a slight shrug, his words from yesterday echoing in my head. Merdon was right about me not wanting Shax's level of nice. But a little bit of nice wouldn't hurt.

No, wait. What was I thinking? I didn't want nice from Merdon at all.

No fey. No way. Yet, I'd broken all the rules that were meant to keep me happily unattached. Was there even a chance that I'd escape the fate that Merdon had planned for me?

"Given the state of the world, the odds aren't in my favor that I'll live to see my nineteenth birthday," I said, thinking aloud. "The chances of me still being single until then are even slimmer. What would you say those odds are?"

"If you stay here? You're as good as claimed already. If you move to Tenacity, maybe you'll be able to stay single. Is that what you want?"

"What I want and what I need might not be the same."

She gave me a small smile.

"It's smart of you to recognize that. But, no matter what you think you need, no woman ever needs abuse. And I'm worried that's what you'll get if you stay here."

I gave her concerns serious consideration.

"I don't think so. I think Merdon's giving me the distraction that I need right now while I try to figure out how to deal with everything that's going on in my head."

"There are better ways to distract someone." She indicated her bow. "And he's stopping you from that."

I grinned at her.

"Is he? Because I'm on my way to practice with you, and he didn't try to stop me once you said I was going."

She sighed and released my arm.

"The fey are far too pushy," she said.

"I agree. But not with women they don't consider their own. You can be my muscle, and I'll be yours if you ever need it."

She snorted.

"Thallirin is a pushover, for the most part. All I need to do is hint at what I want and I get it. Even the freedom to make my own choices about going on supply runs and guarding the walls. Granted, he sticks to me like glue, but I don't mind that anymore. He's saved me too many times to poo-poo his protectiveness."

She made it sound nice and far from clingy. Could Merdon be like that? Give me freedom and distance? I watched him as we approached and somehow doubted that. Merdon would likely be my worst nightmare. Bossy and demanding. Why did my heart stutter at the thought of that?

Ahead, I saw that Merdon wasn't the only one waiting for us. Angel and Shax were already there, too. Before shame and guilt over the previous day's flip out could slow my steps, Angel spotted us.

"Hey, girls!" Angel said with a happy wave. "We ready to shoot some more dicks?"

"I don't like the way you smile when you say that," Shax said from beside her, sending her into a laughing fit.

I couldn't help grinning at his worried frown. When Angel wrapped an arm around his waist and patted him reassuringly, he seemed to forget his worries and bent to kiss her temple in response. It was sweet.

My gaze slid to Merdon, who was standing in all his glorious disapproval off to one side, watching me with an indecipherable expression. Some of my humor faded, and I wondered what he thought of me shooting at dicks. He probably liked it, the sicko. I smirked, and his gaze narrowed in response.

"Ready?" Brenna called.

Angel and I both nodded, and Brenna picked up two bows that were leaning against the plastic pile.

"One for each of you," she said, handing the slightly shorter bow to Angel.

I looked at the one she gave me, impressed by the carvings along the shaft.

"This is beautiful. Who made it?"

"Who do you think?" Brenna asked before launching into instruction.

My gaze slid to Merdon again. He wasn't looking at me. Instead, he watched Brenna demonstrate stance. Holding the bow he'd made for me, I did my best to focus on Brenna as well. It wasn't easy when my mind kept going back to this morning's question. Who was the real Merdon?

As soon as Brenna was done, Angel and I stepped up for our turns.

"I'm so glad Brenna talked you into coming back," Angel said as we took aim. "I don't know about you, but another day spent watching movies might drive me insane."

She released with a twang and groaned when the arrow missed the melted rainbow pile completely.

"I wouldn't mind a day of movies," I said. "Nothing but couch time and buttery popcorn sounds like a dream."

I exhaled and watched my bolt fly true to embed in the plastic.

"You're good," Angel said with a shake of her head.

"I think it's luck," I admitted. "Not something that usually applies to me."

"I disagree. You're here, right?"

I was, but I would never call that luck. I'd call it a combination of fate's cruelty and my unforgivable selfishness.

"Focus," Merdon barked.

I scowled at him.

"I am. I hit the target, didn't I?"

"Do it again."

"Pierce a dick, and prove you're a pro," Angel said with a wink.

"I like that you miss, Angel," Shax said. "Dicks shouldn't be pierced."

"Oh, I don't know about that. If you had a Prince Albert paired with a pubic piercing, I'd never want to leave our bed." Angel tipped her head and pointed to her ear. "The piercings I'm talking about are like the one in my ear. My ear still works and looks pretty with it."

Shax stared at her a moment.

"We would have more sex if I pierced myself?"

The horror-filled hesitation in his voice contradicted the hope in his eyes. She laughed.

"Don't worry, baby. It would take a professional body piercer to do that, and as far as I know, that's a skill that was lost with the quakes."

His disappointment and relief were laughable.

"We're going to Tenacity after lunch," I said. "I can ask around to see if anyone has any experience."

"Whatcha heading over there for? Need any help?"

"Not sure about the help, but you're welcome to come," I said. "Emily is planning on visiting some of the single ladies. She wants to put in a good word for the fey and drum up some volunteers for their dinner dates."

"I heard about those. If you need an extra set of hands, I'm a decent cook. And I'm a great fey interpreter if things ever get awkward."

She looked at me hopefully while Merdon watched us with his stoic stare.

WITH THE BOW in my hand, I ambled back to the house, taking my sweet time without trying to make it obvious.

Brenna was letting Thallirin know her plan to visit Tenacity with Emily and me. Shax and Angel would meet us at the wall after lunch. That meant I had at least an hour to waste. While I knew Emily would have something for us to eat, I didn't want to leave any extra time that Merdon might be compelled to fill with basement activities.

He hadn't said a word to me since telling me to focus, and that worried me. His silence was like the lull before a storm. And, I had no doubt there'd be a storm eventually. I'd escaped his plans for me this morning because of Brenna's intervention, and I'd likely do the same for the rest of the day. He wasn't going to like that. Even now, I could feel his angry stare boring holes into my back.

My spine tingled with the need to look over my shoulder.

When I gave in, he glared at me suspiciously. Given that I'd been looking back at him every thirty seconds, I could understand his mistrust. I quickly faced forward.

The house loomed ahead, too close for my comfort. Tucking my hands deeper into the pockets of my coat, I looked back at Merdon again.

"Any chance I can go look at the cows?"

"No."

"Why not?"

"Because you need to eat."

"I will eat."

"You need to tell Emily that Angel wants to help and that she and Brenna are going to Tenacity with you. Or did you not think of Emily when inviting the others?"

I narrowed my eyes at him, hating what he was hinting at. Yet, he was right. I'd put my need to get away from Merdon before Emily's feelings about her dinner dates project.

Staying the course, I headed for the house. Emily opened the door before I reached it.

"How'd it go?" she asked. The hopeful light in her eyes lanced me with guilt.

"Really well. Brenna's impressed with my aim and says I might have some skill. You should come with me tomorrow." I leaned the bow against the wall, hung my jacket, and kicked off my shoes before following Emily to the kitchen.

"I think I'll stick with baking and let you learn all the dangerous stuff."

"Shooting a bow isn't dangerous."

"What you shoot at would be."

I laughed.

"You know we're shooting at that pile of melted dicks, right?"

She cringed and glanced at Merdon.

"No. I didn't."

"Angel was having a good time. Shax isn't a big fan of the target, though."

Emily slid a plate toward me. It was a simple grilled ham and cheese, yet I knew there was nothing simple about it.

"Bread? Ham? How?"

She grinned.

"The bread was pulled out of a working deep freezer, which is now in the supply shed to help store all the stuff they've been bringing back. So was the ham. The cheese was in someone's fridge. It's part of one of those fancy wheels fully encased in wax."

"I really hope that someone knows how to make cheese," I said after swallowing my first bite. "And I really hope those cows cooperate."

"It wouldn't hurt to ask around about what people can do." Emily looked off thoughtfully. "It'd also be smart to make a list of everyone's skills. I'm sure Matt already started something like that since he knew that Cassie was going to school to be a nurse. We should ask him."

I nodded, amazed how Emily was always thinking about the next thing that would help make everyone's lives better. And there I was, just thinking of ways to avoid Merdon and my own misery. James's words came back to haunt me. I really didn't like who I was these days.

Merdon nudged me.

"Eat," he ordered.

I realized I'd stopped and took a bite. As I chewed, something clicked into place. His barked orders always came when I was lost in dark thoughts.

I paused mid-chew to look at him. Even though he was eating, he wasn't focused on his sandwich. He was focused on me. I'd rarely seen him otherwise.

"What do you think?" Emily asked. "It's called a grilled ham and cheese sandwich."

"It's good. Thank you," he said.

Courtesy. Kindness. How many times had he reminded me to show her the same?

"It's so good," I echoed. "Hey, Em, would you mind if Angel and Brenna tagged along with us to Tenacity? I think Angel's bored and desperate for a way to contribute. When I mentioned the dinner dates, she was quick to offer her help cooking or with the fey to human communications."

"Sure," Emily said. "The more the merrier. I have about five stops planned. Between the cookies and the extra supplies, it'd be good to have a few more hands to help carry everything."

I gave her a relieved smile.

"Good. They'll be ready to meet us by the wall as soon as we're finished."

Emily hurried us through the rest of the meal with her excitement, and we were out the door a few minutes later. Merdon carried a large box crammed with supplies and plated cookies in zip-seal bags.

"Hey, Tor!" Emily called, waving at the fey who was lingering in the street. "You ready?"

He nodded and fell into step with our group.

I wasn't sure we'd waited long enough for everyone else to do what they needed, but Brenna and Thallirin were already by the wall along with Eden and Ghua.

"Heard you're going to Tenacity," Eden said. "Mind if we come along?"

"Not at all," Emily said. "It'll make this a lot easier."

We all understood what she meant when she started handing out the supplies we had to hold while the fey carried us. Angel and Shax arrived before she finished. When the couples started pairing off, Tor came over and picked up Emily.

"Thank you so much for volunteering to do this, Tor. Just remember to keep smiling like you usually do," Emily said to him before they disappeared over the wall.

Holding the supplies she'd given me, I glanced at Merdon, who stood nearby.

"I'm going to have a hard time hanging onto all of this if I'm upside down over your shoulder."

"Do you want to be over my shoulder?"

The way he said it sent all sorts of thoughts through my head. Mostly of the last time he carried me that way and rubbed my butt after he spanked it. A flush started at the back of my throat and climbed to my cheeks.

"I think that might upset Brenna."

He moved closer, eating up the space between us.

"Does it upset you?"

"Sometimes." The word came out a mere whisper.

He tilted his head, studying me, then picked me up and jumped over the wall. The sudden change in elevation made my stomach clench. He touched down and immediately started running. His speed intensified the cold wind whipping my hair and numbing my face. Turning toward his chest, I found refuge and warmth. And something else.

His scent filled my nose.

How did he smell so good? It wasn't soap or sweat; it was just him. Breathing deeply, I relaxed into his hold. His fingers twitched on my arm and thigh, and my pulse spiked in response. He knew I was smelling him.

I closed my eyes and tried not to think. That just made everything worse.

It didn't take long before that feeling of rising and falling had my stomach flipping. As soon as Merdon landed on the inside of Tenacity's wall, he released me.

"Are you ready?" Emily asked. She looked at me, Angel, Brenna, and Eden.

"For what, exactly?" Brenna asked.

"The goal is to try to convince as many single ladies as we can into volunteering for a dinner date with a fey. The cookies are to open doors, and the canned goods are a thanks for hearing us out. No strings attached. We don't want to give the message that they'll only get food if they say yes to dinner. But we do want them to know they'll get a great meal if they say yes. Again, no strings attached one way or the other. We don't want anyone to feel like she's being forced into spending time with the fey for food."

"We're here to be a dating service?"

We could all hear the disbelief in Brenna's tone.

"No. We're here to help improve human relations with the fey. They're more than just guards. They're lonely people with feelings, who are being shunned just because they're different. The dinners are just one way to help people see past those differences."

"I think I'll take Brenna with me to see Matt," Eden said. "I've been meaning to ask him about the last batch of new people. I need to make sure there's no one else I know."

Brenna paled slightly.

"Yeah. I'm going with you."

She handed off the food she carried and quickly split with Eden. It only took two stops to wish I'd done the same. But, I remembered this wasn't about me. It was about Emily and, more largely, the fey. So, I forced myself to stop staring longingly out the window at Merdon and Shax and focused instead on the conversation at hand.

"Tor is just one of the fey interested in testing out his conversation skills. You'd be helping fey like him learn how to interact with us. As a way of saying thank you, we will fix a meal for you to enjoy."

The girl in question side-glanced at Tor, who flashed her a close-lipped smile. He really was good looking, and one of the nicest fey I knew. I didn't understand why the woman was being so standoffish.

"It's not a marriage proposal," I said, my patience slipping. "It's dinner and conversation. If you're not interested, you're not interested. Enjoy the cookies and canned goods." I stood. "We have at least three more stops to make before we have to head back to help Mary with the next test dinner. What's on the menu tonight? Beef Pot Pie with bread pudding and brandied custard sauce for dessert, right?"

I knew I had the woman when she quickly lifted a hand to stop me. Thankfully, she hadn't noticed Emily's panicked look when I'd stood.

"Wait. I'm not saying no. Is that really what you're making?"

"Me? No. It wouldn't be nearly as good as what Emily and Mary make. Trust me when I say you don't want to miss one of their dinners. I had a grilled ham and cheese for lunch that made my taste buds sing, courtesy of Emily. The cookies are hers, too."

The girl looked at the empty plate of cookies she'd inhaled. A full dozen. She was going to be regretting that gluttony later. Or maybe not if she had roommates.

"Okay," she said finally. "Sign me up. But, how am I going to get there?"

"Don't worry," I said. "We'll send a fey around when it's your turn."

"When will that be?"

Emily looked down at her small notebook with an excited smile.

"How does next Tuesday sound?"

CHAPTER TWENTY-THREE

"I can't believe it worked," Emily said, yet again.

I swallowed my mouthful of lobster mac and cheese topped with buttered panko crumbs and waved my fork in the direction of my plate.

"I can't believe there was any hesitation on their part after sampling your cooking. Those women just needed a push in the right direction."

"Thank you so much for being that push." Emily looked at Merdon. "Wasn't she amazing?"

He grunted and continued eating. My stomach flipped nervously, which I tried to ignore. I'd successfully avoided having any time for Merdon's version of training and hoped to keep it that way. Just a few more hours to go.

After my last bite, I executed an exaggerated stretch and yawned loudly.

"What a long day. I think I'm going to shower, read a book, and turn in. I'm beat."

Emily frowned.

"Already? I don't think it's even seven yet."

I shrugged.

"Early day tomorrow. The girls and I are meeting up for practice as soon as it's light because Angel wants to check in with Mary around lunchtime."

"If you're sure," Emily said. "Do you have a book or need a new one? I have several in my room if you want to borrow one."

"I'll grab one," I said, already hurrying from the kitchen.

I didn't think of Emily's locked door until I tried the knob and it swung open freely. Her room, like mine, was devoid of any personal effects. The curtains were open wide to let light in, and her large bed was neatly made.

Going to the bookcase she'd added to the room, I quickly perused the titles she'd collected. Her reading tastes ranged from horror and paranormal suspense to cozy mysteries and sweet romance and everything in between. There was plenty of selection. I just wasn't sure what I was in the mood for.

One title caught my eye. *Dealing with Demons* by Melissa Haag. Grinning, I plucked it off the shelf and moved closer to the window to read the back.

"No, Hannah," Merdon barked.

I looked up in confusion at Merdon, who stood in the doorway.

"Now you're going to tell me what I can read?"

"Stay away from the window."

I rolled my eyes.

"I'm not trying to get out the window. I was just going to read the back of this." I held up the book.

He flicked on Emily's bedroom light, temporarily blinding me.

"Stay away from the window," he repeated.

I blinked at him, toying with the book I held. I knew he

wanted me to stay away from the window because I'd scared him. If I wanted any freedom in my future, I needed to reassure him that wouldn't happen again. More importantly, I needed to give him a reason to believe me.

Crossing the room, I approached him with my heart thundering in my ears. My fingers were steady as I placed them on his chest and looked up to meet his gaze.

"I jumped because I thought there was nothing left. That there was no other way to escape my guilt and shame. I can't say I'm glad you stopped me because you've been a pain in my ass ever since. But I can say that I've learned a lot since then. Life isn't meant to be easy or pain-free. We all have regrets and mistakes we're trying to cope with. I wasn't coping before, but I'm trying to do that now."

His fingers circled my wrist and plucked my hand free of his chest.

"Go."

I didn't understand why there was a low warning in that single word, but I listened to it and hurried to my bedroom. He didn't bother me as I got ready for bed or when I sat up, reading the book. It was good, really good, and spoke to that tormented part of me that I'd been trying to ignore. It also affirmed what I'd said to Merdon. We all had issues. Even the fictional versions of ourselves.

THE HANDS of a dozen infected were holding me down, and I fought with everything I had to free myself as I screamed in desperation.

"Hannah, you are safe." The firm words penetrated the

remnants of the dream, and I untangled myself from the restraining sheets.

Panting, I looked around the room wildly.

"You're safe," Merdon repeated, reaching out to run a hand over my hair.

A full-body tremble shuddered its way through me, and I leaned into his touch hard before I came to my senses and scrambled from the bed.

I held up my hands as he stood, a shadow among shadows.

"No, I'm good. I'm fine." The hitch in my voice said otherwise.

"Hannah, you have one minute to tell me what's wrong before I throw you over my shoulder and take you downstairs where we will stay until you talk."

"That sounds a lot like you're asking me if we're going to do this the easy way or the hard way?"

"Because I am."

I groaned and turned a slow circle, shaking out my arms.

"Why do you always have to push so much?"

"You need pushing."

"Do I? How do you know? What if I just need some quiet time?"

"You had quiet time before bed. It didn't help. You're still acting different."

I stopped turning and sighed.

"Different. That's a nice way of saying freaked out that all my freedom is going to be stripped from me forever."

He tilted his head at me.

"What do you mean?"

"I mean you. I heard what you said to Emily in the kitchen. This isn't just some fey crush. You have your sights set on me. *Me.* You've staked your claim and chased all the other fey away while my head was swimming with all my glorious narcissism. I didn't see it, but now I do, and I want it to stop."

He stood and stalked around the bed. I crossed my arms stubbornly, holding my ground now that I'd said my piece.

"Your freedom has already been stripped away from you forever," he said softly. "You are mine, Hannah. No more running. No more hiding behind your past. You are mine."

My bravado left me with the intensity of his words.

"No. Not me. I'm too messed up." My nose tingled a second before the first tear slipped free. "Pick someone normal. I'm mean, remember?"

"I like mean."

My pulse gave a jump, and I guiltily acknowledged that I wanted him to want me just as I was. Faults and all. I couldn't change my past, and I didn't want to let him go so he could find someone better.

"Are you sure?" I asked, sniffling.

"I want you with every breath and beat of my heart. But I've seen how you use other fey. I won't be used, Hannah. You will not manipulate me."

He wiped one of my tears away and gripped my chin.

"I'm going to sit down, and you're going to come to me like you should have in the first place. If you don't, we go downstairs. Do you understand?"

His attempt to intimidate me was far too successful because I could barely inhale, never mind speak.

"Do you understand?" he repeated with soft menace when I didn't respond.

I nodded jerkily.

"Good."

He went to his chair and sat like he'd said then watched me

tensely, an angry, challenging light in his eyes. Did I want to fight him? Yes, but not in the dumb basement. I hated basement time. Not only did it physically exhaust me, but all of the touching confused the hell out of me now. Yet, sitting in his lap would do the same.

I'd hesitated just a little too long because he started to rise. With a startled yip, I scrambled onto his lap. He grunted, probably in pain because I wasn't being careful, then settled into the chair, wrapping his arms around me.

A shaky exhale escaped me the moment his hand stroked my hair.

"You're safe," he said again.

From infected? Yes. At least, I was for now. But was I safe from him?

Definitely not.

I woke in my own bed, alone in my room, well after dawn. Yawning, I forced myself to get up and brush my teeth. If I didn't hurry, Brenna would likely show up at our door again.

Finding the energy to move any faster than a crawl was impossible, though.

Every time I'd tried to climb off of Merdon's lap to return to my own bed during the night, he'd tightened his hold on me. I'd finally given in to sleep after hours of fighting it. And drifting off in Merdon's arms had been sublime.

I was in so much trouble.

Finished in the bathroom, I threw on something warm and went downstairs. Emily was sitting at the island alone.

"Morning," I said. "Where is Merdon?"

"He left."

I let out a relieved sigh and sat next to her.

"Be easy on him," she said. "He's struggling too."

I snorted.

"How exactly is he struggling? He's always getting his way."

She gave me a long look as she got up and went to the oven.

"He told me that he talked to you about how he feels."

"Uh...that's not how I recall last night's conversation. He told me he wanted me but that he wouldn't let me manipulate him." I tiredly rubbed my hands over my face. "And that was after I started crying because I told him he should pick someone else. He's told me repeatedly that the other fey don't want me because I'm mean. It's like he's being stuck with me. I don't want to be someone's last resort. I want to be wanted for me as screwed up as I am."

"You're not screwed up, and you're not mean. You're dealing with a lot and just need a little help, time, and understanding. He's giving all of that to you."

I gave her the best what-the-fuck-are-you-talking-about look I could muster.

"He's helping you stay sober and keeping you distracted. He wants you but isn't acting on it because he knows you're not ready. And even when you have a moment and lash out, he doesn't get upset. He knows you're hurting."

I stared at her as something else clicked into place. Merdon wasn't the only one giving me help, time, and understanding.

"So, is there any chance that you like him back?" she asked after a moment of silence.

"Do you really think it's smart for me to like anyone when I still hate myself most days?"

"Yes. Because before Merdon, you hated yourself every

second of every day. Now, there are moments I see the real you showing through. The girl before the quakes. If Merdon's the reason for that change, hang on to him and don't let go."

I looked down at the plate she set before me.

"You didn't know me before the quakes."

"No, but I'm guessing that back then, you didn't walk around with a haunted look in your eyes while you tried to hide behind a beautiful smile. In these last few days, you've changed. A lot. When you smile now, it's real. And I'm positive that's who you used to be."

I took my first bite of the homemade cinnamon roll and almost died.

"Screw Merdon. Marry me, Emily. Be my bwife."

"Bwife?"

"Baking wife. You're too talented for your own good. Some fey is going to take a bite from the wrong dish, and you'll be hidden away in some house, feeding him all day long."

She giggled.

"Unless I start serving raw meat, I doubt I'm in danger. But because you're so sweet, here. You get a second one."

I inhaled every last gooey crumb then licked the plate, which she quickly grabbed from me.

"That's gross. Go grab your bow and get out of here."

I grinned, sucking the sweet residue off my fingers as I left the counter.

"Please wash your hands before you touch that pretty bow."

"Yes, Mom."

She grinned at me, and I scrubbed away the gooeyness before grabbing my hand-carved bow and headed out the door for practice with the girls.

The sun was shining, the wind just warm enough for me to

smell a hint of spring on the air, and the snow was melting from the blacktop. A great day to be outside. Soaking it in, I smiled at a few of the fey and hurried toward the meeting spot.

Merdon was already there, leaning against a house not too far away.

"Sleep in?" Brenna asked.

"I'd hardly call this sleeping in," Angel said with a yawn.

"You're the one who wanted to meet this early," I said.

"Next time, remind me how much I didn't like it." She grinned and lifted her bow. "I'm ready to be deadly with this thing. Or, at least, look intimidating as hell before my target figures out that I can't hit a thing."

"Hannah, see if you can pick up from yesterday. I'm going to work with cupcake over here."

"Cupcake? Well, I like you too, Brenna," Angel said with a wink at the girl.

"I can hear the cellophane crinkling when you move. You're probably not hitting anything because you're afraid of smooshing your food."

Amused by their banter, but not letting it distract me, I focused on what I wanted to hit, waited for the wind, then exhaled, and released. I missed, but not by much. Leaving the bolt where it struck, I tried again. And again. And again, until my arm cramped with strain and I had to take a break to stretch. Merdon and Shax were gone.

When I looked over at Angel, she was eating a cupcake.

"What?" she asked. "The baby was hungry."

I rolled my eyes. "I'm not fey, and I'm not buying."

She grinned.

"Shax doesn't buy it either, but he doesn't try to stop me from eating. He likes that I'm getting rounder and that the baby kicks when I'm well fed."

"Maybe the baby is kicking you to tell you to stop," Brenna said with a smirk.

"Be jealous, girls. I don't mind." She licked her fingers clean, wiped them on her pants, then went back to her bow.

Movement down the road caught my eye before I could do the same.

"Are they carrying someone?" I asked.

Brenna stood beside me for a silent moment.

"It sure looks that way, but something's not right. Does that person seem stiff and lumpy?" she asked.

"Are you sure you're talking about a person?" Angel asked with a snigger.

"I'm starting to notice a pattern in your conversation," I said. "It's either sex or food with you, isn't it?"

"On good days, it's both."

Grinning, we watched a trio of fey jog our way. Brenna's observation about the person over Merdon's shoulder proved correct. Only, it wasn't a person.

"Do we even want to know why you have a scarecrow?" Brenna asked.

"It's not a scarecrow. It's a knife dummy. Ryan suggested it."

"Shax, is that thing wearing my comfy sweat pants?"

"I will find you comfier ones. I promise."

She gave Brenna and me a dry look.

"He calls them my 'no sex' pants because when I put them on, he knows I'm not in the mood for 'fun time.'"

I covered my mouth to hide my grin at Shax's guilty look.

"Baby, I'm not mad," she said, sidling up to him. "But you are going to have to make that up to me. It's not okay to get rid of my pants because you don't like them. I wore those when the baby was moving around inside of me and making things uncomfortable. They gave me comfort. Something your magnificent manhood can't do when the little monster's doing its best to make me miserable."

"I'm sorry, my Angel. I didn't understand."

"I know. It's okay. You can make it up to me later."

He was so wrapped around her little finger it wasn't even funny. The sad thing was that he seemed to be loving it.

I glanced at Merdon, who was watching me closely.

"I think the real question we should be asking is, 'why do you have a knife dummy?'"

"A bow is good," Thallirin said. "It can be used from far away." He looked at Brenna. "Distance is safety. But sometimes, distance can't be kept. I want you to learn to use a knife."

My brows rose.

"A knife?" I asked Merdon.

His grunt paired with his expression spoke volumes. Yes, we'd be learning with a knife, and he didn't like it. He was worried I'd do something stupid.

"Don't look so skeptical," Angel said. "I bet this will be fun. Are you going to show us how to throw it?"

"No," all three of them said at the same time.

"We will show Brenna and Hannah how to hold it and how to use it to kill an infected."

Angel frowned.

"Just Brenna and Hannah? What about me?"

"It's too dangerous, my Angel." His gaze flicked to her belly.

"Don't be naive, Shax. Do you think an infected will be like, 'Oh, sorry, Angel. Didn't see that you were preggers. I won't chase you and try to eat your face anymore.'"

315

Brenna quickly turned her face to look at the wall behind her while Angel scowled at me.

"There's no need to be mean."

"So I've been told. But I'm not trying to be mean. I'm being honest. Learning to use a knife on an infected is a survival skill everyone should know."

"And," Angel said loudly before looking at Shax, "Hannah is right. I've had to run from infected more times than I can count. I'm getting too big to outrun anything now. Even my bladder these days."

"So didn't need to know that," I said under my breath.

"It'd be smart for me to learn something that could save us both."

She patted her stomach, and I knew she'd won without even having to look at Shax's expression. She was carrying the ultimate weapon for swaying fey thinking.

We stood back as the guys set up their dummy a fair distance away from the dildo pile. When they had it securely mounted to the rod Thallirin had rammed into the frozen ground with scary ease, Merdon removed a knife from his belt and held it out to me.

I looked at the blade glinting in the sunlight and felt guilt and fear surge forward.

"Focus, Hannah," he barked.

"I am," I snapped. "Does this mean I get my razor back?"

He said nothing, just continued to offer me the blade. I snatched it out of his palm and marched over to the dummy. Letting my audience fade from my mind, I tried to imagine the dummy was a real infected. If it were coming at me, what would I do?

I planted my left hand in its chest to maintain distance and thrust the knife upward into its stuffed head.

"Good," Merdon said.

And it was good until I tried to pull the knife free, and it snagged on the cotton batting.

Just like Katie, my mind screamed.

My lungs ceased. I released the blade as if it had burned me and stumbled back a step.

Hands gripped my shoulders. A face crowded my vision.

"Stop," Merdon said, giving me a slight shake. "You are safe, Hannah. You are here with Brenna and Angel. Breathe."

I lifted my hand, showing him the empty, clean palm.

"It stuck." The words trembled on unspent tears. "Just like last time."

He pulled me into his chest, his arms wrapping around me. His fingers delved into my hair, rubbing my scalp and playing with the curls in a soothing way.

"Leave the past," he said softly. "Stay with me."

CHAPTER TWENTY-FOUR

I LEANED INTO MERDON, SHELTERED FROM THE MEMORIES BY HIS embrace. Slowly, the panic and fear faded, and my breathing steadied.

"Better?" he asked.

I nodded but didn't pull away.

"I heard there's a fight club forming," a voice called.

Lifting my head from Merdon's chest, I saw Eden and Ghua approaching along with a few other fey. Reluctantly, I stepped away from Merdon as Angel waved and answered.

"You're at the right place. We're shooting dicks and cutting cotton. You want in?"

"Heck yes!" Eden grinned even as Ghua winced.

I stood back and let the other girls have a go at the dummy as the gathered fey gave pointers to help with technique and execution. When it was my turn again, I was better prepared mentally and managed a few slick jabs.

Knife work wasn't too difficult. Eden, Brenna, and I all had real world experience. We already knew there were only a few stab points that would work on an infected.

"We should teach them to remove the stupid ones' heads," a fey suggested.

"Not going to happen," Eden said. "Way too much strength needed and far more splash-goo than any of us can handle."

Angel gagged and held up a hand.

"No more," she begged.

"Sorry. Didn't know you were that sensitive."

"I think it was the cupcake I ate. Too gooey." She gagged again.

While Shax rubbed her back, the others debated what we should learn next.

"Hand to hand," Merdon said finally. "The infected are getting stronger, faster, and smarter. We kill the ones we find. But if we miss any, the females need to know how to face them."

His gaze slid to me.

"And they need to know how to fight in the snow and cold."

Aw, hell. Outside basement time? I thought. *At least I had more bite padding on.*

"Okay," I said. "What are the rules?"

Less than an hour later, I was panting as I watched Brenna circle me. When Merdon said "fight," I'd thought I'd be fighting him. No. Instead of the fey coming at us, they had us girls fighting each other. Even Angel got in on it, but she had special rules. Like no knocking her down because no one wanted her to go into labor yet.

"You know," she said from the sidelines. "Add some jello and fewer clothes, and we could charge for this."

My gaze flicked to the fey spectators who'd gathered and were currently cheering us on. That momentary distraction was all Brenna had been waiting for. She launched herself at me. As I fell back under her weight, I was already planning my move. Using the momentum, I kicked my legs up and tumbled us so she was on the bottom.

I snapped my teeth in her stunned face then grinned at her.

"You win," she said. "Where'd you learn to do that?"

"I've been tossed around a lot these last few days." I lowered my voice even though I knew all the fey would probably hear me anyway. "A glowing ass is motivation to learn."

She cringed sympathetically.

As the loser, she stayed in the muddied circle and waited for Eden. I gratefully moved aside and rubbed my neck. While that move had done the trick, it sure did a number on my body.

Strong hands closed over my shoulders and began to rub. I almost groaned.

"Thank you," I said, glancing back at Merdon.

He grunted.

"That was some pretty impressive work," Nancy said from nearby.

Uan held her in his arms. The pair had arrived not long ago. I was sure word was still spreading about our training sessions, given the slow trickle of fey that continued to appear.

"Thanks. I've had a good teacher."

She smiled and nodded.

"The fey sure know what they're doing when it comes to infected and fighting. I'd like to talk to you if you have a minute."

Something about the way she said that last sentence made me feel like I was about to get some really bad news.

"Uh, sure?"

I glanced back at Merdon, who seemed clueless as well.

Uan carried Nancy toward the road, and I followed. When I saw her chair ahead and a shoveled path down on the blacktop, leading away from where Nancy lived, I knew this walk had been premeditated. As soon as Uan had her comfortably resting in her chair, he jogged back to the circle of fey.

"Brenna's told me what Merdon's been doing," Nancy said without preamble. "She doesn't like it. And I agree. It doesn't sound good. But sometimes we don't need good. Sometimes, we need a wakeup call."

She propelled herself forward, and I kept pace.

"The old me would have minded her own business, but times have changed. We've changed. There are less of us to watch out for one another. So, if what I have to say pisses you off, that's fine. Tell me. But, I'd like you to hear me out."

"Okay," I said when she looked at me.

"I don't know what Brenna's said about what happened to me, but I know she told you I had an accident and I drank a lot because of it. That's oversimplified. The accident took my ability to walk, but left me alive. Not everyone who was involved was so lucky. There was a young boy. He'd only been driving for a few months. A car hit me. I hit him. He died. I didn't.

"People kept telling me that it wasn't my fault. That there was nothing I could have done differently. But, fault doesn't matter when it comes to survivor's guilt. I couldn't stop the what-ifs. What if I'd stayed home that day? What if I'd sent Russ out instead of me? Would he have been able to avoid what I hadn't? What if I'd stopped at the store first? What if I'd let the lady go ahead of me at the post office? The questions about what I could have done or should have done differently don't stop."

"Ever?" I asked.

"They fade. They become less frequent, but I still think of them. Not so much about the accident now but about what happened to Russ and Brenna because of those men."

She stopped moving and looked up at me.

"What you're feeling is normal. It's not easy. Some days it'll feel like you're tearing yourself up from the inside, but that's normal. Let yourself feel it. It's the only way to move past it. Drinking, no matter how much it calls to you—and trust me, it'll still whisper to you on your bad days—isn't the answer."

I looked off at nothing for a minute, letting what she said bounce around in my head.

"Survivor's guilt?"

"Yep. That's what my fancy therapist called it. Don't try to deal with what you're feeling alone. Talk to someone who's willing to listen."

I focused on her.

"You?"

She gave me a wry grin.

"Everyone needs a mama-bear in their corner. I'm more than willing to fill in for yours because I'd want someone to do the same for Brenna if she were as lost and suffering as you are, honey. I'm here if you need me. To listen. To tell a fey to back off. Whatever."

She reached out and clasped my hand, her grip strong.

"Thanks," I said.

She nodded, turned her chair, and headed toward Uan.

I wasn't ready to tell the world what I'd done, but knowing that Nancy understood my pain helped me feel a whole lot less alone.

"You're up," Brenna called when I got close.

The fey cheered, and I groaned.

The fey needed a new hobby.

I LAY ON THE COUCH, staring at the ceiling, my belly pleasantly stuffed from another amazing lunch. After the morning I had, I should have been sleepy. Instead, I was bored.

"If you keep sighing like that, he's going to find something for you to do," Emily warned me softly.

The "he" in question was currently absent from the house, which was probably part of my boredom. Not that I wanted Merdon annoying me. I just wasn't sure what to do with myself when he wasn't bossing me around.

"Nancy was there today. She asked me to go for a walk with her and offered to be my surrogate mom."

Emily set down her book.

"Wow. That was really nice of her."

"Yeah. Brenna talked to her about how Merdon's treating me. Nancy seemed less concerned about that and more concerned about—"

I broke off, not sure exactly what I wanted to say to Emily.

She remained quiet, waiting for me to sort it out.

I sighed and rolled so I was fully facing her.

"She talked to me about survivor's guilt. She had it with her accident and again when her husband was killed and Brenna was taken. I didn't know that was even a thing."

"Is that what's going on, Hannah? You feel guilty for surviving?"

The pain crawled in. It would be so easy to say yes and to try to absolve myself of everything. But, Nancy was wrong. She just didn't know it. There was fault. Katie was dead because I'd let her die.

"I wish the answer was that simple," I said. "But, it's not."

"Merdon's right," she said, looking at me. "When you're idle, your thoughts eat at you. As much as I hate you two fighting in the basement, it keeps you focused on things you have control over rather than dwelling on a past you can't change." She gave me an apologetic look before scaring the shit out of me by yelling for Merdon at the top of her lungs.

"Was that really necessary?" I asked, sitting up, heart pounding.

Before she answered, Merdon burst through the door. His fluid movement didn't pause as he surveyed the room and located me. His gaze swept over my face as he came to a stop on his knees before the couch.

"Did you hurt yourself?"

"No. I'm fine."

"She's not fine," Emily said. "She's doing that thing you said she does."

"What thing?" I asked.

"You lose yourself to the past," Merdon said. "The past is dark and no place for you."

He stood and extended a hand.

"Come."

I made a face.

"But I don't want to play spank-and-bite right now. My belly's too full."

"You can walk downstairs on your own or I'll carry you over my shoulder. You're choice."

I glared at him, shot Emily the same glare, then slowly stood.

"I'll walk to the basement, but know that my compliance is only under duress."

"Just get down there," Emily said. "You know you'll feel better afterward."

"Says you. You haven't had Merdon spank you yet, or you'd know that's a lie."

Neither one seemed to care about my protests as I made my way downstairs. I looked at the mat and let out a whine.

"Seriously, I'm going to get a belly ache. Had I known you'd make me do this, I wouldn't have eaten so much."

"No, you are hungry. You need to eat."

"Yeah, well, I'm going to be throwing up all that important food the first time you do that weird 'toss the Hannah' thing you do."

I turned to face him and found myself sailing through the air exactly the way I warned him not to toss me. The landing was marginally softer this time, though.

Groaning, I looked up at Merdon, who was carefully pinning me with just his hips.

"See? You didn't throw up."

"And what would you have done if I had thrown up."

"Feed you again."

I couldn't stop my grin at his absurdity. As he stared down at me, something shifted in his expression. And in his pants.

It wasn't a small twitch, either. The thick length of him grew against me, giving credence to Mary's claim of a rolling pin. He was huge. Like, bludgeon something with it, huge.

My smile faded. Teasing thoughts fled, replaced by an image of a different kind of wrestling we could do.

Gaze flicking to his mouth, I recalled the last time he'd kissed me. It'd been angry and intensely hot and had left me breathlessly confused and tingling in all the right places. Would I feel the same way if he kissed me like that again? My heart fluttered behind my ribs, and my breathing grew shallow.

Without thinking things through, I threaded my fingers in his hair and lifted my lips to his. He jerked in my hold but didn't pull away. I brushed my lips against his. They were warm and firm with slight bumps due to his longer canines.

My fingers brushed against his ear, and his hips jerked against mine, sending a rush of heat through me. And a warning. I was playing with fire.

I pulled back and looked him in the eyes.

"I don't know what I'm doing."

"I know."

"Should I stop?"

In answer, he dipped his head, nipping at my bottom lip. I returned the favor then licked the spot. He growled and pulled my hands from his hair, pinning them to the mat above my head.

I looked up at him, seeing his tense jaw and the way his pupils had dilated. Was this what Emily meant when she'd said he was struggling? Was he fighting his fey urges to bury his face, or other parts, between my thighs?

My insides clenched at the thought, and my body had a mind of its own in response. My legs wrapped around him as my hips arched into his. Cradled against my sweet spot, his hard length rubbed me just right. I gasped and went to do it again.

Except, he wasn't there.

I lay on the mat, spread out like a starfish, and he stood near the base of the stairs with his back to me. I scrambled to my feet.

"What's wrong?" I asked. "I thought you wanted that. I thought you wanted me."

He didn't say anything, just continued to stand facing away.

"What do you want from me?" I asked, my hurt and anger creeping in. "You say you don't like being mean to me but yell at me all the time. You claim to want me, but you've taken off twice now. Dealing with my everyday Hannah thoughts is confusing enough. Don't expect me to guess correctly about what you're thinking or feeling if you're unwilling to clue me in."

"I already told you," he said lowly. "I won't be manipulated."

"You think that's what that was?"

His silence spoke for him.

"It sucks knowing you think so poorly of me. I'm not trying to manipulate you. I'm just trying to figure out how I feel."

"How do you feel?"

I thought about it for a moment.

"Free. Alive."

He turned toward me, a tempest of emotions in his gaze.

"Don't toy with me, Hannah."

"I'm not. I won't."

He stalked across the room and grabbed the back of my neck.

"My patience is limited."

"I know." I grinned at the irony.

His gaze dipped to my mouth, and a moment later, I was the recipient of another of his hot, intense kisses. It robbed me of thought and air. It ignited my whole body on fire.

When he pulled away, I could only blink at him stupidly for a minute.

"For the record," I said when I could find my voice again. "I have never used my body to get my way. I knew that would be crossing a line I didn't want to cross."

"You offered hugs."

"A hug was not what I was offering you just now. You know that, right?"

He grunted and looked into my eyes.

"You can't offer what's already mine." His hands slid down my arms, prickling my skin in their wake. "I'll have what I want... when I'm ready."

He kissed me hard again then left me alone in the basement.

"PLAYING with it won't make it taste better. Just put it in your mouth," Merdon said.

If only he was talking about something else and not the food on my plate.

I gave Emily a reassuring smile.

"Dinner's amazing. I think I just ate too much for lunch."

I could feel Merdon studying me. Did he know I'd just lied? I sincerely hoped not.

"You're restless. Do you want to go back downstairs?"

My fork slowed its idle poking as I stared at him in surprise. He hadn't commanded it or said it angrily. In fact, he'd sounded downright hesitant.

"No. I think I'll go read."

He grunted and went back to eating his meal. I wrapped mine for later and fled to my room. While I might have evaded more basement time, I couldn't escape my thoughts about what had happened down there.

I paced and tried to decide how I felt about how I felt. It was crazy to be attracted to Merdon. He was too much. There'd be no getting my way in any relationship with him. Did I care? I hadn't gotten my way so far, and things were good. Well, except the spankings. I thought of the butt rub after the last one and amended even that thought.

So I liked everything he'd done to me? Not really. At least, not at the time he'd been doing them. But now, looking back, I saw his actions for what they were. An angry, intense man willing to do anything to save the woman he hoped to someday make his. If she lived long enough. And if he managed not to fill her with irrevocable hatred for him.

There'd been so many ifs in his plan when it came to the outcome of my feelings for him. But two things had never been ifs in his mind. The first was saving me. The second was that I'd be his and no one else's.

I liked that. All of it. He took care of me even when I couldn't or wouldn't take care of myself. He put my needs first. Granted, I'd be overjoyed if he'd put my wants first, but Nancy had brought up a good point today. What I wanted wasn't always what was best for me. Was I okay with giving up that control to someone else?

That was the real question. It wasn't about how I felt about Merdon but how I felt about what being with him would mean for me.

Pacing my way into the bathroom, I got ready for bed then settled in with the book. It was the perfect distraction until my door opened.

Once Merdon entered, I couldn't focus on anything but him. He looked me over then went to sit in his chair. I turned off the bedside lamp and studied him. Even in the semi-darkness, I saw the line of his strong jaw, the thick length of his thigh, and the enormity of the hand resting on it.

"Do you ever sleep while I sleep?" I asked.

"Planning on running?" he asked in return.

"No. Not anymore. I'm asking because it's not right that you go without sleep just to keep an eye on me. You deserve sleep, too."

I moved over and patted the empty side.

"There's plenty of room, and if you're lying next to me, I'm betting you'll feel every move I make. There'd be no sneaking past you. What do you say? Want to sleep with me?"

CHAPTER TWENTY-FIVE

JUST AS KATIE AND I RACED THROUGH THE TREES IN OUR DESPERATE attempt to outrun the infected, Merdon's fingers stroked over my hair and woke me. I rolled toward him, needing the comfort of his presence. His arm wrapped around my middle and pulled me even closer to him.

"I like this arrangement better," I whispered.

His hand smoothed over my back in answer.

"Will the dreams ever stop? I hate reliving what I did. I hate being that person. Mean. Selfish."

"You didn't kill your sister."

I lifted my head to look at him.

"I stabbed her. I can still feel the blade in my hand; the way it stuck in her."

"She was dead long before the knife. The infected killed your sister. Hate them. Stop hating yourself. Then the dreams will stop."

I laid my head back down.

"I killed her by running. I should have—"

"No," he said firmly.

"If you'd died in her place, she likely would have died alone shortly after. You weren't mean; you were surviving. Let go of the blame and the hate for yourself."

"I'm not sure how."

He grunted and continued to run his hand over my back. I exhaled heavily and soaked up the feel of his chest under my cheek.

"How do you live with your past?" I asked.

"I stay busy and do what I think would make Oelm proud."

I closed my eyes and tried to believe what he was saying. Would Katie have died on her own? With sorrow, I acknowledged she would have. After all, she'd died because she hadn't been fast enough. We both hadn't had the survival skills. We'd started developing those out of necessity. If the RV group hadn't found me, I would have died on my own. Hell, I'd almost died with them.

Yes, I'd left my sister behind. But it wasn't that decision that killed her. The infected had killed her. And our ineptitude.

If Katie were there right now, would she forgive me? I sniffed against Merdon's chest, knowing I'd never have that answer. I realized that whether my past choices were right or wrong didn't matter. What mattered was I hated that I'd chosen myself over her, and I needed to figure out how to forgive myself for it.

Merdon was gone. It shouldn't have surprised me, given he'd been letting me wake up on my own most mornings now. But I'd hoped I'd wake up snuggled against him instead of alone.

Motivating myself to move, I grabbed clothes and shut myself in the bathroom. When I showered, I saw a razor waiting for me. I stared at it with a growing smile. Shaving would be nice. The trust that razor represented was even better.

It took me a lot longer than usual to get ready for the day; but when I emerged, I felt surprisingly like the old Hannah. The one from before the quakes. Relaxed. Happy. Ready.

With a bounce to my step, I headed downstairs and found Merdon and Emily having a quiet conversation at the kitchen island.

"Morning," I said with a smile.

Emily stared at me.

"You look..."

"Amazing? Well-rested? Ready to make up for skipping last night's dinner?"

"Happy."

"I kind of am. Thank you to whoever left the razor. I feel transformed." I looked at Merdon. "Basement time's going to get trickier now that I'm more aerodynamic."

Emily snorted. Merdon didn't look very amused. He didn't look angry, either. He seemed rather indifferent.

I frowned.

"What's wrong?" I asked.

"I'm leaving."

"What? Why? For how long?" I could feel my panic rising. Whether he'd meant to be or not, Merdon was my anchor.

"I don't know."

"No. You don't get to just up and leave. Remember all that dominant male chest beating you did? I'm yours and all that bull? You're here for me. You stay for me."

He gripped my shoulders.

"I did not beat my chest. You are mine. And I am leaving. You will be here, just as you are, when I return. Do you understand?"

I stared up at him, my gaze trying to read his. He was afraid. He didn't want to leave.

"Don't go," I whispered.

"We are both strong and will do what we must. Make your sister proud."

He leaned in and pressed a kiss to my forehead then left.

I stared at the front door, dumbfounded.

"What just happened?" I asked, looking at Emily.

"I don't know. He was a little quiet this morning, but I figured it was because he was tired." She looked a little sheepish. "He told me he slept in the same bed with you last night and it was everything he'd hoped it would be."

"Then why in the hell would he pick today to leave? Did I drool on him too much or something?"

She shook her head and gave me a clueless shrug.

"Whatever. I don't have the headspace for his games. I'm going to go practice."

"Oh, no you don't," Emily said in a scolding voice. "You barely ate dinner and now want to skip breakfast? I don't think so. Sit."

It wasn't just annoyance in her gaze when I looked at her, but worry. I quickly sat.

"Sorry. I forgot. But I promise my stomach would have remembered before I made it a block down the road. Please tell me it's another cinnamon roll this morning."

Her expression relaxed a little.

"No. It's baked oatmeal. I thought you could use something with a little more energy after hearing what practice has turned into."

"You should come with me today. Just to spectate."

"Maybe I'll stop by. We'll see how much time I have. Mary and I are doing the final preparations for tonight's dinner date."

"Tonight's the first one?"

She grinned.

"Who is the lucky pair?"

"Newaz and Mila," she said.

I recalled Mila was the next Tuesday girl.

"Does that mean today's Tuesday?"

"I have no idea. But it sure sounded official, didn't it?" She grinned. "I sent Tor over with a handwritten note to expect her escort just before sunset."

"Before sunset? How is she getting home?"

"Mary and I went back and forth on that. These girls are hungry, and we want them to know that these dinners aren't just a hookup."

"Even though they are," I said teasingly.

She inclined her head at me.

"But we don't want them to feel that way. So, the note explains that it'll be a long dinner and to pack an overnight bag. It stresses that she would be staying over at James and Mary's place as a guest and would be provided breakfast before the fey takes her back home. I said that if any of it makes her uncomfortable, the fey would return her at any time with a full escort so she would be safe."

"No one's going to want to be outside the walls after dark."

"Exactly. And everyone will get two meals out of the experience."

"And get to see that people are living well and harmoniously with the fey."

She nodded.

I couldn't help but be curious about what Mila's reaction would be tonight.

"Need any help, or just want some company as you eavesdrop from the kitchen door?" I asked.

She hesitated to answer and started playing with her fork.

"It's the alcohol, isn't it?" I said.

"Yeah."

I thought about how to put into words what I was feeling about my ability to stay away from temptation.

"I drank to forget. But it was getting harder and harder to achieve that point of peace. Looking back, I can see what a mess I was. The things I did and how I hurt people. I know why you don't want me to go back to that. Honestly, I don't want to, either. Most of the time. And I know it's the 'most of the time' that's a concern.

"You and Merdon can't be with me every second of every day. Especially now."

I glanced at the door, missing him and wanting him back. Emily set down her fork.

"I know that. He does too."

"Good. I feel better now, up here," I said as I tapped my head, "than I did back then. Nancy told me I'd be tempted to drink again, and I think she's right. However, I think I'm in a place where I can walk away from that temptation. And I'll be with you and Mary and James, and we'll all be very focused on something distracting and, hopefully, upbeat."

"I really want you to be there. I just don't want to jeopardize all the progress you've made."

"And I don't want my past problems to put a damper on what should be a crowning achievement for the matchmakers of Tolerance."

"Okay," she said decisively. "You're in. I'll feed you lunch then let you wash up. After that, you're my assistant."

Happy, I finished the oatmeal, which was amazing, and headed to practice. The sun shone like the day before. The wet drips from snow melting from roofs could be heard all around. And it smelled like spring. I knew not to believe it. Spring was a fickle tease like that, whisking in and out with the northern winds. But it still gave me hope that the world would warm and turn green again soon.

Shax and Ghua waited with Brenna, Eden, and Angel at the practice area. I caught the tail end of Brenna's comment as I approached the girls.

"I just hate when they go off on their own."

"Who?" I asked.

"Thallirin and Merdon."

"Where did they go? Merdon was pretty close-mouthed about it all."

"I don't know. Thallirin just said they were going to hunt."

"They are looking for infected," Shax said.

"Yeah, Mya and Ryan were talking about how it's not natural for us to be infected-free for so long, especially when the traps Ryan's been encountering during his supply runs are growing worse," Eden said.

"Worse how?" I asked.

"The infected are hiding in places, waiting for the group to split up, trying to take out the trucks so the humans can't leave. Stuff like that," Brenna said. "It was intense before I took a break from it. I can't imagine what it's like now." She looked troubled for a minute. "When Thallirin's back, I might go on a few more supply runs just to see."

I couldn't help but look at her like she was crazy.

"Why on earth would you want to do that? You just said it was worse."

"That's exactly why. I'd rather leave the protection of the wall on my terms, and know what the state of the world is, than try to hide from it and have the truth forced on me."

"Like breach day," I said.

"Exactly."

While her logic made sense, the idea of willingly stepping outside the walls still made my insides quiver. There was so much out there. And, Merdon and Thallirin had just run off into it by themselves.

"Do you think they'll be okay?" I asked.

"You both have nothing to worry about," Angel said. "Thallirin and Merdon are survivors and will be just fine."

"Less talking and more practicing," Shax said, looking pointedly at me.

"Why didn't Shax go with them?" I asked after sticking my tongue out at him.

"He's afraid of missing the pez dispenser action," Angel said, patting her belly. "This will be the first birth ever for the fey."

"That's still weeks off, right?" Brenna asked.

"Yep. But Shax's still worried. We've talked to Cassie all about the birthing plan, which will probably include him breaking down their door, pulling Cassie from her bed, getting hit in the face by Kerr for touching Cassie, Cassie's kids screaming in terror at the commotion, and me giving birth all by myself."

"I will be calm, my Angel," Shax said. "I swear."

Angel looked at us with an instigating smile.

"He's totally going to be a fainter."

Eden sniggered.

"That's why I've okayed a few other fey to be there. If we can manage to summon Cassie in a reasonable manner, she's going to leave the kids under fey watch and bring Kerr with her. Shax gets to choose one other fey to witness the actual delivery."

"Three guys watching you give birth?" Eden asked. "Bless your heart."

Angel just grinned wider. "You know how they share information. I don't want to rob them of a chance to learn what getting a girl knocked up means."

"Good idea. Maybe they'll stop wanting to knock up all the ladies when they see what it's really like," Brenna said.

"Be sure to scream and swear," I added.

Angel's smile lost a little of its luster.

"You guys are making me nervous. Let's focus on practicing."

Without Merdon, I didn't push myself as hard. I still shot well, but I declined to use the knife dummy. The only thing I couldn't take it easy on was the hand to hand because Eden and Brenna wouldn't let me.

"I like Angel as a partner better," I said after landing on my back.

"Don't be a baby," Brenna said, extending her hand. "I need someone I can toss so I can practice that move you pulled on me."

"Then pick on Eden."

"She already did," Eden called from the sidelines.

Noon couldn't come fast enough. When everyone agreed it was time to call it quits and head home for lunch, I grabbed my bow and jogged to the house.

"Honey, I'm home," I said, opening the door.

"Good. I think I have everything ready. While you eat, look this over."

She set the sheet of paper she'd been reading next to the plate on the counter. Hungry, I didn't need to be told twice. I kicked off my shoes and hurried to my ham and cheese sandwich with extra mayo and sprouts.

"Seriously, how did you get sprouts?" I asked around a mouthful of sandwich. "This is fantastic. I didn't realize how much I was missing fresh green stuff."

"I've been spending a lot of time in the supply shed and noticed a bag of seeds that was labeled sprouting seeds."

"Sprouting seeds? What's that mean?"

"It means they're seeds specifically meant for eating just like that."

"So like bean sprouts."

"I won't bore you with the kind—"

"You're afraid I'll stop eating it. What is it?" I asked, talking over her.

"—but I will tell you it's good for you. So keep eating."

We had a stare off, which she won because the sandwich was that good, and I didn't want to stop eating it even if I was consuming something weird.

"How much more of this stuff is there?" I asked, finished with my first half.

"Mary and I only grew a small batch. We figured we're probably going to need all the seeds to set up food plots when the weather turns. But we have enough for me to use a little to test out some recipes."

"So, you're thinking of sandwiches for your dinners?"

"That's why you're eating one. Does the flavor make up for the lack of fancy?"

I slowly chewed my bite then nodded.

"I think it does, but you need to make sure you're serving it to someone who likes greens. You know how fussy people can be." I added that bit with a grin because I knew she'd found me fussy a time or two.

"If you like it, I think most everyone else will. But you have just given me an idea. I should probably include the menus of what we'll be serving. It might help anyone who's having second thoughts."

I shrugged and continued eating my sandwich, happy to let her think through the pitfalls while I reaped the benefits. When I was finished, I went upstairs to shower and change then helped carry supplies to Mary and James's place. Emily talked the whole way, mostly worrying about what to do if Mila decided not to show, or how she could help with conversation if things felt stifled.

"You worry too much," I said when we were just about there. "It'll be fine."

"I hope so."

THE KITCHEN WAS DEADLY QUIET. Both Mary and Emily had one ear to the kitchen door so they could hear what was going on in the dining room. The gesture wasn't necessary.

I could hear the soft murmur of conversation coming from the other room. While it flowed easily enough, the casual discussion circling the weather made it hard to know how Mila felt about Newaz.

Emily straightened, disappointment tugging at her features.

"They aren't using the cards," she whispered.

"The cards are a little personal," I said. "If you want things to get to that level, you need more wine."

She gave me a worried glance.

"Not for me. For Mila. Tipsy frees inhibitions, and you're not going to make an alcoholic of her in one night. Look how a little spontaneity helped Farco with Cheri. You know Mila will be fine."

Emily looked at Mary.

The old woman made a face.

"Don't look at me to say no. I'm all for whatever will get that poor guy laid faster."

I choked on my laughter even as Emily sighed and grabbed the bottle of wine from the table.

"Just leave it out there," I whispered.

She nodded and left. As soon as the door closed behind her, Mary focused on me. Since arriving to help, she'd slowly forgiven me for publicly laying into Merdon and had even started asking all sorts of questions about my relationship with him. The top winning question had been if I'd seen his jumbo-sized feybymaker yet.

"You should clog the drains on all the other bathrooms but yours. Then, when he's in there taking a shower, just pop in like you hadn't heard him.

"I'm not breaking things so I can sneak a peek. It's not like we have a plumber on speed dial."

"Hmm. Good point. You might just have to go with the direct approach and ask him to show you his happy stick."

"I thought it was a rolling pin."

"Oh, it'll be many things to you if you use it right."

"I think I understand why James chose to spend the evening in the basement."

Mary snorted.

"He's had fey over for days, helping him turn that into a

sanctuary. He can't even make it up and down the stairs on his own. I don't know why he bothered."

"Probably so the fey you keep peeking at have a more private place to stay."

She looked thoughtfully at the basement door, and I could have sworn I heard, "someone's getting a spanking tonight." I really hoped, for Mila's sanity, she drained the bottle before Newaz left.

Emily reentered the kitchen, her hands moving nervously.

"I think Mila's bored," she whispered.

"I'll give Newaz the signal that it's time to offer a face ride," Mary said, starting for the door. Both Emily and I made a mad grab for her.

"A what?" Emily asked.

"A face ride. Apparently, one of the fey overheard a conversation where one of the girls said someone should ride a fey's face like a horse until the girl was screaming the fey's name. Newaz wasn't sure what that meant, so I explained it to him. He's very willing. Not with me, of course."

I wanted to curl up into the fetal position on the floor for so many reasons. Foremost, was the image of Mary sitting on anyone's face. Second, was knowing it'd been my conversation with Angel that had caused this mental anguish.

"If you need to drink tonight," I said to Emily, "I'll understand."

She made a pained sound and steered Mary to a kitchen chair.

"You stay right there."

"Fine, but things would move along faster if he—"

"Mary, we're also trying to change perceptions, not just match people up. If the fey start propositioning during these meals, no one would ever volunteer to attend the next one."

"Or maybe they all would."

"Not everyone has your drive."

Mary gave Emily a considering look.

"Is that why you haven't settled on a fey? Because you have a low drive? You should consider doing a little self-discovery to get your motor going. I heard some of the dildos missed the burn pile."

Emily's shocked gaze swung to me.

"Don't look at me to jump in and save you. You've pimped me out to rolling pin man. Have at her, Mary."

"Hannah," Emily hissed as Mary chuckled with glee.

I shrugged.

"It's only fair that it's your turn."

Emily crossed her arms and gave Mary and me the same steely look.

"I started this with a single goal. To help the fey and humans live together more harmoniously because we're all that's left. If people couple up, that's great. It'll only help my goal. Until I see that goal come to fruition, I refuse to put my own wants first. That includes any kind of romantic relationship with a fey or a human. Now, stay focused. Both of you get started on dessert. We can't draw these meals out forever."

Mary got up to help me at the stove and leaned close to whisper, "Add a little extra brandy to the brandy sauce. I think Emily will need to sample it twice."

I snorted and stirred.

CHAPTER TWENTY-SIX

"THANKS FOR YOUR HELP TONIGHT," EMILY SAID, CLOSING THE DOOR behind us.

I hung up my jacket and nodded. Both our moods were a bit dejected. Hers because of the epic failure of tonight's dinner. Mine because a long night stretched in front of me with no Merdon to distract me from my thoughts.

"Do you want to watch a movie?" I asked.

"I think I'm going to soak in a lavender bath and read for a bit." She started for the stairs.

"They won't all be insta-attractions, you know. Heck, most of the fey-human couples that are together now started out not liking each other. Don't write off Mila and Newaz yet."

She glanced back at me with a tremulous smile.

"Thanks. I hope you're right. I just thought for sure they'd hit it off. Their personalities are so similar."

"Maybe you need to go for opposites."

"Maybe. G'night."

With a growing sense of desperation, I watched her leave. Nights were never easy, but I realized how all the time in the basement had made them bearable because of sheer exhaustion. What was I supposed to do now? I looked around the room then at the door.

As quietly as possible, I put on my shoes and jacket and slipped outside.

"Anyone out here?" I called softly.

Tor stepped from the shadows and jogged my way.

"Are you sad, Hannah?"

"Sad? No. I just have too much energy. Are you out here because Merdon asked?"

Tor gave me a wary look.

"Will that make you angry?"

"Depends on why he asked you to watch the house."

"He said to make sure you were safe."

"Did he say something about me being sad?"

"When you're sad, you want to hurt yourself."

I looked off into the night, not angry at Merdon exactly but definitely frustrated.

"If he knew I might get sad, why did he leave?"

I was thinking out loud more than asking Tor, but he answered anyway.

"I would not have left you, Hannah. Even if you did try to bite me and hurt my testicles."

I scoffed.

"I didn't hurt his testicles."

"Twice," Tor said. "But it was still a touch, so it was not all bad."

I shook my head at him. The fey were twisted in so many ways.

"I was thinking I'd go for a run. Will you come with me?" I asked.

"Why do you want to run?"

"I'm hoping it'll use up some of this energy and tire me out enough to fall asleep. Plus, it's good to be able to run more than ten feet without gasping for air, you know?"

I regretted those words two blocks later as I leaned over to brace my hands on my knees and panted for air.

"That was much farther than ten feet. You are doing so well, Hannah."

I rolled my eyes and wished I had the strength to knock him down.

"I KNEW I should have been there," Angel said. She looked off into the distance. "Do you think Mila is still at Mary's? Maybe I should go and talk to her now."

I shook my head while stifling a yawn and watched Eden practice her stance and draw.

"I doubt it. She wasn't too keen on spending the night last night, despite a full bottle of wine, and was pretty adamant that she wanted to leave as early as possible."

"Not with Newaz, though?"

"No. She asked if another fey could carry her home. She was nice about it, saying she knew they all wanted a chance to help females."

"Help?"

"Yep. Her words."

Angel sighed. "It's not about being helpful; it's about having a chance to impress them and spend time with them. Seriously, when are the people over there going to wake up and see that?"

"I think, on some level, they already know. They just don't want to acknowledge it."

"The dinners aren't enough, then. We need to do more."

"Like what?"

"Are you two going to spend the whole time talking, or are you actually going to try to improve some skills?" Brenna asked.

"Hold onto your tights, Robin Hood," Angel said, already waddling forward. "Your merry women need breathers."

"Breathers or snack breaks?" Brenna asked.

Since Angel had just finished a single serving sized bag of chips, Brenna and I both knew the answer to that question. At least, for Angel. The break suited me for other reasons.

Even after all the running around I'd done with Tor, who'd been a great sport about it, I'd still had a hard time falling asleep last night. I hadn't realized how aware of or comforted I'd been by Merdon's once obtrusive presence until it was gone. His absence had crawled into my dreams, twisting the memories into a hopeless cycle that had woken me twice before I gave up the pretense of sleeping.

I stifled another yawn and stepped forward to take my turn at the lumpy, rainbow target.

We worked on archery for a bit then switched to the knives and hand to hand when more fey started to gather. With so many shouting out tips and encouraging us to move faster and work harder, sweat coated my upper lip and exhaustion had me watching the progress of the sun.

While I wanted nothing more than a nap, I knew I wouldn't give in to one when I got home. I just hoped all the practice would pay off later tonight.

We called it quits just before lunch.

"My arms feel like they're going to fall off," I said to Eden.

She agreed with a groan. "Whose dumb idea was it for me to join fight club?"

"Yours," I said with a laugh. "At least you have someone at home willing to rub your aches."

"Yeah," Brenna agreed. "I'd kill for a massage right now."

There were a few startled looks from the fey.

"She doesn't mean that literally," Eden said.

"No," Angel said, looking thoughtful. "But it's a great idea."

"Um, you think killing someone for a massage is—"

"Not that. Getting massages. We're lucky because we have fey willing to rub us down whenever we want. There are a lot of other people out there who aren't so lucky."

I knew where her mind was going.

"I volunteer as a sacrifice," I said quickly. Anything that required my time helped keep my mind from dwelling where it shouldn't. And if I happened to relax while doing it? Well, that was just a bonus. Especially if I could arrange for the practice massage just before bed.

Several of the spectating fey started vehemently denying my offer, dashing my dreams, while more still stepped between me and Angel.

"You cannot kill Hannah, Angel. Killing humans is wrong," Shax said. "You know this."

Angel nearly peed herself with her laughter, and it was up to me to explain.

"I wasn't suggesting that she kill me. She was suggesting that we teach you all how to give massages so you can offer them as a service to the people in Tenacity. In order to do that, you need to learn how to give a massage correctly. I was offering to be the person you can practice on."

The no's quickly changed to a bunch of yeses. Except for Shax, who called for quiet.

"Hannah is Merdon's."

Angel dried her tears and patted Shax on the chest.

"Actually, I think we four girls are the perfect volunteers to start because we belong to someone else. The fey who are learning will be more aware and respectful of how they are touching us."

Shax was already shaking his head.

"The type of massages I'm suggesting wouldn't be like the massages you give me. No happy ending, okay? Just gentle pressure to relieve stress and tension like when I work too hard after these practices."

He grunted and seemed to calm down.

"We will talk more about this at home."

I was a little bummed I wouldn't be able to get a massage right away but waved my farewell and told Angel to "call me" when she was ready. She laughed and promised she would.

Emily was in a flurry of activity when I got home, and the house smelled like heaven.

"The fey found yeast," she said without preamble. "A lot of it. Mary knows a ton about bread making. I just helped her mix more dough than I ever thought possible. Because we're cooking the dinner there, I brought all of the dough here so it could finish rising and we could bake it."

My mouth watered at the idea of bread fresh from the oven.

"What can I do to help?" I asked, already kicking off my shoes.

Mary didn't just know things about bread, she possessed some kind of powerful voodoo, too, because the bread that came out of the oven several hours later was pure magic.

"Stop stuffing your face and help me wrap this one up," Emily said with a laugh. "We need to get to Mary's for tonight's dinner."

We left a few loaves cooling on the stove and wrapped the rest to carry with us. They warmed my arms and teased my nose as we walked. It didn't matter that I'd already eaten half a loaf. I wanted more.

Unfortunately, not all the loaves made it to Mary's house, so I had no hope of a second round of gluttony. Emily had given several loaves to the fey we encountered along with directions of where they were to be delivered.

"But why?" I asked as the third to last loaf left us.

"Because if people taste what we can do, I'm hoping a few will be interested in taking up the task. It's a skill that more of us need to learn."

"You mean, you hope someone will step up to be a full-time baker for the community?"

"Exactly. There are so many idle hands right now. Angel's idea about teaching the fey how to provide a non-sexual massage is a great one, but it's just the tip of the iceberg. We need to think bigger if we want to become self-sufficient. We need a bakery."

Emily had been more than a little intrigued when I'd retold that morning's events. Angel's suggestion had sparked an explosion of ideas in Emily's head. She seriously wanted a list of everyone's skills to determine what roles people could fill, and she wanted to find out what the skill levels were so she could determine what kind of cross training needed to happen.

A fey jogged past and gave us a friendly nod. Emily smiled and said hello then turned on me with an urgent expression.

"And people who know how to sew. Clothes that fit will make the fey appear less intimidating."

I looked around at all the fey. Most of them wore items that were too small.

"I don't think they look intimidating. They look two seconds away from pointing the direction of the nearest beach, though."

She snorted.

"Look further south for intimidation," she said from the side of her mouth.

I did, and my mouth popped open a little. The fey who no longer wore his leather leggings had opted for cotton joggers, likely because the material stretched more than jean. And jeans in fey sizes were nearly impossible to find. That meant the fey's one-size-too-small pants were plastered to the impressive lengths of his flaccid meat stick.

"If you look too long, it moves," Emily said, elbowing me in the side.

Averting my gaze, I tightened my hold on the bread.

"Why did you have to show me that? I was walking around in a beautiful state of ignorance."

"Ha. No, you weren't. You're the one who pointed it out to me when we first got here."

Well, that explained why I couldn't remember. My drinking had been escalating hard by then. I shifted my thoughts away from drinking.

"So a baker, a tailor, and what else?"

"We already have a doctor, but we should maybe talk to Cassie about taking someone under her wing." Her expression lit up. "That'd be perfect."

"Talk me through your epiphany."

"Kerr's already learning things because he's her assistant. The fey aren't squeamish. I mean, obviously, right? They rip off heads like it's nothing. If Cassie can teach another fey, because I don't think Kerr would be willing to leave Cassie to do house calls, we'd have a fey doctor who could help treat humans at Tenacity."

"Anyone sick over there would probably just ask for Cassie," I said.

"They get what they get," Emily replied stubbornly.

"I think it's a good idea. Not the forcing who they see part but getting people to learn different skills. You're right that we need to think bigger. Someone who knows how to care for animals and to watch over them would be good, too. Maybe, someday, even a butcher?"

Emily nodded. "Now you're thinking."

Mary was already busy in the kitchen when we let ourselves in with the remaining bread.

"It looks beautiful, Emily," she said. "You've got the touch."

"We should find out who else has the touch," she said. I tuned them out as she explained her growing plan to not only integrate the humans and the fey but to cultivate important shared skills that would give the fey and humans purpose beyond surviving. And a skilled workforce was something we desperately needed once the pre-existing food supplies ran out.

"The fey are plenty strong to plow fields," Mary said at one point. "Hung like plow horses, too. If they're willing, we'd never run out of wheat even if we couldn't use tractors."

I shook my head. No wonder Emily was noticing fey dicks. She was hanging around Mary too much. That older woman's fascination with male parts was concerning.

They continued to brainstorm as they worked on the dinner for the lucky couple. The cream of asparagus soup, which would be served to start, was thawing in its jumbo plastic bag. A pot roast with root veggies already waited in a crockpot and would be served as the main meal along with Emily's fresh bread. I sat at the table, happily licking out the pot from the pie filling for the pecan pie Mary just put in the oven.

"Maybe you shouldn't have too much of that," Mary said. "The sugar might keep you up again."

"Again?" Emily asked.

"Tor said Hannah had to go for a run last night because she couldn't sleep."

"Hannah, why didn't you tell me? I would have stayed up with you and watched a movie."

I finished licking my finger, cursing Tor's big mouth, and rolled my eyes at the pair.

"Sugar has nothing to do with my inability to sleep. And I did ask if you wanted to watch a movie, but I can't expect you to stay up half the night with me."

That was Merdon's job.

I frowned at that random thought.

"Besides, Tor seemed more than happy to keep me company. After he unintentionally mocked my feeble lung capacity, he came up with his wish list for his dream date."

Emily gave a rueful smile.

"He's so excited for these dinners." Her humor faded. "What if I'm just getting their hopes up?"

"One rocky date doesn't make this a hopeless effort," I said. "Stop killing the odds before they have a chance to do it themselves."

Mary chuckled. "They seem to have a knack for putting their foot in it. Such sweet men, though. I wish the Whiteman people would be more open-minded." She patted Emily's cheek. "Don't give up on this. What we're doing is important. And your idea about doctoring and Angel's idea for massage is good, too. If we keep at this, Whiteman will be opening their arms and legs to the fey before they figure out what's happening. You'll see."

I gave Mary a look that Emily caught. She stifled her laugh and agreed with the older woman.

"You're right. There's no point in making it this far and giving up now. What's left to do for dinner?"

We had everything ready by the time the doorbell rang.

"I'll get it," I said quickly.

Emily wasn't fast enough to beat me to the kitchen door, and I grinned in triumph.

"Fine," she said. "But tomorrow night is me."

The door swished shut a moment before I reached the entry and let Sain and a very uncomfortable Jackie in.

"Hi, Hannah," Jackie said. "Can I walk now?"

"Absolutely."

Sain, the fey carrying her, looked a bit crestfallen that he had to give up his shiny new toy. Unfortunately, Jackie saw his reluctance as clingy, unwanted fascination, which I understood too well.

"Sain, remind me to take you up on a lift tomorrow after practice. I should have asked for one today. Everything still hurts."

"I will remind you," he said, putting her down.

"What practice?" Jackie latched onto the conversation, as I'd guessed she would, and moved closer to me.

"Yeah, the fey are teaching a few of us girls some survival techniques. You know, in case we're ever chased by an infected again. I think I'm getting pretty good. What do you think, Sain?"

"You're good at knives. Eden is better at evading. Brenna is the best with the bow."

"I'm going to tell Angel you left her out," I teased.

"Angel is good at snacking."

I laughed.

"I'm so telling her that." I turned and started leading the way to the table. "Did you find anything on today's supply run that you'll be able to use to bribe yourself back into Angel's good graces?"

I pulled out the chair for Jackie, something Sain was supposed to do. He didn't bat an eye at my "slip" though. Rather, he continued to focus on me as he considered my question.

"Do you think she will like more of those cakes?"

"Yep. But do you know what would really get her? Candy bars. Any kind. Any flavor."

"Yes, I have those, too."

"Wait," Jackie interrupted, "You have candy bars?"

"I'm betting he has a whole bunch of stuff stashed at his house. They're stockpiling in case they end up with a roommate. They know we humans like our food."

I patted my tummy.

"Speaking of food..." I rattled off the menu for the night, poured her a healthy glass of wine, not missing Sain's watchful gaze, and hurried to the kitchen.

"You didn't let him pull out her chair," Emily admonished once the door closed behind me. "They've all been practicing that."

I waved away her concern.

"I gave him something better. I helped him seem interesting to Jackie and less desperate and clingy."

Emily considered me for a thoughtful moment then sighed.

"Why didn't I see that?"

"Because, like them, you're trying too hard. Now, let's hustle out some soup instead of drawing it out and making this meal as uncomfortable as last night's."

As I'd hoped, Jackie's natural impulse for self-preservation had kicked in through the course of the meal, and she'd asked Sain if she could see his house before he returned her to Mary's later. We all knew that Jackie was interested in a tour because I'd gotten him to talk about his food stash in front of her, but Emily and Mary didn't care.

While they were still in the kitchen, cleaning up and celebrating with a few drinks, I wandered the roads, not yet ready to go back to the empty house. The alone time gave me a chance to think. This time, my thoughts weren't entirely centered around me.

I couldn't help but dwell on Jackie. She was probably staring at Sain's hoard of food and asking herself if shacking up with a fey was worth it. The old me would have said, "hell no," and educated her in all the ways she could get what she wanted without putting out. The new, healing me saw things a little differently. Probably because I was missing the hell out of Merdon and trying desperately not to think about it.

The man had forcefully wedged his way into my life when I'd been too sick to take notice. When I had noticed, I'd protested in mean and angry ways and received a lot of well-meaning lectures by people who'd made valid points. The fey weren't bad, and they weren't asking for much. Just our time and maybe a little consideration for their loneliness. In return, they gave us everything. Food, clothes, shelter, and safety, all at the risk of their own lives without hesitation.

I'd taken all that they'd offered in the beginning because I'd needed it. I'd given back my time and attention, never intending to delve deeper than platonic with any of them. Likely, Jackie would find herself doing the same. However, the need to survive wouldn't diminish the feelings that would evolve on their own. Rather, it would probably fan the flames. It had for me.

A cow shifted in the shadows nearby, and I nearly screamed.

"Do you want to run again tonight?" Tor asked.

This time I did scream, smothering it to more of a startled yip. Even terrified, I knew better than to make too much noise.

"Sorry, Tor," I said, noting his startled expression. "You came out of nowhere, and I was lost in thought. I think I'll pass on the run for now. My legs are sore from last night."

He grunted, looking disappointed. I could feel his loneliness echoed in my own.

"Want to walk with me for a bit?"

"Yes."

He fell into step beside me.

"Do you know when your date night is scheduled?" I asked.

"It isn't yet. I'm waiting. Newaz held out the chair and didn't talk about her pussy, but Mila still did not like him. He thinks he should have just asked if she wanted to ride his face like a horse until she screamed his name. Do you think that would have worked?"

I died a thousand deaths on the inside but managed to keep a straight face.

"No, sweetie, I don't think that would have worked. It seems to me that all our relationships start a little rocky. Look at Drav and Mya. They were the first, right? Did she fall into his arms and declare her love for him at first sight? No. She ran. He persisted. That's what you guys are really good at. Calm persistence. You just need to make sure that doesn't turn into stalker clinginess. No girl wants that, ever."

He gave a frustrated sigh.

"The list of what females don't want grows, but there is very little on the list of what they do want. Food and for us to leave them alone. How does that help us?"

I patted his arm.

"It doesn't. The best advice I can give you is to be yourself, but don't act desperate."

"That is what Angel told Shax, too. I hate lying. I am desperate. I want what Uan, Shax, Drav, Kerr, Byllo, and Ghua have."

"Don't forget Thallirin," I said unhelpfully. "He seems pretty happy now, too. And his relationship also proves my point. Another rocky start, there. Don't lose hope. There's a girl out there somewhere for you."

"But when will I find her?"

CHAPTER TWENTY-SEVEN

I PAUSED AT THE INTERSECTION AND LOOKED UP AT TOR'S frustrated face.

"You've lived a thousand lifetimes in those caves and only a few months on the surface. So much has happened in those few months. You discovered women. Learned you're compatible with them. And, there's a high probability you can spread your immunity from infection to them. While I know all that is front and center in your every waking thought, it's not in ours. We humans are living in terror of starvation, infection, and being eaten by hellhounds. It's hard for us to think romantic thoughts when we're so filled with fear, you know?"

He considered me for a long moment.

"I did not consider that."

I hadn't either until it was happening to me.

"Give humans some time. The longer we spend with you, though, the more we'll start to see what each of you offer."

"What's that?"

"A future," I said, thinking of Merdon.

Brenna and Tasha's quiet voices drew our attention.

"What are you two up to?" Brenna asked, seeing me with Tor. "More running?"

I looked at Tor.

"Did you need to tell everyone about our midnight run?"

"I didn't. I only told Shax and Newaz."

Rolling my eyes at him, I answered Brenna.

"No running. Just walking around. It's too quiet at the house."

"Yeah, mine too. Want to come hang out with us? Tasha agreed to a sleepover to keep me company."

I looked at the younger girl, smiling and happy, and felt a stab of pain and guilt.

"Yes, we would love to hang out," Tor said.

Brenna smirked as I shot him a look.

"It's no big deal if you'd rather pass," she said. "You can still come with, Tor."

Tor's torn expression had me sighing.

"If I don't go, you can't go. Am I right?" I asked.

"I promised Merdon I would watch you at night. Shax and Emily are keeping watch during the day."

Of course they were.

"Come on, Tor," I said, not having the heart to deny him the company he craved so much. "You can study us as we have a girls' night. Maybe you'll learn something useful."

I WOKE WITH A START, smothering my scream. It didn't matter that I knew I was inside Tolerance's walls or safely in my house surrounded by wandering fey. I still looked around my room, searching the shadows for infected, or worse, my sister.

My gaze landed on the chair beside my bed. Impulse had me

pulling back the covers. I needed comfort, but there was none to be found in a vacant seat. I curled into a ball and remembered I was alone. Merdon had left me. Why, just when I'd started to need him so much?

Listening to the thunderous beat of my racing pulse, I tried to tell myself it would be okay. Empty shadows couldn't hurt me. Yet, the dark corners of my room weren't the only thing I feared. How long would the chair beside my bed remain unoccupied? What would I do if he never came back?

I closed my eyes and tried to think of something else. Anything else.

The evening I'd spent with Brenna and Tasha rose to my mind. We'd watched a movie and enjoyed some popcorn and soft drinks. It'd been so normal, something I would have done with my own sister, and it hadn't hurt. Instead, I'd watched the occasional flicker of devastation that flashed in Tasha's eyes between her smiles. Unlike me, her smiles weren't faked moments of joy. She was finding what happiness she could. But, like the rest of us, she was hurting from all that she'd suffered. Her grandfather had been killed by the men who'd tried to take her twice, according to the fey rumor mill. Would that have been Katie's fate if I'd died in her place? I shuddered to think it.

Unable to go back to sleep with those thoughts circling in my head, I got up and went downstairs to watch another movie. By the time it ended, the sun kissed the horizon, and scuffles of noise from upstairs told me Emily was awake.

She didn't seem surprised to see me on the couch when she came down.

"Rough night?" she asked.

"Yeah. As usual. When do you think Merdon will be back?"

She paused in her process of pulling out ingredients for something and gave me an odd look.

"Missing him?" she asked.

"Yeah. I don't get it myself, but I'm missing him like crazy. Staying busy is the only thing keeping me sane."

She was quiet for a moment.

"Do you think you love him?"

"Love him?" My tone said the idea was crazy, but the way my heart raced and the wave of heat that engulfed me from head to toe made me stop and think.

"I don't know," I said after a moment. "Everything is still so confusing. My dreams. Being alive. It doesn't make sense to fall for someone right now, you know?"

"If he were a human, I might agree. But he's fey. When he leaves these walls, you don't have to worry about whether he's coming back or not. Why wouldn't you want to fall for someone who's that stable?"

"If he's so stable, why'd he leave?"

And I knew that was only part of the issue.

"Why, when I'd just started to feel things for him?" I asked softly.

"I don't know, but the hurt on your face makes me want to kick him in the nuts. I don't regret letting him in, though. I haven't agreed with most of his decisions when it came to you, but he's been so good for you, Hannah. Let's be patient and see what he says when he comes back. And if a nut-kicking is in order, I'm your girl."

I snorted a laugh and helped her throw together a quick oatmeal bake.

"What are we going to do if he is the one for me?" I asked, leaning against the counter. "Does that mean you and I need to stop being roommates?" Most of the single fey had their own houses in preparation for the females they hoped to have one day. Merdon didn't, and I had a feeling that meant he planned to stay here.

"I think Merdon won't care, either way. I mean, you remember how they dropped their pants in front of us all by the lake, right? And how they tell each other everything? They don't hold to modesty and privacy like we do."

"What about you?" I asked. "Would you want to stay here?" I didn't quite manage to keep my feelings out of my tone.

"Yes, I want to stay," Emily said, coming around the counter to hug me tightly. "I'm not ready to leave you, and I'm glad you're not ready either. But when you are, you can tell me to take a hike, and I won't mind at all because that'll mean you're happy. That's all I've ever wanted for you."

I could feel that pre-cry tingle in my nose and quickly pulled away from her.

"Good. It's settled. Merdon can move in, but he gets to sleep on the couch until we decide how hard to kick him in the balls."

She let me escape to practice and promised to have lunch ready when I got home.

Outside, the air had turned colder again, but I didn't mind. Two warmer days in a row had been enough to melt the snow from almost everything. Avoiding a cow pie in the middle of the street, I made my way to the practice lot and waved to the girls already waiting for me.

I smiled at Tasha's tired yawn.

"How late did you guys stay up?" I asked.

"Brog saw you and Tor leave last night and knocked on the door to ask if he could watch a movie with us, too," Brenna said.

"Then one fey multiplied into twenty," Tasha said.

"Heard you introduced them to some zombie movies," Eden said.

"Yep. Only the comedy ones."

"Because she thought I'd be scared. Like the movies are any scarier than real life," Tasha said, rolling her eyes.

"Hey, girls!" Angel called from Shax's arms as he jogged toward us. "Heard you all had a party last night."

"Yep," Brenna said. "Party at your house tonight."

Shax said no as Angel said yes, and we all laughed.

Brenna didn't let us stand around for long, though. We stretched and settled into what was becoming our morning routine. We paired off for archery and hand to hand. I was with Eden, and Tasha paired with Brenna while Angel sat on the side and ate her first snack of the day.

I couldn't say I was getting any better at anything, but given it'd only been a little over a week since my first archery lesson, my progress seemed reasonable. I still missed about fifty percent of the time when it came to the bow, and hand to hand saw me on the ground just as often as the other girls. But I was getting smarter with my moves. And I was reacting faster without having to think things through. So that was something.

I was already thinking of a nice long soak in Emily's tub when Brenna called for the first break of the morning.

"Thank God," Angel said. "I'm starving."

"You just ate an hour ago and barely did anything," Eden said.

"You try growing a baby. It's hard work."

While we rolled our eyes, the fey who'd slowly gathered all shouted out offers to get her something to eat.

"Whoever said licorice sticks, I want those," Tasha said.

A fey jogged off, happy to oblige her.

"Is he really going to get me some?" she asked Brenna hopefully.

"Yep." The way Brenna looked at Tasha with a sad tenderness had me turning away from the pair.

Both Brenna and I had normal childhoods filled with holidays, family gatherings, and whatever food we wanted. Tasha would never have that. She'd never have a normal first kiss or senior prom. She'd never graduate from high school or go off to college. That she was so excited over the possibility of what should have been a simple sweet treat broke my heart for her, and Katie...for the innocence of the lives they'd both lost even though one still lived.

"I wouldn't even care if it was a little dirty," the girl said.

"It won't be," Brenna said, wrapping her arm around the girl's shoulders. "These guys find the good stuff."

Tasha grinned, her anticipation-filled gaze remaining fixed on the direction the fey had run.

"Do you want anything to eat, Eden?" Ghua asked from his place on the sidelines.

"Nope. I'll be fine until lunch."

When she glanced at me, I caught a hint of something more to that conversation in her eyes but knew better than to ask. Not right then, anyway.

"Want to do a girls' lunch at my house?" I asked.

"Yes." Her quick answer confirmed that something was up. I knew Emily wouldn't mind the extra company especially if it involved a story. I wouldn't quite call her a gossip, but she sure liked to know what was going on in people's lives. That's why she and I got along so well.

Tasha let out a happy noise then a groan.

"That's not him, is it?" she said.

Brenna's smile grew.

"Nope."

I looked and saw two fey jogging our way. Their silhouettes were unmistakable.

Thallirin and Merdon were home.

My heart leapt, and I hungrily watched for the first glimpse of Merdon's face as he neared. His gaze locked on mine. I smiled, and unable to hold still, took a step in his direction. The closed expression on his face shifted a little, and I could have sworn his lips tipped at the corners ever so slightly before the hint of happiness disappeared again.

I wasn't sure if that glimpse was enough to save his balls.

Brenna let out a little squeal and jumped up into Thallirin's arms when he reached her.

My greeting for Merdon was more subdued.

"You're back," I said when he stopped before me.

"I am."

"I think I'm mad at you for leaving in the first place."

"Why?"

"Because I missed you, you idiot. There was no one there for me at night."

"I was there," Tor said. "We went jogging, remember?" He focused on Merdon, who still watched me. "You are right that she forgets things."

"I didn't forget," I said. I looked at Merdon. "But it wasn't the same. The chair was empty. What was so important that you had to leave?"

A terrifying sound reached my ears before he could respond.

A soft mewl.

I stepped back as he withdrew a small kitten from inside his shirt and held it out to me. It couldn't be more than a few weeks old.

"You left to find a cat?" I asked.

"I left to find you hope."

I stared at the small puff of grey fur and recalled our conversation about cows and chickens. He'd left to find me a reason to live because I was his new reason to keep going. Lifting my gaze to meet his, I felt myself melt a little further for the man.

"It's yours," he said, still holding it out. "And there are more animals where this one was. We couldn't carry them all, but we will get them for you."

"I'd trade my candy for a cat," I heard Tasha whisper.

I looked at the young girl.

"You can have mine," I said.

Her mouth dropped open. She looked equal parts excited and guilty.

"Every kid needs a pet," I said, assuring her. Then I looked at Merdon. "I'm having all the feelings right now because of this gift, but I can't accept it. I'm allergic to that kind of animal. Like throat-closing, red, watery-eyes, gasping for breath kind of allergic. Thank you so much for finding it, but it needs to go to someone else. And you need to take a shower so I can give you the hug you deserve."

He looked down at the cat, at me, then passed it off to Tasha.

"I'll take a raincheck for lunch," Eden said. "Go help him clean up."

I nodded, not taking my eyes from Merdon, and grabbed my bow.

"We will leave at first light," Thallirin said. "There are many animals. We spoke to Drav. He will send Ryan and trucks so we can get the creatures quickly and return the same day. We will need thirty volunteers."

"Can I go?" Tasha asked Brenna while already snuggling the cat to her face. If I tried that, my face would look like a marshmallow within a minute.

"We don't have any cat supplies here, and I'm betting there are some where they found it," Tasha added.

"We'll talk to Mom, but I'm sure she won't stop you from going if that's what you really want," Brenna said.

"I do," Tasha said, kissing the top of the kitten's head.

"Are you serious?" I asked. Mine wasn't the only shocked face. Eden looked equally concerned.

"This is the world we live in," Brenna said. "Hiding from it won't help us survive it. Besides, there will be thirty fey to keep us safe."

"Us?" Thallirin echoed.

"I'd rather be with you than home alone, waiting," she said. "It sucked being left behind."

He pressed his lips to her forehead. That was it. End of discussion. The fey were going to let those two go with them? Out there beyond the wall where anything could happen?

My gaze locked on Tasha. I could feel the tightness in my chest growing.

"Come," Merdon said. The command in his voice cut through my growing panic.

"She can't go," I said. "You know she can't. It's not safe."

"Hannah, what do you think we're doing here? An apocalyptic version of aerobics class? We're learning skills to survive an increasing threat. It doesn't matter where we are. Out there? In here? The risk follows us because the infected are after *us.* Don't let yourself believe for a minute that these walls are what's keeping us alive."

I could feel it, the panic from the woods the moment I'd realized Katie and I would die. Brenna's words echoed what I'd said to James over two weeks ago. Only then, I hadn't been sure I wanted to live when I'd realized my imminent death. Things had changed, though.

"Hannah," Merdon said sharply.

I turned on him.

"I'm not a dog. Stop trying to command me."

"And I just held a cat that will make you not breathe if I touch you."

"I don't see how the two are related," I said.

"You're upset, and I cannot physically remove you from what's upsetting you. Let's go home."

I stared at him a moment, then glanced at Brenna.

"Let your mom know I want to talk to her before she makes up her mind."

Brenna nodded. I could see she was worried, but not for Tasha. For me. She'd seen my breakdown. She knew I had some kind of baggage. And she'd obviously connected Tasha's desire to go outside the wall with that baggage. How could she not? I'd been close to freaking out again.

"How do you always know?" I asked Merdon as we walked away.

"Because I know you."

I believed he did. And I thought, just maybe, I was starting to understand him.

"Thank you for going out to look for animals, but you didn't need to do that. You've been giving me hope all along. Little bits that I don't think either of us noticed."

He grunted and glanced at me like he wasn't sure what my angle was.

"What do I need to do for you to start believing I mean what I'm saying? That it's not some game or ploy to manipulate you into getting my way? Because I don't like how those speculative looks of yours make me feel. It's annoying, and I have enough crap on my plate to deal with. I thought I've always been real with you."

He was quiet for a moment.

"You have. But is it because I won't allow you to treat me as you have the others or because you don't want to?"

It was my turn for silence. He asked a good question that led to deeper self-reflection. Was I just being real because he wasn't letting me get away with anything else? What would I do if I thought I could pull something over on him. The little devil in me got excited by the idea. Not because I wanted to get away with something but because I wanted him to stop me.

His spankings had warped me. That was the only explanation for it.

The remainder of the walk to the house was quiet.

When I opened the door and called out that we were home, Emily's response was immediate.

"Nuts or no nuts?" she asked, popping up from behind the island.

"I hate when you do that, you weirdo," I said. "And nutting isn't necessary. He left to find animals for me."

Her expression lit up as she looked at Merdon.

"Did you find any?"

"Yeah. A cat," I said.

"Ooh." She made the oh-no face to go with the sound. "You better go shower. Hannah's allergic."

"How did you know?" I asked.

"One of the many rounds of spin the bottle. I asked what hurt you. You said cats."

"Ah." She had probably hoped for a far different answer when she'd asked that question. Maybe, someday soon, I'd talk to her about it. But I wasn't there yet.

Merdon started for the guest bathroom downstairs, and I watched him leave.

"Glad he's back?" Emily asked.

"Yeah."

"Did you tell him he gets the couch?"

"I'm thinking about offering the other side of my bed."

"Mmm," she said, the non-committal noise giving me no clue what she was thinking.

"Are you being judgy? Because if you are, I'm going to tell Mary that you're desperate for a man in your life."

"Ha. I'm not judging. I'm wondering what reason he gave for going out to find an animal for you, especially a cat, that has you protecting his nuts after all those spankings. It must be something good to upgrade him from the couch to the bed."

"When I first saw the cows after I sobered, it gave me hope. Hope that we weren't just sitting inside these walls, waiting for our turns to die. Hope that there was a possible future and a purpose to keep going. I think he went out to find more reasons for me to live."

"Wow," she said softly.

"Yeah. Wow."

I looked down the hall at the guest bathroom's closed door.

"Did you tell him how that made you feel?" she asked.

"I told him he needed to shower so I could hug him."

"Come on, Hannah. You can do better than that. Go make his day."

I looked at Emily, a small smile curving my lips. Hadn't I just admitted to myself that I had a little devil in me? It seemed my friend was just as bad.

"Fine, but you better beat down the door if you hear spankings and me screaming for help."

CHAPTER TWENTY-EIGHT

I PAUSED AT THE DOOR, LISTENED TO THE SOUND OF THE SHOWER and splashing water, then let myself in. The splashing stopped.

"It's just me," I said. "Want company?"

I meant that I would sit in the bathroom with him while he showered; but as soon as I said it, I pictured both of us behind the flowered shower curtain.

Without overthinking what I was about to do, I pulled my shirt over my head, tossed my bra aside, and unzipped my pants. I hesitated at my underwear then decided I was being stupid and took those off as well. He'd been around me when I was naked countless times. Why worry about it now?

"Does silence mean a yes?" I asked. "In my world, silence doesn't mean consent, so I really need you to say something." I opened the curtain enough to peek in at him.

Merdon stood there, a grey-skinned god with rivulets of water running over his chiseled form. I may have drooled a little in the time it took my gaze to do a slow, head to toe sweep of him. The man was huge everywhere. And I meant, everywhere. My regard lingered on the thick length of his shaft that lay heavily between his legs.

"I hear that a woman with big boobs hates running because the bounce makes her boobs hurt. How do you run with that thing?"

"Snug pants."

I finally looked up, meeting his heated gaze.

"Can I join you?"

"Yes."

Stepping behind the curtain, I stood in the steam-filled space at the back of the tub and received the same close study I'd given him. While I'd been naked in his presence more times than I could count, this was the first time he purposefully looked at me. The heat in his gaze warmed my middle, but his silence made me nervous.

"Have you already used soap?"

"Yes."

"Thank you. I hated that you left me. A lot. I was lonely and miserable without you. But, why you left makes up for all of that."

Merdon reached out, the heat of his hand branding my waist as he slowly tugged me forward. The touch of his chest to mine sent a shiver through me. He not only felt it, but he saw it...just like he saw everything when it came to me.

His hold changed, and his fingers gripped my chin, tipping my head back. He studied me for a moment then slowly lowered his lips to mine.

It wasn't the same as the angry kiss or as demanding as the second one, but the way his lips brushed tenderly over mine was far more potent. I tipped my head farther back, hungry for more.

His fingers played with the ends of my hair then trailed down my spine to grab my ass at the same time his tongue traced the seam of my lips. Another shiver raced through me, and I opened them for him. He hungrily delved deeper, his need taking the kiss to another level. His hips arched against me, and the thick length of him twitched between us.

I lifted my hands from his waist, hooking them around his neck and trailing my fingers over his skin.

He broke away for a moment to look down at me.

"I'm afraid to trust this."

"Because you're smart. You see through my bullshit. You always have. Right now, this is real. And, I think it'll stay real for me. That doesn't mean I won't have problems. That doesn't mean that everything will be fine with me. We both know that I have issues. But this is good for me. You're good for me. Just make sure I'm good for you. If I ever get to be too much, I'm telling you now, walk away from me. Save yourself."

"Never," he growled before his lips claimed mine again. The intensity and anger were back. I loved it. I loved his sweet kiss too. I was pretty sure I loved all of him.

The hand on my ass moved lower, slowly sliding from my backside to my folds.

I squeaked at the exploratory invasion. I hadn't thought we were to that stage yet. Heck, I hadn't thought he'd know how to navigate that part. But he managed beautifully, skimming over my channel and going right for the sweet spot. He circled my clit twice, came close to gliding over it, and dodged at the last second. I squirmed, trying to chase his fingertip.

"Be still, Hannah," he said, nipping my bottom lip just as he slid a finger inside of me.

I howled. Or maybe it was a moan. I couldn't be sure. My eyes were rolled back, and my heart was thundering in my ears. He moved it in and out of me a few times as if taking my measure, then added a second finger and more pressure.

"Yes," I groaned. "Yes. More."

"Shh," he whispered against my ear. "Stay quiet or I will stop."

I nodded and lifted my lips, begging for another kiss.

"No. I will watch your face. Your lips can lie. Your face does not."

He withdrew his fingers, and I opened my eyes to scowl at him. He grunted.

"That makes you sad and almost angry."

"Of course it does. I wasn't done yet."

His finger skimmed over my clit, and I jerked at the sensation.

"That makes you happy."

"Stop narrating, and put your finger back where it belongs, dammit."

He grunted and, oh so slowly, slid a finger back into me. I ground down on it, and he swatted my backside. It wasn't the stinging slap from the basement but a quieter, gentler version.

I scowled at him again.

"What'd I do wrong now?"

"Stay still. Your movements are distracting me."

"Well, your lack of movement is annoying me. It feels like you're not into this like I am."

He tilted his head and looked down at me.

"What do you mean?"

"I mean, do you want me or not? Because I can't tell right now. It seems more like I'm a plaything. Shiny new toys are quickly forgotten. Or broken."

He leaned over me, taking my chin with his free hand while his other hand played with my entrance.

"You are a plaything. My plaything." His finger delved deeper.

"And I have waited so long to touch you. To watch your face and learn what makes you happy." And deeper still. "To see what makes you want more.

"I will not forget you, and I will not break you."

He added the second finger again, and the pressure made my eyes want to close. I dug my fingers into his hair and did my best to focus.

"Do you promise?" I asked, breathless.

"I swear."

I gave myself over to him, trusting him in a world filled with shattered dreams and walking nightmares. Because with him, I felt safe. With him, I *felt*.

His fingers teased me relentlessly as he stared down at me. My legs shook with need, and I let it show. His gaze devoured every nuance in my expression. He learned just where to touch me and just how much I could handle before I teetered on the precipice. Pleas poured from my lips.

He growled low and kissed me hard, leaving me panting and so close.

"You are mine, Hannah. Always."

I agreed. Anything for him to end my torment.

He set his lips to my shoulder and pinched my skin with his teeth, the sting sending a jolt through me. I clenched around his fingers, and he grunted.

"Enough playing," he said.

Without warning, he dropped to one knee, pressed me against the wall, and set his mouth to me. I shattered at the first flick of his tongue, his fingers still buried deep inside of me. My eyelids fluttered closed as the rolling waves of pleasure consumed me.

He continued to kiss me slowly as the aftershocks stole the

strength from my knees. His grip stayed firm, holding me in place. I never wanted it to end but was too spent to keep myself upright.

Hands on his shoulders, I managed to open my eyes and look down at him. His knowing gaze met mine as he withdrew with a final lick.

"Was it as good for you as it was for me?" I tried to joke.

"Better."

"We're not done yet, though, right?"

He stood and stared down at me.

"For now," he said.

"We have company. I will get you some clothes. Stay here."

Just like that, he left me leaning against the tile, ears still ringing from a mind-blowing orgasm after dropping a bomb that there was someone else in the house.

I stared at the door, which he'd considerately closed behind him, and imagined him walking bare-assed in front of Emily. I smirked.

She was the one who'd invited him in.

A few minutes later, he returned with a handful of clothes and was already dressed.

"Hurry up," he said.

I shook my head at him and dressed quickly while wondering if he'd always boss me around. Probably. But I also knew I wouldn't always listen. The anticipation of how he'd retaliate had me grinning as I tugged my clothes on.

Decently covered, I emerged and found Uan and Nancy waiting in the living room with a very pink-tinged Emily. Not one to be left out, I quickly joined Emily on the sofa, my hue matching hers. Uan sat in the chair, Nancy comfortably seated on his lap.

"Ah, sorr—"

Nancy waved away the apology.

"Don't. I've been there. There's no point in apologizing." She glanced at Emily. "You might want to have someone find you some earplugs, though. It doesn't get out of their systems for a while."

Emily gave a weak smile of agreement before Nancy focused on me again.

"I heard you wanted to talk," she said.

"I do. But I was willing to come to you."

"And rob me of an opportunity to get out of the house? Nonsense." Nancy looked around the room. "It's very nice in here. Cleaner than I expected for two girls your ages. In my college years, the place I lived in was a shithole."

"Different world," Emily said.

"Which is why I'm here," Nancy said, looking at me. "I heard you don't want Tasha to go out tomorrow."

"It's too dangerous out there."

"Go where?" Emily asked.

"To get the animals we found," Merdon said. "Tasha believes there will be food there for her cat. What do they eat?"

"Dry kibble, meat, milk, stuff like that," Nancy said. "Some of which we have but need for ourselves."

"I'm sure the fey can find what she needs," Emily said.

"I'm sure they can, too. But Tasha's leaving isn't about finding the supplies. It's about finding her place in this world. Are we only here as bed warmers, or are we here to participate in some way, however small, in remaking this world into what we want it to be?"

"Participate, of course," I answered, "but that doesn't mean we need to allow children outside the wall."

"Brenna told me she already pointed out that it's not the wall that keeps us safe. Uan will go with Tasha and thirty other volunteers. If they can't keep her safe out there, nothing will."

"I heard that Brenna was almost bitten twice," Emily said softly. "And that was under Thallirin's watchful eye."

"The infected are getting smarter," Nancy acknowledged. "But so are we. The humans who go out wear layers of thick material that's hard to break through with teeth."

"And when the infected get smart enough to cut it away?" Emily asked.

"Then we'll learn to adapt to that, too. But I'm hoping that the fey who go out at night are making the world a better place, one headless infected at a time."

I looked at Uan then Merdon.

"Fey are going out at night?"

"Yes, we kill any infected that gather."

"Are there a lot of them?"

"No. Very few since they came here and killed so many."

"I hate not knowing where they've gone and why they're staying away," Emily said softly.

"Exactly," Nancy said.

I didn't see how Emily's concern proved her point, and Nancy must have seen the confusion on my face because she smiled at me a little.

"Staying inside Tolerance's wall, we're clueless. What if the infected are doing something out there? What if they're learning something? Or worse, what if they're all gone? What if the hellhounds killed them?

"How is that worse?" I asked. "Isn't wiping out the infected what we want to do?"

"It is. But if they're all gone and we're living in fear in here, missing the opportunity to find survivors, supplies, animals that will help us rebuild into something sustainable, isn't just sitting here worse?"

I hated that I could see her point. We didn't know what we didn't know, and staying here wouldn't help us in any way. Yes, the fey were going out, and they were smart, but there were things the fey still didn't know. That was why humans who understood the world needed to travel with them.

"But it doesn't have to be Tasha," I said. "She's too young."

"The infected are evolving. If I keep her here, she won't evolve with them. She'll be like me. An easy target. I can't do that to her. Instead, I can send her out with a personal escort and hope that she comes home to us. And, hope that I'm still here when she does."

Uan hugged her closer, and I was reminded of the truth again. We were all going to die. Some of us had accepted that and had already given up, a path I'd been on for so long. Some, like Nancy, acknowledged their impending death and were determined to fight for every day they were given. Yet, there were others who still hadn't caught on, and I pitied them for the harsh reality they still had to face. It would be no kinder than the one I was facing now.

I forced myself to see the truth in what I'd known all along. The safety inside our fey-built wall of cars was an illusion. Anything could happen inside the wall just as well as it could happen out there. My fight to keep Tasha here was as pointless as my belief that I was safer here.

My gaze locked on Merdon. He was my safety.

"I'm going with you tomorrow."

He grunted at the same time Nancy smiled.

"You're smart, Hannah," she said. "I'll be going outside the wall myself, once the weather warms. I hate this feeling of false security. I feel lulled by it even though I know better. Staying sharp means staying alive. Stick with my girls and the fey. You'll be fine."

She looked at Emily.

"What about you? Will you be going?"

"No. I'm content to stay. We're like the cows. Keep the herd divided and hope the infected don't attack all the places at once. That way, at least some of us will survive."

Nancy nodded slowly.

"I guess we are." Her fingers played with the edges of Uan's shirt. "We should get going. I want to spend some time with my girls before they go out tomorrow. Be smart out there. Keep your eyes and ears open. See if you can figure out where the infected went or, better yet, where the animals are all hiding."

Uan stood with her.

"Thanks for hearing me out," she said.

"Thanks for talking to me," I said.

Merdon got the door for them then turned to look at me.

"I'm going," I said before he could object. "I hated being left behind. It didn't feel safe."

"You will do nothing to hurt yourself while we are out there," he said.

I almost smiled at the command.

"Not intentionally. But we both know this world isn't a safe place."

He grunted.

"You bring her back, Merdon," Emily said, her strange tone drawing my attention. "Swear to me. No accidents. I couldn't live through a second one."

"What are you talking about?" I asked.

"Tell her," Merdon said. "It's time she knows."

I glanced between the two of them as he crossed his arms and gave me that stern look he usually gave when I'd done something wrong. This time, like so many others, I was clueless.

"What'd I do?" I asked Emily.

"It's not what you did. It's what my sister did."

For a heartbeat, I thought her sister had done what I should have, sacrificed herself for Emily.

"She died in a car accident two years before the quakes," Emily said softly. "She was my best friend. My twin. And she left me."

The pain in her eyes cut a knife through my middle, and guilt hurtled through me.

"We always did everything together. Except the day she died. She ran to the store for some chocolate icing for our birthday cake."

"Emily, I'm so sorry."

"Do you know what her name was? Hailey Anna Belle. My family called her Hannah-bell. I called her Hannah." Her gaze held mine. "I died that day, too. My life wasn't the same. I went through the motions. When everything fell apart, I thought, 'finally, I can let go.' But no matter where I went or who I was with, it was never me who died. It wasn't until I met you that I understood there was a reason. I might not be the sister you lost, but you're the sister I found. I can't lose you."

It wasn't the first time I'd heard her tell me she couldn't lose me, but it was the first time I fully understood it.

Eyes watering, I leaned in to hug her hard.

"I don't want to be lost anymore. I'm so glad you found me."

"Do you mean it?" she sniffled. "Even though I broke the rules."

I pulled back and held her face in my hands.

"Especially since you broke the rules. Thank you. For being there. For caring and never giving up. For everything."

"I'll be back for dinner," Merdon said quietly before leaving.

I released her.

"Why is he always doing that?" I grumbled. "He just got back."

"I think he's trying to give me some time with you. I mean, he just had some time with you. A good time, based on what I could hear."

I gave her a sheepish smile.

"Sorry about that. Still want to be roommates?"

"Yep. The noise you make will keep everyone else away."

I snorted. "You mean all the other fey. And I doubt that. They'll probably be drawn to it."

"Still not changing my mind."

I gave her a grateful smile.

"Thanks."

We ate lunch together, and I felt bad that Merdon missed it. The regular cheeseburger was amazing and something I thought I wouldn't have again.

Most of the day, we just talked. Emily ended up telling me more about the sister she'd lost, and I told her a little about mine. She already knew that Katie had been attacked by the infected, thanks to the fey rumor mill. And though I couldn't bring myself to tell Emily about me letting go of Katie's hand, I told her what happened later. How Katie had found me and I'd had to kill her.

We both cried, and Emily hugged me. I felt guilty about the comfort, but Emily shared the same sentiment that Merdon had.

"If you hadn't made the choices you had, I wouldn't be here now. I would have given up a long time ago. Maybe I'm selfish, but I think it was supposed to be you who survived, Hannah. Don't let guilt rob you of the chance at life you've been given."

As promised, Merdon returned just as Emily pulled dinner from the oven. With his perfect timing, I suspected he'd been watching us through the windows but didn't call him out on it. How could I? I'd enjoyed every moment I'd spent hanging out with Emily even if a few of them created a deeper hurt. I now understood just how much she'd been starved for me to treat her like the sister she'd become. The sister she'd wanted me to be. I vowed I wouldn't go back to the selfish person I'd been. That each day, I'd get a little better. For her. And for Merdon. Because even though he'd left again for all the best reasons, I'd missed him like crazy.

We ate a companionable dinner, enjoying light conversation until Emily set her fork down abruptly.

"I can't keep pretending that you never gave your word, Merdon. If taking her out is that dangerous, don't do it. She's just as important to you as she is to me."

"No. She's—"

"All right, you two, no fighting over me. I get it. I'm important to both of you," I tried to joke. But Emily wasn't having any of it.

"I want your word," she repeated.

"I swear, we will both return unharmed."

She stared at him for a moment then left the kitchen. The soft click of her door was like a gunshot in the quiet.

"She thinks I'm not coming back," I said.

"I know."

I snorted at his typical answer but couldn't truly feel any humor. Emily was scared. Something I understood all too well because I felt it too. Yet, Nancy was right. There was no more safety in staying here than there was in leaving.

My mind in turmoil, I finished my dinner and wrapped up what was left of Emily's like she'd done for me countless times. Merdon watched me in silence. Patient but all too observant.

"Am I being stupid for wanting to go?" I asked.

"No. You are brave."

"Not at all. I'm sticking to the one person I know wants to keep me alive. I feel safer when I'm with you."

His gaze searched mine for a moment, then he wrapped me in his arms and smoothed his hand over my hair. Setting my cheek to his chest, I let out a shaky exhale.

"I feel safe when you're with me, but when you hold me like this, I feel like I'm home again," I whispered. "I don't want to hurt Emily, but I don't want to leave you. Any chance you'd consider just staying here tomorrow and letting Thallirin lead the group to the place where the animals are?"

The movement of his hand slowed.

"Emily will not be hurt when you leave. She will be afraid. That is her choice. Yours is to continue to live in the dark world your mind has created or to face your fears and build a better world." He tipped my head up to meet his gaze. "I hope you face your fears, but know that I will live with you in whatever world you choose."

I nodded slowly, understanding what he was saying. I needed to decide for us.

It weighed heavily on my mind as we went upstairs and got ready for bed. So heavily, in fact, that I didn't realize he was sitting in his usual chair until I'd slid under the cool covers.

Rolling to my side, I looked at him. After what we'd shared in the shower, I'd assumed there'd be a continuation tonight. Had

Nancy not arrived, we probably would have picked up where we'd left off immediately after the shower, given what I'd heard from the fey. When women said yes, it tended to be a green light for a sex-fest. Yet, Merdon was in his chair, calmly sitting there, watching me back.

"Why are you over there?" I asked. "Wouldn't you rather be right here?"

I patted the empty spot beside me and didn't miss the hunger that flooded his gaze.

CHAPTER TWENTY-NINE

Thoughts of the next day vanished as Merdon stood with a slow prowl that set my heart racing. He removed his shirt in a fluid motion and tossed it aside before reaching for the band of his pants. There, he hesitated, his gaze sweeping over my face. Whatever he saw caused him to join me under the covers without undressing further.

He pulled me close, and with a sigh, I rested my head on his shoulder. Safe and comfortable in his arms, and not as distracted as I'd hoped I would be, my worries returned.

"What are we going to do?" I asked.

"What do you mean?"

"Even if we find animals, how are we going to continue to live? How long do solar panels and water heaters last? Eventually, what we have now will break, and we'll be back to depending on fire for warmth. How will we get water when water pumps start to go? None of that stuff is going to last forever. What happens when we have to leave Tolerance more than we do now in order to survive? What will the next generation do? How will they feed themselves through long winters? Will they need to migrate south just to be able to continue growing things?"

His hand stroked over my hair.

"My first memory is of a soft glow in the darkness. My brothers and I didn't know where we were. We had no food, few weapons, and almost no light. We survived in the caves with much less than what is on the surface now. We will survive again. This time, we will do so with the humans at our sides."

His words gave me a little hope, and only further proved that I needed to face my fears and leave Tolerance. Yes, I'd left it plenty of times to cross to Tenacity, but never to gather supplies. I'd left that risk to others.

Knowing that we'd be leaving in trucks that made noise, which attracted the infected, terrified me. My hold on Merdon tightened.

"Why'd you leave your pants on?" I asked.

"I want to be your focus, not your distraction from fear."

"I'm pretty sure I would have been very focused."

He grunted, and I ran my fingers over his bare chest, teasing the skin as much as I was memorizing it. He let me go for a bit before he caught my hand and laid it over his rapidly beating heart.

"Go to sleep, Hannah. Dawn comes early."

I smiled to myself, liking this version of Merdon better than the one who spanked me with no good reason. Well, not any reason I'd liked. Although, he'd been right about the sting of pain motivating me. I cringed, recalling the few times we hadn't been on the mats and his hand had still smacked my backside. I'd earned those for being a brat. Still, I wouldn't have acted so badly if I'd known what was going on. I'd thought he was just acting like a mean son of a—

My eyes went wide, and I lifted my head to look down at him.

"Can I ask you something without getting spanked for it?"

His eyes narrowed suspiciously, but he nodded. I almost grinned but managed to withhold it.

"I swore at you so much and called you so many names, which I'm sorry for, by the way. Mostly."

He grunted, and I could see the hint of a smile tug at his lips before he smothered it.

"No matter what I said, you never lost your temper with me. Except for one phrase that earned me a spanking every time. Why did 'son of a bitch' get me in trouble when all the others didn't?"

"I have no memories prior to my life in the caves. None. No father. No mother. But I am someone's son. I can endure your disrespect of me, but not my parents. That I cannot allow."

In the dim light, I studied his serious expression and melted a little more for the man.

"I'm sorry I hurt you."

He tugged me down for a gentle kiss then coaxed my head to rest on his shoulder once more.

"You were hurting, Hannah. When you hurt, we will hurt together."

With those words, I acknowledged what I'd felt for some time now. I was Merdon's, and he was mine. Heart and soul.

I drifted off a while later, comfortable in his arms. How long I remained that way before my familiar nightmare woke me, I couldn't be sure.

Heart racing and covered in sweat, I jerked from Merdon's hold.

"You are safe," he said as I looked around the room.

I nodded and put my head back on his chest even as my eyes continued to search the shadows.

"It's like Katie's still there, waiting for me to take it all back. To make things right," I whispered.

He ran his hand over my arm as I continued to tremble.

"Nothing can change the past, Hannah. You know this."

I did, and I hated it.

Lifting my head again, I looked at him in the dark.

"Can you be my distraction just for a minute?"

His hand stilled.

"And I don't mean taking me to the basement. That's not the distraction I want."

I trailed my hand from his chest to his stomach, reveling in every twitch along the way. He stopped me just after I passed his navel.

"Please," I whispered.

He growled, and a second later, I was pinned under him. This time I reveled in the feel of his weight pressing down on me even as his lips brushed the skin over my collarbone. The sensitive spot was one of the places he'd often nipped while we were on the mats. My breath quickened, and I threaded my fingers in his hair in anticipation. He didn't disappoint. A zing shot through me at the first nip of his teeth, and I moaned. He licked the spot and moved further south, his lips caressing my skin until he reached the scooped neckline of my cami.

He lifted his head and looked down at me.

One little nibble and a trailing kiss already had me panting. Merdon was no mere distraction. He was the air I breathed.

"More," I whispered.

He dipped his head again, bit my shirt, and tugged it low enough to expose one breast. The hot, flat stroke of his tongue set me on fire, and I let out another groan when his mouth closed over the peak.

When he pulled back, I took his face in my hands and leaned up to kiss his lips softly.

"This is me focused on you, Merdon. I will choose to face my fears tomorrow, but don't let me do that without experiencing you. All of you. Life is fragile, and neither of us knows what will happen. Give me this. Please."

He growled and kissed me savagely. His tongue stroked mine, each thrust imparting his need for me, and I knew this wouldn't be sweet lovemaking. Not this time. He proved me right by grabbing the front of my cami and pulling hard. The straps bit into my shoulders before the material gave way.

Breasts fully exposed, I waited for him to end the kiss. He didn't. He continued to consume me hungrily as his hand roved to my shorts.

I broke away.

"Wait," I panted. "Clothes aren't endless. Let me take them off."

He pulled back and looked down at me. The angry light in his eyes and dilated pupils made him look feral and out of control. That didn't bode well for my shorts.

I tried removing my hands from his hair, but he grabbed my wrists and held my hands over my head.

A knee wedged between my legs, separating them. The second joined the first. Then he settled his hips against mine. Each movement was a methodical exercise in control that heated my blood because I could see how much he was struggling.

The devil in me demanded we test him and the thick feel of his length pressed against me. Merdon read my intent in my eyes, though, because his free hands clasped my hip and stilled me before I even started.

"Do not move, Hannah."

His rough voice abraded my senses, and I shivered with need.

He bared his teeth at my reaction and forcefully arched into my hips, giving me what I'd wanted. A whimper of pure bliss escaped me.

"You are mine. You will listen to everything I say and do nothing until I tell you. Do you understand?"

I nodded, tingling in anticipation from head to toe.

"Now and always, Hannah. In bed and out of bed. Do you understand?"

I nodded again, not caring what I was agreeing to. I was that desperate for him to touch me again.

He dipped his head and took my other breast into his mouth. I panted then squeaked when I felt the gentle scrape of his teeth.

"Quiet or I stop."

I did my best to remain silent as he did his best to get me to make a noise again. Liquid pooled between my legs, and I ground against the hard length nestled there.

"Be still," he warned.

It nearly killed me not to rub against him again as I lay there, throbbing with need.

"Please. Let me take my shorts off."

"No."

He released my hands, skimming his palm down my side and hooking his fingers into the waist of my bottoms. He tugged them down slowly, his mouth skimming from my breast to my stomach to my navel as my shorts traveled the length of my legs.

I was shaking by the time he had them off and his breath was fanning my core. He drew my right knee up to my chest, caressing my inner thigh along the way. Guiding me, he had me hold that leg then the other until I was spread wide for him.

A flash of embarrassment over the position passed quickly when his tongue caressed my soft folds and his fingers found my entrance.

"Quietly," he whispered.

It was the only warning he gave before unraveling my existence and reshaping me into a new version of myself. A version that couldn't imagine a world without Merdon. A version that needed his touch more than it needed its next breath.

He brought me to the brink again and again until I forgot to hold my legs and my hands roved wildly over his head. When I accidentally brushed his ear, he bit my inner thigh in warning. I almost came then.

"Please," I begged. "Please."

He growled and was on top of me. I tasted myself on his lips as he kissed me savagely and settled his naked weight on my hips. I didn't have time to wonder when he'd ditched his pants before the head of his massive erection was pressing into my center. Slick from my need, my body welcomed him even as my channel stretched to accommodate his size. In and in he slid. I felt every ridge and bump stroking me, building the fire burning inside of me until he was fully seated.

He shook on top of me, and I looked up at his strained, shadowed face.

"Do not scream," he warned.

"Why would I—"

He pulled out and thrust back in, no coaxing or patience left in him. My eyes went wide, and my mouth fell open when he filled me to the point of pain. Then he retreated again, only to return.

I gasped at the bruising force even as more heat flooded me. He growled, paused, and wrapped one of my legs around his hips to adjust my angle. The next thrust, while no less forceful, seemed to have more room. He grunted in satisfaction and proceeded to drive into me ruthlessly. I held on for dear life, letting the building pleasure in my core pulse my inner walls. He set a wild pace.

The bed squeaked and hit the wall, but I remained silent as promised. I wanted to be loud. I wanted to howl my pleasure, but I was too afraid he'd stop and rob me of what I wanted most.

I could feel him getting closer. His head swelled. His thrusts grew shallower. My insides tightened. The first jerk of his cock inside of me set off fireworks in my body and behind my eyelids. His lips muffled my scream as I came apart in the mother of all orgasms. Then, his lurching strokes slowed when he emptied himself completely.

Heart thundering in my chest, I lay under him, completely spent and unable to move.

He claimed my lips for another slow kiss and rolled us on our sides so I was curled in his arms.

"Sleep now, Hannah."

It was an easy command to follow.

HE WOKE me before dawn with his hand splayed over my belly, stroking my skin.

"If there was time, I'd lick your pussy again," he murmured in my ear, "and thrust into you until you quiver around me."

My insides clenched.

"I like when you quiver."

He nipped my ear.

"Do you remember your promise, Hannah?"

I blinked, trying to focus. He was doing things to my ear that no one had done before, and it was beyond distracting.

"What?" I breathed.

"You promised to listen. To do exactly what I said. Do you remember?"

I nodded, eager for round two.

"Good," he said with a light swat on my backside. "Get up and shower. Be downstairs in five minutes. We need to leave."

He rolled from the bed, leaving me turned on and confused.

"What?" I asked sitting up. "We have to go already?"

He paused, his heated gaze sweeping over my breasts. I let him look his fill, then reached up to caress my nipple.

"It could be fun," I said, watching the thick length of him harden.

He considered me for a long moment and slowly shook his head.

"You are my distraction, too, Hannah, and today, I need to focus. We will have more fun when we return tonight."

He showed his commitment to self-denial by tugging his pants back on.

"Are you going to let me make some noise then?"

"No."

"Why do I have to be quiet?"

"It upsets Emily when you scream."

That didn't seem like Emily. She was more the type to either high-five me or quietly leave the house to give us privacy. She'd never begrudge me having a good time.

I frowned at him, wondering why he thought that until I remembered the conversation I'd overheard in the kitchen.

"She didn't like hearing me scream in pain and fear when you spanked and bit me. The screaming I'd do now would only be from pleasure. That wouldn't upset her. Well, not the way the basement time did."

He considered my words and grunted.

"I will ask her to be sure."

I snorted.

"You do that."

Getting out of bed, I looked over my shoulder at him.

"Why do I have to shower and you don't? You could join me."

I loved the way his gaze heated at the thought.

"I will shower later when I can kneel at your feet and taste you until you beg and say my name. Then we will return to the bed and I will—"

I held up a hand.

"Nope. You're just teasing me now. You better deliver on all your promises or you're the one who'll get bitten next."

Even under the straining confines of his pants, his dick twitched. I grinned and walked away, already thinking of what I'd bite first.

It wasn't until I was headed downstairs that I remembered what awaited. Leaving. The idea scared me, but not with the complete hopeless terror that had ruled my life for so long.

I still knew there was a very real chance I could die out there. But I'd also heard what Nancy was saying yesterday. I couldn't keep hiding from my reality. Like the drinking, hiding wouldn't make the truth go away.

Emily had hot cinnamon rolls waiting on the counter for me when I appeared.

"Any chance you'd rather stay here and help me make more of these today?" she asked.

The dark circles under her hopeful eyes made me feel guilty. Instead of sitting, I moved around the counter and hugged her tightly.

"I need to go. I don't want to be the person I've been since I got here, anymore."

"But you're not."

"I'm starting not to be. But I need to finish. I need to face the reality of what's out there and stop hiding from it. Let me do this."

She pulled back and looked into my eyes before nodding.

I gave her another quick hug and grabbed my roll to go since Merdon had already finished his.

"We'll be back before dark," he promised Emily.

"Okay."

She looked so sad and unhappy as I started for the door. I couldn't leave her like that.

"Hey, would you mind if I screamed a little during sex?"

Her expression went blank before disbelief then humor painted her features.

"I'll pound on the walls if I want you to take it down a notch," she said. "I'll make sure it's loud enough that you'll hear it over the bed squeaking."

I laughed as I left and hoped I'd return in the same mood.

Merdon carried my bow and a quiver I'd never seen before so I could finish eating my roll. It sat heavy in my stomach and churned with my worry, but I didn't regret eating it. If I was going to die today, I'd die happy. Merdon and I were good. So were Emily and I. Even Mary had pretty much forgiven me for my bad behavior, even though the behavior that set her off hadn't been my fault.

I licked my fingers clean then took my things from Merdon.

"Are you worried?" I asked him.

His gaze lingered on my face before he focused on the road once more.

"I will always worry about you," he said. "I worry less knowing that you will listen."

I grinned slightly.

"I think I like getting bossed around in bed. I'm not sure about daily life, though."

His scowl deepened.

"Do not test me, Hannah."

"Wouldn't dream of it."

We reached the wall and found the volunteer fey already mingling there, having quiet conversations. Brenna and Thallirin were still missing.

"How many humans will be on this trip?" I asked Merdon, my gaze on the excited Tasha, who was talking animatedly to Uan.

"Five. You, Tasha, and Brenna will ride in the two trucks with Garrett and Ryan."

It reassured me to know there wouldn't be many of us. That meant more fey paying attention to our safety.

As soon as the missing members joined us, Merdon picked me up and jumped over the wall. The sudden drop to the other side didn't help settle my stomach. I tucked my face into his chest as he ran and waited for the second jump.

Matt was waiting inside Tenacity's walls when we arrived.

"Morning," he called. His observant gaze caught on me. "You look like you're doing better, Hannah."

"I am. Thank you."

He nodded and handed Ryan two keys.

"They're all yours. We're ready to welcome whatever stock you want us to watch over for you."

"How's the last haul of feed holding up?" Ryan asked.

"Good. That farmer has been a real help in educating all of us on how to care for the cows. This plan to share knowledge is a good one. The three fey who've been coming over daily seem to be more accepted now than when this all started. Hopefully, the other things that Emily's working on will help too. How's Mya?"

"Getting better now that she's almost out of the first trimester but still a little green around the edges."

Matt nodded.

"My wife was the same with our first. Morning sickness completely went away during the second half."

I realized then how little I knew about Tenacity's leader.

"I'll let Mya know there's hope then," Ryan said with a grin.

"There's more hope today than there was yesterday. That's all we can ask for." Matt shook Ryan's hand then headed toward men stationed at the wall to help them with the new, heavy gates.

We loaded into the trucks and pulled out of Tenacity as the sun broke over the trees. The clear sky and brown spots poking through the snow in the fields gave me plenty of hope for a good day. That, along with the complete absence of infected, almost made the world seem normal.

"First time on a supply run?" Garrett asked.

"Yeah. I'm trying not to overthink it and freak myself out. Last I heard, the traps were getting worse for you guys."

"Yeah, the infected are trying harder, but we're still smarter. All they're doing is helping the fey thin their numbers before they run off."

"They run off?"

He nodded. "They're smart enough to know when a trap is failing. Those that can, bail."

"It reminds me of something my dad said about fishing."

"What's that?"

"You release the big ones so they can breed and make more fish."

I tore my gaze from the landscape and looked at Garrett.

"Completely different, though, right?"

"Right."

The second he'd hesitated before answering was more honest than his response.

I told myself I had nothing to worry about as I looked out the window at Merdon. He would keep me safe. They all would.

He and Thallirin ran side by side, leading the caravan as the rest of the fey spread out around the trucks.

We drove for almost three hours before Thallirin signaled with a lifted arm. The trucks began to slow with the fey. Merdon continued on at the same pace. My heart clenched to see him running away from me.

The stretch of road appeared clear. Yet, that wasn't what worried me so much as the tree-lined ditches. I understood that Merdon was probably scouting ahead because we were getting close.

"Why does Merdon have to go alone?" I asked softly.

"Because he'd rather the rest of the fey guard what's most important to him while he's not here to do it himself."

I glanced at Garrett and offered him a weak smile.

"Who's going to protect what's most important to me?"

"He will. Don't worry. He knows he needs to come back. He wouldn't have brought you out here if he thought he couldn't keep both you and himself safe."

I focused on the trees as Merdon veered off the road. For several moments, there was nothing. When he reappeared, though, I could see the dark stains on his clothes even from this distance.

He signaled it was clear, and Garrett eased the truck forward after the fey. Merdon didn't run ahead again but waited for the truck to pass him and jumped up next to my window. Blood dotted his face.

I set my hand to the window as if I would touch his cheek.

"You be careful," I warned through the window.

"You will do as you're told."

I rolled my eyes even as my insides clenched.

"I already promised. What exactly do you think I'm going to do? Jump out of the truck and go running through the trees? Hell, no. Been there and still have nightmares about it. Give me some credit. I'm smart, no matter what you say."

He tilted his head at me.

"You're smart when you think, not when you react."

"Gee, thanks."

He grinned at me then jumped down. I stared after him in shock as he ran to catch up to Thallirin.

"I think that's the first real smile I've seen from him," I said to Garrett.

"And I think that's the first real smile I've seen on you," he said.

I realized I was smiling and settled back on my seat.

"It's weird," I said. "I thought life was over. Instead, Merdon's proving I've barely begun to live."

My heart thrummed with the possibilities of a future with him, and I remembered the way his hand had rested over my stomach when I woke this morning, and my pulse stuttered erratically. I didn't want a baby. I was too scared and unsure who I was yet. But, someday, maybe, I'd be able to give Merdon the world he wanted.

"Shit!"

Garrett braked hard.

I'd been so caught up in my hopes for the future that I hadn't registered the scene as the truck pulled into the long, gravel driveway.

A trail of blood and dead cows led to a cluster of infected grouped around the barn near the silo. The way the infected rocked slightly as they stared at the structure was beyond weird and not how I remembered them behaving.

My gaze flicked to Merdon, who studied the infected with the rest of the fey. With his back to me, I couldn't see his face. Why weren't the fey telling us to run?

The dead cows disturbed me. But the way the infected were acting, swaying and ignoring the sounds of the idling trucks, terrified me. They didn't do that. Noise drew them. Always.

Garrett seemed to have the same thought because he cut the engine.

In front of the fey, the infected stopped swaying.

One by one, they turned. Over one hundred milky white eyes focused on our caravan.

A small, panicked noise escaped my lips.

CHAPTER THIRTY

"It's okay, Hannah," Garrett said, reaching across the seat to take my hand. "The fey won't let them get near us."

He'd barely said the words when the majority of the fey positioned themselves around the trucks.

Merdon looked back at me, and I shook my head at him because I already knew what he was thinking about doing.

He tapped his ear and pointed at me. And the truck. He wanted me to remember my promise to do as I was told and stay in the truck.

I put my free hand on the windshield, a plea and a promise. He'd said that he'd live in the world I chose. Well, that went two ways.

"Don't you dare die," I whispered before removing my hand from the glass.

He tipped his head at me then faced the infected. Thallirin said something to him, and they both strode forward together.

The infected didn't surge in their direction as I expected but stayed right where they were.

"Is that weird?" I asked, still holding Garrett's hand.

"Yep."

I could tell the infected were watching the fey, but they weren't moving more than their heads.

"I don't like this," Garrett said.

"You're not helping."

Thallirin grabbed one of the infected by the head and decapitated it with one forceful jerk. The body fell. None of the surrounding infected moved.

Merdon and Thallirin shared a look then rushed forward, removing heads and throwing bodies. The savage brutality should have upset me, and maybe it would have if it'd been humans dying rather than infected. As it was, I felt nothing but relief that Merdon and Thallirin were killing so many with ease.

A single, mournful bellow echoed outside the windows.

I jumped, and Garrett's hand tightened on mine as the infected finally surged into motion, swarming the fey.

Panicked, I looked to the right and saw Tor. I slapped on the window to get his attention.

"Don't let him die," I called.

Some of the infected heard me. They broke away from the main group and ran at the fey positioned around the trucks. But they had no chance. Two fey quickly beheaded ten.

When I looked toward the barn, very few infected remained upright in the decimated mass of headless bodies. Those who did gave a loud moan then fled just as Garrett had said they would.

Two fey ran after the ones trying to escape.

"Hopefully they won't get far," Garrett said.

The truck door opened abruptly, giving me another startle. I looked over at Tor.

"Stay in the truck. We will move the bodies and make sure no heads remain attached. I will tell you when to get out. Merdon says to listen."

I nodded. The door closed, leaving me inside with Garrett.

"Is it like this every time?" I asked.

"Ryan usually doesn't hold my hand this long, but pretty much."

I wrinkled my nose and released my death grip.

"Sorry."

"Nah, don't worry about it. Just glad no one noticed. The fey are possessive and jealous, if you didn't already know."

"I heard about your near miss with Shax."

"And Thallirin," he said. "I don't know why they keep putting you girls with me. I mean, I don't mind the company at all. I'm just not a fan of the risk."

"Oh, come on. It's not that bad."

He snorted, watching out the front window.

"I have dreams I'm being carried away without a head, and not because I am infected. I pity any guy who gets between a fey and his crush."

I followed Garrett's gaze to where the fey were removing the infected corpses. Then, I looked at the dead cows in front of the truck.

"Do you think there are any animals still alive in the barn?" I asked.

"I do. Why else would they have stood there like that?"

"I don't know. I've just never seen them go after animals. It's always been people."

"I hope there weren't people in there."

I nodded in agreement and watched the fey haul away the dead cows. Ryan gave the carcasses a lengthy look and shook his head as he walked toward the barn with a large group of fey. They disappeared inside for several long minutes before the group reemerged. They had clearly encountered some infected inside, based on the red on their clothing. Not Ryan, though. He still looked clean as he jogged toward our truck.

Garrett rolled down his window.

"Half the cows are dead, but it looks like a few broke free and are roaming the space behind the barn. There's a pig pen around back, too. I'm going to try to pull closer to that pen so the fey can carry the cows there and drive them into the back of the truck, all at once." He raked his hand through his hair. "This is going to be a zoo. Keep your eyes open, and watch your truck."

Garrett nodded then rolled his window back up. Before he could comment on what he thought of the arrangement, Merdon jogged up to us. Shiny dark bits stuck to his hair. I made a face that had him slowing. Not wanting him to stop, I put my hand on the window again. He continued my way.

"You're extremely dirty," I said when he stood next to my door.

"I know."

I smiled and tapped my hand against the glass.

"You're also a bossy know-it-all. But I'm glad you're okay. I heard there's still some animals alive."

"Yes. You can come out and see them now. We checked the barn and there are no more infected."

He stepped back and let Tor open the door for me.

I hopped down and gave them both a grateful smile. Merdon's gaze swept over me as if checking to make sure I was still in once piece. My stomach dipped at the simple display of how much he cared.

"Stay close, Hannah."

"I'm sticking to you like glue," I said before amending, "Well, maybe to Tor like glue. You're a little gooey for close contact."

He grunted and looked at Tor.

"Not too close."

"Told you," Garrett said from the other side of the truck.

I shook my head at him and hurried after Merdon with Tor close on my heels. Behind us, I heard the other truck doors close and Tasha's excited whispers.

The gravel, bathed in glistening red, painted the way to the barn's entrance door. Despite Merdon saying it was safe and having him go first, I still hesitated before advancing into the shadowed underbelly. The scent of manure and silage clogged the air, and I coughed lightly as I entered.

The main area of the barn was far from empty. Dead cattle littered the pen to our left. Based on the pile of infected bodies and the bloody smears on the central aisle, a few of the infected had been inside, waiting for the fey. That or we'd interrupted them killing the cows.

I frowned at the thought.

"Is this where they found the cat?" Tasha whispered.

I glanced back at Uan, who had an arm around the girl's shoulders in a fatherly, loving gesture that was anything but a casual embrace. His gaze shifted around the space restlessly as he listened to her. He took "protective father" to a whole new level.

"This is where we found the cat," Merdon said, motioning to a room near the entrance. He ducked under the pipes hanging overhead and entered the space first.

"It's a milk house," Tasha said. "My grandpa told me about them."

She started looking around the room, opening cabinets and the refrigerator in search of cat food.

"Nothing," she said, disappointed.

"This place is pretty clean, and there's no litterbox," I said. "Maybe this isn't where the cat was kept. Maybe it just wandered in here?"

She nodded.

Shouts and male laughter rose outside.

"Is it smart to make that much noise?" I asked.

Merdon's typically serious expression turned even more grave.

"The animals are frightened and do not want to be carried. One kicked Hanno in the thigh. He is limping."

I cringed. "Maybe we should wait in the trucks."

"Can we keep looking for cat food?" Tasha asked.

Uan and Merdon shared a look before Merdon nodded.

"Yes. Do not lose sight of Hannah. I will return when the animals are in the truck."

"Not a fan of you ditching me," I said when he and Tor started for the door.

Merdon looked back at me.

"Uan will keep you safe while we gather more animals for you."

When he said it like that, I didn't have much reason to feel abandoned.

"Fine. Just don't stay away too long."

He gave me a measuring look then nodded.

After I watched him leave, I focused on Tasha.

"Where should we search next?" I asked.

The three of us checked the milk house again then searched the hallway and the main barn. Through a door at the other end of the building, I saw a fey carrying a pig that squealed and wriggled like crazy. The poor fey was having a hard time keeping a grip on the creature.

"Hey," Tasha said, tugging at my arm. "I think that's cat food."

I looked to where she pointed, a shelf in a little nook off the main building that led to the silo we'd seen from outside. The bag rested on the top shelf, untouched.

"That's perfect," I said. "Good eye."

Uan lifted it down just as shouting broke out somewhere else in the building.

"What's going on?" Tasha asked.

Uan poked his head out the doorway for a moment before answering.

"A human is calling for help. They are trying to find her."

"Do you think it's a trap?" I asked.

He tilted his head at me.

"The stupid ones can't talk, but they've used humans before. We should return to the trucks."

I didn't argue with his logic because I'd been thinking the same thing.

He picked up the food and started toward the door at the same time Tasha and I both heard a low whine.

"Wait," she said.

She turned toward a metal chute and pointed at what looked like a sea of grain inside the opening. Pieces, previously undisturbed, began to move, and a few fell to the floor.

"I think there's a puppy in there. We need to get it out. What if it can't breathe?"

Blatant pleading shone in Tasha's eyes as she looked back at Uan, and I knew he'd cave.

The whine came again, more urgent, and additional bits fell.

Though the surface churned, there was still no sign of fur or anything.

"That's a lot of movement for a puppy," I said, retreating a step. "Why would it be in the grain?"

"It was probably hiding from all the infected. Please," Tasha begged.

The big fey sighed at her pleading gaze, set the bag down, and went toward the chute. The sea of grain continued to stir in an agitated fashion.

Fear crawled up my spine, a feeling too reminiscent of the days before I'd joined the RV group. I snagged the back of Tasha's jacket and pulled her toward me. She glanced at me with confusion, saw my face, and took my hand.

"It'll be o—"

The grain exploded outward as a hellhound launched from the opening.

Time slowed.

Tasha made a sound, her fingers twitching in mine. My heart froze at the sight of the beast's glowing eyes locking on us. Grain rained down on Uan as he twisted and grabbed the hound around the middle in midair.

Uan's biceps strained as he locked his arms around the beast. The creature thrashed, mad with its need to get to us.

I stumbled back toward the doorway, pulling Tasha with me even as, within the chute, a decomposing arm rose from the grain. Then, an infected's head.

Uan grunted as the hound twisted and went for his face.

I didn't think. I gave in to instinct, turned, and ran, pulling Tasha with me.

We needed light. We needed more fey.

My wild gaze swept the empty barn then locked on the exit.

"Hellhound," Uan roared as our feet pounded on the cement. "Save the girls."

His warning was too late. A moaning call echoed, and I glanced over my shoulder. Three infected ran agilely behind us.

Tasha's wide, terror-filled gaze locked on mine, and the old memory rose over the current moment. I felt the slickness of Katie's fingers against mine and the way she struggled to keep up, struggled to breathe.

I ran farther while keeping a tight hold on Tasha's hand. Behind us, the sound of the infected drew closer.

My own breath grew shallower as I focused on reaching the exit. Panic consumed me along with a single thought.

Not again.

We burst through the barn door and into the light. However, the truck was still too far away for us to make it.

But, I saw Brenna standing on the top, her bow ready.

I refused to relive the past a single moment more.

"Save her!" I yelled.

Then, I pulled hard, dragging Tasha in front of me. The girl's eyes locked with mine as I pushed her toward her sister.

"Run!"

Without waiting to see if she'd listen, I turned and faced the oncoming infected. The first one crashed into me. I brought my arm up, wedging it against the infected's throat as we fell backward. The impact knocked the air from my lungs. I struggled against the stars dancing in my vision and the infected's weight but kept my elbow locked and my hand braced against its shoulder.

A rancid smell clogged my nose as the thing pulled back what was left of its lips to snap its teeth at me. My arm quivered. I hadn't thought this through. By the time Merdon got me to this position on the ground, if I had my arm up, I'd won. If not, he flipped me and either spanked or bit me. There'd never been a next step to get out of this position.

The decaying woman moaned loudly again and grabbed for my hand on her shoulder. Her inhuman strength pried my fingers from her tattered shirt. My forearm started to slip despite my effort. Her teeth snapped again.

Closer.

My pulse stuttered, and a rage-filled scream erupted from me.

I didn't want to die, not like this.

A bolt suddenly appeared in the middle of the woman's forehead, and she went slack. Her weight left me abruptly, and an extremely pissed Merdon stared down at me.

"Get up."

I scrambled to my feet and looked around, ready to run again. I didn't need to, though. The other infected all had arrows protruding from their heads as well. I looked back at the truck where Brenna stood, ready with another bolt, and my tears started to fall.

Thallirin had already tossed Tasha up by her sister. They were both safe.

A tight grip on my upper arms pulled my attention back to Merdon.

I'd never seen him so angry or so bloody before.

"Why did you leave?" he demanded.

"Are you kidding me? A hellhound came out of the grain, followed by all these infected. They chased us while Uan—"

The hellhound burst out of the barn door's entrance and into the daylight. Snarling and slavering, it stopped, two broken spears protruding from its middle, not that it seemed to notice them. Or the sunlight. Smoke rose in slow spirals from its holey, blackened hide.

The hell beast didn't run away. It growled, its red eyes locked on me.

Merdon stepped between us and tensed.

An infected moan echoed in the yard.

The hellhound twitched then looked away from us toward the trees beyond the house. With a last snarl in our direction, it bolted. More than a dozen infected poured from the trees to follow it. One infected, wearing the remains of a tattered blue jacket, stood watching us for a moment before running after the hellhound.

"Tell me that's not normal," I said.

"It's not," Merdon said as he straightened and looked back at me. "Are you okay?"

"I'm not bitten if that's what you're asking. But I'll be having new nightmares for a while, I think. Where's Uan?"

Several fey ran inside, and I looked up at Merdon as I realized what had just happened. I'd saved Tasha. She'd been struggling to keep up, and I'd done what I'd wished I'd done every waking moment since I released my sister's hand. I'd held on. I'd pushed her in front of me and stayed to face the infected.

"I didn't leave her behind," I said hoarsely. "Not this time. I couldn't do it again."

I'd been willing to sacrifice myself. My elation that I hadn't repeated my past mistakes slowly faded as other thoughts crept in. I'd been willing to die for her. No hesitation. Was I not better? Did I still want to die? My arms and legs started to shake, and tears flooded my eyes.

Merdon looked at me hard, then strode to the side of the milk shed. The crazy man turned on the hose and proceeded to spray himself while I stood there doubting my sanity.

Before Merdon finished cleaning himself off, a group of fey emerged from around the barn. One carried an unconscious man. The others carried supplies.

A woman trailed in their midst, walking beside Ryan. Black, straight hair cascaded down her back from under her bright red hat. The fey were completely captivated by her and couldn't stop casting glances her way.

"Did someone yell hellhound?" Ryan asked.

"Yes. And not enough fey came running," I said. "If not for Brenna, I'd be dead."

I looked at all the fey.

"You guys are shit for protection. I understand finding new people is amazing, but don't sacrifice the ones you already have."

There were a bunch of apologies, including one from Ryan.

"We were under a lot of concrete and couldn't hear."

"The fey by the trucks heard. Am I that useless? That much of a bitch that I'm not worth saving?" I didn't ask it out of anger at them. I was still struggling to understand everything that had just happened. Tasha and I should have been safe in the midst of all these men, but we hadn't been.

"They were told not to leave the trucks under any circumstances," Ryan said. "We've been tricked before. Infected bait them away from the trucks then try to disable our only means of escape. I'm truly sorry, Hannah. It was my order. Usually, there are two fey assigned to each human. We weren't prepared for how hard it would be to load the animals or to hear a yell for help."

The woman paled.

"I'm so sorry," she whispered. Her sun-kissed complexion paled as I met her deep brown eyes.

"It's not your fault. It's theirs. If they want to keep us alive, they need to plan better."

There was a grunt from behind me before I was turned and pulled against a sopping wet, freezing chest.

"Forgive me," Merdon said against my hair. "Because I will never forgive myself for what almost happened."

I wrapped my arms around his waist and burrowed closer, not caring that he was soaking my clothes.

"I forgive you."

He exhaled heavily and continued to hold me. Behind us, Ryan started talking.

"As you can see, we get along with the fey. They have the speed and strength necessary to quickly kill the infected."

"And the dog things? Can they kill those?" the woman asked.

"Yes. It's not as easy, but the fey are the only things that can kill the hellhounds."

"Fine. We'll go with you."

I pulled back from Merdon.

"You know that Emily is going to be pissed at you when I tell her what almost happened."

He actually winced before grunting.

"I know you said you won't be manipulated, but how do you feel about groveling? I think a lot of that's going to be necessary over the next few days."

He sighed and released me. Hand in hand, we walked back to the trucks.

"Emily is not the only one who will receive my groveling," he said as we stopped by the door. He lifted my hand to his mouth. "I will convince you that I will keep you safe, always. I will protect your body and your heart, Hannah. Believe in me." He kissed my knuckles then jerked back to stare at my hand.

"Why do you smell like Garrett?"

"Ah, shit." There was a flurry of movement on the other side of the truck. Merdon tried to lift his eyes, but I captured his attention by tugging on his sensitive ear.

"Because I want you to take me home and make me smell like you."

A slow, wicked grin spread his lips.

"I know."

EPILOGUE

AN ARMY OF BUTTERFLIES TOOK FLIGHT IN MY MIDDLE AT THE sound of a knock on the door. Already in position to answer it, James winked at me before pulling the door open.

"Just the fey I wanted to see," he said.

"Tor said you needed my help," Merdon answered.

Wearing a pair of fitted jeans and button-up shirt that barely contained him when he moved, he stood on the front step, illuminated by the porch light. From my position in the dining room, I could see his chiseled features and the concern openly displayed there.

"About that," James said, motioning for Merdon to enter.

It took half a second for him to spot me standing beside the candlelit table. When he did, he prowled toward me. James chuckled and shut the door.

My pulse kicked into high gear as Merdon's gaze swept over my dress and then lingered on my face. I'd gone all out for this. Last time, I'd been covered in puke and had acted like a complete bitch. This time, I wore some light makeup and had taken time to do my hair.

"What are you doing, Hannah?" he asked suspiciously when he reached me.

"Would you like to have dinner with me? A real dinner date?"

"Why?"

"Say yes!" Mary yelled from the kitchen.

I grinned up at Merdon.

"Because having a nice dinner is what normal people do when they like each other. And because I screwed up the last time we tried this, and I want to make it up to you."

He considered me for a moment then stepped around me and pulled out my chair. I sank into the seat and tipped my head to smile back at him. He surprised me by leaning in close and inhaling deeply near my ear.

"Did you lie to me, Hannah?"

My stomach dove to my toes. Yet, my pulse raced and my breathing quickened with a thrill of anticipation. I was a little twisted when it came to how I responded to Merdon.

"About what?" I breathed.

"When you said you needed time to prepare for tonight, you knew what I thought." His hands settled on my shoulders, and his lips brushed the side of my neck, showing me what he meant, just in case I was completely clueless. I wasn't.

The entire duration of the three-hour drive home, Merdon had continually glanced at me through the truck window. Given what I'd suggested before we'd left the farm, I'd known what was on his mind. He'd been planning exactly how he would make me smell like him instead of Garrett. But my mind had gone a slightly different direction.

"You disappeared while I was showering, Hannah. What am I supposed to think about that?" The low rumble of his voice continued to wreak havoc on my pulse and breathing.

His fingers flexed on my shoulders.

"Was I too rough with you last night?" His nose brushed against the shell of my ear, and I shivered. "Was I not rough enough?"

James cleared his throat loudly.

"I'll let Ma know to hurry up the meal."

I blushed as he hurried toward the kitchen and waited for the door to close before I looked up at Merdon.

"Behave, Merdon," I said, using the same warning tone that he'd used on me countless times. I knew it wouldn't be enough to get him to sit, though. "I wanted to make tonight special for you. Give me a chance to show you I'm not the Hannah I was last time we tried this. Please."

He released my shoulders and cupped my chin.

"I already know who you are."

"Let me guess. I'm yours?"

He grunted then claimed my lips in an aggressive kiss.

"Behave, my Hannah," he said when he finally released me.

I blinked stupidly at him, panting for air while struggling to form a coherent thought that wasn't centered around us getting sweaty. The corners of his mouth tilted as he took his seat across from me. He knew exactly what he'd done to me and waited in anticipation for how I'd react.

Reaching out, I plucked up the cards I had waiting on the table.

"First question," I said. "What's your favorite color?"

"Yellow." He leaned across the table and tugged one of my curls.

My heart melted a little.

"What's your favorite color?"

"Grey."

He grinned and settled back into his seat.

"Next question. What's your favorite food?"

"Pus—"

"Food's here!" Emily said, popping out of the kitchen with two bowls. She set them down and stole the cards from my hand.

"For Mary's sake, maybe you should wing it."

I snorted a laugh as Emily rushed back into the kitchen. When I faced Merdon again, I found him watching me closely.

"I see what's inside of you."

"And what's that?"

"Life."

I smiled and reached across the table for his hand.

"Thank you for never giving up on me."

He squeezed my fingers in return.

I LEANED AGAINST THE FENCE, momentarily distracted from my search by the new animals and the progress the fey had made overnight. The pigs roamed their own pen that had a separate entrance to the shed the fey had erected. Not only would the building keep the pigs warm, but they'd even added roosts in case we found chickens. The horses had stalls. As pretty as they were to look at, I knew better than to get too close. They were still skittish, and I could only imagine what they'd gone through before we'd shown up.

It was the birds that really fascinated me, though.

A fey had found them nested in the loft of the barn where they had been trapped when the hellhound had arrived. They weren't domesticated but wild. The first wild animals I'd seen since before the earthquakes.

"I thought you would sleep later."

I tore my gaze from the animals and watched Merdon close the distance between us.

"I might have if you'd been in bed too. The girls told me that they barely left their houses the first few days after they gave the green light to their guys. Why'd you leave?"

He looked out over the animals.

"I have no memory of a horse or a pig. They are interesting."

"They are. I like the birds best, though. I haven't seen any wild ones since before the earthquakes."

"The new female said the birds appeared in their barn a few weeks ago."

"Do you think they'll stay?"

"The man wants them to stay."

"I meant the birds," I said with a laugh. Though, I understood why he'd thought the other way. Finding another human female was a big deal, especially one who wasn't wearing a wedding ring.

"Perhaps. If they don't, a fey will try to follow to see where they go."

We watched the animals in silence for a few more moments.

"Are you going to answer my question, Merdon?"

He continued to study the animals.

"Yesterday was filled with many things for you. You needed rest and comfort."

"Okay, but I'm still clueless why you left me alone in bed this morning. Are we only going to be a once a day couple? I mean, it's fine if that's all you want, but I was kind of led to believe I'd be walking with a hitch for the first week."

My teasing smirk faltered when Merdon's heated gaze landed on me.

"I left so you would be well-rested for today. Are you well-rested?"

I hesitated a bit too long.

"Do you need help deciding if you're well-rested?"

A grin parted my lips, and I slowly nodded.

In a familiar move, he crouched low.

"Run, my Hannah."

My eyes went wide, and I pivoted, not needing to be told twice. My laughter trailed behind me as I sprinted for the house. I barely made it ten yards before he grabbed me around the waist and spun me around and over his shoulder. I landed with an oof and squealed when his hand smacked down on my butt.

"You're going to pay for that," I said.

He rubbed the skin, sending tingles to all the right places.

"I will pay and pay until you scream my name," he promised.

I couldn't wait for him to keep his word. Today. Tomorrow, and every day afterward.

AUTHOR'S NOTE

(prepare yourself…it's long!)

First and foremost, thank you for reading! I truly appreciate each and every one of you. Your reviews, emails, and comments begging for more books are the reasons I keep writing. They're also the reasons for this very long note.

I have so much to say about Hannah and Merdon, but first I wanted you to know that I've heard you. Some of you have reached out to me personally. Some of you have left reviews with your thoughts and feelings. I appreciate everyone sharing, and I want to address some of your concerns.

First, I'd like to address the age of the characters I've been writing. Although the books written under MJ Haag are labeled "adult" romance because of the steamy content, they actually fall into the New Adult category because of the characters' ages. As is typical for that category, my characters range between 18 and 25. (The exception to that age bracket is the Beastly Tales, which take place in a fantasy world that shares many aspects of an older, pre-industrial Europe. That includes the notions that maturity is obtained much earlier and that 16 is considered an adult and old enough to marry.) If the age of the characters written under M.J. Haag bothers you, New Adult fiction probably isn't your thing, and that's okay.

Second, I'd like to address the maturity of my heroines. I strive to write unique characters. That includes diverse maturity levels. In this series, each and every character has had some kind of trauma or profound event that has shaped them into the person they are on the page. Brenna's family suffered a great deal of trauma before the earthquakes because of her mother's accident. I've known teens who've had to help care for a loved one, and the maturity they displayed because of those times has left a lasting impression. That's not to say they're now exempt from making youthful mistakes, just that they are more likely to handle the fallout more reasonably than the average teen.

Characters, like real people, aren't defined by their age but by their life experiences.

Now, for the hot mess that is Hannah. She didn't suffer any trauma before the quakes and struggled to make just about every choice that faced her. I'm not sure what else to say about her. When we started the series together, Hannah was all sunshine and rainbows. Then, as things progressed and we got to know her a little better, we saw some behavioral changes, a common trait with alcoholism.

Alcoholism is a serious topic, and most of us have been, or will be, touched by it in our lifetimes. It's a multifaceted disease that can be so different from person to person. While Hannah is a fictitious character, I did my best to walk the line between realism behind her compulsion to drink, its effects on her and her recovery, and the timeline and constraints of the Resurrection world.

While one of the major signs of alcoholism is behavioral changes, Hannah's couldn't all be contributed to her drinking. The post-traumatic stress from what happened to her sister was also a major issue. Hannah had been hiding who she really was as well as the deep pain caused by even deeper secrets. Some issues just won't stay buried. PTSD is some serious stuff in how it impacts mental health and behavior.

The complexity of Hannah's situation and character made her difficult to write, especially during a world crisis. Her thoughts were heavy and dark. Yet, I deeply feel that her story needed to be told.

Hannah's guilt ate at her. She couldn't cope with the choices she'd made and turned to drinking. With the drinking came the blame. Part of her healing was seeing the truth of her situation and how *her* actions were playing an active part in the way the people around her were responding to her. Even as she was healing and dealing, she was still trying to blame. It's human nature to not want to own up to our faults.

We are not perfect people, but we have the ability to redeem ourselves and our past mistakes through our current and future choices. By being open to the fact that all of us have flaws, we can work on our own imperfections instead of focusing on the imperfections of others.

We can strive to be the best version of ourselves possible, no matter the circumstance.

And...that's enough heavy thinking and topics for now.

While this book might seem like it's all about Hannah's problems (that's what she'd want you to think), it's more deeply about the Resurrection world community that's been building since the end of the third book. Becca and I destroyed the world in book one, and even though I love writing in a broken world, leaving it like that wouldn't make for a good conclusion to the series. So, I wanted to start putting some of the pieces back together and give you a glimpse of what the future will be like for the Resurrection world when the series does end.

The next book, as you've probably already guessed, will be about Tor and a new girl, June. As I've mentioned above and as the end of *Demon Disgrace* has hinted, the world is changing. Because of the big changes occurring in the next book and the direction the characters are currently steering their story, I see another long book in my future.

I'm hoping their story will be filled with a few more laughs, but I never really know the direction they'll take until I'm writing it. Like my kids, my characters are rarely influenced by my wants.

However, for those wondering what happened to Uan, you will get more information about him in the next book since the timelines will cross a little (just like the timeline in Demon Dawn crossed with Demon Disgrace).

I'll post a poll in my newsletters to ask if you all want the book after Tor and June's story to be the end of the series next (a.k.a. where in the hell did Molev go?), or if you'd like to hear about one or two more fey first. Be sure to weigh in! Every vote counts!

Until next time, happy reading!

Melissa